MW00614261

LEAVING THE HOME FRONT

The personal experience novel of a boy from the heartland to World War II

by *Jay Karr*

Kingdom House Press
Fulton, Missouri
2005

I

Copyright ©2005 by Jay Karr

All rights reserved. No part of this publication may be reproduced, or transmitted in any form, without the prior written permission of the publisher, except in the case of brief quotations embodied in critical articles or reviews.

Leaving the Home Front is a novel mingling a true historical chain of events with fiction. In this story real people, both public figures and private persons, interact with fiction characters. The names of some private persons have been changed; in the case of widely known public figures, both the names and the facts of their lives are true to public record.

Printed in the United States of America.

LIBRARY OF CONGRESS CATALOGING-IN-PUBLICATION DATA
Leaving the Home Front: the novel of a boy's life from the Heartland to World War II by Jay Karr
KINGDOM HOUSE is an imprint used by Jay Karr
E-mail: jkarr@sbcglobal.net
First printing:ISBN 0-9609926-5-0

Back cover: oil portrait of the author by Jane Mudd.
Front cover: trooper &1953 Mercury by Jay Karr.
The author acknowledges his debt to
Martin Northway for proof reading,
and to Christian West for electronic editing.
Kingdom House books are available at special bulk wholesale discounts in the United States. .
Contact: Kingdom House Books, Fulton, Mo.65251.

Rock a bye baby on the tree top
When the wind blows the cradle will rock
When the bough breaks the cradle will fall
And down will come baby, cradle and all.

(A frontier nursery rhyme)

Acknowledgments

Thanks to Lt. General E. M. Flanagan, Jr., U. S. Army, Retired for permission to quote passages from *Airborne.* His history, and his personal advice taught me much I had not known about my own outfit, the 11th Airborne Division.

Further thanks must go to Bennett M. Gutherie, a jump master in the assault on Corregidor, for his history of the 503rd Regimental Combat Team in the South Pacific, and his invaluable advice on my description of the jump. Thanks also to heroes of that jump--which I considered suicidal when I saw the tattered chutes on the blasted trees of Topside--who responded to my queries in Don Lassen's *Static Line* with their own horrendous experiences of the jump and the assault that followed.

Many thanks to C. W. Gusewelle, author and airborne veteran, for his pre-publication criticism and encouragement on this novel.

Thanks for permission to use the passages from Nile Kinnick's diary entries for December 7th and 8th, 1941, must go to Rhonda Wetjen, of the University of Iowa Press.

And to Todd Stocke, Editorial Director, Sourcebooks Inc. For "fair use" confirmation of permission to quote Edward R. Murrow's on-the-spot description of the parachutists' jump from a C-47 over Operation Market Garden in *World War Two On the Air*.

Thanks to Ada M. Hoots, Editor, for the story, told by two descendants of Caleb and Rachel Clark, Elizabeth Smith, and Opal Elderkin, in the *History of the Clark Family in Madison County, Iowa,* 1937, of the dead Indian baby interred in a tree near the settlers' first camp on Clanton Creek in 1846.

For Phyllis, who was patient and enduring
And for all the missing. May they still turn up.

VII

Prologue

Rock Force, February 16, 1945

Call me 37758380, he thought, no one even knows my name; except the last few days Jankowski had started calling him "Shucks" because he was from Iowa, and the squad had picked up on it. That meant he was beginning to settle in with them a little. But he was uneasy with the jump because he had only been assigned to the 503rd ten days ago, the last guy pulled out of the gang of paratroop replacements he had come all the way from Ft. Benning with and sent solo to the 503rd on Mindoro to replace a trooper who had broken a leg in one of the last tune-ups before the mission. So he had only had a week to try to fit in with a close-knit company of veterans before the jump. All he had seen of the Philippines was the town of San Jose he had come through on the trucks on the way from the landing, which had been like the back of beyond in the *National Geographic,* something the Incas built and the Spaniards had destroyed, elephant-eared green jungle already swallowing the thatched huts on stilts--and the rice fields with their levees, and the mountains beyond. He would like to describe this to Fairy. But he had told her in his last letter that he was going to the 11th Airborne, and it nagged at the back of his mind relentlessly now in the air, that the unfinished letter saying it was really the 503rd was still in his pocket. So, no one knew where he was.

He was uneasy loading, because he had never jumped with the extra equipment the others had already jumped a mission with--only the standard rifle pack and rounds at Benning--and now he was loaded with the bi-pod and a bandolier for Jankowski's A-6 machine gun, and grenades, and clips in each side pocket, and wore one of the Mae West flotation vests which he knew from the Dog Island jump were a fickle savior for a water landing (if you panicked and pulled them before you unfastened your chute harness, they crushed your chest, but if you released your harness first they saved your life). The upper pockets of his jacket held his rations and his glasses cased and buttoned in. Someone said you went up the ladder into the plane doubled over like a woman eight months pregnant--but this time she was overdue; he must have weighed 280 lbs., and Jankowski had boosted him from below.

In training the jump sticks had always been twelve men--one stick out the door on the first pass, the other the second time around--but for Corregidor they told you off in sticks of six men each, because they would only be six seconds over the Drop Zone with water on both ends, "So, leave that reserve chute behind, my man, at 300 feet you won't even have time to say *rip cord*!" And he was the last man in the first stick. No one liked being the last man in the stick.

In Europe you were in the air for hours and slept on the way, but Corregidor was only 200 miles from Mindoro, and through the open door he now saw on the brown water below the V wake of a torpedo boat high-tailing it east, and a pall of smoke on the horizon where the 11th Airborne had fought through the Genko line, and the Japs had tried to burn the old city of Manila before they died.

He had the queasy feeling because he had never jumped without a reserve chute, so he shouted at the top of his lungs, "It's combat, Dumbass!" and Jankowski beside him looked around and said, "Yo!" And he yelled again just to shout down his churning gut as the plane suddenly turned turtle in the air, doing that familiar rolling stop down to eighty miles an hour. And his stick stood up and hooked up and checked backpacks and stood in the door. No waiting. The jump light; the jumpmaster slapped the first man, and they ran into thin air like sprinters running with cramps, bent over and grabbing the equipment bundle strapped like a big-bellied fetus where the reserve chute

2

should have been, and the prop blast peeled them away from the tail.

He didn't need to look up for the canopy. The white silk streamer popped and the chute filled, and every part of the harness seized him and slammed him to a stop in the air. This was always euphoria--but not this time. He had a momentary pinwheel view of Topside and his DZ in front of the Milelong barracks tilting away and going under him too fast to try to slip the chute, and he just raised his eyes to the horizon for the landing when the windborn canopy yanked him straight between the clawing trunks of two smashed trees.

And the landing shock didn't come at all, and he saw the toes of his boots clear the lip of a cliff, and he was high in the air again, over the ocean now. As he drifted down, the wind spun him backward and he faced the rocky cliff, and as if he'd jumped from a skyscraper and fallen past a window with someone in it, he met the eye of a Jap sighting a rifle at him from a cave hole, and the muzzle popped off smoke and his backpack cracked like a flag in the wind, and he felt a hot track across his side.

He supposed he was wounded, but he hadn't had time to feel anything when he knew he was going way over the beach. He got rid of the rifle pack, and popped open the buckles of the harness, and hung free in just the harness under his arms, and pulled the Mae West and took a great breath just as he hit the water. Home free.

But the jacket only hissed and stayed empty because the Jap had holed it, and he kept going down. He shucked the helmet and got rid of the grenades and the bandolier, and tried to get at the flap pockets and dump the clips. He couldn't open the right one, and had to double up underwater and get the knife out of his boot and slash the pocket open.

The clips tumbled out and he still kept going down, because there was still the bi-pod strapped under the belly

3

pack, and he worked on that in growing frenzy, slashing away the twenty-pound pack, and when it went down into the very darkness, he was clear and kicking upward.

But his uniform was heavy as a wet sponge and the boots were God-awful heavy, and he had used up so much of his air that bubbles he couldn't help were coming out. But he was starting slowly up toward the sunshine when a glaucous vision of Fairy came through layers of strangely clear water above him, her body laced with rippling sunshadows on her little polka dot Chili Williams suit and her flickering legs languidly kicking, with her head bent down toward him and her lips speaking silently in the music of long glimmering chords at the pool on his birthday once, and her hand reaching down to draw him up.

Before

Miles Morgan was born in Des Moines in 1926. A few years later, when he was about nine, listening to a radio quartet called *The Sons of the Pioneers,* that came on WHO before the evening news, he was suddenly visited by a revelation, "My dad was a pioneer, and my mom was a daughter of the pioneers!" It was 1935, and the turn of the century had been a little late for pioneering in the Midwest, but it had been a peculiar history on both sides in that respect.

His father, J. Arthur Morgan, was a civil engineer, called Doc because his voracious curiosity nourished a strain of didacticism that compelled him, when he was in the throes of reading up a new process, to explain it to everyone, particularly hitchhikers. His round head, prematurely bald as a billiard ball from the high fever of the polio that had almost killed him at eighteen, contributed to the professorial impression. But, he had earned his pioneering credentials as a young boy on the brink of his teens, when he had accompanied his mother and two brothers on a latter-day homestead claim in western Nebraska. The homestead had been Mary Ellen Morgan's contingent solution, when her alcoholic husband deserted her and the five children on a small farm in western Iowa and returned in a rented buggy on a Sunday afternoon a few weeks later and shot up the house: she had placed the two girls with relatives in Atlantic and taken the three boys to Nebraska. The homestead lasted till J. Arthur was fourteen.

Before he was five, Miles had endlessly studied two black and white snapshots from that time. The one of that little matriarchy, Mary Ellen, Parker, Chester and J. Arthur in front of a low house made of sod laid brick fashion, with grass growing out between the layers of sods, the land in the background as barren as a seascape. The boys in the foreground holding clarinets. In the other photo, his father, then fourteen, and not remotely resembling Randolph Scott--his idea of a pioneer--stands wearing moleskin pants, a tight little jacket over a white shirt, a Tom Sawyer straw hat, and carrying a small valise. His foot is on the step of the caboose of a stock train. He is also unmistakably wearing a large black pistol in a holster on his hip. Miles knows his father is about to take the caboose to Chicago with a load of cattle. J. Arthur had once explained that the gun was to protect the check he would bring home for the sale of the cattle. He told Miles that it had been too heavy a responsibility for a boy of fourteen, and though he had brought the check home safely, whatever had happened on the trip induced in him a permanent mistrust of the "city of the big shoulders."

Shortly after J. Arthur's mission, Mary Ellen gave up the homestead and returned to settle permanently in Des Moines. There the boys had gone through school and taken up professions: Chester, pharmacy (he now had his own drug store in Des Moines); Parker, optometry (he had opened a business in Detroit after the Great War)--and J. Arthur, civil engineering (his first job was surveying for the Rock Island railroad).

But when J. Arthur had returned from Peoria in the spring of 1916, he had already been sick two weeks. The item in the *Des Moines Register* says that he had infantile paralysis, and mentions that it went undiagnosed until he got back to Des Moines. In a snapshot of him taken late in his convalescence, he sits in the sun on a park bench showing his shriveled calf and looking as wasted as a castaway. This young man, dressed in a light suit several sizes too large for him, sits with his head bowed staring at his folded hands, his former profusion of dark, curly hair, now reduced to four thin strands combed across the middle of his pate. Paralysis had toyed with the right leg. Six weeks earlier a good doctor had told him he would never walk again. Two canes rest against the park bench by his side. He had just returned to the Rock Island. Ferne says he bucked till they moved him from draftsman back to his survey crew to prove to him that he couldn't do it. But with a cane he went torturously up and down the ditches of the right of way till he could go without it. Then he took a surveyor's transit again. By the summer of 1920, he had started to play golf and tennis again, not well, but as he was fond of quipping: like the dog that played checkers, it was a wonder he could do it at all.

When he could walk with a barely perceptible limp, he had taken a job with the Iowa State Highway Commission and had begun the westward trek with Highway Six near Iowa City. And by the time Miles was three, J. Arthur had been for several years the supervising engineer on the first "modern" paved highway across the state, Davenport to Omaha, and the family had already moved with the progress of the paving from Iowa City to Grinnell to Des Moines, where they moved in with Mary Ellen Morgan in her house east of the state capitol while J.

6

Arthur commuted to the job, at first by the week, and as the paving approached Des Moines, daily.

Mary Ellen was tall and angular with an androgynous face that bore a striking resemblance to a British prime minister of the period, a likeness accentuated by her steel-rimmed spectacles and shadowy moustache. As a small child she had been brought to her grandfather's farm in Sheffield, Illinois from her birthplace, the Yorkshire mill town of Greetland. Her daughter-in-law always maintained that the deep imprint of Mary Ellen's baptismal church, of the Primitive Methodist denomination, still accounted for her many rectitudes and prohibitions, and later told Miles she would not look at him when he was born from disapproval of his mother's "flapper" vices of bridge playing and golf. Though by the time Miles' memory began making a sketchy record, he had become her favorite, and there had developed a rivalry for his father's favor between Mary Ellen and Ferne, which, with small-animal cunning, he was already adept at exploiting: If Mary Ellen condemned the chocolates his mother brought home from an afternoon of bridge, the English tea, with a cookie on the side, which Mary Ellen laid out for him as soon as Ferne was out of the house, came to represent for him the distinction between the English style of a pioneer woman and the modern American woman (tea vs. chocolate).

Of course, Mary Ellen taught him at these *tete-a-tete* teas that, after bridge, "mixed" dancing--whatever that was--was the next step on the downward path, and drinking, her former husband's vocation, was almost there. Playing cards led to drinking and dancing and another abomination, which she represented in Miles' presence with a facial rictus of aversion. Her sons, unashamedly acquainted with all of these vices, were beyond reproach, but Ferne was not so lucky.

7

She would bitterly complain to J. Arthur that Mary Ellen was overbearing because the English had always oppressed the Scotch, and her maiden name had been Gordon. Though she wasn't so uncouth that she would grasp a chicken by the head and twirl it like a cowboy twirling a lasso till the body flew off, as Mary Ellen would do if the ax wasn't ready to hand. She had good reason to suspect that Mary Ellen and Miles conspired together, after tea, to terminate certain chickens in this style, Miles the studious apprentice gawking in wonder that they could actually get up and hop around that way without their heads.

Once on her high horse, Ferne would declare, even with Mary Ellen in the next room, that her ancestors, if you please, were here on the Middle Border waiting when Mary Ellen's family arrived in Sheffield. She declared that it was a matter of record that her ancestors, the Clarks, were the first white people in Madison County, southwest of Des Moines. She regarded it as a misfortune that her father, restless with land hunger at the close of the frontier, had improvidently traded a quarter section of good Iowa farm land for an undeveloped section in western South Dakota. She had finished high school there, but all of her sentimental memories were of Winterset. When Miles was four, most of the other families stemming from Ferne's great grandparents, Caleb and Ruth Clark--the rest of the Gordons, Husses, Clantons and Westmorelands--were still living around Winterset, and had recently built a three-story stone tower in the city park in honor of their forebears. The brass plaque above the entrance said that Caleb Clark, and Ruth (nee Clanton, b.1818, in Quincy, Illinois) came down the Ohio river on a raft, settled briefly near St. Joseph, and in the spring of 1846, made up a family wagon train that broke a trail north-east into central Iowa.

Ferne's *Clark History* says they had already been dwelling in a lean-to on Clanton Creek for about two weeks when they encountered the second settler, one Hiram Hurst. Her great-great aunt, Mary Adeline Clark, b. January 1847, was the first white child born in Madison county. In that history, her older sister Elizabeth tells of an Indian child's corpse interred in a tree near their lean-to:

While the Indians camped here, a little baby died. They took a hollow tree, cleaned it out and put ends in it. They put the baby in it and tied it up in the top of a tree with hickory bark. They put a little tin pail with it. The bark soon rotted. It fell down and the pail fell out. Our parents wouldn't let us touch it. The high water came and washed it away.

In time (how was there ever time?) Caleb built a real cabin from trees he cut down and split with an ax, held together with wooden pins and roofed with hickory bark. He had followed the trade of stone mason in Pennsylvania, and the third home he built twenty years later, in Winterset, referred to as The Old Stone house, was still inhabited when Miles visited Winterset with Ferne the day before he went into the service. Caleb and Ruth Clark had fourteen children, born in Illinois, Missouri and Iowa. Miles' Grandfather Gordon's mother was one of them.

Miles didn't remember when he learned that his father and mother met and married because a row boat in which several young women on vacation from their jobs in Huron, South Dakota took shelter from a sudden thunder storm under one of those boathouses that used to line the beachfront south of the resort hotel called The Inn on West Lake Okoboji, was joined by another boat in which one of several young men from Des Moines was J. Arthur Morgan. Having met, the pair courted somehow at long distance--as Des Moines was then about five hours southeast of the lake and Huron was a half day's drive northwest of it. They married in Sioux Falls in 1924, and Ferne nee Gordon returned with J. Arthur to Iowa, the state in which she had been born and where she had lived into her teens.

Who can say that a return to the neighborhood of her childhood had not been part of Ferne's dream of an ideal marriage? But the summer and fall she spent as a reluctant tenant in Mary Ellen's box of a house on the high lot near the Iowa capitol was anything but idyllic. Even Miles remembered his parents' squabbles when they were trapped in their stifling room-and-a half upstairs nights as the tent revival Mary Ellen always invited to use her empty lot across the alley rent free in August built to its regular hysterical climax, and the howls of people "talking in tongues" prevented them from moving downstairs to sleep on the cool front porch. He remembered being carried downstairs after the revival--past the shadows of Mary Ellen's musty living room, its saggy sofa, upright piano (reserved for hymns), tasseled lamps and blocked fireplace decorated with tinsel--covered china elephants that sparkled in the candlelight, and when his parents were finally asleep on the double daybed in the early morning wind from the west, he dimly remembered lying in his trundle bed across the porch, building dreams on the groan and hoot of the trains in the switchyard below Capitol Hill that made up before dawn for Omaha, Denver, Flagstaff and such exotic western places. Much later, when he felt his impending service in the war coming close and weighed his choice, as though he had any, between Europe and the Pacific, those nights on the capitol hill above the rail yards listening to the quintessential train whistle blues would always nudge him to go west to the Pacific.Until the Thirties, J. Arthur seemed quite happy that his job was enshrining the last trails of the frontier in the concrete of the first paved highways across the state. His highways

were filling an indispensable piece of the grid that would--
"You watch it happen still in our time!"--make one
uninterrupted high-speed thoroughfare from coast to coast.
In those first years; when J. Arthur took his son to the job,
Miles was just old enough to feel the expansive satisfaction
his father took in the place he had made for himself. He
had been wasted by polio, but had taken up his bed and
walked; he had once been a homesteader, but was now a
MODERN man through and through with his *Scientific
American* under his arm, looking, when he could ever
glance up from his inspection of a bridge job swarming
with men driving the pilings at his direction, past the
yellow D-7 Cats shoving the hills out of the way at his
direction, to a new silver Lockheed monoplane bearing the
mail across the sky to Omaha once a day.

Sometimes he would wax eloquent at the dinner
table on the theme that Mary Ellen's aborted pioneer dream
was being fulfilled by the new air routes that were already
playing leapfrog with his highway system before it was
even complete. Would everybody be flying by the end of
the 20th century and make his highways obsolete? Well,
this summer just in case, he planned to work in some flying
lessons.

Naturally, in the summer of 1930 when J. Arthur
Morgan took the vacation he had planned for a year, they
went west. He traded his old Dodge for a Buick, and they
took route 66 over western highways more primitive than
the ones he was building, where no bridges spanned the
flash-flood creek beds in the deserts, but the road ran down
one steep side of a dry wash and up the other. They stayed
in tourist "courts" with a single wall between the men's and
women's sides of the shower, and his mother took him to
the women's side to scrub the road dust off, and he tried to
peep through a hole beside the pipe into the men's side and
met a man's eye looking back at him. And J. Arthur made a

great row about it at the office and got the fellow thrown out.

In Los Angeles he saw the ocean from the harbor he would one day ship out of for the Pacific Theater of World War II--and saw the famous stair in Los Angeles where Laurel and Hardy had struggled all one hot afternoon to deliver a piano which kept falling back down, and where the wonders of the new West were epitomized by a Goodyear blimp hovering in a searchlight beam over a filling station opening. When they returned and settled in a rented home in Adel twenty miles west of Des Moines, the Depression had already preceded them.

PART ONE

Hard Times

Leaving the *Home Front*

1

A Middletown

J. Arthur Morgan's obituary in the *Dallas County News* in January 1950 says he had been in Adel eighteen years when he died. But Miles' Sunday school diploma shows that he was promoted to the Beginners' level in September of 1930, so it was twenty years that the Morgans had been in town.

Adel looked almost like the usual midwestern county seat town when you came over the brow of the hills from any direction and saw it in the "dell" below at the confluence of two branches of the Raccoon River. The tower of its courthouse pierced the trees and you could read its clock at your hilltop eye level of a hundred and twenty feet. The courthouse had been built of white Bedford stone with a red tile roof that also capped the castle turrets at each of its four corners (its design by the firm of Proudfoot & Bird copied a French chateau, with castellated corners and an Independence Hall type tower). Built on the scale of courthouses in Des Moines and St. Louis, it proclaimed the prosperity and optimism of the county in 1902.

As you descended the hills from Highway 6, or Highway 169 which intersected it here, you would begin to identify two communities: the white-siding town with its courthouse, four churches and the pretty, elm-shaded Riverside park (later to be renamed Kinnick-Feller Park, after its two great athletes, who were young boys growing up in the county at that time), and at the far west end, a red campus clustered around a large tile factory sprawled across the Milwaukee track. To a small boy, the factory was a fantastical mix of medieval-looking, futuristic towers with conical tops, a street of low kilns like giant brick Jell-O molds, and a flat-roofed factory building. Its narrow-gauge electric railroad ran into the woods a mile or so to a deep clay pit. The tile plant had had its own infrastructure of managers, foremen and workers who lived in a kind of color-coded suburb made of its own red industrial brick.

But when the Morgans arrived in Adel, the factory had been shut down for a year and its towers gave the impression of a grand design stopped in its tracks and deserted. The small electric train and several hopper cars that had carried clay from the pit sat on the track rusting. The company streets were empty and the storage yard was stacked high with acres of unsold brick and tile.

There had been some labor trouble. The previous year, a handful of its former workers had tried to take over and restart the plant, but the takeover had collapsed. The company had threatened to evict them all, but as there was no one to rent the homes, had allowed them to stay and deferred their rent indefinitely.

When they rented a house, possibly because J. Arthur was unsure of his own job in the first shock of the Depression, the Morgans took an empty brick bungalow in the factory town. Thus, they were "factory people" for their first six months in Adel. When J. Arthur moved the next spring into a middle-aged white house across from the school in the main part of town, Miles cried, simply because he was leaving his first friends--the five Rhodes boys next door, whose favor would prove to be an unreckoned blessing in due time--and there was only one pre-school boy his age in his new neighborhood.

This was a moody fellow not as congenial as the Rhodeses, who would cause him a good many knocks and "Uncles!" before they became friends. His name was George Kinnick, and after their mothers had introduced them, George would stop by mornings, and they would set out together to explore the neighborhood. But before they had gone far, as it was vacation time, they would cross paths with a gaggle of older boys who would, out of boredom and a desire for wholesome diversion, incite them to a "boxing match", which George, who had two older brothers, would win. He would end up sitting on Miles' chest, and Miles would have to say "Uncle!", and go home in tears. There he would sulk for a day or so before his loneliness induced a hopeful amnesia, and he would go rambling with George again, often to the same effect.

Early on, when the Kinnicks went on vacation, Miles was at loose ends, and Ferne quieted him by reading *Anthony Adverse*, a thick popular novel of the day to him. But when she wrote letters to her sisters, he pestered her to let him write, and she taught him to hold the pen and scrawl wavy lines across a blank page.

In his mock writing, he would always place a period at the end of his scribble, and ask her to read it back to him, as he had trouble making out what he had said. Nor could she, but George Gallup was just then inventing scientific polling, and the idea that the audience might tell an author what he was saying occurred to Ferne, too, and she began to interpolate family stories into Miles' scribbles: "Here you tell George that my great aunt Elizabeth Clark saw the Indians bury a little dead baby by hanging it over a stream in a hollow log," she would say solemnly.

"I do?" "Yes, you say they cleaned the log out and stopped up both ends and hung the log up in the tree with hickory bark." After she had told him the story several times he could carry it on, "And here I say they put the baby's little tin pail in with it--but the bark rotted and the cradle fell into the water," he would add sadly, astonished with his writing gift.

"You should tell George when you see him that that was almost a hundred years ago," Ferne would add. "The Kinnicks might be interested, because George's mother's name was Clarke, too, though it is spelled with an *e* at the end. Don't forget to put the *e* at the end when you write George's mother's maiden name. And don't forget that his Grandpa Clarke was the governor of Iowa. When you see him on his walk, you must always say, 'Good morning, Governor Clarke, sir.'"

At the end of the summer, when Miles had begun to nearly hold his own with George in their boxing exhibitions, school started, and the two boys were separated. Miles marched across the street to the first grade at the Adel elementary school while George's mother, who may have had a better education than anyone in town, began schooling George at home.

Unknown to Miles, the children's loyalties on the playground were first to their neighborhoods and then tied to consanguinity, which, like the Mafia's connections, often crossed the neighborhood fault lines. Along with the factory kids, there were the "south enders" and the "farm kids" and the "river end" kids. Miles knew nothing of this system, but because George was at home, and Miles was the only boy from the central west end, he had to fight the first day. When he was pushed off the teeter-totter by a boy from the south end, he waded in the way he was accustomed to fight exhibition matches with George, and took him down and sat on his chest. Before the recess bell, he made Bud say "Uncle!" and taunted his friends with the victory hoot, "Nya-ya!" and trudged back to class with a marked strut.

After this, he sailed unchallenged through his first months immune to "new kid" challenges, not because of the respect he thought his fight had earned him, but because J. Arthur with his talk to his neighbors in the west end about economic recovery was well liked in the factory town, and the stair-step Rhodes brothers had quietly thrown a protective umbrella over him.

But there was really no entire immunity from the jungle law of the playground in an elementary school that

18

granted no "social" passes to children who failed. Those who could not pass were compelled to keep trying until they could. For various reasons, some failed year after year until they were almost old enough to vote, and these often made recess the kind of terrifying minefield for the younger children that a prison exercise yard is for a green convict. There was probably no way that Miles, too oblivious to notice this, and too callow to be quiet, could always have his bodyguard of Rhodes brothers around him, and one day when he was in third grade, something happened on the playground that took him out of school and reunited him with George Kinnick.

That noontime there were no Rhodeses about when Miles crossed the street from lunch at home and joined four or five first and second grade boys crouched around a three-foot ring drawn on the ground for marbles. It was the simple game in which all the players ante one of their own marbles into the ring, and each shooter in turn gets to keep anything his shot knocks out of the circle. A dispute had started about one boy's shooter, which was a "steely," a ballbearing about three-quarters of an inch in diameter. Much heavier than any of the others' glass shooters, it sent whatever it hit, sometimes several marbles flying out of the ring. Someone had just raised a protest about the use of the "steely," and a lively argument was under way, when a shadow fell on the boys squatted around the circle.

Two boys--more precisely youths--who had recently transferred into the school were standing over them. Their names were Clifford and Nels, and they were much too old for elementary school. They were almost the same size, close to six feet tall, and very thin. Fifteen or sixteen years old, they had missed a lot of school in other places and were in their first week in third grade with the semester more than half over.

Clifford wore ragged jeans and a denim shirt. Nels wore bib overalls and a shirt that may have fitted him once but now left his wrists bare halfway to the elbows. On the sides where the bib of the overalls began, his hip bones were visible. There were other ragged children in the yard, but they were half Clifford and Nels's size, and they all wore socks and some sort of underwear.

Clifford had a long jaw and prominent cheekbones that gave him a western look, and Nels, who bore him no resemblance, though they were half-brothers, had a round face whose bulging eyes had a glassy sheen. He seldom blinked. The brothers' reputations preceded them, and when the younger boys looked up, the argument stopped. After a few moments of silence Nels said, "Le'me see it," and pointed at the steely. Nobody did anything, and after a moment he said, "Give it here," and held out a big dirty hand. The owner of the steely, a boy named Jack, looked at it regretfully and gave it up to him. Nels rubbed it on his overalls and started to put it in his pocket. When the boy named Jack said, "That's mine," in a small, funny voice, Nels bent down and held the steely temptingly under his nose and smiled. When Nels smiled, Cliff slapped the steely out of his hand. It fell in front of Miles and Miles snatched it up. Nels turned his glistening eyes to Miles.

"It's not yours. It's Jack's," Miles snapped, and thoughtlessly looked Nels in the eye. The creepy stillness of the strange light eyes gave Miles his first inkling that he had said something he would like to take back.

J. Arthur had been standing on the front porch talking to Ferne before returning to his office, and he had been watching the boys from the corner of his eye. At that moment, his voice rang out across the street, "Miles, give Jack his marble!"

Miles instantly obeyed. Clifford took Nels's arm and turned him away, and Nels went reluctantly, looking back at Miles over his shoulder as if memorizing his face, while his half brother spoke to him in a low voice. The next day, Miles was kept home, while J. Arthur went to talk to

the principal and the third-grade teacher, who was afraid of
Nels. Monday when Ferne got him ready for school, she
took him across the corner to Kinnicks' house, where he
would finish the year with George under the tutelage of
Frances Kinnick.

Her maiden name was Clarke. She had attended
Drake University and Northwestern. Nile, Sr. had attended
Iowa State College. He had been a football player, and
George boasted that his father owned the record there for
points-after-touchdown converted by drop kick. (The type
of kick, executed by one player without a holder, in which
the kicker drops the ball and kicks it at the instant it strikes
the ground, has long been abandoned for the more
dependable place kick, and it is said that Nile Kinnick, Sr.
still holds the record for extra points by drop kick at Iowa
State.) When he graduated, Nile, Sr. married Frances
Clarke and came to Dallas County to manage the family
farms. Of course, now it was Depression in the Midwest
and everyone was hand-to-mouth, but the Kinnicks'
situation was especially serious in the spring of 1931, and a
part of the reason his parents took Miles out of Nels' way
was probably to help the Kinnicks with the small tuition
they paid Frances for tutoring him. Though Frances' father
had been governor of Iowa till 1917, there were heavy
debts; farm crops were bringing next to nothing and
foreclosure of the farms was threatened.

The Kinnick home was a huge, white, three-story
house on its own half block with a cathedral-sized attic,
and a big barn (testifying that it had been a farmhouse at
the edge of town at the turn of the century). Miles had been
to the house with George several times before he began
coming every day for tutoring: One rainy Saturday they
had played in the attic, which was filled with a marvelous
surplus of old clothes. Because there were cutaway coats
and top hats there, Miles decided the house had probably
belonged to Governor Clarke and his wife, Arletta, when

he had been governor. That day he met a girl whose nickname was Punky there, who took the role of the governor's wife, and they acted out a pretend inauguration with Miles holding a coverless book and George being sworn in as governor. Later, they went back down the narrow stairs from the attic and on down the main stairs, which had a stately turn, and descended along a wall of yellow-gold antique paper showing castles on heights overlooking a river which was supposed to be the Rhine in Europe.

On school days, George and Miles worked together on opposite sides of a card table in the living room till Frances declared recess and gave them cookies and milk in the kitchen under the wall posted with blueprints of a sailing sloop. Sometimes George's older brothers would be there, and Miles met Nile, Jr., 14, whom everyone called Jun, and Ben, thirteen months younger. Jun was the Morgans' morning paper boy, and that year Miles thought Jun Kinnick won the *Register & Tribune Iowa Paperboy of the Year* award, because Jun biked up Morgans' driveway every morning at seven and delivered the *Des Moines Register* into J. Arthur's hand as he stuck it out the screen from his bed.

So, Miles was in awe of Jun, though he took an immediate warm liking to Ben, who was witty and had a way of teasing that didn't hurt. Ben's smile, droll and mildly ironic, had a personal focus on you, while Jun's wide and totally doubtless grin, shaped into an animated plus sign by the deep cleft in his chin, radiated a general benevolence on everyone at once. George, as if he felt a premonition of a heavy destiny, seldom smiled.

Frances Kinnick worked the boys on math in the early afternoons. They used textbooks passed down from Jun and Ben, which may have been the same books used in the classes across the street. Later, there were history lessons from Frances on subjects like Thoreau and Walden, which Miles would not hear about again until high school. And the last period of the afternoon was devoted to the study of general science, for which Frances produced simple demonstrations of the inclined plane and centrifugal force. Then if she approved their workbooks, she released them to the side yard where a football game would have already started and would go on until dark.

These games, organized by Jun Kinnick and usually captained by Jun on one side and Ben on the other, were real football rather than the usual playground pick-up touch football games. There were standard kickoffs and marked sidelines, and a line across the middle of the yard that conferred a first down, and though every boy who wanted to play was claimed by one team or the other, Miles and George were too small at first to do anything but stand on the sidelines and watch the teams of six or eight boys struggle.

Then, one day when George and Miles came out of the house from their afternoon with Frances to stand yearning on the sidelines as usual, Jun Kinnick, who was destined to become *American Athlete of the Year* in a few years, took a time out to teach them to hold the ball for kickoffs, and rehearsed them till they could keep their finger on the ball right through the kick, and not let it fall over, the way Lucy does to Charlie Brown in the comics. From then on the "squirts" had official positions, Miles holding for one team and George the other.

Late in the fall, when constant wear had made a grassless hardpan of the pounded turf in the side yard, the game changed to basketball, and the teams went to the old barn where Nile, Sr. had put up a rudimentary backboard and hoops at each end of the hay mow. Then, till dark school days, and on Saturday mornings, the teams pounded the ancient alfalfa dust up from the clattering boards of the haymow into clouds so thick that the sun motes from the pigeon cupola at the top of the barn seemed filled with some sort of smoke screen through which the teams rushed back and forth like a frenzied mob till Miles thought he would suffocate or fall through the rattletrap floor, and the two boys, too young to even toss the ball as high as the hoops, retreated back down the stairs for a breath of clean air.

In the fall when Jun Kinnick was a high school freshman, and Ben in the eighth grade, and Miles had started school with Frances again, one Saturday morning George persuaded Miles to run away with him to Alaska to hunt for gold (they had heard about the Gold Rush there, but not that it was over) and they set out, prudently enough, walking downtown to "buy" supplies at Art Hynen's dry goods store. Art himself helped them select two of everything, mackinaws and mittens and long underwear and arctics, and he even picked out their socks, while his female clerk discretely withdrew to phone their mothers.

Ferne and Frances came and picked them up and scolded them all the way home, but to Miles it seemed they were punished very lightly for such an awesome transgression as buying supplies for a trip to Alaska without money (certain that their credit was good, they had merely given Art Hynen their names). Actually, the Kinnicks' credit was not good. Though Miles did not know it yet, George's motive for gold digging in Alaska was that the bank had foreclosed on the farms Nile, Sr. managed, and George, ardent to repair the woe at home which he dimly understood, had set out for the gold mines to restore his family's fortunes.

Soon after the aborted gold expedition, the Morgans rented a house in a different neighborhood near Riverside Park. Nels landed in reform school for breaking into houses, and Miles returned to the public school. And in the fall of 1932, Jun Kinnick's freshman year in high school, the two brothers and the veterans of their sandlot football games began to bring Adel a winning football season, the first in a while.

In The Tullis House

J. Arthur moved the family from the house across from the school to the third house from the park on Ninth Street. What they always called the Tullis house was a two-story house with four bedrooms and a bath upstairs. It was technologically obsolete even for a small town house in the Depression. There was a hand-fired furnace in the basement, but no means of forced air circulation. In the winter the heat rose straight up to the first floor by means of a 36-inch register situated directly over the furnace between the living room and dining room. Above this register in the first-floor ceiling was a small register twelve inches square which was meant to heat the entire second floor. Ferne and J. Arthur's room was on the front of the house, the first to catch the morning sun; the southwest room belonged to a girl named Constance, who came from a farm to live with the Morgans while she finished school. She was a long-boned blonde girl who helped Ferne around the house and sat with Miles when his parents went to a movie or a party. Miles' half-converted storeroom on the northwest side caught the prevailing wind and was frigid from November to April.

When an arctic cold spell came early that fall, by some private agreement between Ferne and Constance which he was not party to, Miles was moved to Constance's room, and they began to sleep together in Constance's double bed with every extra blanket available pulled over them. Miles nestled in the center of the big brass bed impatient for Constance to come to bed and fall asleep and make a cozy cocoon around him. In the mornings their breath steamed out in a cloud in the room to set them running first for the little register in the hall and

25

then by turns for the bathroom where Miles' father had put a small space heater.

The Tullis house was not insulated, and since there were no storm windows, the humidity made frost castles on the insides of the windows in the night. When Miles brought his clothes downstairs to dress, he would imagine fairy stories to fit the fantastic landscapes on the living room windows and scratch his name in the frost on the inside of the glass, and run back to stand at the edge of the big iron register in the center of the house where you could always get warm. Though the roaring furnace just below made the register too hot to stand on with bare feet, Miles found that he could send a large gob of spit down through the grating onto the top of the red hot furnace and cause a sizzle of frying saliva that would fill the downstairs with an aroma both intimate and obnoxious, and could bring his mother running from the kitchen, holding her nose and yelling.

Most of Miles' impressions of the several years in the Tullis house seemed to relate to the coming and going of winter. Early fall brought the home football games which were played Friday nights under the newly installed lights of the field half a block from the house. J. Arthur and Ferne walked to every home game, and his father praised the Kinnick boys' talent--(Nile, Jr. could kick and pass the football fifty yards with either hand). But Miles was less interested in these real games since he and George had no part in them any more, and spent most of the games playing imitation football with a scrum of boys his age behind the bleachers.

Some time in October J. Arthur harvested the green-skinned walnuts from a tree in the back yard. He jacked up the car in the entrance of the little dirt-floored garage and started it with its rear wheels off the ground. He put it in second gear, set the throttle and fed baskets of unshucked walnuts into a trough in front of the spinning wheels, which peeled the walnuts and sent them out the back like bullets, to the peril of anyone passing on the sidewalk in front of the house. When they stopped rolling, miraculously cleaned of their nasty husks, it was Miles' job to collect them in a basket.

The walnut scheme was a sign of J. Arthur's essential character: If he had had a choice to be some famous figure from mythology, J. Arthur Morgan would have certainly chosen to be Daedalus. The master of all artificers was right down his alley. Mathematical and mechanical talent counted tops with him, and he admired that kind of ingenuity most when it provided a short cut around some old-fashioned laborious process--as did the assembly line of Henry Ford. Thus, his walnut shelling scheme, and his love of mathematical puzzles, chess, navigation (though he was land bound), photography, wood working (for which purpose he bought a lathe and produced a profusion of beautiful table and chair legs, though never a whole chair or table), and his love of a practical joke of a certain high style which must not hurt or offend the victim, but must leave him in a state of helpless mystification--or his need to perform certain stunts on a borrowed bicycle in the back yard, riding backwards and standing on his head on the seat (boyhood revisited) for his family's wonder and amusement. These were the spitting image of the man. That winter he took up Morse Code and began to study ham radio.

At Christmas of 1932, after a protracted argument about money with Ferne, he bought a console radio wholesale. In music, his tastes were eclectic as far as from *"The Hall of a Mountain King"* to Gilbert and Sullivan-- but no closer to popular music than the occasional waltz or fox trot for Ferne's dancing pleasure. So Miles was set to learn the flute rather than the saxophone or trombone, which he would have much preferred. Miles, on the other hand, loved lilting popular songs like *The Music Goes*

27

Round and Round, and *My Heart Belongs to Daddy*, which he thought was a children's song. He already considered his tastes modern, and his father's old fashioned.

In the Tullis house as Miles began to mark his father's ways and become better acquainted with himself by noting the differences between them, he noticed that J. Arthur was unhappy when a fine scheme contracted complications, as when the fusillade of walnuts flew down the driveway half-shelled and the car had to be continually lowered as the deepening trough under the wheels flung them out in a nasty mess, which Miles was conscripted to correct by finishing the shucking.

Politics was a far more complicated matter. It was a precarious time to come to political awareness, particularly in the Morgan family, where national conditions inflamed partisan personal conflicts among siblings on his mother's Gordon side. One of the Gordon brothers, a mason by trade, was a union organizer in South Dakota and started to campaign for the state senate on the Farmer Labor ticket. Early in the campaign, the husband of Ferne's sister Hazel, who was county attorney, accused him of being an anarchist and threw him in jail. He was running for the same office. Later Ferne would complain that her brother-in-law, Bill House, had assured his seat in the state senate by keeping her brother locked up during the campaign.

Yet in the Morgan household, political differences were often stunned silent by a general consternation with the times. Working on a model boat or drawing at his card table in the corner of the dining room, Miles often snatched his understanding of national affairs out of the air that carried his parents' discussions between J. Arthur's chair in the living room and his mother in the kitchen. Yet both parents often joined in that common gesture so many people used to express their bewilderment with the aberrations of the Dirty Thirties; they threw up their hands in mutual dismay, and groaned, "What's the world coming to?" They did this over the Farm Holiday movement that blockaded the roads and forcibly dumped milk on the way to the dairies. They did it about the mock hanging of a "foreclosing" judge in northwest Iowa, and on Huey Long, and on Bertrand Russell, a Nobel Prize winning guest professor at the University of California who advocated free love and was fired. They agreed he was crazy, only in a different way from Father Coughlin, or Adolf Hitler, another crazy man who, J. Arthur said, "ought to be watched." Then there were 11 million jobless Americans, and the price of corn sank so low that some courthouses burned corn that winter because it was cheaper than coal.

In May, Ferne was feeding hoboes who drifted down from a jungle near the tile plant and stopped at assorted houses to ask for handouts. There had been a bumper crop of them headed for the Veterans' Bonus March on Washington. Ferne and J. Arthur argued about them. J. Arthur, who picked up hitchhikers indiscriminately, sided with the downtown merchants who complained that the "hoboes" lifted milk and canned goods from their shelves. He tried without success to discourage Ferne from making sandwiches for them because there were "degenerates" among them, and cited the kidnapping of the Lindbergh child.

In July, when the army burned the veterans' tent city at Anacostia Flats and General MacArthur blocked their march around the White House, J. Arthur sided with President Hoover, but Ferne fed the ragged men again as they came streaming back across the Midwest.

Two Ford V-8s

Miles had started going out to the Modlins' farm to play after the Lindberg baby's body was found and the mothers of Adel stopped letting children play in Riverside

Park. The Modlins' farm was at the dead end of a half-mile lane that ran west under the tile plant's railroad to the clay pit. It was deeply eroded land there, and the Modlins raised corn, kept a dairy herd and delivered milk in town. There were four boys, Dave, the eldest, down through George, and Jack, to Bob, Miles' contemporary.

The Modlins were a working family, like most farm families then: everyone old enough to follow instructions put in a day's work with livestock, chores or crops. There was time for Miles to play with Bob, because Bob was below the age of responsibility, and there were already three able-bodied older brothers to do the work. Dave, George and Jack went about their business, and yet there was always time to fit something in that was an immense adventure for a town kid who had never known an animal larger than a dog. You could not wait till tomorrow to bring the cows in--Miles helped with that--and they had to be driven into their stalls and milked by hand--Bob did some of that. But the brothers were all old hands by now, and knew how and when to cut up.

So Miles got lessons on the one-legged milk stool, cheek against the flank of the cow and learned how you could make the milk sing in a rhythm in the bucket if you closed your fingers on the teats from the top down in sequence, right hand, left hand, one-two, one-two, and learned how often it was okay to fire a shot into the mouth of the patient cat who always came to admire the work and sat where he made an inviting target. And he learned which cows liked to knock over the bucket, and you with it, as though they had a streak of rebellious mischief buried somewhere in there, and also which were the real outlaws and would poop on you if they got the chance, and put a hoof in the milk bucket if they sensed you were a guest conductor, and wished to show you that they didn't like your touch.

And sometimes there was an outbreak of squirt-gun war with tracers of milk crossing under the cows. But Miles just got elementary milking and the smell of the cow, and managed his few dribbly squirts and got out of the way because it took a powerful and practiced hand to empty a cow in a few minutes, and they all had to be done in time-- and the cream separated by Mrs. Modlin, and the milk bottled and delivered to the grocery stores and the homes in town by Dave and George and Jack in an old Essex with a cut off top.

John Modlin was outrunning the Depression by working from pre-dawn till noon, listening to the market reports while he ate lunch, and sitting in his chair in the sparsely-furnished living room after lunch (which was called dinner because breakfast had been at five) and reading *Successful Farming* and *Wallace's Farmer.* At one he went out again and worked till dark. But he kept a couple of ponies for the boys to herd the cows with, and one of them was as high as a horse, red-brown and white, and capable of a wonderful gallop, but gentle as a maiden aunt when she carried Bob and Miles. She knew the two boys, their frivolities and their weaknesses, and when they would fall off in a laughing fit, she would stop and wait for them to lead her to a stump and climb aboard again.

By the time he started spending time on the Modlins' farm, necessary work and responsibility had carried the boys beyond the kind of burdenless boyhood Miles was going through, and they were generally patient with his fecklessness, except when they invited him to take a turn wrestling a calf. He knew he would lose what little credit he had earned with them if he played Freddy Bartholomew and stayed out of the pen to keep his clothes clean. So he learned first hand what a calf is built like, how much bumpier they are to wrestle with than another boy the same size, and how dense their bones are, as though the strength they are coming into is latent in them from the

31

beginning. But he found out how you could tip them over, nonetheless, if you got hold of the right place. And he got acquainted with their smell, rank, pungent, but not filthy like pigs, since cows are vegetarians, and carried it home on him and was scolded by his mother, but moderately, because she cherished her own farm girlhood.

But when he kicked the pony in the flanks, and she bucked and ran away down the narrow lane under the low-hanging limbs with him and Bob aboard, and exploded into the pasture with them barely plastered to her neck and went flat into a right-angle turn bounded by the drop-off of the clay pit, and he saw the hooves kick clods over the cliff, Dave, George and Jack didn't tell their father on him or ban him from the farm as he deserved, but patiently explained that he could die of such shenanigans, or worse, injure the pony.

They seemed to have decided among themselves to salvage something worthwhile out of him, and in August, the week after his birthday, they invited him to come along on an overnight camping trip and persuaded their mother to call Ferne and get her permission. That day, the Modlins packed a tarpaulin, old blankets and two pup tents, ran the milk route early and picked up Miles with his hot dogs and buns, three cans of fruit cocktail and an opener--his price of admission--and set out for a wilderness park near Redfield instead of the old log cabin near town where they had told their parents they were camping. It was about ten miles west of town, and turned out to be a momentous change of plan.

The older brother was elsewhere, and that day George Modlin became their leader. Half a mile east of the one-track lane into the park, they left the car in a farmer's yard and took their packs and forded a low creek that separated the park from the farm and took off overland. Miles and Bob acquired sticks to impersonate rifles and straggled along after George over an invisible track through the woods toward a ridge that George said overlooked a little shelter house in the center of the park.

Climbing the last hill, George acted the lead scout and went ahead to look at the clearing. He was good at stalking for a big fellow, and disappeared for twenty minutes and then popped out of the undergrowth behind them while they were gabbing and cutting up. George said there was already a car parked by the shelter; someone else had gotten there first, and they would have to make camp in a little clearing he knew of this side of the ridge where they wouldn't interfere with them. Finding someone already there seemed to upset him a little. He had been playing along with their games before, but he suddenly stiffened up, and when they made their camp below the ridge he made them curb the nonsense. They had pegged out their tents and roasted the hot dogs and eaten the potatoes they covered with clay and cooked in the coals, but when the two boys wanted to sing songs like *Home on the Range* around the fire, George shut them up. He stole off again to check on their neighbors, and when he came back he told Jack that another car had come in and there were more of them down there now. He had counted five cigarettes. His broad, amiable face looked grim when he told Bob to douse the fire, and he made Bob sleep in Jack's tent, and put Miles in his tent so the two boys would not be able to get together and start horsing around. They called him a wet blanket, but Miles overheard him outside telling Jack in a low voice that he had seen a man with a gun in the doorway of the shelter, but that it was too dark now for them to pull out. After that, Miles was quiet and spent a long time lying rigid listening to the strange forest sounds and looking at the crack of the tent flap. The next thing, his eyes seemed still to be open, but the dawn was squeezing through the tent flap, and just when he started to crawl out to pee, the other side of the ridge erupted in fireworks like a Chinese New Year.

Gunshots clapped from the trees on the ridge a few yards above them, and more came from a distance. They lay flat in the tents and heard a distant car rev through the gears. A machine gun chattered from below and incited a whole barrage from the hillside. Then there was a lull. Miles said, "What the *hell!*" and tried to get out, and George jerked him back by the ankle as the fusillade started up again, and he got really scared when George's big square face a couple of inches away from him turned blue-looking and grim. It seemed that he watched an ant for a long time struggling to carry a part of a grasshopper across the little clods under his nose while the shooting went on. Finally it stopped and men's voices sounded from the hollow yelling and cheering as though they'd won a big game.

George crawled out, and Bob and Jack followed him, crouching the way George did, up through the bush to the ridge line. There they looked down on a crowd of armed men milling around excitedly, some with shot guns broken over their arms, others were poking in the hut with drawn pistols. And they recognized Sheriff Knee down on the bank of the creek angrily stamping up and down and pointing into the timber on the other side and giving orders.

"God a' mighty!" Jack hissed, "Look there!" Just off the track half way between the shelter and the one-track lane, a Ford sedan had run into a tree and was tilted to the side with its tires flat and all the windows shot out. There were hundreds of holes in its doors like wormholes in old wood. The other Ford had gotten almost to the creek. Its doors were hanging open and men were looking into it. A station wagon and two cars emerged from the woods on the one-track lane and stopped at the riddled car by the tree and there was a long parlay. Finally someone got in on the other side and helped get a body out. Then they pulled out a woman. She was wearing riding breeches and dark glasses, and when she saw the body, she began screaming and flailing her arms. They put the body in the back of the station wagon, and the woman in a car, and the two vehicles pulled around and disappeared back down the lane. People were beating the bushes across the creek, but there didn't seem to be any hurry now.

"Who were they?" awed Miles asked George. "They're two Fords ain't they?" George said, "Let's go".

They crouched back down the ridge and folded up the tents quiet and quick and made tracks back to the creek. George wouldn't let them cross till he watched up and down, then they got the Essex and drove in the other direction, south to the highway, and back to town. The two Ford sedans and the Tommy gun had tipped George off last night. "Clyde Barrow wrote Henry Ford that he won't use anything but Fords for his getaway cars."

"I guess they won't be using these any more." Jack said. "I guess they got 'em this time."

The Modlins swore Miles to silence on his honor when they let him off at home. "If you tell them we were there there's going to be trials and stuff and we'll be in hot water forever for taking you to Dexfield! Now you be quiet, Miles! *Swear*?" Miles swore.

Dexfield Park, a rugged, uncleared stretch of timber, ten miles west, had briefly sheltered one of the deadliest gangs in the Midwest. Miles, who had been there, and was afraid to say so, learned when his father came home that night that Clyde Barrow and Bonnie Parker, and a henchman named W. D. Jones, had somehow abandoned their riddled car and crossed the creek and escaped. Clyde's brother Buck died of wounds in the hospital in Perry; his wife, only wounded in the eye by flying glass in the Missouri shootout the week before, was in custody. Sheriff Knee later said that the gang had intended to lie low in the deserted park till their wounds healed, but the radio news of their flight from the Missouri shootout had alerted a farmer who reported the five strangers with two cars

35

camping in the Dexfield shelter. While the four boys were heading for the park in the Essex, the sheriff had recruited a posse of fifty armed men and come to Dexfield Park to take the Barrows dead or alive.

It was Bonnie and Clyde whom George had seen returning in the late afternoon from a trip to Perry to get medicine for Buck and Blanche. And Sheriff Knee, who was later appointed commander of Iowa's first highway patrol, had deployed his posse on the hills above the cabin without a hitch. The little camp of four boys was doubtless in more danger from the posse than from the Barrows, but their east end of the hollow was a *cul-de-sac* and sparsely staked out. At dawn, when the Barrows went to get water at the creek, every gun on the hills had opened up. Buck Barrow got his wife in the car and tried to make a break, but was soon mortally wounded. Bonnie and Clyde and Jones abandoned their riddled Ford and made it across the creek. They stole a farmer's car and got away.

Miles only caught up with this the next week, when the entire window of the Southside Drug was devoted to a display on the Barrow ambush. He would remember most vividly the big glossy black and white blowup of Blanche Barrow in a man's white shirt and riding breeches, straining in the clutch of two strong-arm deputies, her face behind her black-lensed pilot's glasses a Medea mask of defiance and despair. "That's when they just told her Buck was dead," a man looking at the window over his shoulder said. The bizarre figure, everyone in the county's perfect conception of a hardened gang moll, was an innocent farm girl who had fallen in love with Buck Barrow and walked into several lifetimes of bad luck. The black glasses concealed her wounded eye filled with glass splinters that would ultimately destroy its sight.

That day he and Bob Modlin and Jim Mitchell went from the drugstore window to the Ford garage, where Jim borrowed Golden Mitchell's key to a small airless room in the rear of the garage where Buck Barrow's "death car" had been stored. For a minute they would stand in awed silence in the heat and dust motes still smelling faintly of blood. Then they would step forward and place their fingers gingerly in the bullet holes in the sides of the car.

The next year Bonnie and Clyde were killed in an ambush on a country road in Louisiana.. Miles and the Modlin boys had come within an ace of making their acquaintance. True to his oath, Miles kept the secret of the adventure till his freshman year in high school when the Modlins took another farm out of the county and moved away. One night he almost told the story in a crowded car on the way to a music contest, but the fact that everyone in the car would know the outcome the moment he started to tell it made him substitute a fanciful Halloween story instead.

The first week of the new school year Miles discovered by chance that he had become a New Deal Democrat, and a violent one at that. When the Morgans had visited J. Arthur's brother Chester in Des Moines one Sunday during the presidential campaign, his cousin Kenneth, several years older, had treated everyone after dinner to a rendition of a Republican campaign verse about possession of the White House that was then going around his school.

> *Hoover at the front door talking to a lady.*
> *Roosevelt at the back door crying like a baby.*

Miles brooded about the verse on the way home, as he had sensed his mother's displeasure with his aunt's effusive praise of Herbert Hoover. The next time boys started bantering about the election in the school yard in Adel, he turned the slogan upside down and sang it ya-ya style in the face of a boy named Fred Gibbony who had come out strong for Herbert Hoover:

Roosevelt at the front door talking to a lady.
Hoover at the back door crying like a baby,

.

That evening after school, he and Fred met alone in a grim rendezvous on the lawn of a house across the street from the high school. They abused each other's candidates, then each other, and when Fred called him a "rich kid," Miles pushed him, and they fought. It wasn't the last time he would be called this despised name (though at that time J. Arthur's salary was $150 a month) or the last fight he would have about it, for although Roosevelt was the favorite of most of the children at school, Ferne continued to buy Miles' school clothes at Frankel's in Des Moines, where J. Arthur bought his suits, and sent him to school dressed like Freddy Bartholomew--the snooty English child actor popular at the time--and in a year when perhaps a third of the parents of his friends were out of work, and the paper claimed *11 MILLION JOBLESS*, "rich kid" was the ultimate dirty name.

Most people were focused on the home perils, and when Roosevelt won the presidency by a landslide and said we had "*nothing to fear but fear itself*," people took it that he had a plan by then for putting *thirteen million* jobless back to work.

But Miles' parents also listened to the pulse of the world, which was limping dangerously. Japan invaded Manchuria, and J. Arthur explained to Miles the difference between the Japanese (small-statured, militaristic, island people who were a rising naval power in the Pacific) and the Chinese, (the oldest civilization, who had invented fireworks, but were peaceful people who made the delicate bamboo junks for coffee table decor that Woolworth sold). In January, Adolf Hitler became the German chancellor, and J. Arthur called Hitler an international gangster. Ferne wondered why the Nazis were boycotting Jewish

38

businesses and expelling Jews from professions, from state jobs, from teaching in schools. The *Des Moines Register* said concentration camps were being created to imprison Jews.

An American heavyweight named Max Baer, who had killed a man in the ring in 1930, fought the German Max Schmeling in Yankee Stadium, in August. The Morgans all listened to the broadcast because the prize fighter's cousin lived in Adel a few blocks away. Miles listened because his mother did--it surprised him, since she affected to deplore men beating each other for sport---that when the American pounded Schmeling so badly that the fight was stopped in the tenth round, Ferne clapped her hands and cried, "Take that, you Nazi!"

Perhaps Max Baer's victory was the bright spot of a winter when no one knew what was coming next, or from what quarter. Miles heard *15 MILLION UNEMPLOYED*, but a more painful sign of the Depression deepening in his restricted orbit was Christmas when he had asked Santa for three cars for his American Flyer and received only one.

The new president, Franklin Roosevelt, declared a "bank holiday," which Miles learned was not a picnic but a harbinger of national bankruptcy, "Collapse!" moaned J. Arthur. "Wait and see," said Ferne, "He will turn it around!" She loved Roosevelt, and maybe his wife Eleanor even more. And she pointed out that Uncle Bill House, who had been tapped by Rex Tugwell, the president's brain-trust boss, for a post in the new administration, had rented his house in Huron and moved the family to a suite in the Mayflower Hotel in Washington. "Our new First Assistant Postmaster General Bill House will soon have the Depression well in hand," she said, with irony that even Miles picked up on.

George Kinnick and Jim Mitchell often came to help Miles run his train on the weekends that spring when Frances Kinnick was at work and George's two older brothers moved their endless football game to the Park. One sunny Sunday afternoon when George was helping run the train, a red dusk settled on the town and blotted out the sun. J. Arthur passed the parlor where the track was and turned the ceiling light on, "It's Kansas blowing away," he said cryptically. The following week the National Land Bank transferred Nile, Sr. to Omaha, and he started living there during the week and driving home on weekends. The rest of the family would stay in Adel through the school year, Jun's sophomore year, Ben's freshman.

The *Dallas County News* gloated that Clyde Barrow and Bonnie Parker had finally been ambushed and killed outside Shreveport, Louisiana. It said they had murdered more than a dozen people.

In June, the prize fighter Max Baer, whom the media called a playboy, was serious long enough to win the heavyweight crown from Primo Carnera in the eleventh round after knocking down the gigantic Italian twelve times. J Arthur mentioned that a house on Rapids Street next to Max Baer's cousin's was going to come on the market next fall; perhaps they would buy it. Miles thought it would be a thrill to move in next door to the world champion's cousin.

Before October, the Adel football team shook the little town wide awake. Every Friday night in the fall, at home under the lights a block from the Tullis house, or at Dexter, Dallas Center, West Des Moines or Winterset, Jun's side-yard pick-up team, now in leather helmets and black-and-red jerseys, won a game, sometimes by forty or fifty points. Jun Kinnick threw touchdown passes to his brother, and with his compact brick-like frame bursting through his line of farm boys and factory roughs, ran through all the opposing secondaries to a score of touchdowns. J. Arthur marveled that his paper boy completed passes for forty and fifty yards repeatedly, and once punted the ball sixty yards.

People arrived for the games from farther out in the county every Friday night and forgot their hard times for two hours, and came away celebrating the best high school team they would ever see. Sportswriters from the city came to the last games of the season to watch the "corn belt comet" and decide that Jun Kinnick would be the first sophomore to ever make all-state. Ferne pitied Nile, Sr., who had to drive two hours from Omaha every Friday evening after work to see part of the game his boys were winning. And Miles, who truly did not comprehend that he was watching a national athletic career take off like a rocket (as who did, in the fall of 1933?), affected an old-boy unsurprise when he told kids from defeated schools that "Jun Kinnick's just our paper boy."

For some disobedience, and "insubordination" he was condemned to stay home from the last game in November, which would decide whether Adel had won the mythical state football championship. Miles' parents went off to the game and left him with Constance. She studied in the living room while he sat at his card table looking in *Popular Mechanics* at the silhouettes of warships on a graph showing how the Japanese were defying the naval limitations placed on them by the Europeans and the Americans. There were silhouettes of battleships and cruisers and submarines which he tried to draw, and then called Constance to come and admire, absorbed in ships and insensible to the wild cheering that rose to a crescendo from the field at the end of the block.

At nine-thirty a stream of honking cars poured out of the field and down the street, and a boisterous crowd passed on the front walk heading down town to celebrate in the cafes or the speakeasy near the Rock Island tracks. His parents stopped on their way to a victory party, and he saw his father actually do a jig from excitement, twirling around in the kitchen on one foot and yelling, "Adel's Iowa State Champs!" He grabbed Miles up and swung him around,

41

"You should have seen those Kinnick brothers tonight!" Ferne took Miles upstairs and put him to bed.

Then he was alone in the big bed, too excited to go to sleep and waiting like a dungeon prisoner for Constance, who, this fall, had taken to dressing for bed in the bathroom. When he heard the stealthy creek of the door after ever so long, and she slipped in under the covers, not bothering to ask him if he had said his prayers, as she did when they went to bed at the same time, it filled him with a wild troll-like glee to lie still facing the wall pretending to be asleep and counting two hundred while she settled down on her side facing away from him. Then, still with his eyes shut, he suddenly turned over and snuggled up tight to her back, now he the spoon and she the "spoonful," and flung his arm over her and tried to hug her closer. He felt something strange when he groped over her ribs, and a kind of a bomb went off in his head, and Constance kicked violently and sat up shrieking, "Miles Morgan!" in a voice he had never heard from her, and which made him burn with guilty glee.

But suddenly a strange new perplexity caught in his throat, and he retreated silently to his own side and turned to the wall. He was still awake ever so much later, still simmering in a feverish consternation--what was *that* he burned his fingers on?--when he heard his parents come home, and sensed Constance awake too, far over on her side.

The next day Constance was gone to school before he woke, and when he came home from school, his mother said they had had "a little talk," and they had decided that he was grownup enough this year to go back to his own room. Ferne had already made up his old bed.

The rest of the winter he slept alone; things were changed between him and Constance, not in any way specifically, but a strange sort of abashment affected him in her presence, and though they had laughed much together almost like friends before, from that time on she seemed to keep a certain barrier between them that stifled her smile at his pranks and the show-off stunts she had laughed at once. Ferne's reaction, too, deepened his mystification, as something he had done--which he did not know and she did not specify--seemed to have embarrassed her before Constance. Yet, he detected a note of suppressed bravado in her voice through the bedroom wall when he eavesdropped on her telling his father about the incident. But on his father's side, there was no doubt that whatever he had done had earned J. Arthur's furious disapproval.

In the spring of 1934, Constance graduated and married her fiancé, a young farmer, and went to live on a place just off Highway Six on the way to Des Moines. After that, from time to time the Morgans would stop to visit with Constance and her husband, and he would always feel a little tongue-tied in her presence because he never got over the suspicion that she had married and moved away because he had somehow failed her as a bed companion.

A large pile of sand, and ranks of brick from the Adel tile factory were unloaded at the gate of the football field in the spring, and a crew of bricklayers worked for a month to build an impressive eight-foot brick wall ramped up to a brick arch across the entrance to the football field, and connected to a tidy brick building with two dressing rooms for the football teams. On the concrete medallion set into the base of the arch it said, *1933 UNDEFEATED TEAM*. The keystone at the top said that it was in memory of C. S. Macy, whose family financed it. It was tall and impressive, but the Depression overtook it, and there was no money left to outfit the dressing rooms with showers and lockers. The water was never connected, and the Macys moved to California. Miles and his friends ran on top of the walls and climbed to the top of the arch to look over the park. The unfurnished locker rooms became shelters for homeless men passing through, and the walls became soot-covered with the smoke of the small fires they lit to cook their stews.

In the summer, the eight-year-old Dutch colonial on Rapids Street became available when the widow of the former owner of the New Rialto movie theater decided to follow her children to California, and J. Arthur bought the house on installments. Nile Kinnick, Sr., had found a modest house in Omaha and moved Frances and the boys there, and soon word drifted back to Adel that Jun and Ben Kinnick had made the football team at Omaha's Benson High.

2

Down so Long

In 1934, a month after Max Baer became Heavyweight Champion of the World, the Morgans moved into the house on Rapids St. across from a brick church with no steeple, a block north of the courthouse, and next door to the fighter's cousin. It was a compact jewel box of a house, a small pre-Depression Dutch colonial, every builder's feature of it top of the line, from oak floors and beveled glass mirrors in the oak doors to a fine glassed-in sleeping porch elevated over the driveway by square columns, which made a portico for the side entrance. But for Miles, the ultimate luxury feature of the house was a furnace which sprouted pipes carrying heat to the registers in every room, upstairs and down. The next winter his principal winter chore would become tending the new stoker that augured the coal into the furnace from a hopper that had to be filled every two days.

The living room ran the depth of the house, with two large front windows and a bank of windows along the east side, beneath which, from a reclining hideout on the padded window seat, he covertly studied the three Baer girls next door as they carried on their complicated social life from their open front porch. He could compare the actual girl with the ideal by turning his glance to the picture in a gilt frame above the fireplace, where Ferne had hung a Maxfield Parrish print of a bevy of wan beauties clad in see-through scarves who trailed their fingers in a marble reflecting pool backed by distant rose-hewed mountain peaks. At the Tullis house, he had often studied the scene and wondered if it was somewhere on the grounds of the

Taj-Mahal. Here he wondered if the maidens were harem girls.

The Morgans' new address was close enough to downtown Adel that the unemployed men on their way through by thumb on Highway 169 who perched like a flock of ragged crows on the pipe railings guarding the stairs to the barber shop under the bank, found Ferne's backdoor handouts within easy walking distance. They seemed to know the Morgans were good for a handout right off, and Ferne would complain that she could watch them saunter past every other house on the block to turn straight into her driveway and knock on her back door. She still fed all who were willing to do a little work in the yard or split some kindling, but was so mystified that they knew her house that she sometimes walked up an down across the street looking for their chalk mark on her steps. J. Arthur never told her that they kept track of the Morgans through their grapevine in the jungles going in and out of Iowa along the Milwaukee line.

What these men got was what the Morgans were eating. And, watching them as they sat on the back steps munching the leftovers of the Morgans' lunch made Miles aware that the Morgans were now dining less often on "Depression food", such as mush and milk, fried mush with sorghum (eaten like pancakes) and chipped beef on toast, and that the occasional austerity entrees of bread and warmed up gravy had ended.

Now the pot roasts reappeared (with potatoes, carrots and onions), and pork chops, and fried chicken with mashed potatoes and gravy, or chicken with dumplings and homemade noodles.

Years later, when he was in the service, a passing whiff from the battalion bakery, like the olfactory inspiration of Proust's Madelaine, would resurrect the memory of Ferne's homemade bread, and raise a mirage before his eyes of a winter day home from school when his first breath in the house was of pans of bread and clover-leaf rolls rising under tea towels on all the hot air registers.

And then the baked hams, which, with the help of the hoboes at the back door, the family soon reduced to casseroles of scalloped potatoes and ham, and finally to a ham hock that would flavor a three-day pot of navy beans that was Miles' favorite of the sequence and worth working diligently through the preliminary metamorphoses of the ham to finally reach an inch-thick slice of home-made bread piled high with a steaming ladle of ham and beans, and crowned with a giant wedge of farm butter that swam around on top till it dripped down the beans in golden rivulets and spread out on the soup that filled the plate.

Yet, the simple cooking of a steak remained Ferne's downfall. She still bought the round steak or occasional sirloin in the Depression quarter-inch cut, and in approved farm tradition, fried it till it was dead brown all the way through. Steak was the only kind of meal that defeated her, and J. Arthur knew better than to complain, though his son had seen him devour an inch-thick Porterhouse with gusto when Uncle Bill House bought his dinner at the Ft. Des Moines Hotel on one of his flying visits from the East.

Though J. Arthur continued to frown on the hoboes who came to the Morgans' back door for handouts, he often came home with a new kind of paring knife that would "cut paper," or a patented apple corer he had purchased from one of these men who carried such items and would sell them on the square when they could attract a customer. He was a soft touch for their pitches, perhaps because of his Republican credo that prosperity was generated by individual enterprise, which he was encouraging by buying their trinkets. He occasionally loitered with them on the railings till dinner time, soliciting their opinions as guest experts on vital topics of the day such as how to avert a shortage of beer now that

Prohibition was over. And one evening, he had hoisted himself with the rest of the "loafers" onto the saw teeth that had been bolted to the pipe railings to discourage them from blocking the light to the basement businesses--which their restless bottoms had long worn shiny and blunt--and had come home late for dinner chuckling about watching Dr. Mershon un-park his Ford, "Quite a show!"

Body Shop: All Makes

He said that at six the doctor had come down and gotten in his car, which was always parked diagonally in front of the Rexall Store below his office. The doctor was in his eighties, and the car had been a late and unsatisfactory replacement for his horse and carriage--so it was his way to start it, put it in reverse, and when the engine was shrieking, pop the clutch and send the little sedan shooting backward across the street until it bounced off the opposite curb or jumped onto the courthouse parking. J. Arthur said the downtown people knew this and kept the parking spot on the other side of the street open in the late afternoons so that no harm was done, but Ferne said she could think of ten reasons it was dangerous.

A few days later, Miles and Jim Mitchell were on their way home from the square at six. As they passed the loafers' corner, they noticed a larger, livelier crowd than usual sitting on the railings, and saw that diametrically behind the doctor's little Ford in its usual place in front of the Rexall drug, a large black sedan with white sidewalls and California plates was parked at the courthouse curb.

They altered course and went into the drug store out of curiosity to see the tourists and observe how they would cope with adversity. They both picked up comic books from the magazine rack near the front window and peered over them at a well-dressed couple finishing ice cream sodas in a back booth. (After the fact, their parents had

48

scolded them for not introducing themselves to these guests of the town and warning them about the placement of their car--but the boys, with the age-old wisdom of children, already knew that the young may advise their elders, but never influence them a whit, and they had simply waited, whispering and standing on one foot and the other from impatience and suspense.

The doctor, a trim little man with a white moustache, came out of his door and got into his Ford while the prosperous California couple paid Mr. Cozad at the register and paused at the door to consider chewing gum. To Miles' companion, who was already a tireless booster of his father's Ford garage, and always had a stack of its business cards, *Mitchell Motors: Golden Mitchell--Ford, Mercury, Lincoln--Ford Trucks,* it presented a natural business opportunity, and he fished one out of his pocket. As he hesitated to polish his sales pitch, Miles snatched the card and intercepted the Californian in the doorway.

"I'm giving out these cards to friends of Ford today, sir." he said, and bowed a little as he extended one. The Californian took the card, gave it a perfunctory look and handed it back.

"My car is that new La Salle. Ford is not..." he said, and pointed at the shining sedan across the street just as the doctor's car roared to life, and the tenants of the railing across the corner stood up in unison.

"*Body shop!*" Miles said, "*All Makes!*" The rest of his sentence was drowned in the shriek of the doctor's engine. The nimble little Ford leaped like a kangaroo and crossed the street backward in less than a second and smashed the rear of the La Salle.

"Ho-ly smoke!" The Californian cried. He put both hands in his hair, and started toward the wreck, but then did a pirouette and took the card from Miles and ran across the street as the doctor shifted into low, his normal driving

49

gear, and started for home with the big La Salle hooked to his bumper.

The accident had been noted from the sheriff's office in the courthouse. No doubt they had been keeping casual watch on Dr. Mershon's parking problem because a deputy came right out. The loafers came from the corner and milled around the two cars helpfully and stood on the locked bumpers and bounced them. When the Ford garage tow truck arrived, Miles went home and told his parents about the La Salle and its owners who would be spending the night at the Arlington Hotel.

George Kinnick had returned for part of summer vacation to stay at the old governor's long gray stone house at the head of Court Street, and before the Morgans went on vacation, Miles would often ride his bike up to see him. If he timed himself to arrive around eleven, George's grandmother, Arletta, would invite the boys to ride with her in her electric car while she made calls. The electric was tall and shiny black, and from a distance looked something like an early Model T Ford, except that the little suitcase-size trunk was the same at both ends. Front and rear were just alike, and in the middle the passenger compartment was like a greenhouse with tall windows all around, and the same kind of windshield looking both ways.

Inside, it was also the same at both ends; upholstered seats about the width of a love seat faced each other. Arletta Clarke would face forward on the outward leg of the trip, steering with a tiller in the middle of the floor. When she was ready to return home she did not turn the car around, but reversed the tiller and latched it and placed George and Miles on the opposite seat and drove home backward.

One July day Miles tried to eke out a longer ride by persuading Arletta to drive past their new house on Rapids Street. He said his neighbor now was Max Baer's cousin, and offered to introduce George to Lester Baer if they saw him on the porch. But George already knew about Lester Baer, and he was unimpressed by Miles' attempt to prove that Adel still had sports celebrities after Jun Kinnick. He said his brother, who had again made All State in Nebraska, was auditioning for various college teams, while Max Baer had clowned away his heavyweight crown to Jim Braddock. When Miles countered that, Bob Feller, 17, who was now pitching semi-pro baseball out of Des Moines, had recently thrown a pitch that beat a racing motorcycle, George said he had only beaten the motorcycle because its top speed was ninety. He told Miles that when Nile had been catching for Bob Feller on the Legion team, he had once put a round steak in his mitt and brought it out at the end of the inning perfectly tenderized. After that, Miles became uncharacteristically quiet and turned to the window to watch the town pass by in slow motion.

Under the great elms by the river, Adel nodded through the heat wave of the summer of 1936. Because the W.P.A. was building Adel's first swimming pool, and Ferne would not let Miles swim in the Raccoon River, the family went to Lake Okoboji and took a cabin for ten days.

When they returned in the middle of August, George had gone home to Omaha, and it was a major disappointment that Miles could not show him the new Gabby Hartnett catcher's mitt he had gotten for his birthday. He had chosen to be a catcher because Jun Kinnick was a catcher, and it was a genuine, grown-up catcher's mitt, which he had mounted a big campaign for. And now that he had his mitt--of course he would not allow anyone else to use it--he felt a certain destiny for the position. Though he knew he was still a chubby, squarish fellow who could seldom hit the ball over the infield, he felt that Coach Townsend was satisfied with the steady chatter of baseball pepper talk which he copied from the semi-pro players, and favored him running his mouth behind the plate to bolster the pitcher and pep up the team.

51

But the fact that words flew out of his mouth before he thought about them had recently begun to bother him a little. In fact, his too-ready tongue had made it a stormy year at school. He had been punched in the face till his eyes watered by a tough girl who had taken offense at a slur against her sex which he had blurted out without even knowing what it meant. And a boy named John Hall, whose basketball style of launching a no-look pass into the stands had inspired Miles to do a comic imitation of him in the locker room (intended in good fun) had recruited a posse of two other boys he had also offended, and chased him home all spring.

Then, in late August after a baseball practice: when he had got a hit that had rolled through the fielder's legs, and for once had beaten out a double, and all-in-all, had had a good day, he separated from his friends on the gravel that curved both ways out of the park, and was trudging past the arch of the Undefeated Team dragging his bat and swinging his new mitt on his wrist, when he heard a car coming into the park from Twelfth Street. He looked back and spotted an old junker sedan coming down the hill making more dust than speed. As it got close to the little clump of his four friends, he saw it swerve at them and make them dive for the ditch. He was instantly filled with some towering righteous outrage, and as the car approached him, he turned and faced it, "You could have hit them!" And when they swung at *him* in the same way and shook their fists out the window, he spat in their eyes just the kind of a gob he had been spitting into his new glove all afternoon. The glimpse he got of them ducking his spit made him start to laugh, but after the old jalopy roared away down 9th Street and turned out of sight, he soon heard it rising again from afar like an angry wasp, and he picked up his pace.

He was on the walk in front of the Tullis house by the time it tore out through the gate behind him and ground to a stop at the curb. It was a big old bus of a kind not made any more, rustier all over than anything he had ever seen outside the junk yard.

"You spit, piss ant!"

He looked over his shoulder at the Tullis house. A sprinkler was working on his former front lawn, but there was no one in sight on the block.

"Aw naw!"

"You did. Why'd you spit?"

"I got a cold." He tried to fake a cough, but there wasn't anything there. In the car they started muttering among themselves like a bunch of judges deciding what to do with a condemned man. The guy riding shotgun was someone from the factory. The shadow inside the car kept him from seeing any of the others except the one on this side in the back whose face was turned away talking to the driver. Something unpleasantly familiar about the big head. No boy. When it turned toward him, the round face with its pop eyes made something go sick at the pit of his stomach. It was Nels who had tried to take the steely from him in the school yard once. Nineteen or twenty he must be now. The others were still quibbling, but Nels shrugged them off and got out.

"Sucker, you spit on me," Nels wiped the back of his hand across his face, and a weird straight-across grimace that came out from under it made Miles take a half-step back. He was locked on the eyes, glassy and empty as a fallow field with a kind of question pointed inside, not at him. Miles now remembered that Nels had been in the reform school. "Yeah, you did,"

Miles went backward another step and felt the sidewalk. He could hear the sprinkler hissing with a relentless sylvan sound in the dismal sunshine. For a moment, the world was empty except Nels standing over him like a tin cutout, and the old thing with the steely starting over where J. Arthur had stopped it. "What you got here?"

"Nothing," he said, holding up the bat.
"Naw, *that*," Nels pointed at the Gabby Hartnett mitt. "Here." Nels put out his big dirty hand for the glove.

Miles saw that Nels was going to have his new mitt, not to look at, but to keep as a kind of payback for the spit. He looked back wistfully at the Tullis house, but the windows were empty and his father was a long ways away. Something like a clairvoyant vision of the next ten seconds came as clear as a scene in a crystal ball. He wasn't going to give up his mitt. But he had the bat. That was what he had. But the mitt was on his left wrist. If he dropped the mitt to use both hands on the bat, he would maybe get in one swing. If one swing didn't do it, it would be Nels's turn at bat. In fact, in that bulging-eyed gawk, he could tell Nels already saw this, too, and was watching with interest for him to decide.

He took a breath. The ten seconds started. But he would not drop the mitt. He was locked to it like the monkey who starved to death because he wouldn't let go of the handful of nuts in a narrow-necked jar. But just as he knew the time was up, the car door creaked and someone crossed the parking and did what the half brother had done that other time--put a hand on Nels's shoulder, "Come on, let it be. Someone's coming."

Nels didn't move, but it broke the bubble and he looked away down the street.

Miles' salvation was Bill Rhodes. Gingerly, he turned Nels and led him back to the car. Somebody in back shouted a dire threat about his future. But Bill Rhodes got behind the wheel and drove away.

A week or so after it happened, he started to tell his mother a version of the incident beginning with Bill stopping Nels from taking his new mitt. Ferne was driving to Perry--the town where Buck Barrow had died--where

54

Miles took a swimming lesson twice a week. When he mentioned Bill Rhodes, she asked him if he remembered Bill's family living next door when they lived up in the west end, and wanted to know how those boys were doing in the summer band. The Morgans and some other parents, she said, had put in to help the Rhodes boys rent their band instruments because their father was still out of a job. Miles decided on the spur of the moment not to tell the story of Nels, since the point he had had in mind was how Bill Rhodes saving his bacon with Nels, the jailbird, showed how much Bill liked him (even if he spat at his car?). He said they were doing fine in the band.

Signs of the Times

The New Rialto now had air conditioning, and all the kids went to the Friday night Western with someone like Tom Mix or Joel McRay doing *The Way West* or *The Alamo* or a reprise of the range wars.

Various swash buckling chronicles of the British Empire began to come along. *The Lives of A Bengal Lancer, The Charge of the The Light Brigade, Gunga Din* and *Four Feathers,* introduced dashing heroes with a sense of humor--which western stars like Randolph Scott lacked. Sophisticated and ironic, though comrades to the death, Franchot Tone, Errol Flynn and David Niven, Douglas Fairbanks, Jr., and a very young Cary Grant were as cool as Tom Mix was hot.

Moreover, since the shootout with the Barrows in Dexfield Park, Miles and the Modlin boys and Jim Mitchell and Herb Robbins had started to see real life in the doom-bound wiseguys like Jimmy Cagney and Edward G. Robinson ("Can this be the end of Rocco?") and had begun to play Cops and Gangsters.

Though Gary Cooper was the strong, silent pioneer type, Clark Gable was the best kind of really *modern* American hero, a slick-haired, street-wise man's man, whose moustache caught women's attention and whose wise cracks reeled them in (could a kid ever learn to do that?). When he saw Clark Gable with Claudette Colbert in *It Happened One Night*, where the unemployed reporter and the runaway rich girl team up hitchhiking and spend the night in the one-room tourist cabin, and Gable rigs a curtain wall with a sheet to oblige Colbert's maidenly modesty, Miles began to get an inkling that something more than his roughhouse snuggle had prompted his eviction from Margaret's bed.

Yet, before any main feature, he took in news flashes of the simmering European cauldron from Pathe' newsreels and *the March of Time*. They brought glass-jawed Mussolini posturing over his invasion of the Ethiopian kingdom of Haile Selassie *"The Lion of Judah,"* who became America's sympathetic hero.

They provided cuts of Hitler hosting the 1936 Summer Olympics in Berlin, where the necessity of presenting three gold medals to a black American athlete, Jesse Owens, discomposed him so much that he left the stadium and went into seclusion. Everyone despised Mussolini on sight, but the fork-tongued Fuehrer, who had hidden his concentration camps and taken down "No Jews Allowed" signs for the sake of Olympic public relations, confused many--not only Neville Chamberlain, but also Charles Lindbergh, the transatlantic hero, who came back from a celebrity tour of the Reich and announced that the Nazis had some swell ideas and that their air force could whip the French and British combined.

Newsreel sports showed the latest champion flagpole sitter and dance marathons from the West Coast. And Miles, who had become the sometime playmate-sometime pet of the three Baer girls next door, went into mourning with the whole family after seeing Max Baer, who had clowned away the heavyweight crown, knocked out by Joe Louis, the Brown Bomber. Miles, and Jean, the youngest daughter, two years older than Miles began walking to the Friday night movies together when Jean couldn't find a date.

Newsreel Football always featured Ivy League teams, Yale vs. Harvard, or Brown against Colgate, games which the film maker could cover by sending newsreel photographers to the games by car from New York. These films always implied Ivy League football was the best in the land, which Midwesterners were beginning to realize was baloney. To lighten things up, serious sports reels were garnished with bathing beauty contests from Coral Gables, Florida and ranks of surfboarding beauties in brief one-piece bathing suits.

When the Spanish Civil War began, the Russians helped the Loyalists, and Hitler helped the Rebels. Some Americans organized to fight for the Loyalists but America was non-interventionist, and they were forbidden to go. Loyalist was a good name. Republican was an even better, but Fascism and Communism were both bad. Midwesterners didn't have a clue. Miles had never heard of Ernest Hemingway, a tough-guy writer in Wyoming who announced he was going to Spain to find out. He went to Madrid and found his third wife.

J. Arthur watched the sitdown strike at General Motors that started on Christmas Eve 1936 and went on for forty-four days. All Miles remembered of it was the big picture of the Flint, Michigan plant which the *Des Moines Tribune* published the day the strikers won, with workers waving improvised victory flags out of all the windows, and their wives on the streets outside cheering them. Ferne preened over the labor victory because J. Arthur had been predicting they would vandalize the plant, and they had not. After that, they still squabbled about it, but J. Arthur let up on his jeremiads against organized labor a little. After all, the Wagner act had legalized labor organization and picketing. When there was a steel strike in Chicago on Memorial Day of 1937 and fifty strikers were shot, some of them women and children, Jay Arthur shook his head and condemned the police as vehemently as he had the American Nazi rally in New York that had protested the boycott on Nazi imports.

On the other side of the world, the Japanese bombed and strafed an American gunboat, the Panay, sheltering diplomats from the Japanese army, which was raping Nanking. (Though it remained unknown in the West that the Japanese had butchered 300,000 Chinese noncombatants with their three-body swords there, when millions of Americans saw newsreels of their bullet-riddled Panay with its gunwales awash, they felt the first ghost of an inkling that the Japanese would ultimately turn our way).

Going to the Adel Public Library was the only one of his habits his parents encouraged, and before sixth grade Miles had devoured a history, *The Great War*, read up the Lafayette Escadrille, and begun a series of new sea novels about the adventures of the crew of a Liverpool-registered tramp steamer that plied all seas. The deckhand and the oiler and his mates talked in a cockney dialect, and soon Miles could blurt out their favorite expletives at the dinner table. "*Gor blimey*!" he would say if the soup was too hot, and Ferne would invoke her ban on profanity, though J. Arthur hazarded that he thought it meant "God bless me."

Three novels on the U.S. Army Air Corps and the hero's adventures through training and qualification as a fighter pilot at Rantoul Field, Illinois, prompted Miles to decide on a career in the Army Air Corps. Being eleven, he could do little about it but amass a rag tag squadron of balsa airplanes which he and his friends would take on cross country formation flights around the block. He began to put into his nightly prayers the request that the Lord favor his vocation as a pilot, after invoking blessings on his parents and friends. Lately when his Uncle Maurice Gordon's family left their failing South Dakota farm and headed for the West Coast in a new car, but without enough money to get there, he added them before the ah-men.

Doubt and Death

He was accustomed to say these prayers in his bed, but he had heard Ferne tell his father that Hazel had said that Uncle Bill House got down on his knees beside his bed in the Mayflower Hotel every night to say *his* prayers no matter how drunk he was when he came home from politicking, and he began to think he ought to try it on the floor because not much faith welled up in him in the bed.

Since his grandmother had died just into the new year, Death had started a kind of crisis of belief in him.

For Christmas, Mary Ellen, who was dying of lymph cancer, had given him an expensive hard-cover book full of black-and-white photographs of dioramas of the life of Christ sculpted by one Dominico Mastroianni. The three-dimensional scenes were done in great detail against bas-relief backdrops of Jeruselem and the Sea of Galilee and Golgotha. In them an ascetic, Nordic-looking Christ was portrayed with ferocious masochism bleeding under the Crown of Thorns, being lashed through narrow streets by a brutish throng and hanged up nailed to a cross between the two criminals. Miles could not make himself read the text, though it was in large type, nor sit still while Ferne read it to him. After his grandmother died in January, the garishly lighted crucifixion of the cadaverous, anguished Christ, with the grieving women beneath the cross, overwhelmed the Resurrection and the Ascension scenes for him, and began to give him bad dreams.

While at the same time at school--his room was now in a corner of the junior high floor of the big building--their teacher, Miss Johansen, plain-faced, bespectacled, dressed in nail head suits and crepe soled shoes, prowled the aisles from the back rows taking spitball marksmen from the rear as she lectured about Socrates as if he had been a personal friend of hers.

Socrates was ugly--perhaps resembling Miss Johansen herself, with the same high balding forehead--and he went around the courthouse square in Athens proclaiming that he knew nothing. (Knowing nothing caught Miles' attention--he had been there--and woke his dreaming mind's eye: what did Socrates *mean* by that?) Supposed to be a teacher, Socrates, instead of "lessoning" his students, asked questions, which Miss Johansen quoted while looking at the ceiling, doing the dialectic from memory. And Miles began to see that the questions led Socrates' students, who did not know the answers, to stumble inexorably into the correct conclusion. He began to see that these conclusions mercilessly unmasked baloney, and were softened neither by the power nor position of their targets. It had never occurred to Miles there could be courage of the *mind*! For which, Miss Johansen said, the philosopher was tried and condemned.

Like Christ! he thought, as if he were the first to think of it. Though Miss Johansen was positive that it had happened a good deal before Christ. Yet, his judges had allowed Socrates to poison himself with hemlock. And as the poison worked slowly, he had spent his last hours quietly talking to his friends and disciples. While, on the other hand, Christ was killed with sadistic savagery that allowed him to say almost nothing? Were the early Greeks more civilized than the later Romans and the Jews?

Here he lost Miss Johansen's story and went on alone. Thinking that maybe the crucifixion's barbarity wasn't really more sadistic than Socrates' self-immolation because Christ's cruel execution wasn't a *real* death. Wasn't His time on the cross more like hanging a high school coach in effigy, entirely symbolic, since Christ, unlike Socrates, was part of a three-person God--and if he was--how could He not know it?--and if He did know it all along, how could the pain be real? But Miles remembered, *"Why hast thou forsaken me?"* as though He had only *thought* he was God, but then found that he must really die? Or could the Father make Him go through it all to the point of his very death just so that Christ could see for Himself what it was like to be a man and have to die--and then just say something like, "Come here, son, just kiddin'!"

But long before Christ, Socrates, also, made no protest or struggle--and said he was going to a better place. Like heaven? Or Olympus? Miles thought Miss Johansen had said Socrates came after the Greeks stopped believing very much in Olympus and before they knew about heaven. Socrates was still a pagan. And since heaven had not been invented, he was not eligible for heaven. None of the pagans were--back even thru Neanderthals. So--was heaven always waiting there with locked doors like a movie house in the morning while eons of men, and pre-men before them, went to perdition because the main feature had not started yet? Of course, Mary Ellen's ferocious Methodism would have made sure *she* was there on time.

But what of Miles' friend Paul, who had not yet been baptized, like Socrates?

The White Night

Paul Hensley had been Miles' new friend in the spring. Herb Robbins' parents were friends of Paul's folks, who had a farm a couple of miles from town. And though Paul was in the next grade lower, Miles had played with Paul a couple of times when they were both at Herb's. Paul was a small, nimble boy, with a wisp of blond hair above lively eyes and a quick, wide smile. In May, Paul had chased his dog into the gravel road in front of their house before school one morning and had run head first into the side of a car. The door handle of the front door, pointing forward, caught his head like a spear, and Paul died before he fell down. When Miles came home for lunch and said Paul had not been to school that morning and there had been some kind of huddle about him among the teachers, Ferne said, "Miles...Paul was hit by a car this morning." She didn't want to tell him, but thought it was better that *she* do it than the impersonal way it would be announced in class that afternoon.

It was only a few days since he and Paul had become real friends, friends in a way he had thought would stick right through school--since the recent evening Herb's parents had invited him to ride along with them after supper out to Paul's farm.

Fred Robbins, Herb's dad, told J. Arthur that they would come by after supper and pick Miles up, but they had got a late start and it was around nine when he heard the chuck-chuck of the Robbinses' Model-T Ford out front.

Just riding in Fred Robbins' car was like a ride at a theme park. It was a special car. Like Arletta Clarke's Electric, it was more than old, it was almost a museum piece. Not just a Model-T, but an early one that Fred Robins kept in flawless condition, it was a coupe with a rumble seat. Herb's parents rode inside, and he and Herb rode in the rumble seat of the shiny black antique car that putted through the dusk at thirty miles an hour on the gravel road out to Paul's farm.

He and Herb paid their respects to Paul's parents in the parlor--and Miles remembered that it was already dark enough inside that the lights were on as the elders sat down for their visit and Paul took his guests outside to show them around the farm yard.

62

The three boys had gone out onto the porch of the farmhouse and stood there a moment deciding to play Cops and Robbers. But it was different that night because Paul didn't have any toy guns, and since it was dark and Paul knew his way around, they made him the leader and they were all three on the same side. And they pretended it was some phantom after them, like the Vampire, not a robber or a gang.

As they started down to the barnyard they were talking, but when they began to whisper, the sound of the night enveloped them with the shuffle and grunt of animals in the stalls nearby, and a murmur and burst of laughter from the house and the regular deep tolling of the shaft of the windmill like a funeral cadence played by a sub-human hand far underground, intermitted with a tiny whine like a mosquito, of trucks on the grade of the highway to the east.

Paul had started to run, and they had run between the looming barns as if they were chasing something, or running away from something. No one said which it was, but he could feel it there, something around them in the black shadows, because ever since his grandmother's death, black night had something breathing in it.

Then when they paused panting at a board gate, he suddenly noticed that the blackness was caused by the moon. He looked up and was almost blinded by it. Partly up the sky, it was large enough that he could clearly see the features on its face, though it was too bright, almost as blinding as the sun, to look straight into. And from it the light came down as thick and heavy as rain in front of a street light. And he suddenly thought, "That's why moonlight *falls!*"

From the top of the fence they had climbed up onto a low building, and then stair-stepped to another higher up, and on the lip of the roof Paul pointed his finger down like a gun, and they all made a sound, not a bang, but like a Roman candle going, "Chuff!" into the black. Then everything way below, the old tractor, and the slats of the wagon, was suddenly aglow from inside like phosphorus lighting the numbers on a watch. You could see colors, but strangely altered. And from the lip of the roof he made out the shadows of their three figures dancing on the edge, their steps making a music of moonlight which their feet played like black and white piano keys on the ground.

They had long gone mute except the sound of their feet drumming on the roofs when the voices of the parents called them from the house. The voices half woke him from the spell. He could recognize waking because he could suddenly smell the farm again, alfalfa and manure and grease again. And the three of them climbed down and went silently to the house.

In the light of the living room, talking to the elders, Miles could tell that Paul and Herb were coming down from something, too. Herb now had his feet on the ground because he had never been entirely off it, not all the way. He was perplexed--a fisherman who had felt something on his line that he had lost before he could see it. But when Miles looked at Paul, he knew *they* were the same with it; he and Paul had let themselves be moonstruck, and were still half dreaming. Though by the time they said goodnight on the porch and were back in the old car, it was totally shredded and gone.

It was just a farm, and it was just moonlight, not a silver country of death, luminous and abysmal.

Miles knew the next day that it had moved him, that he had been *somewhere else.* Maybe Paul, too, so he naturally thought: *the next time we get together at school maybe we will talk about it.* But they never had, and now of course, they never would.

In all his youth, he was to feel the moon spell twice more, but never quite as an ineffable charm, a transvaluation of life and death. Later, when certain signs and countersigns seemed to vibrate harmonically between

64

him and some music or a painting, he suspected that the work came from that same inchoate place: Moon struck were Van Goghs, Ravel's Bolero, Hopkins' wild poems, Dostoevsky's Inquisitor, Fitzgerald'a Gatsby, Sherwood Anderson's village, a Faure' requiem, and a Chagall, a Stravinsky, and some of Chirico.

He asked Ferne if he could skip school that afternoon. She told him he could, though he would be home alone with the dog. Would he be all right? He said, yes, and when she had taken the car and gone to one of her bridge clubs, he dug out some of his toy trucks and a toy bulldozer that he had not had out of the window seat all summer, and took them outside. In the driveway, he began to push dirt around with the bulldozer and load it in the trucks and haul it to another place. After a while, when they remained little tin toys in a driveway, he sighed and gathered them up and went inside and put them away in the window seat. One day, years later, when he was about to leave for the war, he opened the window seat and saw them there just as he had forgotten them, and Paul.

But today the dog went off somewhere, and he lay on the sofa for a long time looking up at the chandelier and wondering if he himself ever died, if he would see Paul and ask him if the moonlight had been that way because he was going to die. He had decided that, baptized or not, Paul would be there, as would Socrates. Then his insides all felt swollen, and he lay wishing he had gone to school.

The Highest Lake in the Bighorns

That spring, J. Arthur Morgan committed to amateur radio with his usual fervor, giving up wood working, navigation, lens grinding (for an astronomical telescope) and photography (though not golf), passed his examination for a class C license, W9TGK (as a qualified telegrapher), and began building his first rig in the back hall of the new house on Rapids Street.

In June, when Miles went with him to some one of his jobs around Des Moines, J. Arthur began parking him with a radio magazine in the fly blown lounge area of the storefront Iowa Radio Inc. while he bought parts and picked the brains of some of the men who worked there, all radio men. The word "fanatic" would not be a misnomer for them. Though they came from different walks of life, as with most technical men, the only prerequisite for entrance into their fraternity was an active fluency in the language of the chosen subject, here amateur radio, and an ardor to chase the galloping strides of its new technology. It was a fraternity of hackers in electronics before the word existed, still in the time when new types of radio tubes were on the breaking wave of the science.

The smell of Iowa Radio was burnt bakelite, a non-conductor of a million uses, and though J. Arthur's radio friends were sometimes rich men, they tended to smell of bakelite, and their appearance was characterized by an indifference to shirt tales, shaves, coats, and ties. J. Arthur's particular friend was a brilliant radio man named Teasdale. With his wisp of hair sticking up from the crown of his head, and a vague visionary gaze from behind his soldered glasses frames, he would have looked like a Dagwood Bumstead except that Alfred Teasdale was missing the end of his nose. He had burned it off, turned it into a flat, poreless, chalk white pit, in winning a contest at a radio convention to determine who could hold his nose for the longest time in the spark that sizzled between two charged poles. He had won, but the spark had fried away the front of his face.

By now J. Arthur had learned enough of the technology from Teasdale and others at Iowa Radio to build a rig with which he could broadcast and receive Morse code. He had bought a fifty foot utility pole in the spring, cajoled his friends with the Power and Light truck to set it in deep by the corner of the Morgan garage, and returned to church a sufficient number of Sunday mornings to persuade the pastor to let him string an antennae two hundred feet from the top of his pole to the top of the chimney of the church without a steeple. He then began to "work" amateurs as far away as New Zealand on a regular basis.

Miles dimly understood that when Mary Ellen Morgan's house was sold and the estate settled in June, it enabled J. Arthur to trade the old Chevrolet for a Mercury demonstrator, and made possible their vacation trip in convoy with two other radio friends and their families on what the *Des Moines Register* called the first two-way radio caravan across the Midwest.

J. Arthur's "rig" was not portable; and only the other two cars operating with home-built two-way radios powered by extra batteries in the trunks, were able--with considerable interference--to talk to each other, mostly, J. Arthur claimed, on the subject of keeping the Morgans' Mercury in sight between them and steering them clear of wrong turns into the sand hills, which J. Arthur said he, having lived there, knew far better than they. They turned north from Laramie and drove to Casper, where they picked up another radio family, an oil geologist named Long, who had lost his wife two years before to cancer, and their son, Carl, Miles' age. They then set off in four cars-- Ed Long, who knew northern Wyoming from business and many Scouting trips, leading the way--into the Big Horn Mountains. Late in the afternoon, beyond the switchback highway and at the end of a track that turned off it and ran close under peaks through a narrow pass, they left the cars at a bridgeless stream. Fifty yards across the stream was a new Boy Scout lodge the geologist had helped to build in 1936 for his son's Boy Scout troop. It was a one-story log cabin with an open front porch at the base of a mountainside peppered with an avalanche of barn-sized boulders arrested eons ago in a cataclysmic tumble toward the bottom of the valley. They portaged their supplies and sleeping bags across the stream on stones that were the scattered vanguard of this ancient avalanche, and made their headquarters in the cabin.

Ed Long cooked all the hot cakes, eggs and bacon breakfasts, and they hiked in the mountains for three days in quest of a phantom mountain lion. Besides the four men, there were Ferne and the two other wives and three pre-teen girls and Ed Long's boy Carl, a sunny-headed freckled thirteen-year-old the same size as Miles. The men and two boys slept in sleeping bags on the porch, the women and girls inside. Out there the first night tenderfoot Miles was sure he would not be able to sleep under the great boulder poised over the lodge. (Ed Long called it Scarface, and said it was probably embedded three stories deep for its fifty foot height.) But Miles had watched the stars begin to move like Roman candles above the opposite ridge and then slept better than he ever had before.

By the time they returned to Casper the following Monday and started back east, Miles and Carl had decided to keep in touch by mail and send urgent messages back and forth through their fathers' radio contact. Which they did, until the next summer, when a raft with three Boy Scouts aboard was caught in a freak storm on Lake Solitude, the highest lake in the Big Horns, and Carl was drowned trying to swim for shore. The other scouts survived, but Carl's body was not found.

One day Miles told George Kinnick about Carl's death to prove that he already had two friends in his life who had died on him. Later he was deeply ashamed of himself because he had said that certain omens which foreshadowed Carl's death had happened the summer they met, though they had only been ordinary mishaps that Carl's drowning had colored in retrospect. After that, he began to notice that whenever he told Carl's story, he exaggerated some of these things to heighten the effect.

3

Good News of 1938

NEWS BRIEF: January: still 7.8 million jobless. March 12, German troops enter Austria. April 19, General Franco's Rebels are winning the Spanish Civil War. June 22, Joe Louis over Max Schmeling on third knockdown in the first round. June 22,Reich issues special identity cards to Jews. Sept. 30, Prime Minister Neville Chamberlain returns from Munich; at Heston Airfield waves treaty with Hitler's signature. Proclaims "Peace for our Time!" Nov. 1, Seabiscuit beats War Admiral. Rose Bowl: California over Alabama, 13-0.

So, at the first of the summer, when he was still twelve, Miles often went with his father to the construction for the day. On the site, J. Arthur kept him in the state Ford out of harm's way while he crossed the excavation to talk to the foremen. Miles watched the Le Tourneau drivers burned black to their undershirts, looking over the back of their rigs at the blade carving up great bites of sod, or jerking the levers of the big yellow D-7 dozers as they rode them tipped 20 degrees on the hills like cowboys riding broncos. J. Arthur said sometimes the Le Tourneaus turned over and killed a driver, and Miles waited with morbid expectation, but it never happened on his watch. He did not realize that there were no old hands driving these rigs because the technology of big diesels and man-high tires was less than twenty years old.

Other days, when he didn't go to the new pool, he would help his mother feed the mechanical wringer of the Maytag and then dawdle with the chores she set him in the yard. Ferne and Marie Robbins traded watches on their boys, and while he was in Herb's sandpile, Ferne would be at bridge till four: Thursday bridge, K.K. Club, Women's

Club, Garden Club, then home with groceries starting dinner.

Summer Sunday afternoons J. Arthur took them for family rides in the Mercury in the vain hope that the increased speed of the wind coming in the open car windows would cool them off. They would ride down into the Boonville bottoms to look at the new highway starting west out of Des Moines, or to Winterset where Ferne would visit with her Gordon aunts while the men sat by an algae-choked goldfish pond and smoked. Once they drove deep into the timbered end of the city park and climbed the stone tower there built by their descendants to honor Caleb and Ruth Clark, the first settlers of Madison County.

Or, bored with the ride, he would stay home, lie on the livingroom floor under the big revolving fans J. Arthur brought from the office on the weekends, and read the Sunday adventures of the *Katzenjammer Kids* and *Blondie,* absorbing the basement cool from the floor. After three, he would slope up the hill against the heat to see the Bradleys' Sunday poker party. Doc Bradley had been the Morgans' and everyone else's doctor till he left his wife and went to another town with his nurse. John Bradley and his brother had lived in Des Moines those years. Now the doctor was back with his wife and restarting his practice. Now again unfamiliar license plates parked Sunday afternoons along the street in front of the doctor's house. Often from other counties, and frequently out-of-the-state, several big old roadsters with leather seats of makes familiar to the Twenties, and a dark blue sedan with a spare tire encased in a chrome-trimmed wheel well, squatted like alien spaceships in front of the Victorian house.

Miles would follow the two brothers in past several tables where the women wore hose rolled to the knee and held their cigarettes in the corners of their mouths while they assessed their poker hands with one eye squinted against the smoke. He had a wandering glance, and looked at their knees and whatever else he could see without bumping into the chairs. The boys would loiter in the kitchen till they were alone, and then snitch drinks from a pitcher in the Kelvinator. The Bradleys allowed Miles only a shot glass or two, as it wasn't real lemonade, and he was deemed too young for a whole whiskey sour. Then they went out the back and around to the cars and sat on the curb and discussed the upcoming World Heavyweight grudge rematch between Joe Louis and Max Schmeling.

Joe Louis had knocked out Max Baer after Baer had lost the championship to James Braddock. Then Louis had knocked out Braddock for the heavyweight crown. Now, in the middle of June, the national excitement over the upcoming rematch in Yankee Stadium between Louis and the German Schmeling was building to a pitch of national suspense "never before equaled" by a sporting event. Propaganda from Germany claiming a second Schmeling victory foregone because of Lewis' natural (racial) inferiority was reported in the American press. While Hitler and Goebbels lionized Max Schmeling, the phlegmatic Lewis expressed personal hostility against an opponent for the first time because of the racial slurs. Once again, as in the 1936 Olympics, Hitler was making race an issue for Americans; would we choose his Aryan contender over a black American champion?

As the boys sat on the curb wiping the road dust from the indented red hexagon on the hubcap of the Packard, they favored Louis--along with the consensus of American fight fans, who would make him their overwhelming favorite before the fight. As for Miles, warmly lubricated and more fluent than usual from the shots of whiskey sour, he claimed the certification of his handshake with Max Baer last winter (when the Baer brothers had visited their cousin) conferred on him the omniscience to call the fight for Louis by a knockout in the fifth.

Dragging his feet homeward at sundown, he meditated on the families' different styles of drinking. Unlike the Bradleys, all *his* relatives--except Mary Ellen, the Primitive Methodist, and Uncle Bill, who claimed to drink only from a sense of professional obligation-- practiced a certain straightforward hypocrisy in which the men of the family deferred to the women's ban on strong drink in the house and convened before dinner on holidays in an unheated barn or garage and stood in a circle passing a bottle of whiskey around over Miles' head and blowing out great puffs of fragrant breath after each heroic swig. While Ferne kept the family liquor, a dusty-shouldered bottle of Crème de Menthe and J. Arthur's Haig & Haig, on the high shelf in the kitchen broom closet--the same two bottles that had already been to several New Year's Eve parties, and which would endure till Miles would polish both of them off the night he got his call-up for the service.

Senate

In July, his cousin May Senate Howes came for an extended visit from Washington, D. C.--an agreement set with Ferne's sister, Hazel, so that "the child" might renew her acquaintance with wholesome smalltown life during her summer vacation. Hazel, who had driven back to Huron the first of August on family business, would pick Senate up on her way east.

Miles, who was four years younger, put on a sulk when he thought he would have to drag her around with him everywhere. He needn't have bothered. May Senate, who had been so named because she had been born during Uncle Bill's first term in the South Dakota legislature, was now unrecognizable as the gangly tomgirl he had played with several Christmases ago. Since then, Uncle Bill's luck had picked her up from the parched prairie of South Dakota the way the whirlwind picked up Dorothy from Kansas, and set her down in the nation's capital, where her life had caught a political counter- current of the Depression that flowed with good fortune and high connections.

Though her mother drove to Huron, Senate came to Des Moines by plane (by plane!). But of course Uncle Bill, First Assistant Postmaster General--and special czar of new air routes--had made this happen. Yes, and fixed it so she could bring her new puppy, a chow named Tang, which Senate had bought with her own money, won at a casino in Havana last Christmas holiday.

Nor was her school a public school like Miles'. It was National Park Seminary. And from her home suite in the Mayflower she apparently sallied forth with Tang on a leash and made indelible impressions on handsome young men, as she was now tall and willowy, and according to Ferne, already taking assured possession of a certain style of glamour.

Senate, of course, took what was happening as her due. She showed Miles mementos of her recent conquests like an Indian showing scalps: dance programs from several proms at Seminary--all filled--and the white ensign's cap that had been thrown in the air, to *her*, by a young man when he graduated from Annapolis. These were merely keepsakes of the first installment of her brilliant future. Now, the young officer was on sea duty--out of sight out of mind--and one morning when she caught Miles trying on the ensign's cap in front of her dresser mirror, she tossed it to him as he left the room, as casual about it as she would be when she married him two years later, when he began flight duty as a submarine patrol pilot.

So much for the drudgery of chaperoning his Washington cousin: they moped on foot to the swimming pool and back exactly once, and they stayed at home exactly one evening, the first, reading to each other alternate chapters of L. Frank Baum's *The Wizard of Oz.* And after Miles had gone to bed, Senate had used her little

green address book and phoned the wives of certain of
Uncle Bill's connections in Des Moines whose sons' heads
she had turned at a political black-tie affair last winter in
Washington.

And these young men began arriving in Adel the
next day. On Tuesday morning, Senate had already left
with one of them for a Des Moines golf course before
Miles got up. After that, on Ferne's orders, Senate took
Miles as chaperone on most of her dates. With little protest,
as she had less interest in these young men *per se* than in
their adventures, and Miles shared her interest, and they hit
it off: thanks to Senate, he rode a roller coaster and a tunnel
of love at Riverview Park and drank a mock mint Julep and
swung his mother's golf club for the first time. One of
these young men, the son of a Des Moines auto dealer, was
smitten sufficiently that Senate took possession of his
roadster for three days and ran the wheels off of it with the
Baer girls until J. Arthur made her give it back.

Miles had not read F. Scott Fitzgerald, though he
may have seen a movie Fitzgerald had written, but several
years later when he did read *the Great Gatsby*, Senate's
was the first face suggested to his mind's eye by Jordan
Baker, Daisy Buchanan's pal, the "liberated" golf champ,
though May Senate wouldn't have left the borrowed flivver
with the top down in the rain and lied about it as Jordan
Baker had. Senate was his first experience of the self-
sufficient girl the War would soon create, from Rosy the
Riveter to Barbara Hutton. But before Miles finished high
school, Senate's husband, whose ensign's cap he still
prized, would go missing on submarine patrol in the
Bermuda Triangle, and Senate would already be sailing
into a run of dark years.

The posters for the movie *Good News of 1938,* on
the corner of the New Rialto, featured art work of a
streamlined ocean liner crossing the waves at great speed,
leading Miles to believe that it would be about a

modernistic ship, and he lobbied Senate into taking her date to see it at the Rialto. But the picture was so corny that the three had forgotten it by the time they left the theater and came out talking about the newsreel, which had shown an Irish dignitary presenting a new compass to a tousle-headed young American who swore he had tried to fly his wired-together Curtis Robin monoplane from New York to California, but had accidentally ended up in Ireland because of a broken compass. He had replicated Lindbergh's trans-Atlantic flight "unintentionally," and was dubbed "Wrong Way Corrigan". Senate's date, who had just gotten his pilot's license, kept schmoozing her to fly to "California" with him--and see Dublin.

Senate had been with the Morgans three weeks when Hazel arrived from Huron to take her back to Washington. Hazel, whatever she had been like before Washington, had by now seamlessly melded her own style with the fashionable chic of a capital-wise matron. Like certain women Miles had seen on the pages of fashion magazines, she wore permed brunette curls waved close to her head, and smoked cigarettes in a holder like Norma Talmage. Yet, her unique endowment was the Bogartian whisky growl with which she laid out in all confidence the state secrets of the New Deal world of which she seemed to be the center. Miles thought she was glamorous, and took her stories at face value because he had seen the clippings from the society pages of the Washington papers in which Hazel *was* shown pouring punch at Eleanor's side. Now, she was in a hurry to get back to the capital in hopes of arriving--as Ferne put it--before Bill House forgot to come home for his prayers some night. About Senate's visit Hazel was effusively appreciative with scarcely a trace of condescension, "How can one raise a child in a hotel suite? Three weeks in Adel have done Senate a world of good! The Baer girls, they're down-to-earth real people! Senate's just a country girl at heart."

77

"Some country girl," Miles muttered.

Hazel and May Senate got the Buick tuned at Mitchell Motors and stayed an extra day to cross paths with Wayne Gordon, who was stopping overnight on his way back to Seattle from rowing for the University of Washington in the Poughkeepsie Regatta. He had been a raw-boned fourteen-year-old in overalls that smelled of sour milk when the Gordons left for the West Coast without enough money to take them all the way. Now he was a senior at the University of Washington, and had pulled an oar for the first scull the West Coast Conference had ever entered in the Regatta. He and a crew mate were driving two new cars west for a Seattle dealer.

That night Hazel and Ferne put together the kind of Sunday dinner "we used to help Mama cook back in Winterset," and they all sat around the table afterward talking family, Wayne not smoking, but Senate manipulating one of her mother's Kools ("which are not harmful to your wind like a real cigarette").

Wayne would join the Navy Air Corps after graduation next spring. He said, "Did you ever think Hilda would have a Japanese friend? This family has a nursery up the hill. But, there's a lot of sentiment against them. People say if Japan acts up, whose side will they be on?"

Monday early, J. Arthur took snapshots of everybody, with the two West Coast men in front of the twin Buicks, and Hazel and May Senate and Ferne with their arms around each others' shoulders, and Miles in front, and the Baer girls rubber necking from their porch. Then Wayne Gordon and his crew mate left for Seattle.

Hazel and May Senate said goodbye and headed east. Miles wouldn't see any of them again before the war. But the visit had etched a certain truth in his mind as vivid as a neon sign. Maurice Gordon had a year-round painting contract now; Hilda worked in downtown Puyallup; all of the boys had found jobs in the canneries, and their sister

78

Eileen was an accountant. They weren't rich yet like Bill and Hazel, but every one, as Wayne boasted, would go to college now.

It dawned on Miles that however thin things still were in Adel, in Iowa, in the Midwest, in the wake of the dust bowl, in the tail of the Depression, things didn't have to be that way anymore. "Look at them," he said to Ferne. "They left that farm with nothing and had to wire Hilda's folks for money to get there. Now, they've got themselves a whole new deal!"

As he walked toward the band concert that evening, it seemed that the truth about America was that you didn't *have* to find your roots in digging up buried Troys as Europeans had to do; they were right there on the surface of the country. Americans took their roots with them, and the future here was a current that never passed the same place twice. And your sweet tomorrow was in the flow--if you were an American kid.

Gone With the Wind

All at once, it was the dead shank of summer, and the droning of locusts started up in the early afternoon and the air smelled like the chaff of baking straw, and his cousins had returned to their exciting lives, and there was nothing to do in his life again but trudge to the pool every afternoon with Jean Baer and play water tag and let her try to teach him how to kiss under water--a colossal bore.

The Baers lived in the yellow two-story house between the Morgans and the highway. There were two daughters older than Jean, who was fourteen. Lester was a mail carrier. He had been a semi-pro baseball player once. Though he was long retired from playing baseball, sports of all kinds were still his exclusive interest, and he often spoke of young baseball players he was "bringing along," for whom he had got summer jobs with Highway Maintenance running mowers while they played for Adel in the semi-pro league in central Iowa and tried to get discovered. These young men often hung around the Baers' front porch to be near one or the other of Lester Baer's older daughters. And Lester Baer monopolized their attention with sports stories of his cousin, Max, who had lost his killer instinct after a man he had knocked out died, and had clowned away the World Heavyweight Championship, and Max's younger brother, Buddy, a coming heavyweight almost as big as Primo Carnera.

Lester had put up a professional punching bag on his lower basement landing, and would sometimes take the young men away from the girls and give them instruction on punching the bag, at which he was accomplished. Miles, in fact, received a lesson on the bag, but preferred to hang around with Jean on the front porch and follow the talk of the boy friends. The sisters had a windup record player, and would often bring it down from their room and dance to current hits, *And the Angels Sing*, and *My Dear Mr. Shane* (*Bei Mir Bist Du Shoen*).

One day, when he arrived, they were all talking at once about the announcement of a national competition to find the girl in the whole United States who was right to play the role of Scarlett O'Hara in the movie of Margaret Mitchell's *Gone With the Wind.* The press releases from Hollywood said that none of the established stars like Katharine Hepburn or Joan Crawford had the right combination of fire and innocence to play the role, so David O. Selznick had decided to send talent scouts across the nation to discover the right girl. The Des Moines paper announced that these talent scouts would be holding auditions for the part of Scarlett O'Hara in a suite in a Des Moines hotel on a given date, and all three of the Baer girls decided to compete for the part--which was exactly what most other girls of Scarlett's age were deciding to do across the country.

The Baers' front porch soon became an impromptu dramatic workshop where the girls prepared for their auditions by continually changing their hair styles and applying new shades of nail polish and lipstick to go with their new audition outfits. Gladys, enshrined in the porch swing with a cigarette, weighed the possibilities of the Gibbs girls from up the street, and sent them home. Then she set up a sort of filmschool agenda exclusively for Gail, Beverly and Jean. The hang-around boys were sent to the basement to work the bag with Lester, while Miles-- considered a zero romantic distraction--sat at the wicker table by the front door impersonating a talent scout and asking the girls questions which Gladys wrote out for him in the style of auditions she had seen conducted in show-business movies. The girls were to enter, introduce themselves, and utter Scarlet O'Hara lines culled from the book. Miles sat at the table, and Jean came through the door and drawled:

Fiddle dee dee! Fiddle dee dee! Wah! Wah! Wah! This wah talk's spoilin' every party this spring! I get so bored I could jes' scream. 'Sides, there's not going to be any wah!

Her southern accent so exercised him that he broke up and rolled on the floor and was sent home, while the girls, all three of whom had robust figures, went inside to try on some old corsets that Gladys had brought down from the attic.

When the red-letter day arrived, he watched from his parents' bedroom window as the Baer girls, transformed and harshly glamorized in their new dresses and high-heeled pumps, wobbled to the car, and with Gladys at the wheel, set off for fame and fortune.

They returned before dark looking bedraggled and quelled, and would never talk to him about the tryouts, though Gladys confided to Ferne that there had been an awful crowd and much jostling and cutting-in in the hotel hallway outside the audition room. The actual tryouts were apparently short and perfunctory, the "scouts" were a hard-looking set and Gladys wondered if they were real Hollywood people at all. Some months later, when it was announced that a young English actress had won the part, Gladys said it had just been a publicity stunt to get everyone to see the movie, which it did.

A New Way of Looking at Things

After Labor Day, Miles trekked up the hill to the brick school building again. During the summer his navy blue band uniform suddenly looked less as if it had been handed down by a departed giant. The only other flute player was a senior, so Miles became, he assumed by default --though he still had another year of junior high--a full member of the band. So, when the band began rehearsing *Ballet Egyptian*, the new overture for the music contest, it surprised him that Mr. Fardel assigned him the premier part in the long flute duet.

In the first week, before school had settled into its seasonal grind, Miss Trout announced that the junior high would see a demonstration of "*television*," a new electronic device for broadcasting a live picture onto a small movie screen in your own home. The junior high would watch it downstairs in the gym in the late afternoon.

You couldn't ever have called her a spinster. Miss Trout was thirty-one and had already been principal of the junior high five years, but everything else about Alice Trout contradicted the fact that she had grown up in a country village in northern Iowa and attended the state teachers' college: She looked like a miniature Rockette, at school always perfectly groomed, wearing on her high-breasted, wasp-waisted dancer's body one of her crisp little suits with a skirt no longer than it had to be and a bolero jacket over a frothy peek-a-boo lace blouse that hardly any other woman in Dallas County would have dared wear. And she would set it off with one of the vivid paisley scarves she adapted into ties. She was partial to striking color combinations, bright red with beige or chocolate to cool it down, magenta skirts with concertina pleats from the hips down. Her telegraphic signature, those pumps with four-inch heels--sonic devices of self-announcement whose swift, staccato rim shots, like a pair of drummers proclaiming the arrival of a royal, established her authority to all the children in the gym before she even turned the corner at the landing of the stairs--were to play a large part in the new medium's destruction of her dignity that afternoon. Coming downstairs she had seemed perfectly prepared to go before a camera--but she was late for the class, and her subsequent debut on TV before the whole junior high was entirely one of those misadventures that happen from time to time in high schools, erotic Freudian slips of the collective unconscious.

The junior high classes had trooped down the stairs from the first floor, turned a blind corner in the ground-level vestibule by the west door and descended a half flight to the basement hall with the men's locker rooms at one end and the women's at the other. They had trooped with much disorder through the entrance to the cracker-box gym in the center. There, they had been placed on the front risers near the centerline of the basketball court by Miss Laffler, who announced that Miss Trout would come after the "show" and take roll.

There was considerable excitement at first. A temporary curtain had been stretched across the middle of the basketball floor, and on one side of it a high school girl was sitting near the top of the free throw circle in front of

83

some sort of camera. The camera was wired to a small movie screen facing the students on the other side of the curtain. The inventor, a man named Farnsworth, who had recently perfected the first practical home scanner and taken it on this cross-country introductory tour, scurried back and forth with his assistant for a few minutes making adjustments. Then he stepped in front of the small glass screen, which was now showing patterns, and explained that they would focus the camera on the girl, and her image would be transmitted by the wires to the picture screen on the other side of the curtain, where they would see her image as a live moving picture.

The girl, Theodora Clarke, George Kinnick's cousin, was instructed to wave her hand and stand up and sit down. She did this, and on the other side of the curtain, a small image replicated her, moving in a shimmery black and white on the screen.

All the students went "ooh!" and "aah!" It was truly the first time anyone in Dallas County had ever seen a live television image, and the inventor urged them to imagine a day soon to come when this mechanism would carry from afar to just such a screen in their own homes events like the Hindenberg disaster or the San Francisco earthquake, while they were actually happening. It may have been one of Farnsworth's earliest demonstrations, because, as moving pictures were much larger and clearer than his small screen, and everyone present could see the real Theodora in living color on the other side of the curtain, the children soon became bored and noisy, and Mr. Sinift came down from the back row and conferred with the inventor. Mr. Farnsworth then announced that there would be a brief break to move the equipment, and Theodora's picture would be sent to the screen "long distance," from another part of the building.

After the high school football team stampeded in the west door from practice and clattered downstairs into the men's locker room, the janitors helped the technicians move the camera and lights up to the vestibule of the west entrance through the doorway from the top row of the gym.

Just as the inventor stepped in front of the little TV and began to announce that Theodora's picture would now come to the class from "long distance", he was interrupted by a sudden wild hoot like a Rebel yell and the clatter of football cleats running back up the basement steps from the locker room. Suddenly the image of a boy in half a football uniform flashed across the screen and skidded out of sight around the corner of the landing, disappearing up the stairs to the junior high floor. *"Come back with my jock strap!"* bellowed someone in hot pursuit, and at the same time, before the children had time to titter, Miss Trout's percussive heels proclaimed her regal arrival from the junior high above.

"Come back with it, you!" With surprising clarity, the screen blossomed with the rear view of a young man as naked as Michelangelo's David who had obviously heard Miss Trout's stacatto steps on the stairs and was flailing his arms like windmills in an attempt to reverse his momentum in mid stride before she materialized. *Impossible!* And as the principal of the junior high rounded the corner and collided with him, more or less head on--the naked fullback's feet flew out from under him, the teacher's spike heels left the floor, and all the junior high, now glued to the screen, leaned forward as one to see the football player in a state of nature and the smartly dressed young woman in a concertina skirt, sit down spread-eagled on the floor of the landing like two children to a game of jacks.

Though there was scarcely time for us to catch the whole picture before her image dissolved in a piercing dot of light, most of the junior high got the impression of Miss Trout with her hairdo down and her iron mask ajar, as an endearingly human girl of limited experience, quite all-eyes before she remembered to scream. Then, those who were quick enough to look over their shoulders through the lower gym entrance caught a glimpse of some portion of the football player, who ducked by attempting to preserve his incognito like September Morn, with his hands partly covering his thatch of bright red pubic hair.

Shortly, Miss Trout would retire to her office upstairs without taking roll. Miss Laffler, her powdered cheeks aflame, would dismiss the junior high. Mr. Sinift would stride across the hall to beard Coach Stollard in his office. And the junior high children would skip home to extol the wonders of the new television medium to their parents over dinner.

The Ventriloquizer[*]

That fall, not long after the collapse of the long Maytag strike in Newton--where J. Arthur had so many friends among the workers from his days on the Highway 6 project that he took labor's side for once, and he and Ferne mutually deplored the strife rather than taking their usual polarized positions--Miles found himself in serious trouble in school. Of his various recent delinquencies in class, this was the first one to infuriate a teacher so much that she demanded his suspension. As to the reason Miss Laffler was as offended by his ventriloquist "trick" as if it were some sort of personal attack, he hadn't a clue till he had spent an hour cooling his heels in the superintendent's outer office in the late November afternoon, more or less eavesdropping on the pandemonium the young teacher was raising inside and watching a steady procession of his schoolmates pass in, summoned by Superintendent Weir to testify against him.

---

[*]Copyright applied for, 1937

The previous day, an English teacher had read to a senior English class a widely popular new short story entitled, *Address Unknown*, which dramatized the wave of Nazi-sponsored anti-Semitism sweeping over Hitler's Germany.

Miles was unaware of the reading, but Miss Laffler had heard an animated discussion of it in the teacher's lounge, and she had begun Miles' American History class that morning by trying to counter the groundswell of American hostility she thought she sensed rising around her against the country from which her parents had come, and against herself. She had held up before the class a clipping from the *Des Moines Register* with a photograph of Prime Minister Chamberlain descending from his plane at Heston Airfield waving the treaty he had just signed with Hitler in Munich, exclaiming, *"Peace for our time."* She had translated part of a recent letter from her grandmother in Bavaria which echoed the Fuehrer's assertions about Germany's peaceful intentions. And she had passed this letter, which was written in German, around the class. Miles' attention had played hooky early in the class. He had already seen the newsreel of Chamberlain, and with the majority of Americans, had made up his mind that Chamberlain was a Casper Milktoast knuckling under to a bully. So he had spent the class drawing pictures of a patented device guaranteed to throw your voice, and thus entertain your friends and make you the life of a party, which he had just received by sending a two-dollar money order to the address of a classified advertisement in *Popular Mechanics*. It was called a *Ventriloquizer*, and it looked like a cricket call. The directions said that if placed properly under your tongue, it would make your voice seem to come from someone else as far as thirty feet away. At lunch, he failed to mention Miss Laffler's lesson in international affairs because he had forgotten it, and he spent the rest of the hour in front of the mirror in his room with the Ventriloquizer under his tongue, trying to say words without moving his lips.

That afternoon in the study hall at two, when everyone was half asleep and Miss Laffler, at her desk on the platform, was doing her nails, he ducked down and placed the Ventriloquizer under his tongue. His home desk was located in the middle of the seventh grade, with four girls, Punk, Gloria, Molly and a new girl named Joann Jackson around him and he intended to "throw" his voice among the boys in the corner of the room. Hopefully, it would seem to emerge from the mouth of Jim Mitchell, who was nodding over a book. It had occurred to him that making his friend speak in a southern drawl would be comical, and he simply used the Scarlett O'Hara quotation he remembered:

Fiddle dee dee! Fiddle dee dee! Wah wah wah! I get so bored I could jes' scream! 'Cause there ain't goin' to be any wah!

Everyone in the hall looked straight at him, and he knew he was merely talking in a loud voice with a lisp. But Miss Laffler on the platform dropped her nail brush and pointed a crimson finger at him. Her face, under her heavy powder, flushed from her throat up: "Miles, you come up here!" she ordered.

When he arrived beside her, she was already losing her composure. She was convinced that she recognized a mockery of her message of peace to her class that morning. "What have you got in your mouth?"

He had kept it in his cheek in an attempt to conceal it: "It throws your voice," he lisped, "Oh, it *does*!" She retorted with high irony, but could not think of anything further to say, because his deed had brought to the surface so many of her recent fears. She put out her hand, and he contritely placed the spit-glistening device in her palm. She pointed to the ceiling, as to God: "Go to the Office!" she said, "and wait!"

At three-thirty, Miles sat in the superintendent's outer office, leaning toward Superintendent Weir's door to try to make sense of some sort of tempest within. He heard Miss Laffler sobbing and repeating his name in some connection with the letter she had passed around, and declaring that if Miles was not suspended, she would pack up tomorrow and leave Adel for good.

In time, when Miss Laffler's agitation subsided, the superintendent sent his secretary for the girls who had seats around Miles in study hall, and they came one by one, avoiding the eye of the miscreant in the outer office, and told Donald Weir that they had heard Miles utter "fiddle-dee-dee." Gloria added that it sounded like something Scarlett O'Hara had said in *Gone With the Wind*.

The superintendant knew the America Firsters were having a convention in New York; he knew that Hitler had recently decorated Charles Lindbergh; he also knew that the short story, *Address Unknown*, about Hitler's state-sanctioned persecution of Jews, had been read to a senior English class. But though he was soon convinced it was merely another of Miles' *non sequitur* follies, Miss Laffler held her ground. Wasn't Miles an habitual offender? Scarcely a week ago, she had sent him to Mr. Weir for passing around a laxative chewing gum in a Chiclets box. Many had taken some and chewed them, including herself.

Miles heard this and felt the balance finally tip against him. Mr. Weir promised her that he would suspend Miles for a day and bar him from all activities for the semester. It was nearing five o'clock when the teacher finally blew her nose on the superintendent's last Kleenex and pierced Miles with such a triumphant glare as she passed him in the outer office that he knew his goose was cooked.

The superintendent's secretary tidied her desk and left without turning on a light. From the twilight, Miles watched the superintendent reflectively turning over the patented Ventriloquizer under his desk lamp and apparently preparing his sentence. Then, as the office clock struck five, Sigurd Fardel burst in from the hall and rushed into the superintendent's office without closing the door. "You've suspended this boy!....No, no; Mrs. Bates just informed me that you've curtailed his music!"

Miles sat up from his condemned slump. Had his Palladin arrived? Mr. Weir was surprised; he had thought he was banning Miles from sports, which would not deprive him, as he was on no varsity team. Music had been furthest from his mind. Sigurd Fardel, the squat, disheveled-looking music man with a broad bald forehead and a thumbless left hand, whose parents had brought him from Alsace as a boy, still spluttered with their accent when he was excited, "Will you destroy our concert? Over a ventriloquist prank?" Until his middle forties, he had been a professional musician playing trumpet with John Philip Sousa. When he married, he had quit the band and entered the state university to get a music degree. Then, in early middle age, he had taken his first teaching position in Adel, and had started the band from scratch. With his assistant, a social studies teacher named Hoffman, by dint of giving each student individual instrument lessons (he was capable of playing all the brass and woodwind instruments including the flute), Sigurd Fardel had in a short time created what was regarded as the best small high school band in the western half of the state. And this reputation had recently secured him the invitation to bring his band back to his *alma mater*, the University of Iowa, early in the new year to be the featured band in a concert of high school music which would be broadcast from the Student Union.

In the superintendent's office, he now began tamping his thumbless stump on Donald Weir's desk in time with his speech. "I have in this band two flutes!" he sputtered. "We have the music for our overture which we have been rehearsing. It is coming along! It is almost fine! We play in Iowa City after new year. And there is a *flute duet*, which is the centerpiece of the slow movement! I have but two flutes in this band, sir! And *he* is to play the first part--and you have suspended him from all activities? Did I hear this incorrectly, sir, eh?"

Superintendent Weir was not a musician. And after a moment's deliberation, he suggested that the flute duet be played as a solo by the other flutist. The band director uttered an explosive sigh and ran his hands over his shiny scalp. "The *duet*, Donald, has been written for *two* flutes! No-no, please, it would be, even if I rewrote it for him, a fiasco, a *fizzle*! Miles has the vibrato. You must allow Miles to play, or..."

Mr. Weir pretended to make a note on his appointment pad of the second ultimatum delivered to him this afternoon, and his patience began to fray as he contemplated his dinner growing cold and his wife's ire, "Because of his *vibrato*?"

"No, Donald, it is--what Miles has got is not simply a vibrato. It is the ripple of a breeze on a still pool, in a manner of speaking, sir! Yes! The boy doesn't even know he has this. It's none of his business. But I tell you..."

"All right! All right! Very well...*Enough!*" the superintendent waved Mr. Fardel aside. "*Miles!* Come in here!" He had discovered the solution of a Solomon that would keep his promise to the teacher and still placate the music man: Because the concert would take place in the second semester, the suspension of activities need not apply to it, nor to the rehearsals in preparation for it.

He curtailed Miles' nonexistent extracurricular activities for the rest of the semester, came down on him

91

severely for the laxative gum and levied a day's suspension.

The first week of the new semester, the band parents took the long drive east to Iowa City and helped set up the band on the stage of the Student Union at the bottom of the steep streets near the Iowa River below the old capitol. That night in the great hall, when Mr. Fardel leaned over the podium and brought the two flutists forward into the intimidating spotlight, it was not merely the auditorium, their families and five hundred strangers, but to Miles a vast radio audience. The vibrato, which he still did not know he had, acquired an exquisite tremor from his excitement. In the passenger seat beside J. Arthur on the way home, with Ferne and two girls in back, he heard a delayed broadcast of the concert over the University radio station, savored the quivery elegance of the two flutes through the white noise of the radio, and nodded off.

J. Arthur tuned the radio to WHO and listened to the announcement that Hitler's troops were Marching on Prague. Neville Chamberlain's gift of the Sudetenland the previous autumn had turned the Czechs' frontier fortifications over to Germany, and now they were cooked. "It took the wolf six months to get hungry again," he muttered. When the lights of Des Moines came up on the horizon, Miles woke up with the complacent thought that he had finally brought off something his father approved of, while J. Arthur contemplated the cloud over his son's future that had just grown to be much larger than a man's hand.

* * *

As usual in the spring, J. Arthur dusted off his golf bag, declared golf his prime hobby and headed for the golf links of Des Moines on Saturday. Once Ferne had played, but she was left-handed, and when she made a hole-in-one using the back of J. Arthur's putter for a driver, he persuaded her to retire. Miles accompanied his father now on Saturdays, and J. Arthur dropped him at the Roosevelt Theater on University Avenue, where he would watch several serials while his father played eighteen holes with his foursome. Last year Miles had seen Buster Crabbe in *Flash Gordon's Trip to Mars*, but this year Buster Crabbe returned as Buck Rogers in a story that was a kind of caricature of how things really were in Europe now, with Killer Kane in Hitler's role trying to take over the world.

This summer, Miles often brought along a friend by the name of Berglund, a boy new in town who was nearly a year younger but a head taller than Miles. Dick was an intelligent, quirky boy without a father, already at thirteen as tall and thin as a cornstalk, with long bones and a profile like the face of a centurion on a Roman coin. Straight on, one eye looked at you, the other, lazy, a little to the side--a defect that his mother could not afford to have corrected. The family had been the victim of early misfortune. Several years ago when he was eight or nine, there had been a growing family; Dick's father had had a store in another town. When the youngest child, Janey, was a few months old, the father had caught strep throat, gone to the hospital for observation, come once to the window of his room to smile and wave at Verna and the children, and had died. The next year, with her small insurance settlement, she had attended a beauty school in Des Moines, and with the help of a sister who was married to a prosperous attorney in Perry, had moved to Adel and set up a beauty shop on the second floor of the brick building across from the bank.

The beauty parlor and the family apartment were in tandem, and occupied the rear half of an upstairs shared with a dentist. The suite began with a waiting lounge of 1920-ish wicker furniture, then the beauty parlor and finally the living quarters of the family consisting of a bedroom, bath and kitchen-dining area. There was always a small, tubby, spayed female dog named Muffy, the scent of whose incontinence, blending with that of Verna's various permanent-wave solutions, gave the hall along the east side of the suite a peculiar astringent smell.

Dick Berglund, coming into his teens, tried to improve his mother's sparse earnings by carrying papers, but he had one of the weakest routes in town where he was often exploited by deadbeat subscribers who hid out at collection time Saturday mornings leaving their radios and washing machines running on their front porches. Instead of making money from his route, Dick, caught between will-o'-the-wisp subscribers and a bullying paper manager who threatened to take his route away from him if he lost business, was soon paying for the subscriptions of twenty deadbeats with his wages from the odd jobs he did around the square. What he earned from opening the Southside Drug in the morning and sweeping out stores evenings, he now gave to the paper manager to pay for his "extras."

He had a quick mind, and his studies were easy for him, and he had begun to hang around the Morgan's a good deal. J. Arthur and Ferne welcomed him as a positive influence on the erratic Miles, and the two boys shared an uncritical love of reading, and flying (though neither had ever flown). When Carl Long drowned in Wyoming, Miles suddenly took notice of his unappreciated friend and started getting up early and biking along with Dick on his paper route. In August, when Dick went to spend two weeks with his Perry cousins, Miles knew the route well enough to stand in for him. He soon discovered the twenty extras his friend was carrying and filled out cancellations for all of them and turned them in. For once he humbly took the blame for something he hadn't done, held his tongue under the abuse of the ranting paper manager, and when Dick returned, gave him back his route cleared of deadbeats, which amounted to enough of a raise that Dick Berglund could afford to go with Miles to the Flash Gordon serials till September.

Courage

Before his birthday, Miles read that Judy Garland was in New York for the world premier of *The Wizard of Oz*. George Kinnick was at his grandparents' and Miles told Ferne he wanted to take George and Jim Mitchell to see it for his birthday. But new films seldom came to town for weeks, and the picture wasn't even in Des Moines yet, so she invited the boys to a birthday lunch. After hot dogs, Pepsi, birthday cake, and cherry pie with ice cream--Miles' menu--the three boys set out and rambled aimlessly into the eastern part of town where Highway 6 and the railroad crossed the river.

Three bridges crossed the Raccoon below the dam, an early steel two-Model-T-wide bridge on the old road to Des Moines, a new bridge on Highway 6 and the old railroad bridge which dated from the late 1800s. They went to the old highway bridge, which kids visited all summer for its overview of the river, and crawled through the hand rail and down onto the prow-shaped ledge on top of the bridge pier. There they sat for a while watching the current twenty-five feet below, and George talked about Seabiscuit, and boasted that Omaha had a real horse racetrack, called Aksarben (Nebraska backwards), and said that Jun had already gone back to Iowa U. to practice for fall football. George said he was keeping a physical regimen Jun had laid out for him before he left; if he could hold himself straight out on a vertical bar by the time Jun came home at Thanksgiving, his brother would give him his second-best suit. George informed them that Jun's ankle injury--a hairline fracture which had spoiled his junior season at Iowa--was healed. He predicted his brother would have a sensational senior year.

95

"The whole team's great, so watch out for Iowa! '39's their year for Big Ten champs!" Miles and Jim both nodded, walleyed at the idea that Iowa could move from the bottom to the top of the Big Ten--where it had never been--in one season.

George watched them and frowned, and suddenly got up and climbed up to the bridge floor and seized the zig-zag braces in one of the vertical girders and climbed straight on up to the top of the superstructure. Miles and Jim came up to the floor and watched him, and then reluctantly followed.

Sitting on top of the big I-beam looking up the river, George said that if you stood up, you could probably get a good view of the powerhouse and dam. The beam was as wide as a railroad tie, and Miles and Jim were satisfied with the view sitting down holding onto the steel. George stood up. He didn't hold on or even stick out his arms for balance.

Miles knew positively that the beam was walkable. He knew his father walked these beams in the course of business all the time, bad leg and all, but he continued to stare down through the bridge at the current. He was higher above the floor of the bridge than the top of a semi truck, and from the floor of the bridge, say fifteen feet; it was another twenty-five feet to the water. He sat watching while a gravel truck crossed the highway bridge fifty yards farther south.

George said stubbornly, as if they'd disputed it, "They're going to be Big Ten champs this year." Miles and Jim said nothing. They were ready to go back down. George said, "I'm going to take a look from the other side." They were silent, looking at the X member that crossed over the road between the big I beams.

"You better not try it," Miles said. George grabbed the rusty steel rod as though testing it. "I'll tell you what--if I make it, Iowa's Big Ten champs this year!"

"Come off it!" Mitchell said.

Miles looked at the rod of the X-member. It was probably only a twenty-foot traverse, but what if you cut your hand on the rust, or snagged it on the X-joint in the middle? If you fell, the road could bust your ribs, and you could fall over the railing and hit the pier, or fall twenty-five feet into the river and smash yourself on the old junk in the shallows. He thought of Carl Long drowning in Lake Solitude, and started to climb down carefully. When his feet touched the floor, he didn't feel queasy anymore and looked up. George was swinging across on the rod like Tarzan, hand over hand, crossing the X to the other side. It was easy for George.

When George came down, they all walked back toward town silently. Neither of them said, "That was pretty neat, George."

Not following George made him feel low, and he asked himself if George had done it just to show them up. But he knew that hadn't had anything to do with it. He suddenly surely knew that he and Jim were not in George's competitive picture at all. George would have hand-walked the rod whether they were here or not, because he was doing it for *Jun*, to establish something in himself in relation to Jun. Miles realized that it wasn't all peaches and cream to have a two-time All State halfback as a brother. He knew that what George had done was something a grown man, even a gymnast, wouldn't have done, *because a man would have to have a reason for doing something risky*, and George's only reason had been to defend Jun by being like Jun. He remembered Nile, Sr. coming home from work years ago when Miles was at Kinnicks' being tutored by Frances: The man had a steel stare that could become a death ray if he thought you weren't matching up, and George wasn't matching up with his school work in those days, and some of the look splashed on Miles like acid.

Understanding this made him feel easier. George *had* to do Tarzan on the bridge, but Miles *didn't* have to-- because there were forces bearing on George that just weren't there for Miles. He decided every person had his own reasons for doing what he did, or not. So, if it was true--even though he would never have an older brother-- when the reasons to do an important thing came, he told himself that he would probably have courage enough to do that thing, even on a high place.

Don't do anything--he told himself--for anyone else's reasons but your own. Have your inside reason, and it will tell you what to do. If you don't have your own reason, you will let other people's reasons push you into doing their stuff and hurting yourself. He was almost sure that it was true.

By the time they reached the square he felt okay about it and took them into the South Side Drug and bought three sodas with his birthday money.

Eleven Golden Helmets

The next week, George Kinnick had returned to Omaha to start school. The closing of the pool was the beginning of fall, and Stalin and Hitler made a non-aggression agreement to signify the kind of fall it would be: Six months ago General Franco had marched into Madrid signaling the end of the Spanish Civil War. On September 1, in sham retaliation for a provocation he himself had staged against the Poles, Hitler sent his Panzers spearing into Poland. On the third, Britain and France reluctantly honored their treaty with Poland and declared war on Germany. Stalin and Hitler, now goodfellows together, agreed on how they would carve up Poland. World War II had finally fallen on Europe like the proverbial other shoe.

Yet most of us were looking the other way. American attention was fixed on the World's Fair in New York and its symbols, the virile "Trylon" and feminine "Perisphere" portraying a serenely futuristic cohabitation of consumerism with applied science: *"Progress for Peace,"* was the theme. In the Midwest, after Jun Kinnick's Hawkeyes ran roughshod over South Dakota in their first home game, Iowans' heads began to turn toward Iowa's new football season. When Mr. Blough, the junior high coach, devoted most of his first team meeting to telling the boys that they were inheriting the uniforms of the 1933 Undefeated Team, the thought that his first season of organized football would move in tandem with his hero's made the hair stand up on the back of Miles' neck. These, Coach Bough said, had been the uniforms of a State Champion, and the junior high had been *chosen* to carry on the Undefeated Team's winning spirit, which still lived in these pants and pads.

At first, they looked at the pile of stained and threadbare jerseys with dismay, but as Mr. Blough waxed eloquent, they began to halfway imagine it. The suits had already been earmarked, and somebody else inherited Nile Kinnick's old uniform. Though Miles was only two inches shorter than Nile now, the knee pads of the pants he got reached the middle of his shins, and his jersey looked like a tent.

The uniforms also had a fetid smell of something brought up from long storage in a dank basement. The rankest odor came from the shoulder pads and helmets because the fabric covering the padding had long worn away and left soiled wads of dingy cotton batting sticking out. The helmets had once been red with a black wing-shaped leather shield above the brow and three leather straps stitched over the shell of the helmet from back to front, though these helmets had been worn out so long that they went flat as a lily pad when you dropped them on the ground. On your head, they afforded the protection of a stocking cap.

In their new-old uniforms, heirlooms of a grand tradition, looking like a detachment of a defeated Mongol tribe straggling over the steppe in front of the high school, the junior highs now took the field every evening to be drilled in organized football for forty-five minutes before Mr. Blough went down to Macy Field to assist at varsity practice.

Their football lesson began with all the players running five yards and throwing themselves on the ground headlong and sliding on their bellies, "to get friendly with the earth," then moved on to "the rolling block," which called for running another five yards and throwing yourself down sideways at a place representing an opponent and rolling while kicking your feet and legs as high as possible

100

so that, hopefully, with his knees kicked, the opposing player would fall down. Finally, linemen got specialized training in coming up from a three-point stance when Mr. Blough said "Hike!" with crossed arms which he promised would produce a kind of forearm upper-cut under the opposing lineman's chin as he raised his head to look around for your ball carrier.

Coach Blough often grew cross with his namby-pamby charges after half an hour, and during the scrimmage that topped off practice, would tend to pick up a slowpoke lineman by the neck of his jersey and the seat of his pants and fling him over the offensive line into the other squad's backfield. The flung boys would pick themselves up with a sort of dizzy elation at having moved so fast, though the coach never threw Miles because, he suspected, he was too fat.

Dick Berglund caught a pass in the first game, and Miles played tackle, but despite their drills, and *the tradition*, they lost to Dexter. On Sunday morning, October 8, the two sat together in Woods' cafe after finishing Dick's paper route, drinking cocoa and replaying the game till Miles got the Big Peach sports section of the *Register* and read about the brilliant upset Jun Kinnick's Hawkeyes had scored over Indiana for their second home win, 32-29.

The next week while the junior high won their first game, the Hawkeyes stumbled over Tom Harmon and the three-team-deep talent of a great University of Michigan football power and lost 27-7. In the diner, Miles read Bert McGrane's description of Jun Kinnick passing to Buzz Dean for Iowa's only score.

The next Friday afternoon, Adel Junior High played the Woodward State Hospital team. On Adel's second first-down play, as Miles and a husky boy named Walt Heimberger, his companion guard, prepared to high-low their opponent, the Woodward player crouching before them suffered a seizure just as the ball was snapped, and

101

the two Adel linemen remained frozen in the three-point stance while the play went for sixty yards. Their opponent had been whisked off the field by two attendants in white coats by the time they straightened up. Adel had made the only score of the game without them.

They had finished their season 2 and 1, and the team watched without regret as the uniforms of the Undefeated Team went into the locker-room laundry bin. They had not betrayed their heritage; but they had not exactly enriched it. Some said that beating the epileptic colony did not count; others said a win was a win. Fortunately, perhaps, their rolling blocks had failed to break their opponents' knees (this block would soon be banned from football), and their forearm upper-cuts had not laid any of their opponents low.

In the middle of October, Miles went to a Halloween party at the home of a girl whose friends called her Punky. Though he had known her since kindergarten, he had only recently begun to call her by her nickname. He strutted about with his invitation in his pocket, feeling big because a pretty girl had invited him to her party. He and Dick Berglund and Jack McCleary went to the party as the famous trio from *The Wizard of Oz,* Dick as the Cowardly Lion, Jack as the Tin Woodman--his body covered with silver-painted cardboard tubes held on with rubber bands-- and Miles the Scarecrow. Dick's mascara whiskers ran down his face when they bobbed for apples and Miles' straw stuffing made the girls sneeze in the hugging game, but as he walked home, he said the girls' names over to himself: "Tiff, Punky, Joyce, Gloria, Joann," and they had a musical sound.

On October 17th, the Nazis attacked the western front with one hundred thousand troops.

On the 28th, Iowa defeated Wisconsin 19-13 at Wisconsin, and the next weekend, defeated Purdue at home. Football suddenly took the foreground in Iowans' focus. All shared the growing frenzy for the Hawkeyes, but Adel regarded the Iowa team as uniquely its own. George's summer predictions about Jun's senior season were already more accurate than the eastern sportswriters' prophecies of another year of bottom feeding in the Big Ten for the Hawks. Not at the bottom by any means, but 4 and 1 so far, Iowa was suddenly the spoiler of the Big Ten.

But Notre Dame, undefeated, and everybody's pick for national champion, was coming to Iowa City on the eleventh. That Saturday, Miles struck a bargain with Ferne when she devoted his day to removing the summer screens and putting the storm windows on: while he washed the storms and replaced the screens, Ferne would move the little Philco from window to window so that he could listen to the game while he worked. In the second quarter, he remained for six minutes standing on the ladder, half-in, half-outside the living room while Jun Kinnick intercepted a Notre Dame pass at midfield, and three plays later, ran over center for "the most important score of his life." After their former paperboy drop-kicked the extra point, Notre Dame fought to a touchdown as time ran out--and missed the conversion. Final: Iowa 7, Notre Dame 6! Playing eleven "sixty-minute men," with only three substitutes, Iowa had climbed to the top of the Big Ten.

For finishing the windows under such stress without breaking any, J. Arthur proclaimed that Miles would have a ticket and a free ride with him and two of his surveyors to Iowa's last home game with Minnesota.

Saturday morning the little town was arrested in a cataleptic trance between dread and hope: Minnesota's nationally ranked "Golden Gophers" were huge men whose line outweighed Iowa twenty pounds per man. The sports pages asked, would it be a grudge game for Kinnick, who had been dismissed as too small for Minnesota's team in a tryout up there after high school?

Late that afternoon, as the shadows chilled the west side of the stadium at Iowa City, J. Arthur and his party watched from the forty-yard line in deepening gloom as Minnesota pushed the smaller Iowa team from one end of the field to the other without ever quite putting the game away. Then, late in the fourth quarter, with Iowa still scoreless and Minnesota a touchdown and a field goal ahead, the held breath across the state had begun to sigh out and the sunshine fans to leave the Iowa stadium. Then, in the words of the *Register's* premier sports poet, Bert McGraine:

Outweighed, overpowered at times, outmanned as usual, the invincible Hawks went into the fourth quarter trailing, 9 to 0, moved the length of the field twice on passes (by Nile Kinnick) and whirled on in the national spotlight with a thundering climax that 50,000 observers still can't believe.

Nile Kinnick's passes resurrected the losing Hawkeyes so late that many paying ticket holders only heard the roar of victory from the parking lots. Miles, for his part, saw none of the first score because he was slumped in his seat with his hand over his eyes when his hero completed the first long pass. He stood up and cheered, but what good would a touchdown do with the ball going to Minnesota with less than four minutes remaining? He was once more slumped over, counting the gum wrappers under his seat through the beginning of crybaby tears, when pandemonium broke out again! This time he looked up in time to see Nile's pass settle in the arms of the gold-helmeted receiver in the end zone! The extra point was good. The final score was Iowa 13, Minnesota 9, and J. Arthur grasped his hand and tugged him through the mass of 50,000 berserk fans to pay their respects to Nile Kinnick in the locker room. That's Miles on the edge of a throng of young fans shown getting their hero's autograph on the *Register*'s sports page Sunday. He is saying to another boy, "I used to hold for his kickoffs!"

The next week, finishing their season 6-1-1, missing the Big Ten Conference championship by one loss, the eleven "60-minute men" were raised to the pantheon of American football. But for Nile Kinnick, the apotheosis had just begun. It is not a reflection on other great athletes to say that he was no run-of-the mill All American. Phi Beta Kappas seldom win football awards, but in the following months, Nile Kinnick, Phi Beta Kappa, won the Maxwell award, the Most Valuable Player of the Big Ten Conference and the title of American Male Athlete of the year over Joe DiMaggio. In December, sportswriters voted him the Heisman Award by a two-to-one margin over Michigan's Tom Harmon.

His acceptance speech for the Heisman at the New York Athletic Club so eloquently moved beyond sports to the larger concerns of the nation about the crisis in Europe that it jumped from the sports sections to the front pages of newspapers across the country: "Kinnick says: 'I thank God that I was born to the gridirons of the Middlewest, and not the battlefields of Europe.'"

*   *   *

Ten days before Christmas, the World Premier of *Gone With the Wind* was held in Atlanta, sponsored by the Union League. Clark Gable, Vivien Leigh and other personages attended. Having devoured the book, the nation now turned its sentimental attention to the motion picture version of a seventy-year-old war. Before spring, the entire Adel school marched down to the New Rialto to see the picture, and Jean Baer told Miles that if she had known they wanted *that* sort of southern accent, she could have played the part as well as Vivien Leigh. Miles thought the film was all downhill after the Union burned Atlanta, and when he and several other boys who agreed with him began to talk and make a disturbance down front, teachers stationed at the back of the theater came down and silenced them with severe frowns as though it were a religious service. Thus, the boys were all ears when Clark Gable said, *"Frankly, my dear, I don't give a damn!"* and repeated it to the girls on any pretext for weeks.

*   *   *

One Sunday early in March 1940, the Morgans drove to Des Moines to have Sunday dinner with Uncle Bill House at the Ft. Des Moines Hotel. He was passing through on his way back to Washington from dedicating an airport in Nebraska. Miles remembered the meal afterward for gustatory reasons. Deaf to Ferne's warning on the way in that the Ft. Des Moines had one of the most expensive dining rooms, he ordered the Porterhouse steak dinner. Uncle Bill overrode Ferne's cancellation semaphores to the waiter: "Let a growing boy have what he needs, Ferne." And, shortly Miles was feasting on the first fine Porterhouse of his life.

Bill House was particularly expansive that day. All through dinner he enthused about the decision of his boss, Postmaster General James Farley, to seek the Democratic presidential nomination. Bill House said that though Roosevelt had been his benefactor and a friend, he did not favor a third term, and he thought Farley could win the nomination. Roosevelt was tired. If Bill stayed with him he was locked in place, but if he hitched his wagon to Farley's star, he would go up with him--and, after all, Farley was his boss. He owed him. He had agonized over it for weeks. Now he had made his decision, and he was sailing with the wind.

On the way home Ferne said Hazel was scared to death that F.D.R.would run again, and they'd be back in South Dakota. J. Arthur, noncommittal, hazarded that Wendell Willkie would probably be the Republican candidate.

4

A Gathering Storm

Earlier in the week, the ceremony for Memorial Day had been cancelled because the Panzers had driven the French and British back across Belgium, and all the places the veterans of the Great War had been singing about for twenty years had been overrun by the Nazis. But, on Tuesday when the English began rescuing their army and carrying them back across the channel in a thousand little boats, they were told it was on again.

Miles stood at semi-attention in his place in the marching band ranks with the bent-wood lyre sticking out in front and the flute sticking out to the side. When he thought about it, he knew he looked like a fool. Earlier, he had put on the blue uniform coat for the first time this spring, and it was so tight that he had to force the gold buttons down the front and they still gapped open; he weighed almost as much as J. Arthur, but the new height notch on the kitchen door had only climbed an inch. Walking downtown with Dick Berglund, who was five feet eleven now, he had felt like Mutt or Jeff--whichever was the runt--stumping along in his certified fat-kid exploding uniform with the coat tails flaring out over his broad-bottomed white duck pants.

The band was drawn up facing the north front of the courthouse and the rows of white crosses that the American Legion Auxiliary had set up early in the morning to represent Flanders Field. To the left, the honor guard in World War I puttees and old inverted saucer helmets stood with their Winchesters at parade rest, and one of the women in a white nurse's uniform with a red cross on her cap continued to stand at attention. Now the speaker, an elderly attorney, was struggling for some meaningful way

108

to work the old war they were memorializing together with the present one they were all thinking about. He wasn't finding one, and he kept groping for it while Miles watched the spring sunlight gradually unveil the Civil War cannon from its leaf shadow on the lawn across from Fred Robbins' barber shop, and wondered what kind of a day it was at Dunkirk for rescuing an army.

Finally, Mr. Fardel stood up and led the band through *America the Beautiful*. Then the minister put something about Roses of Picardy in the closing prayer and Miles had an urge to yell, "That was then! They need help now, before it's too late!" But he knew that no one over here could do a thing, not even Roosevelt, and he kept his head bowed beneath a heavy emotion both prayerful and hopeless until the a-men.

The crowd began to wander away, and the Red Cross lady started gathering up the crosses for next year. "If there is a next year." He looked around and didn't see Dick Berglund. The other band members were heading back to school to drop their instruments at the band room before lunch so he turned away and started home.

Last fall's ecstasies of almost terminal elation when Nile Kinnick had led the roll of all American athletes suddenly seemed like a hundred years ago. Though Nile would still captain the All Star game at the end of this summer when the best of the collegians always played the best of the professionals at Soldier Field, the fizz seemed to have gone out of it, and his hero had been one of the first to say so. He was returning to law school at Iowa in the fall, and had already told George he was thinking about the service. "It's all changing," Miles muttered, "and it's not half changed yet."

In December, when the Atlanta premier of *Gone With the Wind* had been ballyhooed so much as the *WORLD! premier!* that J. Arthur wondered sarcastically whether the Finns would ask the Russians for a truce so

109

they could all go to see a movie about the American Civil War, Miles was still occasionally replaying the Minnesota game with his friends. But in January, the real war had actually taken people's minds off Scarlet O'Hara. The European war was like the faraway thunder of a summer storm that might have a tornado in it, but might miss you after all. Who could say, when the Finns had actually started winning "on the frozen wastes of Lake Ladoga," and had even invaded Russian territory, and the allies were going to help them? And the British destroyer Cossack boarded a German ship in a Norwegian fjord and rescued 300 British sailors, prisoners from the Graf Spee battle off Montevideo? It was all like listening through static to a broadcast of Iowa playing an away game, only garbled voices coming through, but enough that you could tell it wasn't going too badly.

Before Christmas vacation, J. Arthur had moved his radio headquarters from the basement to the back hall between the kitchen and the living room where he had the right size alcove to accommodate a new "rig" he was building, and Miles had transferred his model-building factory back down to the bench in the furnace room by the stoker. He had inherited a comfortable work stool and an old rocking chair and a lamp for down there, and Ferne had turned over her little brown plastic Philco to him when J. Arthur got her a new one for the kitchen. Since then, he had done all his model building and much of his studying and random reading down there while listening to the war news on the little radio.

During vacation he and Berglund had read *David Copperfield*, Berglund reading aloud to polish his elocution for the debate team while Miles worked on a Hawker Hurricane. Dick's model was the radio announcer from WOI at Iowa State, who read classics like *The Moonstone* and George Eliot's *Middlemarch* for an hour, three days a week. The boys also read *The Three Musketeers* to each

110

other from a little book in a new kind of inexpensive binding called a Pocketbook. When Berglund found a scene in which D'Artagnan discovered a *fleur de lis* tattooed on the breast of the beautiful Lady de Winter, they both fell silent, vividly envisioning on the basement wall before them a new aspect of literary sensibility which they instantly considered French, a female breast with a tattoo.

Some time in February one of his mother's books migrated to the basement. They began reading the Book of the Month Club's bonus classic, Fitzgerald's *Rubaiyat of Omar Khayyam,* and Miles was excited to find that a verse he had liked in *Beau Geste* was a quotation of the *Rubaiyat*'s opening stanza. He memorized it, and coming into J. Arthur's presence one morning at breakfast, suddenly declaimed:

> *Awake! for morning in the bowl of night,*
> *Has cast the stone that put the stars to flight,*
> *And low, the hunter of the east has caught*
> *The sultan's turret in a noose of light!*

J. Arthur looked up with a frown and returned to his paper, and Miles realized that, though his father still recited lines he had been forced to memorize in school from Longfellow's *Evangeline*: *"This is the forest primeval, the murmuring pines and the hemlocks..."* he disapproved of reciting poetry just because you purely liked it. Liking poetry well enough to memorize it free, was not manfully Midwestern.

But they found they could use the *Rubaiyat* at school: Sigurd Fardel would turn to the blackboard to put up a Latin sentence, and Miles would whisper, *"The moving finger writes, and having writ moves on,"* and they would snicker. Or, Berglund, would come up behind a girl stooping over the water fountain in the hall and breathe in her ear, *"A jug of wine, a loaf of bread and thou!"* And when she jumped and turned around, he would wink and add, "and *Hold the bread!*"

By the furnace was a good warm place to study winter evenings. From time to time Miles would have to get up and fill the hopper of the stoker with crushed coal, or take a glowing ring of clinker out of the firebox with the long-armed tongs and dump it in a steel tub to smoke. And they always kept the little radio on at a low murmur. During Christmas vacation while Berglund studied Latin and Miles cut and glued stringers pinned down on wax paper, they followed the afternoon soap operas: *Our Gal Sunday* ("*Can a girl raised in a little mining town in the west find happiness as the wife of one of England's wealthiest titled lords?*") and *Ma Perkins*, a widow who tried to run a lumber yard in a town just like Adel, and *Lorenzo Jones*, an odd-ball inventor in a little town just like Adel. And they always tuned up *Mary Marlin* when they heard the *Claire de Lune* theme music because Mary's husband, Joe, a senator, had mysteriously disappeared on a fact-finding mission to Siberia. Which was as close to the real world as the radio soaps got.

But after March, when the Finns finally surrendered, the basement room with its ubiquitous humming radio had become their peanut gallery on the war. Prime Minister Chamberlain preened that in giving the allies months to prepare for war, Hitler had "*missed the bus*." And almost the next day, the Nazis invaded Sweden and Norway.

On May 10, 1939, Winston Churchill finally replaced Chamberlain; Panzers poured into Belgium, and the French *Maginot Line* that *Life* magazine had called impregnable was useless. Holland was overrun and the allied armies were trapped at Dunkirk on the Channel.

When he got home from the Memorial Day program, Ferne had gone to Garden Club and there was no one but Molasses sleeping on the sofa. He left the flute and lyre on the seat in the front hall, and filled the dog's water bowl and went to his room and changed to his regular school clothes. When he left the house he took his music with him.

He had heard there were American volunteers in the Royal Air Force and he hoped the British army could get home and hold the Nazis off till he was old enough to join the R.A.F. But, it might not matter one way or the other, because he hadn't been doing so well at school again. His grades showed that he sat and drew airplanes a lot when he should be looking at the black board. He could remember things he read pretty well, but nothing on the board seemed legible, and he resolved once more to try to look at the chicken tracks up there hard enough to get into the R.A.F.

As he descended the steps to the basement band room, John Bradley was practicing the tuba with a cigarette smoking on the music stand and smoke rings rising from the bell. Dick Berglund, who was not in the band because he had a "tin" ear, was listening with an air of serious respect to three girls gossiping about another girl. Miles looked at the topsy-turvy room with chairs every which way and a maze of music stands like spiders in the corners, and said, "Hey, I*n this battered caravanserai...*"

"*...Whose doorways are alternate night and day!*" Berglund responded.

The girls stopped talking and looked at the boys with their jaws ajar. They were stunned. Then they were impressed, "Aw, you two!" they said.

Berglund had taught Miles that when you mystified girls they were usually favorably impressed. Bradley, however, made his tuba do farting noises. Everybody laughed. Miles put the music in the file and went to class. He felt better about the war when he forgot it and played the fool.

And then, less than a week after Memorial Day, on June 4, the boys would be sitting in Miles' basement room huddled up to the Philco listening to Edward R. Murrow's from-the-last-outpost-of-civilization voice relaying Winston Churchill's apocalyptic declaration of Britain's lonely defiance of Hitler's coming invasion:

> *We shall fight on the beaches. We shall fight on the landing grounds. We shall fight in the fields, we shall fight in the streets; we shall fight in the hills...we shall **never** surrender!. Until, in God's good time, the New World with all its power and might, steps forth to the rescue and liberation of the old.*

After that, they were often in the "war room" following the *Battle of Britain* on the six o'clock news. Miles had become an armchair authority on air power and tabulated the scores of the daily air battles over England and marked them down on a little calendar he pasted up beside the radio.

On his workbench were the models of all the planes that were fighting these battles. When he finished them, he lined them up on the shelves: The German *Stuka*, the dive bomber that had been the terror of the refugees on the roads of central Europe. Obsolete already, capable of only about 180 miles per hour in level flight, *Stuka*s were still being sent across the channel by Goering and were dying like flies under the guns of the British fighters. And a balsa *Messerchmidt* 109-E, the top German fighter that was the equal of the Hawker Hurricane, but not quite the equal of the Supermarine Spitfire. In August, the Germans were sending everything flyable across the channel, and when he heard that the Spitfires were flaming ME-110s at a rate of four to one, he shouted, "Send those 110s!" And the Spitfire, the prettiest fighter you ever saw, had become the queen of the Battle of Britain.

On his birthday, a climactic air battle took place from Scotland to the Thames, and the Germans lost it at the rate of two to one, their downed pilots unable to return to battle, while the downed British pilots often fought again the same day. September 15 would turn out to be the Germans' last major push for superiority in the air over Britain and the Channel. On September 17 Hitler postponed Operation Sea Lion, the invasion. Its curtailment would be permanent, though Britain was still dying, the U-boats cutting her supply lines.

Athlete of the Year

. There is a photograph of Nile Kinnick in *the Dallas County News* which also ran in the *Des Moines Register* in early August 1940. The focus of the picture is a bare-chested Nile Kinnick in khaki shorts and football shoes kneeling on the grass of Riverside Park holding a football. He is surrounded by five boys in their mid-teens over whom he is grinning with his wonderful doubtless grin. The caption says he is giving some "pointers on kicking, passing and running" to a group of neighborhood "hero worshippers" as he tunes up to lead the College All Stars in the annual game against the professional champions at Soldier Field. The others are George Kinnick, Wayne Fritz, Miles, Dick Berglund, and Lowell Dawes, the Adel fullback.

Miles is wearing a half smile, pale and squinty and a little abashed, as if he has just emerged from an underground place and been caught blinded by sunlight, which pretty much sums up his situation. Miles was *not* in the process of getting football pointers from Nile. He had given up such sports in July because he could no longer catch a ball. The Gabby Hartnett catcher's mitt was collecting dust in the basement stair landing, not even broken in. (There was a reason for this, but he did not know it yet.)

George Kinnick had simply extracted him from his hibernation in the basement that day and they had been hanging out with the girls who handed out baskets at the swimming pool office when they had been drafted to help the News photographer make a picture story on Nile Kinnick training for the All Star game.

A few days after the photograph, Miles went to the square with George to eavesdrop on his brother's address to the Rotary Club. There, in the big room above the newspaper office, Nile Kinnick, Jr., *American Athlete of the Year*, graciously dismissed the introductory effusive compliments, made a joke about the famous picture of him with a debutante and his coach, Dr. Eddie Anderson, in a nightclub in New York with a glass of milk before him, and spoke briefly, as he was expected to, of Iowa's championship season and the upcoming All Star game at Soldier Field. Then he smoothly shifted the football talk into a larger topic and said he was already looking forward to a golden post war era when democracy would spread to all the peoples of the world. There was no trace of bombast in the talk.

Miles would see his idol once more after that: One Thursday night in late September, when George Kinnick had phoned, and Miles was wondering as he walked toward Clarkes' if the beginning of the draft meant that America was finally going to answer Winston Churchill's call for "*the new world to come to the rescue of the old,*" a big black sedan stopped beside him, and someone rolled down the window and asked him if he knew where Governor Clarke's home was. He said he was headed there, and the man in front made room for him and introduced everyone in the car. They were all "*Ironmen,*" Iowa team mates of Jun Kinnick, except one older fellow who said he was a sports promoter.

Nile Kinnick opened Clarke's door; they all shook hands, and the promoter said something about the proposition for a new professional football team for the 1941 season, to star Nile Kinnick. Then they all went into the governor's long library room, and Miles and George went down to the diner to talk. Over their nickel Cokes, Miles fervently predicted that George's brother would be governor of Iowa after the war.

(That weekend Nile Kinnick used the car his father had brought him from Omaha to drive to Cedar Falls to introduce the Republican presidential candidate, Wendell Willkie[*], at a rally there. Before the weekend was over he would drive on to Vermillion, South Dakota, to scout the University of South Dakota's football team for an upcoming game with the University of Iowa. Then, returning to Iowa, he would referee a night football game at

---

[*] The Republicans nominated Wendell Willkie in June. At the Democratic convention, a shallow flurry for Jim Farley died under the steamroller draft of Franklin Roosevelt for a third term.. The Houses had only recently quit their long tenancy at the Mayflower Hotel and bought a home in Silver Springs, perhaps in anticipation of James Farley's presidency. Now, Uncle Bill had to beat the bushes for a position that would keep the family in Washington in the manner to which they had become accustomed. He took a post as vice president of Mid Continent Airlines.

Morningside College in Sioux City, and according to his letter to the family, give a half-time demonstration of punting, and passing the football with either hand before returning to Iowa City Sunday night to study for his Monday law classes.)

5

Yarning in Three Tenses

In September of 1940, due to Franklin Roosevelt's manipulation, the United States paid lip service to neutrality while trading fifty reconditioned destroyers to Britain for bases in the West Indies. While the Battle of Britain had been won, the Battle of the Atlantic, to save England from the U-boats, became critical. The losses of British ships far surpassed replacement, and food and war supplies arriving in Britain were less than half of 1939's. Britain was dying. Miles did not know the statistics, but the sense of an ultimate crisis was in the air. Both political parties declared their support of Great Britain's fight against aggression, and everyone now referred to the British as "us" instead of "them." In October, the U.S. Army started its first experimental paratroop battalion. From the time Uncle Bill House had gone down with Farley at the Democratic convention, it had been a foregone conclusion at home that F.D.R. would win. Even J. Arthur went Democratic, deciding "not to change horses in mid-stream." That slogan apparently swayed the dubious. The country began to slowly mobilize.

Miles was drawn out of his basement war room by a number of activities that conscripted freshmen into the small school's vigorous activity program. He left a Grumman Gulfhawk half-finished on the workbench and joined the choir of the church without a steeple across the street when Dan and Mack Rainwater joined, because their father, Ray, was choir director. He could read the music, though he wasn't sure from session to session whether he would be a tenor or a bass. In October his favorite anthem was celebratory:

119

The valleys stand so rich with corn that they laugh and sing!
They laugh! And sing! THEY LAUGH! AND SING!

which the choir bellowed with open throats, imagining the Israelites celebrating a sixty bushel-to-the acre Iowa-style bumper crop. Ray Rainwater liked robust singing. Dan Rainwater had taken up drums and was collecting a trap drum set piece by piece on layover. He had caught a whiff of swing music at his cousin's in Chicago and now carried his drumsticks everywhere and rained paradiddles on most solid surfaces, making himself the prophet of syncopated music in the county. (Miles knew from Dan that a drummer, Gene Krupa, had been arrested for smoking marijuana, but didn't know what that was.)

That fall, a few of Mr.Fardel's music groups began to reach the upper levels of the music contests. Survivors of local elimination contests took to the road to the contests in neighboring towns, and later the few Superiors went on to Winterset and West Des Moines. There was a national contest at the tip of that pyramid, but no one west of Des Moines had ever gotten that far.

In the ensemble events Miles felt no stage fright, but on stage alone with the band director's wife at the piano and the frail flute in hand, he assumed the posture and movement of a rusty Tin Woodman. When a lack of competition passed him through to District in flute solo that year, he prayed that the Lord would give him a non-fatal disease to take him off the travel roster. But the night of the event in late October, a case of stage nerves was the progenitor of the first yarn he ever told--to two parents and three kids in someone's car on the way to Winterset.

It was already dark, and the driver had turned on the headlights, and the chatter between the female oboe player and a trumpeter on each side of him in back had died out and left him gnawing his knuckle and trying to forget that soon, in the bright lights of a strange auditorium, Flora Fardel would be trying to lift him through *The Red Saraband* (#3 difficulty). His panic reflex to stage fright suddenly compelled him to talk, and in a lull, he blurted out:

"Once upon a time about a hundred years ago in Madison County right near here ..." and paused to test the atmosphere in the car. The parents in the front seat stopped talking to each other, and he launched a tall tale, scarcely remembering that his mother had once told him the story of her great grandmother, then a pioneer child, finding the little corpse of an Indian baby wrapped in a blanket with a toy pail and interred in a hollowed-out log in the top of a tree, and how the wind had loosened it and it had all fallen on the bank near their first lean-to on Clanton creek--and how their mother had ordered the children to leave it alone.

Miles improvised a ghost story from it in which the ghost of the dead child cursed the life of the callous white man who cut its corpse down and stole the blanket and pail. He said the curse had continued to blight the lives of the man's descendants from generation to generation. As he saw that they were approaching the lights of Winterset, he finished by making up how he had noticed in the *Des Moines Register* only last week that the man's remaining descendent had died in a mysterious crash on the bridge over Clanton Creek that now marked the spot where the Indian baby had been found.

Perhaps the telling had taken five minutes, and when he finished, there was a silence, the flavor of which he liked, and the woman in the front said, "My my! Is that so, Miles?"

"No, it's fiction, mostly," he said, though for all he knew, the creek they had crossed may have been Clanton

Creek, and the Indian baby's tree burial might have been close to the bridge.

"Oh," she said in a reproachful tone, and he could tell she was mystified--which also pleased him.

He did not rate a First or Second in his solo that night, and was mightily relieved. But he was in other ensemble events which did go to the next contest level. And though the oboist had said nothing about the story to him, when they were assigned their rides to the next District elimination a week later, he found himself with the same people as the previous trip--except that the oboist's parents were driving--and he sensed Doris had pulled strings to put him in their car. Sure enough, when they were on their way and it was dark again, the oboist's mother turned around in the front seat and said she regretted not hearing the pioneer ghost story, and wondered if he would mind telling it again.

He truly didn't remember how to start it out again, and she said she was disappointed. But after they had ridden for a time in silence, he heaved a sigh, as though it were costing him a great mental labor, and said, "I can't vouch for every word of *this* story, because I heard it from an old cowboy at a lodge in the Big Horn mountains of Wyoming....."

It was an entirely different story, which began with a description of Lake Solitude, the highest lake in the Big Horns--which he had never seen--and a boy who, "once upon a time long ago," had been taken by the Spirit of Lake Solitude when he and two others were caught by a sudden violent storm while rafting on the lake. It, too, was a ghost story, and ended with the boy rematerializing at a Boy Scout bivouac at a scout cabin in the mountains a whole half century after he had drowned to warn a present-day Scout troop preparing to sleep there that an earthquake would soon send the great boulder that beetled over the camp crashing down on the cabin. The boulder, which

Miles could see in his mind's eye, was exactly the one their party had camped under with the Longs in the mountains two summers ago.

Though the trip was somewhat longer than the one to Winterset, this story, too, came to an end with the boys escaping from the cabin just as the boulder crashed down-- and the lights of the host high school appeared.

Doris said, "See, Mom!" and the trumpet player sighed with exasperation, and the oboist's mother turned around from the front seat, and said, "My goodness, Miles, I didn't even know you folks went to the Big Horns last summer."

"Oh, no, mam, it was the summer before last."

"Oh? That was when that old cowboy told you that story? "

"No-no, mam, the cowboy part is fiction. But my friend Carl Long really *did* drown in Lake Solitude."

Later, on the way home, there was a certain amount of probing about what was and what wasn't true in the tale, but he declined to explain where the rest of the story had come from, and indeed, he couldn't have.

In the week that followed, there were some signs that the stories had made a few ripples. He overheard an older boy say to a friend in the rest room that he sure wanted to ride next time in that car where some big stretchers were being told. The tone was ironic, so the fellow knew Miles was listening. And his companion said that he sure wanted to *avoid* it, as he usually had a nice nap on the way to contest. But Miles was pleased, and began to think he was onto something he could actually *do*, and started to think about making up an exciting yarn for the next trip.

In any event, the story he subsequently invented about a party of boys out camping who accidentally capture some gangsters and turn them over to the sheriff, didn't quite get told. The first two stories had come out as naturally as breathing. He seemed to have opened his mouth in the dark and there they were. But on the way to Council Bluffs, the girl oboe player, who had taken a shine to the trumpet player, went with him in another car. Miles was stuck in the outside corner of the back seat of a car next to a girl named Joann Duncan, who had transferred from Des Moines in the fall. He had never spoken to her, though they were in some of the same classes. A large fat girl on the far side of the car crowded Joann over against him, and he could feel her trying to make her body as small as she could so as not to touch him in the dark, swaying car.

As he waited for the right moment to start a souped-up version of the Modlin boys and the Barrow gang, Mr. Olson pulled into a filling station and they all got out and stretched. Joann Duncan went to the rest room with the fat girl. When they were under way again, Miles realized that Joann had refreshed the cologne she was wearing, and the tart-sweet floral cloud she exuded had dried up his story in his head. He was tongue-tied. And on the way home when she nodded off and caved over against him he became as petrified-stiff as if he had had a seizure.

At school Monday, he made a point of noticing her. She was light-boned and thin, but with an extraordinary posture as erect as a hussar, which might have been the only mark of physical beauty about her, except for the freckles across a pale little face beneath a pair of somber gray eyes. Her mouth looked as though it would be wide if she ever really opened it, but the lips were pale and had a dry, cracked look, and her hair was unremarkable except for its tendency to fall in her eyes and get peremptorily tossed back every few minutes. Yet, with her vertical, marching walk, she gave the impression of being, not so much older, as beyond the local girls in some canon of experience. And the other girls said that being from Des Moines, she thought she had come down in the world. She

124

lived around the block from Miles on the west side of Ninth and Grove in a low yellow bungalow with a wintered-in front porch. Her father had been notoriously surly to all the children who had come for treats at Halloween and Joann had only one friend.

Of course, he now had a full-blown crush on her, the more acute because there was so little of her showing except the freckle-scattered nose and straight gray eyes. Her soldier posture in the little plaid skirts she wore indifferently, sometimes tilted or halfway turned around, with the blouse tail out as if she'd been dressed by someone else, always tempted him to give their hem a tweak as she passed his desk, to see where they would end up, since they had so little support from her hips.

Before Christmas, he discovered that she brought her lunch and often ate with her friend in Miss Trout's math classroom. So, he had Ferne make his lunch, and he went to eat there, too. He and another boy came before the girls arrived, and Miles printed a corruption of her name on the blackboard: "Joann Junk Can" in huge letters, and drew a garbage can overflowing with trash. On the tilted lid, he drew a face with a freckled nose. When Joann arrived, she looked at his cartoon and turned on her heel and left the room. She did not eat there again. He was disappointed because he had rather expected the drawing to break the ice between them.

During the presentation of the public speaking assignments in English class the week before Christmas, when Miss Grinnell called on Joann, and the girl said she was not prepared, a gush of gallantry made him raise his hand and volunteer to go in her place. Miss Grinnell saw that he had nothing on paper, but she nodded, and he hastily scribbled: "Can We Lose the War in the Air?" on a blank sheet and left it on her desk as he went to the front. He introduced himself as a young American entering the Air Corps and looking over the American air armory on the

125

eve of committing himself to training to fly bombers or fighters. He meant to imply that he was portraying just the kind of fellow whose shoes he would fill as soon as he was old enough to volunteer for the Air Corps.

He said that since last summer, the Defense Advisory Commission had committed billions to expanding America's war production. Wooden rifles were a thing of the past now, but aircraft development was a real bottleneck. "What American plane can he fly if he's called to help win the Battle of Britain?" he asked rhetorically, and noted that *Popular Aviation* had said that the life of the Brewster Buffalo, an American fighter loaned to the British, was about equal to the life of a barrage balloon. "Yes, the Boeing Flying Fortress can hold its own with the Bristol Blenheim and the He-111 now, but if I go to fighters?" he said, hoping that Joann would see him going to fighters, "Well, there's the Curtis P- 40, a strong airplane. But the only thing it can do faster than an Me-109 is dive. And the Seversky P-35, a racing design they are developing into a long-range fighter...fast, but heavy as a locomotive ....No," he said climactically, "We have *one* top plane: Remember *Time* magazine's report on that new fighter, with two engines on a twin-boom fuselage and the pilot in a pod in the middle that broke Howard Hughes' cross-country speed record at 400 plus mph? And ran out of gas and landed on a golf course?"

Several of the boys nodded, "Well, my money's on the Lockheed P-38 Lightning! That's what *I'm* going to fly!"

He was sure that if applause had been permitted in English class, he would have had some. Miss Grinnell cleared her throat and dismissed the class. People filed out. He saw Joann hanging back in the hall, probably to thank him for saving her bacon.

"Can I ask you something?" she said.

"Sure, ask away."

126

"What was the point of <u>that</u>?" She wrinkled her freckled nose and walked away.

Christmas vacation, he moped after Joann like a snubbed pup. Sometimes he stood in front of her house hoping she would come out. Once his patience ran out and he threw a snowball at her front door. After New Year's he saw her father loading their furniture into a trailer backed up to the front porch. Mr. Sinift said Joann was not coming back after break.

The day she moved away was filled with snow, huge flakes coming lazily down out of a still, sunless sky just below freezing. The air was so dense that houses and trees made dim shapes of white on white, and the snow piled up on fence posts in fat eiderdown pillows awaiting another degree of warmth to turn to slush. He saw Joann's car go past without the trailer, and he waded up to the corner of Rapids and Ninth and watched it pull up in front of the yellow house. He had on a mackinaw and a new Christmas cap of Hudson Bay wool, red with a black stripe across the top and retractable ear flaps. He stood on the corner stamping his feet while the snow piled up on his shoulders and began to put a white cap on top of the red cap.

When Joann and her father came out, she was wearing red rubber Cossack boots and a narrow-shouldered little coat over snow pants. Her father waded around to the driver's side and stopped to take a long look his way before he got in behind the wheel. Then the car came slowly along the street toward him.

What did he look like standing hot and transfixed in the mackinaw, a would-be Lochinvar with a cap of snow on his head and his mouth agape like a hole in the snow? He didn't see himself that way.

But Joannn's father certainly did. When the car came abreast, Miles raised his hand. Her father stopped the car and said something to the girl. As Miles began to expect that she would get out and come around through the snow and say goodbye, or give him a note with her future address, her father turned toward him grinning--not a Christmas smile--then got out and picked up two handfuls of snow, patted them unhurriedly into one snowball and took aim and pitched it at him. It knocked his cap off and showered snow on his nose. The man snorted, glared at him and got back in the car and drove on--half a block--before Miles came unstuck and grabbed a handful of snow. But he realized he would be throwing it at Joann too, so he just stood there holding it till it began to soak his glove.

He never saw Joann again, though years later when he was home on leave from the service, someone told him she had lived with an aunt in Des Moines and had finished high school there. They thought she had married and moved away.

Relativity

The first yarn he actually wrote out--a yellowed copy of which surfaced recently after fifty years in the desk where he wrote it—catches better than he ever could have told you, what he felt was happening in the world that year, and what he made of it.

The story's inspiration was a random riff he and Dick Berglund got into in the superintendent's office after class one afternoon about Mr. Sinift's geometry lesson. Mr Sinift, the powerful, bear-shaped principal--who knew more than most of his students ever would think of, and was a fond figure to most of them because he only expressed his disapproval by pinching the tendon between their neck and their shoulder till they stood on tiptoe, but seldom told Superintendent Weir what he knew against them--had a class of eighth-grade geometry that semester. Though, with the approach of the war, he had begun to make his high school classes groan with a sudden new rigor, Maurice Sinift still took the "small potatoes" at a dog trot that left time in Miles' class for a few digressions into "pure" science. These lectures tended to sketch what the edges of physics and astronomy looked like to the *Scientific American.* Everyone liked them because they didn't entail home work, and they left Mr. Sinift with more time to tutor the senior boys who would soon be looking for special assignments in the service.

That day he had been doing Einstein. The name Einstein, of course, was already like an oral X-caliber that mowed you right down. Einstein's light, Mr. Sinift had said, was like a particle but also like a wave. This meant nothing to them, except that it was awesome.

Also, light moved at approximately 186,000 miles per second. They nodded, and wrote that down.

"Imagine yourself moving at the speed of the earth's rotation, which you are--does anyone know what speed that is?" (Silence.) "Well, it's just short of 25,000 miles a day, at the equator--you yourselves can test it, because from where the sun came up yesterday, today you're back around, and it comes up again in almost the same place in 24 hours! Eh? So, you've come 25,000 miles (a hand up in back)--Yeah, okay, 24,000-*plus*, in 24 hours, about a thousand miles an hour. Herb, did you ever think the reason your hair points straight back like that is because we're going so fast? If you could go up in the stratosphere and go 25,000 miles an hour with the earth's rotation, you could hang over the same spot on earth, like a kite, only you'd have to go a bit faster to compensate for your altitude.

"But, anyhoo--if you shoot a light out along the vector with the earth's rotation, will the light go faster than a searchlight you shoot straight up? If so, how much? 25,000 miles per hour faster? ...Don't bother to get out your pencils, boys and girls, not a bit of it! Just the same speed,

129

up, down or sideways! *Wow!* Who says? Einstein says--but it has been tested and proved by other scientists who didn't believe their own data at first. Einstein just told them they were right the first time. Same speed!"

Then Mr.Sinift had capped off the session by revealing that Einstein had proved that time slowed down for you proportionately as the speed of the "train" you were on approached the speed of light.

Berglund was running some dittos for Miss Laffler and his thumbs were purple. He made a pass at Miles' shirt and said, "That guy on the *Coffee Cup* show this morning said his voice was coming to us through the ether. Through the *ether*!" He snorted.

"There isn't any," They both looked superior.

"If time slows down as you speed up, what happens if you get up to the speed of light? Actually?"

"It stops?"

"Time *stops*?"

"Time stops!" They contemplated time stopping. It wasn't at all hard to imagine now. "If you had a twin," Berglund said, "and you left him here on earth and flew at the speed of light to..." "Betelgeuse." They had heard about Betelgeuse from J. Arthur, whose new hobby was astronomy.

"Yeah, Betelgeuse...and you came back..."

"527 light years out, and 527 light years back,"

"But no time would have passed for you."

"Not for me. But my twin on Earth would be dead of old age about a thousand years."

"But *you* wouldn't even need a haircut yet!"

"Think of that! Bozo Kline would be out of business!"

"Or if you went faster, say 600 light years!"

"You might arrive home before you left, and it'd be Valley Forge time! They'd still be crossing the Delaware. *Jeez*!"

"And you'd be rowing!"

"*You* would, you mean!"

They started yuking, and Superintendent Weir's secretary had yelled from the inner office to hold it down.

So, he left Dick Berglund and went down to the locker room and got his stuff together for the track meet the next day.

Saturday afternoon he managed to place in the shotput, but came in last trying to run the mile. It was the best he could do, but Coach thought anyone so slow was goofing off and made him jog up the hill through the park back to school, a penalty he would get used to. So supper was already on the table when he got home. Ferne didn't mind; fine with her if he had been running off some baby fat. But J. Arthur was frowning. Miles thought it was his lateness, but it wasn't. It was something bad.

As he dished up the roast, J. Arthur said, "They caught up with the Bismarck."

"Good!" Everybody knew the Germans' best battleship, blockaded in port by the British navy, had come out and was being hunted.

"But it sank the Hood," his father said.

"Aw!" he made an actual strangled shout of disbelief, "not the *Hood*!" The Hood was the "pride of the British fleet," new, fast, guns to match anything afloat, an awesome silhouette. "What in the...."

"Calm down!" his mother said.

"Blew her up. They hit her magazine or something- -lost all hands. A thousand men--more!" J. Arthur grimaced and returned his attention to his plate.

Miles felt as if he'd actually been socked with a heavy fist. He fiddled with the rest of his meal, then excused himself. "Well. They'll get that Bismarck!" he said from the doorway.

131

"They've lost track of her completely," J. Arthur said. "She can be into those convoys like a fox in a hen house before they find her."

Miles climbed the stairs to his room and flopped on his bed. Things that he had been ignoring since Joann left town got together with the loss of the Hood and welled over in his head. Suddenly totally unrelated goads and losses, the smaller the more baneful, coalesced into a landslide of disgust for his feckless, useless life here: He had been standing with Ferne in Younkers department store before Christmas and Ferne had been buying an expensive blanket of fleecy longhaired wool in a pattern of red tulips on a beige ground. Why was she paying twice as much? "Because it's the famous Holland Tulip blanket, and now that the Nazis have Holland there won't be any more of them." He snapped back that he knew the Nazis had Holland, and they had squabbled the rest of the afternoon. Now, he got it. It came home. No more Tulip blankets, and no more *Hans Brinker and the Silver Skates*, and the Nazis goose-stepping all over Holland. The news reel view of them tramping through the *Arc de Triumph*! He finally got the point of Roosevelt's last Fireside Chat: "*If Great Britain goes down, the Axis will control Europe, Asia, Africa, Australia and the high seas, and we will be living at the point of a gun!*" Now he lay on the Tulip blanket, belatedly getting the point of Roosevelt's, "*Never since Plymouth Rock has American civilization been in such danger.*"

His bedroom was small, with space for what he needed, but not much more. His dour stare took in a closet on the left with a mirror door he could see his prone figure in, and across the room another door that led to the sleeping porch where he slept in the summers in the big old brass double bed Ferne had made up for the season just today. In the sloping front wall was a dormer with two windows, and in between them a study desk with a portable typewriter. A model P-38 hung from the ceiling. He imagined everything taken away, one by one, ending with the Holland blanket, *"Never since Plymouth Rock,"* he intoned, and squinted at the curtains over the windows with some heavy, inchoate emotion till his eyes watered:

What America was supposed to do about that, was to be "the Arsenal of Democracy." Right now it didn't look like it was going to be enough of an arsenal in time. On that Sunday last spring when he and J. Arthur had ridden out with the contractor to look at the site where the U. S. Rubber Co. was to build a huge new arms plant, the two men had looked over empty fields scattered with tufts of snow where stakes with red surveyor's flags were planted, and not a foot of earth had been turned, and there was no earth-moving machinery in sight. And they had talked as though their minds' eyes could already see a gigantic arms plant all but completed. But Miles' mind's eye could see only the unemployed loafers sitting on the railings across from the courthouse dipping Snoose year-in year-out. He could not envision in this part of the country anyway, such people having enough strength to get up off the loafers' railing and be "the Arsenal of Democracy".

He groaned and rolled over, slammed his feet on the floor and jumped up and started pacing around the little room and out onto the porch. He put his hands on the sill of the open window and ducked under the shade and looked out at the street. A horizontal ray of oblique sunlight rested on the chimney of the church without a steeple across the way. The air coming in smelled loamy, and a taint of lilacs floated in it. There was nothing in the street, not even a stray dog. "The Hood's sunk and the Bismark's loose." he said out the window.

He went back into his room, cracked open the window in front of his desk so he could smell the lilacs, and got a piece of typing paper out and rolled it into his little, black Corona. He placed his hands over the "rest" positions and tried to punch the keys forcefully, the way he had been taught in Miss Spagnola's "touch typing" class. He wrote haltingly at first:

> *Michael wondered how they had lost the Second World War. He wondered what had really been at the bottom of it all.*

He stopped typing and Roosevelt's Patrician periods resonated in his head "...*To keep your children and your grandchildren later out of a war...*" He bit his thumbnail and continued,

> *Michael guessed it had been decided long ago when they had turned their backs and stayed home and left the offspring of tyranny to build a towering empire from the ruins of the old world.*

The story now established its situation quickly. Michael was the young American pilot of an unarmed observation "kite," and was waiting in a vast ready room of a final world war among the shades of all the airmen who had gone down in the losing cause of defending the United States from the previous invasions--there had been two unsuccessful invasions stopped by all the pilots who were now gone and unable to answer the last muster. This invasion would be successful. It would soon come by air again, in waves of sub-stratospheric troop transports that carried a battalion of soldiers per ship.

Michael and the sparse figures in the dimly-lit ready room always went on watch in space for a month at a time, supplied from Afantu, a meteor that they had captured and built an annex resource depot on. Propelled by electromagnetic drives, the Kites touched down on Afantu and were fed at almost the speed of light down to their observation positions where they hovered stationary with the earth's rotation in orbit above all weathers, on electronic "watch" over the Euraxis staging areas.

The logistics of the war were long established, the dynamic balance an extrapolation from as far back as WW II. The Euraxis with its great mass of slaves, a juggernaut; the U.S. a less populous enclave of free men armored with superior technology. Early in his career Michael had done missions when the first penetration of the Absolute Mass Barrier had been made, and access to interstellar travel just below the speed of light had seemed to promise interplanetary colonization. This plan had been illusory; the Mass Barrier had proved impenetrable to all but the smallest missions, thus Absolute. Though several of his deep sorties had spanned earth decades, Michael had aged less than a month in that early phase.

Before his first assignment he and Leni had planned to marry. They had both been in their twenties.

But when he returned from Afantu, she had reached retirement age and was giving up her post. Because they had remained in touch, he had known what was happening, that time had almost stopped for him, while on Earth it went racing on. When she was still young, she had wanted to keep their vows, regardless. But he had stubbornly freed her, insisting that she must marry someone else, and have the children they had planned to have. And she had had children, though perhaps in a concession to their lost dream, she had never married.

And when his mission was over, and he returned, her children had already had their children. Only when he saw them did it really hit home to him. When she brought these aging children to a rehab affair the Echelon arranged for returnees debriefing after decades in space that had passed for them as hours, he had thought her granddaughter was Leni. Leni's middle-aged daughters knew something of him from the remote past, but had never met him. Nor did they this time. Her grandchildren must have wondered what they were doing there. He and Leni had had a few minutes alone, and both knew as they embraced that Michael might have been her son; she might have been his mother. She had been a robust young woman; now she was frail. He seemed like a son--who needed a haircut. She had tugged gently on the shaggy hair at the nape of his neck when she hugged him, as a mother would have. He had been the one who broke down--she the stoical one. She had lived her life, while in space they had lived between haircuts.

After that their relationship had taken on a mother-son tone.

Now, when his call came, he left the note to her unfinished on the ready room desk. Someone would send it spacemail, if there was anyone left.

Minutes later, Michael launched with the few remaining kites through Afantu to his station.

At the end of the story, after the wave of lumbering subsonic troop carriers of the Euraxis had brushed aside the American interceptors with few losses, Michael plummets his unarmed kite into the atmosphere, knowing that if it doesn't burn up like a falling star before he crashes it into the leading trooper, his fuel cell will create an electromagnetic holocaust across their front that may turn them back He wrote: "For tonight those who waited below were safe, but the enemy would come back, and next time would not be stopped because there would be no one left to stop him."

He pulled the last page out of the machine, bundled them all together and paper- clipped them. Then he numbered them by hand. He had a feeling of exultation, so he stacked them and evened them again and put the paper clip back on just for the authorial feeling of it. *H

He went downstairs and found J. Arthur sealing some business letters to take to the depot to go out on the twelve o'clock train. He hitched a ride downtown.

The next morning, he turned the story in to Miss Grinnell.

Three days later the British navy sank the Bismarck. The same day, President Roosevelt declared an unlimited national emergency. Congress finally passed Lend Lease, outright aid to Britain. Miles began to ta: "ke a more sanguine view of the war. Miss Grinnell gave back his story with the commentGood description and moving action. Watch punctuation!" He was sure it would have gotten an E if he had not been so inspired that he had to dispense with punctuation and spelling. Dick Berglund read the story, but was not impressed. He said that most of it was "implicit" (his new "lawyer" word) in their talk in the superintendent's office about Sinift's relativity lecture.

6

A Man's Work

June: Summer vacation had just started to fall into its sleepy rhythm with the opening of the pool, and again Miles began to fraction his days out among a few lazy priorities. He often went along on the early morning paper route, which Berglund now delivered on a good bike he had bought with his solvent paper route. Afterward, they would get fresh honey buns at the diner and take them to the Southside Drug, which Berglund opened up every day.

Berglund's new nickname was Racy, conferred on him by Liz Sinden when the other fountain girl turned out the light on them when Liz had taken him to the basement to carry up a jug of syrup for her. "*Mr. Berglund, what makes you so racy?*"

Before customers came in, "Race" would make coffee and put the store in shape for the day's business, while Miles sat at the fountain munching the honey buns and gabbing. Then, as the long dawn shadow of the courthouse steadily gave way to sunlight on the west store fronts of the square, he often migrated to the reading room of the library with a *Life magazine,* or a new *Saturday Evening Post* or *Colliers,* or *Popular Aviation*, or the *Christian Science Monitor* which Frances Kinnick had put him onto. Sometimes he spent a long time scrutinizing the excellent photographic studies of groups of topless African women posed beside objective-looking bearded explorers in pith helmets and bush jackets in front of grass huts in old *National Geographics.*

Toward the end of the month he started getting up at dawn, taking one of his father's golf clubs and a couple of balls and going to chip balls around the park. But he had a tendency to lose them, even on the well-groomed, gently

138

rolling lawns. One evening J. Arthur gave him three cut-up balls and forbade him to use his Titelists.

The tone of his relationship with his father began to take a mystifying turn one day in June when he accompanied J. Arthur to the construction. After lunch in a restaurant in Perry, they had run into Mr. Sears, the contractor who had taken them for a tour of the Des Moines Ordnance Plant site in March. At the cash register the jowly contractor looked up with stage surprise and greeted Miles instead of his father, "Why, if it isn't big J.!" he said, and extended his hand to Miles, "Did you bring little J. to help you inspect the grading?" He broke up laughing, patted Miles on the shoulder and shook hands with J. Arthur, who took his time before he chuckled. Sears said, "I believe the boy has got an inch on you this winter, Doc. Of course, maybe he just looks higher because he has hair."

That evening after supper, J. Arthur had Miles stand against the kitchen door frame for the first time in several months, and marked his height with a kitchen knife. The mark was an inch above the previous one. "Well-well," he said to Ferne, "When they ask for Big J. from now on, call *him*."

But soon Miles had a suspicion that his superior height wasn't that casual a matter with J. Arthur, who had not till now seemed particularly troubled that he didn't have a part-time job or a paper route as long as he did his "chores." Now, however, J. Arthur began to bring home odd jobs that he had drummed up for Miles among his cronies downtown.

He was okay with this at first. He had time on his hands and had squandered his allowance, and he fancied he was learning how the world worked by doing a different job every time. He subbed for a filling-station attendant one afternoon, then worked as a rodman for Roy Cross, the county engineer, for two days. One hot day he worked as assistant to a scavenger who went about digging out clogged septic tanks and emptying full outhouse pits. Though he didn't have to get right down in these pits because it was his first day and he had no boots, he was so fragrant when he came home that Ferne made him undress in the front hall and go directly to the bath while she phoned his new boss to tell the scavenger he could not work tomorrow, or any time in the near future. J. Arthur carped at supper that *he* had done dirtier work as a boy in Nebraska, and it made a man of him. When Miles asked what work was dirtier than scavenging, he got a surly silence.

On Wednesday, J. Arthur brought home a new 21" lawnmower and two lawn jobs he had found for him among his friends. Miles could use the new mower free of charge on these jobs and get the same money he got for doing their own lawn, a quarter, which was the going rate for about an hour's lawn work. "This is more like!" He thought at first that the jobs would make him a dollar or so every ten days if the season didn't turn dry, and maybe he'd pick up more and have a real lawn business.

But he began to realize that J. Arthur picked his lawn clients the same way he selected a hitchhiker--there was an element of altruism in it. One of these "lawns" was a retired widower named Bracher who lived in a large house with a deep, sloping backyard four blocks up Grove Street. When he did his first job on Bracher's lawn, the old man wasn't home. It was high grass and took him two hours, and a quarter finally came home with J. Arthur the next week.

Ten days later, he timed the old man's lawn by when his father told him to mow their own. When he finished, he pushed the mower on up to Bracher's, but he had only mowed two swaths before the man came out on the back stoop and told him to go home and not come back till he was called. Miles said, "Yes, sir," and free-wheeled the mower back home.

When another week with a good soaking rain passed and Bracher didn't call, he took it up with his father, who mused over it a minute, and said that Mr. Bracher was retired on a very small pension, and was also blind in one eye--which had been put out when the trunk lid of his car fell on his head. Miles pointed out that Mr.Bracher had a new Buick, but J. Arthur seemed to misconstrue the affluence point and merely said that it was the trunk lid of his *previous* car that had put his eye out. Miles grumbled under his breath that it didn't take more than one eye to see that the lawn was too high.

But it was Saturday again before J. Arthur came home and said Mr. Bracher wanted the lawn done Monday. On Monday, in back of Bracher's house, the crab grass was knee high. He tried to start where he had left off ten days ago, but when he got into the uncut part, the lawnmower choked to a stop within three feet. He tried backing it up and getting a run at it, and he made five feet, but then the mower choked again, and there was no making the blades move, even when he put all his weight on it. He pulled the clotted grass out of the blades. The sun was straight up and the backyard was baking hot.

Streaming sweat, he stopped and blotted his dripping face with his T shirt and ran at it again, taking much smaller bites, but halfway back across, he began to feel strange, and he saw that there were goose pimples on his arms. He dropped the lawnmower handle and went into the shade of the back porch and sat down. His khaki pants were sopping dark all the way down the thighs. When he looked out at the yard it shimmered like a mirage--or it was his eyes. When he thought it was his eyes, he decided that it was probably sun-stroke coming on. He got up and went to the back door and knocked to try to get a drink of water, but Mr. Bracher didn't answer the door, though his Buick was sticking out of his tipsy garage.

He went back to the mower and carried it into the shade and stood it up on its side and used his pocket knife to cut away at the tight-woven, doughnut-sized wads of crab grass around the axles. When he heard the courthouse clock strike one, he straightened up and pounded his fist on the tire of the mower. "Dang you!" he said, "Christ, shit, dam son of a pup!" and banged the mower over on its wheels and started to pull it home. But the wheels were still frozen, so he dropped it by the front driveway and gave it a kick and walked home.

He drank a quart of \well water and soaked in the bathtub for half an hour. He was drinking more water when his parents came in with the groceries, and J. Arthur asked how the lawn had gone. He sat at the kitchen table still feeling red in the face and said it hadn't.

"Why?"

"You can't mow it; it's too high."

"How much did you get done? Did you just give up?"

When he thought of all he had tried to do as "just give up." He let out an explosive sigh and wailed, "No, I didn't *just* give up. I was there till one, and it was ninety-two today! It was too *high*! I was getting *sunstroke*!"

"Oh, piffle!" J. Arthur exploded, "Did you stop and get a drink?"

"He wouldn't answer the door."

"Well, he probably wasn't home."

"He was there all right. I saw the car."

J. Arthur half-turned toward the living room. He had the evening paper in hand and appeared to want to get to his chair and read it. "Well, I'll go up with you in the morning when you've cooled off and have a look at it."

"Looking won't do any good."

J. Arthur stared at him, "Just as you like; it's your job."

He didn't answer.

J. Arthur started for the living room again. "Did you put the mower in the garage?"

"The wheels were locked. I left it."

"Where?"

"In Blind Pugh's yard."

"Show a little respect! *Mr. Bracher!* "

"Mr. Bracher--the wheels wouldn't turn."

"So its right there, in front?"

"By the drive."

"By the drive? What if Mr. Bracher got out of his car and didn't see it? He's half blind, you know."

"He might fall over it and finish the job."

"Hush," Ferne said from the sink where she was working with her back turned. He looked up and J. Arthur's upper lip had gotten pale and stiff looking. "*You!*" he said, "Get up there and bring my lawnmower home!"

"I can't," he wailed, "The _wheels won't turn_! Why don't you drive me up and I'll put it in the trunk, and we can bring it home?"

"Not on your life, mister, I'd be embarrassed to show Mr. Bracher I had to come in the car and rescue you from a job you couldn't do, or even bring your equipment home yourself. As it is, I'll be embarrassed to take Mr. Bracher's money when it's going to take you another day to finish it."

"I'm not going to finish it."

"You're not?"

"Because *I can't!*" he said shrilly, "Nobody can." He felt like he wanted to cry, caught in the usual no-win corner with his father. He felt the inside of his chest wither toward sobs, the way it always did when his father cornered him between righteous desperation and obedience. But this time, instead of the tantrum, the void in

143

his chest suddenly filled up with something hard. He stood up, rocking the table. "All right, I'll *carry* it home! But then I'm through with your damned lawn business!" He started for the back door.

"Oh, no, you're not! Mr. Bracher asked me to get his lawn done! How will I keep my word if you lie down on the job?"

"You should have thought of that when you let him go two weeks!" He knew insolence was coming, but he blurted it out, "Get your highway crew with the gang mower," he said for a parting shot and ducked for the door.

J. Arthur lunged after him, but Ferne had already turned from the sink and got between them. She gave Miles a push toward the back door and followed him out.

"I'll take him up and get the mower," she said over her shoulder, "Then we'll sit down and talk about this like civilized people!"

Up on Grove Street, Ferne sat at the wheel while he put the mower in the trunk with the handle sticking out and tied it down with twine. The old man had come out on his porch and lurked there watching as though waiting for some overture. But Miles had gone frozen hard toward Mr. Bracher from the moment he knew the man had been watching behind the curtains and would not give him water, and he did not speak to him.

On the way home, Ferne shamed him, "for talking insolence to your father," and said how she had long hoped that he would not succumb to his smart-aleck side. For his part, he vented his feelings in that tone of aggrieved righteousness he always took to plead his case with her when he and his father fell out. But contrition or not, he was determined not to go back to the rotten job, insisted the lawn could not be done without a power mower, and she had seen it; what did she think? She wouldn't take his side, but she said she could see it from the car.

They didn't talk about it anymore. When they got home and he took the mower out of the trunk, his remorse now made him resolve to work all tomorrow morning if necessary to pull the tangle of wire grass out of the wheels. He was still shaky inside from the scare of rebelling to the edge of his father's volcanic wrath, which he had seen heaped on others, but never had drawn down on himself before.

Dinner was late and silent and J. Arthur got up from it and went directly back to his rig in the back room, put his earphones on and was in his other world.

Miles went to the living room and sat in his father's chair. He put his feet up on his hassock, and tried to read the paper. Hitler had hurled his Panzers at Russia on a two-thousand-mile front, and the paper was full of it. Normally they would have talked about it at dinner. Tonight when he finished the paper, he went downtown looking for someone to talk to about it, but he ended by spending his last quarter to go to *The Grapes of Wrath*. When he left the theater, he dawdled on the way home thinking of his South Dakota cousins starting out for the West Coast without enough money to get there, but not having anything like the trouble getting a new start in Washington State that the Joads had in California. Not by a long shot.

7

Eye Strain

J. Arthur was still in the back room with his earphones on when Miles got home. He skirted the living room where Ferne was reading and went on upstairs. On the sleeping porch he had connected an old floor lamp to his bedroom with an extension cord and he went to bed and read *Northwest Passage* for a while. When he turned off the light he asked, "Help me to honor my father more," but he kept going over the quarrel and justifying himself to himself that Mr. Bracher's lawn was un-mowable, and kept turning restlessly till he had kicked off the sheet. It was a warm night, but comfortable enough with all the windows open on three sides, and after the courthouse clock struck the last time, he pushed the pillow through the shoulder-wide bars of the old brass bed onto the windowsill so that the pillow was propped against the screen and he could lie looking straight up at the stars.

When he opened his eyes, there was a full moon that had sneaked up as blindingly bright as it had been the time they ran on the roofs with Paul. He had the feeling that something had awakened him, but there was nothing. The town clock said three a.m.

Then, from a distance, there was the slightest shivery titter, like birds quibbling in their sleep. Turning over on his stomach, he peered down on the moon-bleached street and made out four dim figures running through the leaf-shadows. They burst out in a titter of thrill giggles, and the one in front ran backward with her finger to her lips, and he thought (Wowwee!) they were naked as September Morn! But when he put his hands to his eyes and squinted through the cracks between his fingers, he could make out their breasts jouncing like dancing bull's eyes, and all but one were wearing underpants. Only the leader, when she turned around, showed a dark little wedge between her thighs that wasn't shadow. *She* was naked, you bet! And through his fingers he suddenly recognized them all. They were the girls he had overheard chattering in the next booth at the Southside Drug about going to a slumber party in Florence Wing's backyard. She was the girl who had moved in on the opposite corner of the block, whose dad was the new depot agent. Miles had never met her but thought of her as an older girl because she was a grade ahead.

When they swerved across the street and disappeared, flushed like quail by the headlights of an early milk truck on the highway, he turned over and stared up at the moon again with a cozy sense of forbidden discovery. He had never seen a naked girl (excepting an unsatisfactory view of one who slipped and fell down in the shower at the pool while he was sitting with some of these same girls on a towel near the women's door). But one moonlight night last summer, when he had slept in the tent in the Bradley brothers' yard, six boys had turned out after midnight and run around the block naked. Now he fell asleep hoarding this one insight in the vast hungry vacuum of his ignorance of women: under the sway of the full moon, they, too, sometimes ran naked in the night.

In the morning, the first moment after he woke, it did seem to be a dream until he remembered their names. With a gallant impulse he would soon betray, he made a pact with himself never to tell who they were.

But before noon, half of Adel was scandalized and the other half snickering over the display of a pair of lace-trimmed under panties in the news-office window:

LOST OR FORGOTTEN!

THIS ITEM FOUND LAST NIGHT ON THE
SWIMMING POOL FENCE IN RIVERSIDE PARK.
OWNER MAY RECLAIM SAME AFTER TEN PM
FROM THE DELIVERY BOX BEHIND THE NEWS
OFFICE. NO QUESTIONS ASKED!

Ferne brought the matter up at lunch--J. Arthur was eating at the job that day--and she told Miles she had seen the four girls run past the house in the early morning when she was coming from the bathroom: Had he heard them?

He kept his head down and nodded.

Well, did he know that the constable found an item of underwear on the pool fence and they put it in the window of the *Dallas County News*? She thought it was rather shabby of old Snyder to make a joke out of it. "It looked to me," she said, "like they were all naked as jaybirds."

"Nope. Three of them were wearing pants," he said sententiously.

"Pants?"

"Panties," he said, and blushed.

"Oh, malarkey." They had played a road game this spring, and Ferne had been able to read signs farther away. "If I couldn't see they were wearing panties, how could you?"

Miles put his hands in front of his eyes and peered at her through his fingers, "I zee every-zing!" he said, like the character actor Akim Tamiroff.

She made a rueful smile, "So, if you saw so much, who went without?"

He shook his head, "You'd tell Garden Club."

"Whoever she is, I just hope she *doesn't* try to get them back tonight. You bet he'll have a watch on that alley!"

"She doesn't have to come through the alley."

"What?"

"She lives on the block," he said before he thought.

"Ah, *Gloria* then..." she nodded. "Gloria could just come down the back stairs, eh? Well, I won't give her away." After a moment's thought, she turned around from the sink and put her hands over her eyes and mimicked his squint. "You've been doing that at school."

"What?"

"To see the blackboard? Does it help?"

"Sometimes; not so much as it did."

She frowned and took his dishes to the sink. "Your father's been talking about taking this year's vacation to see Parker in Detroit. Who knows how long it'll be before we have another chance? And Parker can test your eyes while we're there."

He shook his head. He liked his father's older brother, and he liked the idea of seeing Detroit, but he was not keen to take an eye test. They had had an appointment in Des Moines a year ago, but he had dragged his feet and missed the appointment out of a suspicion that fighter pilots did not wear glasses. Since then he had been looking through the chinks between his fingers, which at first had sharpened his focus enough to read the blackboard. Now it didn't work, but he was still applying Kinnicks' Christian Science.

One night in June, when he had been playing catch with J. Arthur in the backyard before supper, a high toss had come down between his upraised hands and knocked him on the forehead. J. Arthur had laughed. Miles had dropped out of baseball. But Ferne had seen it, and now made up her mind that they would go to Parker Morgan's and have Miles' eyes looked into.

By the time they left for Detroit, the unclaimed panties had been replaced in the *News* office window by a display of record-size turnips. All the youth in town knew who the four girls were who had barely escaped the constable's spotlight while taking a moonlight swim. Though grownups still speculated about who "our aquatic Godiva" was, several powerful sermons had been delivered in which the abandoned panties became a metaphor for the throwaway morals of modern youth.

Parker Morgan was the eldest of the three brothers but looked the youngest, partly because he had a head of thick dark hair compared with J. Arthur's bald pate, and also because he had a lively comic side. He liked slipping into his clown persona and doing an impersonation of Groucho Marx in which he would flourish a cigar and walk in a crouch and tell a blue joke. He was six feet tall, slim for his age, looked trim in the suits he wore to work and wore a thick Groucho-like moustache. He had served in the army in 1917 and settled in Detroit for reasons unclear to his nephew. Now he had two daughters in their early teens. He had wanted a son, and immediately took Miles under his wing, beating him repeatedly at table tennis and promising to get him some glasses that would let him see the ball. His optometrist's office was on the fourth floor of a building across the street from J. L. Hudson's, Detroit's largest department store.

For the Morgans' visit Parker had planned a vacation week, and he took time off to show his brother's family the huge, dirty metastasizing city. For three days they stared at the mansions of the Motor City aristocracy in Grosse Pointe and the gray rows of housing slums, like tumbling dominoes, on the edge of downtown, where people lived who had been sucked up from the Deep South by the arms work of the First World War. They went to Henry Ford's Greenfield Village, and visited the strange Detroit airport and marveled at the multi-story oil storage tank between the runways.

At Henry Ford's River Rouge plant, both families peered down open-mouthed from an overhead catwalk as a new Ford car started on the assembly line as a naked chassis and crawled along below them accumulating parts while a crowd of men swarmed over it like the runaway brooms in Walt Disney's *Sorcerer's Apprentice.* Sparks flew from welders, and new Ford V-8 engines came swinging in on their overhead tracks to join the inexorable dance, and the car bodies were hefted in and settled on the chassis and bolted so that the men now climbed in and out of the cars to fit head liners and put in the dashboards, and wheels with tires were slammed on, and the nuts tightened with pneumatic guns in a dense soup of noise, till the last wires were spliced through the firewall and a gray man jumped in and drove away in a new Ford that had come together before their eyes. The Iowans had never seen an assembly line!

On the way home, Parker told them that Henry Ford was going to convert Willow Run to building bombers, "A thousand a day, he says, if they let him do it his way."

"You think he can?"

"Maybe," Parker said, "But a B-24's more complicated than a Ford."

On Friday after lunch, with the moral support of his uncle, Miles got his first sport jacket. (this year he had changed his mind about raggedy clothes, and turned up his nose at his Sunday suit with the sleeves up his wrists). Since he would have bargained with the devil for it, he had promised Ferne that he would begin taking special lessons on the flute and would practice the instrument daily if she would give him the sport jacket for his birthday. Parker took them across the street to Hudson's and selected a green and gray Harris tweed jacket in a man's 38-L. It was fingertip length to Miles, but Parker assured him all the sharp teens in Detroit were wearing them that way, and it appealed to Ferne because he could grow into it. A tailor marked it, and she paid ($15.95: new fall merchandise) and Parker made them fix the sleeves while she waited so they could take it home with them. She was going to meet J. Arthur, and they were going across the river to see Windsor, Ontario.

Miles went with Parker to have his eye test. Walking back to the office, at a stoplight Miles glanced up open-mouthed at a procession of live models parading on some sort of catwalk behind a long window that rounded the corner on the third floor of the building across the street. They all wore evening gowns and fur coats, and were a living advertisement for the furrier whose sign flashed on and off above the window. Miles squinted up at them through his fingers and Parker told him he would be able to see their beauty marks with his new glasses. But a few minutes later, in Parker's examination room, Miles could soon tell that it wasn't going to go well. Parker had begun the examination in a merry mood: When Miles was reading, how far away did he hold a book?"

"About this close."

"Pretty close for a school book, but if it's the *Police Gazette* you need to get all the details, ha-ha! Have you ever read *The Open Kimono*, by Seemore Hair? Heh-heh!

But with the overhead lights out, and a spotlight on the chart on the wall, and Miles looking with one eye, then the other -- "Start with the line of the smallest print you can read" -- he couldn't read the smallest line, or the next line up, or the next, until he was almost up to the **U R** just under the big **E.** Then Parker's merry Groucho mask disappeared and he went on with entirely professional instructions. Miles squinted and squirmed, and was told to try a line below again, and he tried to narrow his eyes to slits to get the sharper focus he got with the chinks between his fingers. With the left eye it was better, and he could feel out some of the letters four lines below the **E.** And he thought he was okay with the light bars that started above and to the side of each other, and came closer together till he said, "Whoa!" When Parker got up from his stool with a sigh, and opened the shades, Miles sat back sweating and rubbing his eyes. He was tired. "Well?"

"Fine," Parker said, without looking up from his notes, "I can correct you to 20-25, and that's almost there-- though the right eye takes some doing. Now I'll send you to the lady across the hall, and you can pick a frame. About Tuesday you'll be seeing some babes around Adel you never noticed before!"

Miles said, "Well, look, Uncle Parker, what are my chances of passing the eye test for the Air Corps when I graduate? Can you, if one eye's pretty good?"

His uncle put down his pen and stood up again and looked out the window. His version of Groucho came back, "Look here, Miles! See here!" He put his arm around Miles' shoulder and pointed across the street and down. "No, the fifth window! Oh, Jiminy Crickets! Do they have anything like that in Iowa?"

Miles saw that the whole side of J. L. Hudson's a floor below their level was women's dressing rooms. The windows were curtained halfway up, but the top half of the windows were clear, and he was looking down at a woman taking off a frock and standing in her step-ins to hold it to the light and examine it.

"What do you say? What do *you* think of that?" Parker said, "If that won't put a flag pole on your club house, we'll have to put a rush on those glasses...ha-ha! Isn't this the best location in downtown Detroit? Look here! Here's another one!".

"I can see her all right," Miles said, thinking that, for all he could see, she might have been the Wicked Witch of the West. He sat down in the examining chair. "But, Uncle Parker, do you *know* if I could pass the Air Corps eye test when I get these glasses?"

Parker too sat down. "Miles, the vision requirement for the Air Corps is uniformly high for both eyes."

"Well, what do you have to have? What do I need?"

"It's 20-20, Miles," he said,

"Then it's only off by five?"

With the silence in the office and the whisper of traffic on the street below, Parker sighed and said, "I'm really sorry, son, but we're talking *uncorrected* 20-20. What you have--surely you had some idea of that--what you have is one really bad eye and one that's not quite so bad. Both are seriously nearsighted and astigmatic."

"How close am I, then, without?"

"It amounts to 20-200 in the right eye, 20-100 in the left."

"Isn't there any exercise--or operation?"

"I'm afraid not. You're lucky we can bring them back to 20-25."

"How about the Marines?"

"Miles, what I'm telling you would be the best news in the world for a lot of men right now. There's a good chance that you won't even be drafted. I know how you feel. But, pulling no punches, Miles, I doubt if you'll qualify for regular service at all. I don't know how you've been getting by at school. But much as I hate to pour cold water on your hopes--I don't think your mom and dad will think this is anything but good news right now."

A Dawn Patrol

The day his glasses came, he went to a dance at the Rainbow Hall that a girl by the name of Hindeman had invited him to before he went to Detroit. He wore the new jacket with a tie. Ferne had tucked his glasses case in his pocket, but he had not even tried them on.

It was eighty-five degrees and humid, and in the Rainbow Hall above the dry goods store the two ancient overhead fans stirred tepid air from the open windows into the heat. The other boys were coatless in open-necked white shirts. Miles stood by the window in his new tweed

154

jacket and sweltered. The chaperones invited him to take it off, but by the time he gave in and hung it on a chair, his shirt was so dark with sweat he was embarrassed to go onto the dance floor. That the girl didn't seem to mind increased his dislike for her. She had a crush on him, and said she was taking up the flute this summer to make herself his protege.

He walked around with her through one number and then told her he had to go home and took his new coat and ducked out and down the stairs. Because she followed him down, he picked a quarrel with her on the walk in front of Hynen's store and made her cry. He started home alone with the new jacket over his shoulder, and when he came to the trash can on the corner by the Rialto, he tossed the jacket onto it. At the corner, he remembered the new glasses and went back. At home he brushed off the jacket with great care and hung it in his closet.

Before Detroit, he had started getting up at dawn some mornings and riding his bike to Riverside Park and hitting a golf ball around. Now, with Mitchell in Minnesota and Berglund working in his uncle's law office in Perry, and the lawn business dried up, he had nothing to do, and he got up when the first taint of dawn etched the shape of the house next door in the darkness, and tiptoed through the house to get an iron and a couple of balls. He made coffee and put some in a thermos and grabbed up the new glasses as an afterthought--to try them out at finding lost balls.

In the park where he usually started, he put the bike on its kickstand and got the glasses out of their case and put them on. Everything jumped out at him, the park entirely more vivid and specific than he had ever seen it. He could suddenly make out individual leaves on the trees along the river a hundred yards away, and when he looked down, for the first time he saw single blades of grass at his feet.

He teed up the ball where the *News* had taken his picture last summer with George and Jun Kinnick, took some practice swings and lofted the ball toward the river. The course he had laid out earlier was one a half-blind man could follow. But Lo! He could follow the flight of the ball now, and after it landed he could even see it roll. By the time the sun was up, he had gone entirely around the park. With the new glasses on he hadn't lost a ball.

The year the swimming pool had opened, Babe Ruth had made an appearance at a semi-pro baseball game and swatted balls into the swimming pool from home plate. Before Miles went to Detroit, he had got the idea from the Bambino of teeing up his ball and chipping his last shot into the pool. He knew the constable might appear at any moment on his sometime dawn patrol, so Miles went through the charade of being surprised, "Why, darn, it's gone into the pool!" and put away his club and wheeled the bike to the pool fence and climbed over and searched along the side till he found the ball. Then he stripped to his drawers and left his glasses on the walk and dived in.

Usually he swam a few laps and lay in the sun till he dried off. When Archy Dillon did drive into the park, he never turned into pool lot, so Miles had stopped scrambling to get out of sight. This morning he turned his laps and stayed longer than usual, testing floating on his back with his new glasses, looking up at the cloudless sky. He had learned somewhere that you could float without treading water if you kept your lungs full and lay spread eagled with your arms extended above your head. With his toes just breaking water he lay that way till he almost went to sleep. The sun was over the victory arch, and he was barely back on his bike when the car belonging to the manager, Coach Townsend, drove in.

Miles waved over his shoulder and pumped on up the hill toward Twelfth Street. He pulled off in the shade at the rustic table beside the collapsing log cabin that overlooked the park and sat at the table drinking the rest of his coffee and watching the empty park. It looked much clearer than he had ever seen it, but he didn't know if he liked it the way it really was, with candy wrappers in the pool lot and some of the trees on the river bearing huge gray webs of bag worms cocooned in their branches.

The war was going badly again. With Rommel holding a thousand miles of North Africa and the Russians reeling back toward Moscow, Roosevelt and Churchill meeting on the cruiser Augusta and declaring the Atlantic Charter as though they already had all the say about it, sounded like bravado. He toyed with the Byzantine "step-on-a-crack-and-break-your-mother's-back" superstition, speculating that *he* was responsible for all the allies' troubles because his eyes had made him useless to his country. Once, he had figured it all out that life had some kind of use for every single person. But, since his eye failure, he had abandoned that cheerful universalism and decided that there were probably some people who would never find a place. Maybe God planned to make enough people so that He could just waste a lot of them, the way He was wasting the Jews in Germany. "If I was Him, I wouldn't do that," he said aloud, and for a moment wanted so badly to do some important, useful thing that his chest ached with it.

He took off his glasses and laid them on the table, and the park became as beautiful as a painting again. Then he put the glasses back on and got on the bike and pedaled through the Twelfth Street entrance of the park and past the quiet houses on the hill to Grove Street.

He had never come this way before, and if he was doing it now because he wanted to go by Mr. Bracher's house on the way home and see if the old man's lawn was being mowed, he was not aware of it. He seemed to have been doing things since he got home in a kind of waking reverie, and when he got to Grove and Thirteenth, he stopped the bike at the curb and looked down the hill for a long time.

157

The first block was a very gentle slope, then it steepened perceptibly from Twelfth to Tenth before the heavy overhanging elms obstructed his view. The street was new-looking whitish-gray concrete with a tiny straight seam running down the middle. At intervals there were manholes, and between them expansion joints crossed at right angles. As he studied the street, he counted: joint-joint-joint-manhole--joint-joint-joint-manhole, till the descending hump of the hill obscured the sequence before the intersection at Eleventh. He had ridden down it before, playing a kind of bicycle slalom by swinging right, then left, back and forth across the centerline at each joint and manhole, but now for the first time he could see the stripe and the joints clearly all the way to Tenth.

He pushed off and coasted slowly down the street without pedaling, letting the bike creep along barely fast enough to keep his balance with his feet resting on the pedals. This time, as he gradually gained speed, he thought how J. Arthur used to ride a bike backwards at the Tullis house, and he took his hands off the handlebars. At the next expansion joint, he leaned his weight a tiny bit to the right and the bike swung a few inches out, and he passed on the right side of the joint, and then leaned to the left, and the bike came back across the line. For a block, he alternated every joint till the bike was going so fast after the Twelfth Street intersection that it was time to unfold his arms and put his hands on the handlebars. Instead, his arms spread out like a high-wire walker to keep the bike from yawing too wide with each swing, and he began to hear the tires suck a little when he banked.

At Eleventh Street, he was still making every cross mark, but it was with that swinging rhythm now of the "Hell Diver" he had taken Parker for a wild ride on at Belle Isle, and he could hear the slipstream in his ears, and he wanted to look up when he heard an engine somewhere, but he was not going to miss a joint, and he had made up

158

his mind to do every single one till he got to Tenth, and then it would be a world record.

Fifty feet from the corner he was watching cracks like crosshairs and gripping the bike with his thighs with every swooping bank when the familiar racket of the old Adel Lumber Co. truck made him look up, and he was staring a red flag straight in the eye. The truck was already past the center of the intersection and the flag was on the end of a load of planks sticking out the back. As though he had already decided everything, he kept his arms straight out and lowered his shoulder and leaned and heard himself say, "Can do!" and barely touched the foot brake and felt the flag swish past his face, and just had time to think it was the neatest no-hands bike trick anyone ever saw, before he was over the handlebars and onto the pavement belly-sliding on the concrete toward one curb while the bike smashed into a tree on the other parking.

His naked arms were the runners that saved his chin. When he stopped, the new glasses were still on the tip of his nose, and he jumped right up and pushed them up and looked around to see if anyone had seen him crash. For effect, he shook his fist after the departing truck as if it was their fault.

The bike had climbed the curb and tipped over against the tree. The golf club was in the gutter, and the thermos was still rolling down the street with a festive tinkling sound of broken glass.

"You damned fool!" he said, and looked at his bleeding arms and knees before he retrieved the club. He picked up the bike and bent the fender away from the front wheel so the bike could be pushed, and walked it slowly to Ninth Street. He turned toward Rapids and stopped and took off his T shirt and used it to swab the blood from his arms and knees. Then he put the bloody shirt back on to spite himself. When he turned into the alley, the girl named Florence Wing, who had had the slumber party early in the summer, was taking a sunbath in her back yard. She jumped up with a scared expression on her face and dropped her magazine.

"Well, what are *you* staring at?" he said so fiercely that she froze till he had limped on down the alley. He came into his yard through the back drive and went directly to the pump and pumped water on his bloody arms and knees.

He was trying to straighten the fender on the bicycle when Ferne flung open the screen door and came out on the back stoop, "For God's sake what happened?"

"Nothing," he said.

Of course, by early in the fall Miles knew from George Kinnick that Jun, who had turned down professional football for law school the previous year, had returned to the University this year without re-enrolling. He would mark time as an assistant backfield coach until the Navy Air Corps called him up. One afternoon in late October, as Miles sat in study hall picking at the black specks of dirt his bicycle fall had tattooed into his forearms, thinking of Jun Kinnick started him musing about his old dilemma, courage and cowardice. He had never considered his smash-up courageous. It had simply happened because he had made up his mind at the top of the hill to break an imaginary record by keeping his hands off the handlebars all the way to Ninth, and he had been too pig-headed to give it up and too determined to think what would happen if he even touched the brake. He knew he had come within a split second of doing himself severe bodily harm. Was that brave? Or was he a showoff? Ferne said he was a showoff.

But no one was watching--so, who was he showing off for? It wasn't showing off any more than George had been showing off when he swung hand over hand on the cross brace of the old bridge. That time, up there high on the superstructure of the bridge, Miles himself had been frozen with fear. But he had decided that he was not a coward that day because to be a coward you had to run away from something dangerous that you *should* have done. And to be brave you had to *conquer* your fear and go ahead and do something dangerous you *should* do. And George had done the Tarzan walk, you might say, for family reasons. So--had he himself had a reason for doing the bicycle slalom? If so, what was it? He wrinkled his brow and tried to think of an inner reason he could have had that would have made the bike slalom brave instead of reckless.

Of course, he had become so accustomed to his glasses that he had stopped seeing the frames at the edge of his vision anymore; so consequently, nothing occurred to him, and he went back to picking the ingrained sand out of his arms.

8

The Childhood of Mankind

True, no one in the Midwest was paying enough attention to the Japanese in the fall of 1941. They had been making war in China in the Thirties. But that fall was an extended geography lesson in Russian names and places in the news. Moscow was the main objective of the German offensive on a 325-mile front. The northern and southern ends of the front were Leningrad (St. Petersburg, the old name) and Stalingrad. The Germans were surrounding one, approaching the other. Which was which? Americans couldn't keep them straight at first, but the same Russian names waxed and waned across the front pages throughout the fall months, and we finally learned that Leningrad was the one that was surrounded; Stalingrad was the city the Russians were stubbornly holding, fighting off the bloodiest siege of the war on the Eastern Front. In September the Panzers reached Azov and cut off the Crimea. In October, Moscow was the prize Hitler all but claimed, but was bogged down in front of in November. The Russian government and the tank factories had been moved beyond the Urals, wherever that was. War historians compared the Germans' drive for Moscow to Napoleon's campaign the previous century. When the Panzers faltered in the first freeze, Hanson Baldwin wistfully evoked the imminence of the Russian winter which had once driven Napoleon out of Moscow and back across Poland. And sure enough, by the sixth of December, the Russian counteroffensive across the whole Moscow line had broken the Nazi front, and the Germans reeled backward under the hammering of the largest tank assaults ever mounted.

Americans were rooting for the Russians, and sent them arms and supplies. It was a symbiotic relationship. People in Sioux City prayed for the survival of Moscow, and their prayers were answered: The German front began to collapse. Till he leashed his rampaging divisions for the first two weeks in September 1943 so that the Germans could destroy the Polish resistance, Stalin looked like a benign Uncle Joe to Americans. But hints of German exterminations in "death" camps, and the revelations of barbaric S.S. reprisals for any German troops killed by the resistance anywhere in occupied Europe came with every news flash: fifty Frenchmen a day for one German until the wanted resistance fighter was turned in, the same with Hungarians, Greeks, Belgians.

The myth of U.S neutrality was cast aside as German submarines torpedoed another American destroyer and sank the Reuben James. Charles Lindbergh had made a speech to America Firsters in Des Moines in August saying that America had better join Hitler or be beaten by him. But the American merchant marine redoubled convoys to Archangel, and James (Jimmy) Doolittle replaced Lindbergh as America's hero aviator.

Miles remembered the day he picked out the music for his contest solo with Miss Mountain because Jimmy Doolittle was going to do a flyover at the Des Moines air show that afternoon, and J. Arthur was running the car in Miss Mountain's driveway, impatient to get to the airport.

Miss Mountain had played a few bars of *Carnival of Venice* and a few bars of the short one that went like an express train, and Miles said he was not ready for *Le Tourbillon (The Whirlwind),* but he still chose it because it was half the length of *Carnival of Venice* and as fast as *The Flight of the Bumble Bee*, and if he *could* learn it he could get off the stage in a hurry. He jogged to the car with the new music wrapped around the flute case.

163

They had been parked at the airport five minutes when a camouflaged monoplane slashed over them from behind the solitary hangar in a surf-crashing roar, stood on one wing, and was gone in an arc like a rocket. It was one of the new generation of American air power just coming on line. It was called an A-20A, and looked like a faster version of the B-25 which, two years from now, would carry Major Doolittle and his sixteen-plane flight from an aircraft carrier in the Sea of Japan on our first air raid on Tokyo. On this day, Major Doolittle made another pass with his new-era twin-engine attack bomber and went back to Rantoul field, and the locals had seen some of the future in the sky. [*]

Then, one sunny afternoon in October, Miles was on his way home from school with the flute under his arm and the sheet music of *The Whirlwind* wrapped around it. As usual, he was walking with Jim Winters, who lived farther down Rapids Street.

Jim Winters' family was impoverished because his father was an invalid from being mustard-gassed in World War I, and his mother held the household together by taking in laundry. Jim, an amiable blond string bean with a good head, was a high school junior. He was six-foot-three, but weighed less than Miles, and was one of those youths of which it was said that he had outgrown his health: his eyes seemed to have permanent bluish shadows under them. Last week he had been injured in Adel High School's humiliating loss to Boone, and Doc Bradley had ordered

---

[*] Charles Lindbergh, a bootstrap elitist in a primal American mold, and originally a man of little faith in the fighting potential of a democracy, finally caught on, rejoined the American Air Force, flew missions in the Pacific and rendered valuable service to the war effort. James Doolittle received the Congressional Medal of Honor and the rank of general for the Tokyo raid, and commanded the American air forces in Europe.

him to drop football. Since Miles--"your royal slowness" to Coach Blough--had been so far down on the roster that he had been sent across the field to run the chain, and was only called back and thrown into the debacle when all was lost, he too had begun to skip football.

The two boys had crossed the brick street slowly, loitering in the Indian Summer sun, at first talking about the U.S maybe entering the war--which Jim Winters dreaded because of his father's wound, and which Miles was still in a hurry to grow into. Now they were discussing Mr. Sinift's last lecture. When John Hall joined them, Jim Winters was attempting to reprise the gist of Maurice Sinift's remarks about evolution.

Back in fifth grade, John Hall and two friends had vowed revenge on Miles for a real or imaginary insult, and for most of one semester had made it hot for him on the way home from school. There had been some close chases and some rocks thrown. Now John Hall's henchmen had moved away, and John Hall, who seemed to Miles to be growing smaller and more light-boned every year, had apparently forgiven or forgotten. He still intruded his snide, smut-rife rant everywhere, and when he found the boys talking about a school subject, tried to steer the focus onto the bodily functions of the female, about which he had a rich store of misinformation.

Jim Winters had just asked Miles if he knew that "ontogeny recapitulates phylogeny," and Miles had insisted on knowing what language Jim was speaking. By then, they had crossed the street in front of the old house the Morgans had once occupied across from the school and come to a stop near the stump by the driveway down which the All American, Jun Kinnick, had once bicycled every morning to deliver the *Register* into J. Arthur's bedroom window. Today Sigurd Fardel had released Miles early from Latin and sent him with Flora Fardel to play *The*

Whirlwind at a bridge club, and John Hall gave Miles' necktie and the music-wrapped flute case a derisive look.

"Well, it means," Jim said, "that the development of the individual repeats the evolution of mankind--somehow."

The extent of Miles' understanding of evolution was about the same as most Iowa kids his age. In the early Forties any boy in the Midwest was likely to use the phrase "survival of the fittest" several times a day as an all-purpose truism that might simply mean "the big fish eat the little ones," or "the better man wins," but which, most were dimly aware, came from the Theory of Evolution propounded by a man named Darwin. The children's presumption did not come from their study of evolution in school so much as from a Sinclair Oil Company advertising campaign featuring dinosaurs. (If a father bought a tank of gas at a Sinclair station, his son or daughter received a card with a color picture of one of the types of dinosaur whose bones had been found in the company's oil fields around Sinclair, Wyoming, and an informative caption about archeology and the age of their bones, and their extinction. When Miles got such a Sinclair card, J. Arthur cheerfully explained natural selection and the Scopes "Monkey Trial." Thus, the Sinclair institutional advertising of the dinosaur-- a kind of *Jurassic Park* of that day-- had rendered evolution non-controversial. Except for the lively arguments that sprang up among Miles' friends as to whether--since man descended from the ape--King Kong could have mated with Fay Wray.

Now Miles absently put down his music-wrapped flute on the stump by the driveway, perhaps to make a gesture, and listened open-mouthed as Jim Winters repeated what he remembered of Mr. Sinift's summary of the primordial artifacts of evolution still retained in our modern bodies--our tailbone, our vermiform appendix, the uniform number and structure of digits we share with all mammals from bats to whales ("Mr. Sinift has a friend who even had a throwback gill in his neck").

At this point John Hall gave a suppressed snicker. "The world was made in seven days," he said. "The Bible says so, in the book of Genesis. And the world is four thousand years old," he added.

Miles recognized John Hall's figure for the age of the Earth from last Saturday morning's rant by the anti-science evangelist who preached on the corner of the square on Saturdays in good weather, and he remembered seeing John Hall standing in the sparse audience.

"And this war is the beginning of Armageddon," John Hall added, "and the anti-Christ is coming out of Russia! That's in Revelation. And Creation was made in seven days is in Genesis."

"Four thousand years ago the Egyptians already had the pyramids finished for about a thousand years," Miles sneered. "You think dinosaurs were running around eating camels?"

"It *was* made in seven days," John Hall repeated, "I looked it up."

"But how long was a day, in *those* days?" Jim said.

"Yeah, you think those days were twenty-four hours?" Miles chimed in. "Do you think it was Greenwich Mean Time? Like, God went to Greenwich and said 'Let's synchronize our clocks, men--I want to do this Creation in six days, no more, no less--and have Sunday for a nap'?"

"A day in the Bible is a *symbolic* time," Jim added. "A day might mean, like the whole Mesozoic Period--about two hundred million years long. Ask anyone."

"You bet," Miles nodded.

"But Sinift says these symbolic *days* are in the same order the Bible has them," Jim added. "There's the light first, then the water and the earth, and then the fish are the first life, then birds, then the land animals, and finally

167

man; so it's the same order as the seven 'days,' *relatively* speaking."

"Yeah, everyone knows that, Dumbo," Miles affirmed, and felt an inner lilt to be mocking someone who had chased him home two years ago.

The same thing dawned on John Hall in reverse. His mouth fell open and he said, "Fruits play flutes!" and grabbed for Miles' flute. He got the tube of sheet music that was wrapped around it, but the instrument case slid out and fell on the ground. John Hall ran off up the driveway toward the back of the house. "Fruits play flutes!" he sang, and stopped to wave the music, and skipped into the backyard.

Neither boy made a move to give chase. Coach Blough was teaching John to return punts because he was the fastest kid on the team. And moreover, Miles, who had once lived in the house, knew that John Hall would have to come out the same way he went in because the backyard was blocked by one of those sprawling barn-garages joined to a tall fence along both lot lines, and as the barn door was always padlocked John's escape route was closed.

Miles picked up the flute case and caressed away the imaginary damage with his handkerchief, and they started at a stalker's pace toward the rear along opposite sides of the house. Though he had been damning *The Whirlwind* for days as he struggled to memorize it, Miles suddenly charged forward with a yell of righteous outrage when he saw John Hall trying to climb the fence at the corner of the shed with his music wadded in his hand. Miles ran and grabbed his old tormentor by the foot and pulled him down and gave him a backward push. "I'd rather be a fruit than an ignorant little *shit* that thinks the world is four thousand years old. Give it back!"

John Hall looked at the music rolled up in his hand, and Miles saw he was going to stamp on it. "Give it here!" he sang again, and gave the smaller boy another push with both hands. John stumbled into Jim Winters, and Jim Winters pushed him back, and the two bounced him between them like a yo-yo before John Hall dropped the music and made a break for the driveway. Jim Winters tripped him and Miles grabbed him by the shirttail and John Hall fell down and tore his shirt up the back.

"You don't appreciate music," Miles said, and nudged John Hall with his toe so that he coiled up like an earthworm and put his arm over his head. Miles drew back his foot to give him a good kick in the ribs, but he noticed Jim Winters turn his back, so he held the kick, and instead pulled off John's shoe and threw it on the barn. Then he got the other shoe and threw it in a high arc after the first.

"Next time I'll bust your nose!" he said fiercely. He picked up his music and they walked back down the driveway. They stopped at the stump and laughed at John Hall trying to climb the fence onto the roof of the barn to get his shoes.

In front of Miles' house they parted and Miles picked up the evening paper. In the living room, he sat down in J. Arthur's chair and looked at the headlines. On the front page, a boldface head said,

"Hungarian officer tells of thousands of Jews deported from Hungary massacred in the Kamaninsk-Podolak region of Poland--2,500 souls."

As to ontogeny recapitulating phylogeny, he wondered whether the textbook could tell how close Mankind was now to being evolved into a grownup state. What if Mankind was still in the relative baby stage, where infants are when they can destroy things but still don't know how to do much else but eat and poop. A baby doesn't realize he is making a mess, but to get him over it you've got to take twelve or fifteen years to teach him to do something constructive. Miles considered how relatively long that might be, and estimated that it might still take Mankind about a million more years of evolution to grow into relative adolescence and stop pooping on life the way the Nazis were doing.

When he put the paper down he sat in the twilight feeling how the rush to kick John Hall had overwhelmed him, and after a while he put the flute together and started playing progressions that he made up. It was sad music.

Nationals

Perhaps the football pasting Boone gave Adel that year had done nearly as much as Mr. Fardel had done to start a fine year for the music program. For a month the instrumentalists had had nothing to take their minds off the music and they ended by bringing home a dozen Superiors from the regional music contest. Running the chain at the Boone game till the last sub went in had certainly cleared Miles' mind of football dreams for the fall of 1941, and he had put off for a while worrying about the burning question of whether he could be a football player and a flutist at the same time. The thought of standing on the stage and failing the flute solo terrified him more than quitting football, and since John Hall had done him the backhand favor of making him memorize *The Whirlwind* in short order, by the middle of the month he could go through it almost like the waterfall Marie Mountain made of it, especially when stage fright put him in overdrive.

Adrenaline got him a ticket to the district contest. Then Marie Mountain turned up at his performance there and came into the green room and bestowed on him her Special Edition Haynes flute to use for the competition. That she took him that seriously made his mind go blank for a moment before his cue, but then the jeweled movement of the Haynes boosted him through the 32nd-note runs as if he had gotten wings.

Afterward, J. Arthur beamed and said the flute went off like a rocket and hit Flora Fardel in the seat of her piano. "Yes, sir, lifted her right off the stool! Which takes some doing!" It was all a blur to Miles, and when the notice went up of his Superior, he remembered thinking he had fooled the judges plenty. Miss Mountain came backstage and actually gave him a cold hug and said he could use the Haynes again at regional; in fact, "as far as you go."

Again at the Regional Elimination in West Des Moines, the judges rewarded their misconception that he managed the lightning fingering by his own efforts, and gave him a Superior. He had begun to half believe it himself, except for the sneaking conviction that State Contest was as far as a sophomore should go, one who would be--anyway, next year--exclusively a football player. Yet, he had settled into a pattern now, and hollow in the stomach, with sweaty palms, he would lift the silver flute and fire off *The Whirlwind* like a Roman candle, and bow and leave the stage before they wised up. So! Sophomore or not, he was going to National!

National Music Contest would be in Minneapolis in 1941, and in the month's interval leading up to it, he practiced an hour a day with the Haynes, which Marie had let him take home, and he started praying to avoid the flu instead of praying to get it. He and Race Berglund still had time to do their homework in the basement and listen to the six-o'clock news before supper, and it was exciting to hear the Russians were overwhelming the Germans, and the British winning back North Africa.

But now they began to notice that the Japanese were rattling their Samurai swords at America. Japan's moderate cabinet fell, and Tojo became prime minister. The news that the Japanese were at the end of their patience with us moved to page one above the fold of the *Des Moines Register*, which explained to Midwesterners that "East Asia Co-prosperity Sphere" meant "Asia for Asiatics and all other Asiatics under the Japanese, and Americans out of the Pacific. President Roosevelt demanded that the Japanese stop pouring troops into Indo China and stopped selling them oil, and the Japanese, who needed oil to run their killer war machine, called his demands "a fantasy (which) left nothing more to say." Yet, the two special envoys the Japanese had rushed to Washington kept calling on the U. S. Secretary of State, Cordell Hull, to continue talks and we still slept soundly in the Midwest.

Berglund stayed for dinner the night before they left for Minneapolis. At the table, Miles said Tojo was a phony, but J. Arthur reminded them of the attack on the U. S. gunboat Panay when the "Jap" army ran amok in Nanking in 1937. "You watch them now. They want some respect. They're an upstart nation having an attention tantrum. Remember when you used to hold your breath? This is their international temper tantrum. Only they'd a lot rather hold our breath than theirs. Asia's their oyster," he said, as he pushed back from the table and lit a Camel. "No, I don't think they're bluffing!"

Though J. Arthur had been grumbling that Miles' lurch to the top of the contest ziggurat had given him a swollen estimation of himself, Ferne had volunteered them to take a carload in the Mercury to the contest. On the first of December, eight cars of Adel band parents and contestants left for Minneapolis at thirty-five miles an hour. Besides Miles, Doris, the oboe player, the saxophone sextet and the brass choir, were still in. In a holiday mood, and blessed with unusually mild weather, the caravan made its slow way north. The band committee had taken advance reservations for them all at the Vendome, listed on highway billboards as "*Minneapolis's Dollar Hotel*."

The Vendome turned out to be an unfashionable middle-aged eight-story brick pile that had seen better

172

days. But, possibly due to the fame of its Dollar advertising campaign, it was full of music-contest parties from half a dozen states. J. Arthur and Ferne had a stingy double bed with a chenille spread embossed with cigarette holes, and Miles set up his folding cot with its foot against the single window. The window faced an air shaft.

As the Adel contingent arrived early, they left their bags in the rooms and went for dinner to a Chinese restaurant next door. All returned at about the same time, raised their shades and opened their windows on the air shaft, and were surprised to see the familiar faces of the others in their party looking back at them, plus strange faces from Minnesota, Nebraska and Wisconsin. Greetings of mock salutation floated in the air above the tarred roof four stories below: "Dr. Livingston, I presume!" and marginal ribaldry, "Oh, honey, do you need a roomie?"

One of the saxophone sextet acquired a pitcher of ice and began pegging the cubes at his friends across the air shaft. One cube missed its target and arced in on a Wisconsin parent just opening a window. That party shouted angrily and attracted a barrage of ice cubes. Her husband gathered up the ice cubes and threw them back. Mack Rainwater leaned out of the window next to the Morgans to pour a glass of water on the head of a girl peering out the window below and J. Arthur, who had perched on the foot of Miles' cot, leaned around and sloshed him with a pitcher of ice water, then slammed the window down and made a strategic retreat to the double bed to read his radio magazine. The melee in the air shaft grew, and squalls of ice water doused Miles' window like rain.

Before dark, J. Arthur came back and raised the window for a cautious look. He was doused from the flank, and ducked away, but half a pitcher of ice water soaked the foot of Miles' cot.

The assistant manager came down the hall with a bellhop, knocking on doors and threatening to evict the whole Adel party. The commotion died down, then broke out again around eleven when strangers who had been to a bar came back to their rooms with a magnified sense of fun and began throwing a variety of trinkets into the well. Handfuls of rice rained on the closed window, and cries of real wrath echoed in the air shaft.

Flora Fardel phoned Ferne and said that Miles was scheduled on stage at seven a.m. at a conservatory in St. Paul. Miles rolled into the swaybacked cot soon after dark like an elderly person. He tried to sleep while his prankish father sat on the foot of the bed raising the window and slamming it down and dodging around. When J. Arthur was the only adult still at play, Ferne told Miles to get dressed; she said they were going to get their own room on the outside of the building. She had the phone in hand to call the desk before J. Arthur realized they were leaving. He and Ferne had a private talk in the hall, and when they came back, J. Arthur was calmer, and donned his pajamas while Ferne went to the bathroom and put on her nightgown. All went to bed.

Miles, trying to find a dry place for his feet, tossed about throughout the night, the noises of combat and celebration flaring up in the air shaft till nearly dawn. Then, before he was really awake, they left for St. Paul without breakfast.

He had naively assumed that each higher level of the contest would attract a larger, more cosmopolitan audience. He had sometimes shivered at the thought of his National performance entailing performing alone on the stage of a vast symphony hall filled with hundreds of twin-cities music lovers eager to hear flute solos. Actually, the large groups with many-parent constituencies, the bands and choruses, were given the choice times in the large halls. Solos, with their few family followers, got fringe times and places. The flute competition was scheduled into a music classroom in a St. Paul conservatory. Here, in the sallow post-dawn electric light, a half-tuned grand piano squatted at floor level with three sleepy judges in the front row of an empty classroom. Several sets of parents made up a fickle audience, drifting in with their children and accompanists and noisily departing when their own children finished playing. There were never more than ten people in the hall. Miles, in the middle of the program, took in the departing audience over the barrel of his flute and lost the stimulant that had always seen him through. He played with sticky fingers; yet, the magic flute, like the bat a baseball player has knocked the lead donut off of after taking his practice swings, had its own souped-up momentum and largely carried him through a mechanical performance. He was convinced it had been a disaster. Only Ferne's furious clapping marred the dead silence of the classroom as he and Flora filed out past scribbling judges.

But an hour later at the hotel when Flora called and informed them he had taken a Second and would get a silver medal--which Jostens would mail to him when the award had been inscribed--his mood cleared up like a sunrise. Ferne gave him an approving nod, but she aimed her recriminating glare at J. Arthur. On the way to Iowa she was talkative and cheerful with the other riders, but when they were in Adel and had let them off, she told J. Arthur that she blamed him and no one else for depriving Miles of "his Superior." Why wouldn't the boy be tired after his father had jumped around on the end of his bed like a juvenile delinquent half the night? How could Miles rest? His covers were wet! "It's a wonder he didn't catch cold and cough into Marie's thousand-dollar instrument!"

Usually his father simply withdrew from the fray, clapped on his earphones and went incommunicado till Ferne cooled off. But this time the next few days were like

175

Death Valley Days at home. Miles was happy enough to see his name in the paper with his second place, and when Jim Mitchell invited him to go with him in his parents' Lincoln Zephyr to the big dance hall in downtown Des Moines on Saturday night to hear Tommy Dorsey *in person*, Miles exploited the silent feud at home to hint to each parent separately that the other approved of his going, as a reward "After all I'm only a sophomore"--and manipulated them for the price of a ticket.

On the way to the Tromar Ball Room, both boys were nearly giddy with anticipation, and they proclaimed to Golden and Ruth that December 6, 1941, would be a red-letter night in the personal history of their whole lives because it would be their first time hearing a great "nationally renowned" band, live! Plus Tommy Dorsey's sensational young crooner, Frank Sinatra. Jim's parents nodded perfunctorily; they were attending a good movie. They warned the boys repeatedly to behave on the way home. The boys were to ride back with Punk and Tiff in the back of Tiff's sister's boyfriend's car.

Certainly Miles had been addicted to the bands on the jukebox at the Sweet Shoppe. He could hum all the popular swing tunes and could banter with Berglund and Mitchell and Rainwater about Tex Benneke's tenor sax ride on *Chattanooga Choo Choo*, and the Modernaires' close harmony, and Tommy Dorsey's solo on *Song of India*. And he knew that this was one of the top bands that was making a deepening rift between his father's kind of music and his own. Everyone under thirty knew that Tommy Dorsey played trombone and that his theme was *I'm Getting Sentimental Over You*. And Rainwater said that *Metronome Magazine* had just ranked Frank Sinatra the most popular swing-band crooner of 1941--over greats like Rudy Valle and Bing Crosby and the Eberle brothers.

So, in his new plaid jacket--which barely came to his fingertips now--and their new neckties, memento

176

souvenirs with sparkly trombones on them which both boys bought before the dance (two for $1.98 at the men's store across the street), they waited in the ticket line among a crowd, all teens, civilian boys and girls and teen soldiers, and so many young sailors that some ancestral memory of the ocean had to have stampeded half the farm youths in the state directly into the navy. Some not much older than Miles had the necks of bottles sticking out of paper sacks in their pea jackets.

As they stood on the edge of the floor adjusting their eyes to the dark that focused on the bright bandstand where the T/D blinds sat up in tiers with an elaborate drum set on the top, their photographic minds marked through the cigarette haze already curling under the chandeliers of the vast blond dance floor, how in dry Iowa the sailors gallantly spiked their girls' drinks below the table top before they chugged a hefty snort straight from the sack, right under the noses of the off-duty cops who loitered in the shadows and waited for someone to start a fight.

Out on the floor, Miles and Jim shouldered through to places under the microphone, and gaped at the side men trickling onto the stand and tuning up. Finally, Tommy Dorsey tapped off the beat for *I'm Getting Sentimental Over You.* And later, Frank Sinatra entered the spot in a pandemonium of applause--a hawkeyed young fellow wearing a double-breasted suit that draped on his thin frame like a men's store tux on a manikin--and gave the breathless girls an insolent once-over, and then seduced them with: *Marie, Blue Skies* and *Blues in the Night,* till they began to rock in unison in a kind of shaman's trance.

Sinatra, who was in his early twenties, had already put his stamp on a personal swing phrasing, which, near the end of the dance, he had applied to a new Harold Arlen tune called *That Old Black Magic.* In the back of the car on the way home, the song and the way he sang it had sparked a divisive clash between the boys and the two girls. The

177

girls, who were still a little wild, brimming over with the throb of Sinatra's voice, saying, "I don't care, there's something *special* about him, *oh, you know! Something!* Oh, Miles, don't say you didn't notice it!"

And the boys saying, "Baloney!" because they knew it *was* something special that made the girls vibrate like plucked guitars. The hair stood up on the back of Miles' neck, and he mooed, *"That old black magic has me in its spell. That old black magic that you weave so well,"* and the girls shrieked, "Oh! shut *up*, Miles! Don't *spoil it,* Miles!"[*]

But while they argued in the dark about Sinatra, their lives were changing under them. The Japanese fleet was already running toward Pearl Harbor at flank speed.

---

[*] Frank Sinatra left Tommy Dorsey the next year under bitter circumstances, and his famous appearance with Benny Goodman at the Paramount in Manhattan, which caused dozens of bobbysoxers to faint at the first performance, and more to pretend they did for pay the next day, was still more than a year away.

PART TWO

A Change of Life

Leaving the *Home Front*

1

The Day in Infamy

From Nile Kinnick's diary (he had entered the Navy Air Corps at Fairfax Airport in northeast Kansas City on December 4, 1941).

December 7:
Attended services at 1st church at 9th & Forest on the East side.

News of Japan's unprovoked attack on Pearl Harbor came over the radio about three o'clock. About a third of us were lounging around the barracks. Everybody accepted it quite unemotionally, seemingly more interested in whether liberties would be curtailed than whether the U.S. could retaliate effectively. Must confess that my own feelings were somewhat similar to the rest. However, I wished my training were already over, & I was ready to go. I am torn between a desire not to miss out on anything, and a feeling that I am better off here.

We saw Sally Rand put on her bubble & fan dance at the Towers Theatre tonight. Can't recommend it very highly. Doesn't begin to compare with Gypsy Rose Lee's performance at the World's Fair in New York. The latter's act bordered on the artistic it was so cleverly done....

Tonight I drove over to town & made a recorded interview for brother Larry Winn's sports broadcast.

December 8:
Heard over the radio tonight that 500 unidentified planes were over San Francisco. Seems incredible that the

181

Japanese would come so far. Really don't believe the report can be authentic.

    ...Now that the U.S. & Japan are at war I shall say this. I expected it but not quite so soon. I expected to be faced with the prospect of serious combat action when I joined up. I am ready for whatever it may be my duty to do. I feel much as I used to when the football season started & I knew Minnesota was on the schedule...

    Miles had been sluggish waking Sunday after Tommy Dorsey. The morning was cloudy bright, and almost warm, and he jogged the last block and came in late and bumbled over old Cozad's feet getting to his seat in the choir while still fastening his robe. But he was in time for the introit. The anthem was *"Behold a Host Arrayed in White."* During the sermon he got the flute out and warmed up the mouthpiece. He stood up beside the piano--Mrs. Caudron accompanying--to play O'Hara's *"There Is No Death"* for the Tithes and Offerings solo.

    The minister was a man of mild and pacific sentiments, and some would later criticize him for his sermon, *"How Much Do We Want Peace?"* considering what was already happening at Pearl Harbor at that very moment. But most remembered the service as though it had been a long time before Pearl Harbor, and refrained from blaming him for sentiments that, for a few hours more, were theirs, too. And the closing prayer was *"For those in the service: for their families: for a just and lasting peace."*

    None of Miles' last night's companions at the dance had gotten up this morning to come to the service. Miles, looking over the schedule on the back of the program as he walked home saw that "Charlene Cross, Worship Leader," was on the Youth Fellowship program tonight to review a recent European novel *The Seventh Cross.* He decided to go, and maybe pick up the debate about Frank Sinatra with Punk and Tiff.

When he got home, he sat down to read the paper without taking off his tie, Ferne's Sunday dinner dress code. But after dinner, he hurried upstairs and changed and took the football and went out looking for a game.

He sat on the courthouse steps for a while waiting for someone to show up, and feeling a sleepy Sunday pall over the empty square. The sky was cloudless and the temperature was almost balmy. The two cars parked on the south side belonged to people he knew lived above the stores, and little came by on 169 but a dribble of churchy traffic. Just as he was going to head for Race Berglund's apartment to roust him out, the tall boy came around the corner, and Mitchell showed up with two others from the west end.

Before it struck two, they had a two-on-three game going on the lawn. But no one else showed, and the box of the square bounced back an empty echo of their yelling, till they finally moved the game to the side yard of the Methodist church up behind the diner.

They weren't supposed to play football there, and the church board had set a steel Maypole in cement in the middle of the lot last year to discourage it. But there was no one about to say no at the time, and when Bob Murray joined the game, they picked up an even number. It was a good game till Mitchell touch-tackled Miles into the Maypole. A glancing blow, but Miles kept limp-winging it till Mitchell agreed to compensate them all with a soda, and they recessed to Woodses' Diner across the alley.

Suzie was in the back and Earl at the grill in the front window frying nickel burgers and worrying a ragged Sunday paper, and the little radio over the cooler was droning organ music. They were all ready to go back to the game, when the *dadada! dah--dah--dah! dadada!* S. O. S. signature of a special bulletin cut in on the organ music and a grim news voice said that this morning Japanese planes had attacked Pearl Harbor. Not much was known. The

183

laconic announcement was repeated, and then the station began an interlude of patriotic band music.

The boys sat stunned silent for a minute revolving their empty Pepsi bottles on the counter. Then Earl Woods turned his back on the grill and delivered an impromptu definition of the Japanese character decorated with a vein of profanity he seldom employed, but which they assumed came from the same authentic place as the tattoos on his arms: his two hitches in the old destroyer fleet out of the Philippines.

Rocking on the counter stools, with dropped jaws and new frown wrinkles on their brows, they listened avidly to the salty jeremiads of a real expert on the black-hearted "Jap" till the old sailor ran out of broadsides and turned back to his smoking grill. The boys wadded up their wax-paper plates and went directly home to quote Earl to their families. Miles noted on his way that there were now cars and pickups dashing past the courthouse, as if everybody who had heard the news was driving somewhere as fast as he could to wake someone else from their Sunday nap and inform them that the war had started.

In one hour Pearl Harbor had united the country in a shared emotion of apprehension and vengeful resolve. Though Miles missed President Roosevelt's short address to Congress the next day requesting a declaration of war on Japan, the family listened together to his *Fireside Chat* with the American people on the ninth as Franklin Roosevelt laid out in English less magisterial than Winston Churchill's perhaps--but honed with a steely promise the beleaguered Churchill could not have commanded--a design for the total mobilization of America to exact a wrathful justice on Japan. Franklin Roosevelt did not understate the gravity of the losses the Japanese had inflicted in the Pacific attacks, nor minimize the expectation of more to come, but he outlined the means of American retaliation undergirded by the resolve of a unified American people to work a seven-day-a-week production regimen and supply America and her allies with sufficient war materials for ultimate victory. He did not scant the sacrifices we would be asked to make, but he concluded with the expression of a characteristically American vision: that the United States was sworn to direct its immense force *to ultimate good as well as against the immediate evil.*

We Americans are not destroyers--we are builders!

In that *Fireside Chat*, Miles caught the lift of something he would never quite feel again, the first prenatal kick of an immense common objective whose birth would charge America with an explosive growth that would last through the war and for years beyond.

Two days later, Germany declared war on the United States, and we declared war on Germany and Italy.

*   *   *

There was a muted quality about Christmas that year, as though the nation were taking a deep breath before starting the long uphill path of the war. The Morgans spent Christmas Eve in Des Moines at the home of J. Arthur's eldest bother, Chester, a pharmacist who had his own store on the central north side. He was married to a pretty woman, a first-generation American, whose parents still spoke English with a heavy Swedish accent. They had one son, Kenneth, now seventeen and a senior in high school. Much of Chester's spare time was spent on the affairs of the Masonic lodge of Des Moines, whose Shrine Chorus his pure Irish tenor adorned for several decades.

The brothers were as close as siblings who had shared hard times on a homestead farm in Nebraska could be. But between Ferne and Esther there was always a kind of simmer of hostility, like that of stranger cats whose fur stands on end when they see each other. The reason was

Ferne's irritation with Esther Morgan's superior rivalrousness about their two boys. As Chester's business had begun to prosper, Esther had more money than Ferne to shower expensive things on Kenneth, and it annoyed Ferne that Esther treated these luxuries as the rightful rewards of Kenneth's personal superiority. Ferne, who would have enjoyed spoiling Miles in the same way, was reduced to aiming darts at her sister-in-law's "pretensions," usually defensive ones, because Kenneth was a handsome boy, amiable and intelligent, who unselfconsciously exploited his two-year age advantage over Miles by being a step ahead of Miles in most endeavors they both attempted. Kenneth was the more skilled builder of model planes. He was the proud owner of a gold-plated trombone which he played in the East High School Band. He was a Boy Scout well along toward his Eagle rating. Moreover, he was placid and non-assertive, letting things come to him rather than lunging for them headlong, as Miles often did.

That night the course of their Christmas Eve, which the two families had been holding at alternate homes for some years, ran true to form. Ferne admitted that Esther, who had learned her repertoire of home-made delicacies at the knee of her mother, a one-time apprentice cook in a Swedish aristocrat's kitchen, was the superior Christmas cook. Her buffet had groaned with rich pastries and tarts, and the men had settled in front of the fire in the living room scarcely able to do more than talk somberly about the wave of massive Japanese attacks across the Pacific-- Guam, Wake Island, the sinking of the Prince of Wales and the Repulse, the Philippines going under (Corregidor, "the Rock" in Manila Bay, still holding out). Later, they had joined the two boys in running Kenneth's Christmas gift, an enormous model train with a boiler the circumference of a stove pipe that chugged noisily around the Christmas tree on a three-inch track pulling several European-looking cars. Miles had only seen an electric train this large running among the dolls in Younkers' Christmas windows downtown, and he wondered later whether it was the same one. Though he realized that his aunt had made Chester get something "better" for Kenneth than the Lionel and American Flyer trains made in America, he saw that the train was much too large to make any realistic train landscape in the house, but still too small to ride on, and he soon became bored watching the behemoth electric train circle boringly around the tree. When he got up and wandered into the dining room, he found his mother and Esther sitting stiffly speechless with some new installment of their old hostility.

Ferne used his appearance as an excuse to terminate the evening. It was time to be on the way home, much as she hated...with the long drive and the possibility of snow. She sent Miles to the bedroom for their wraps, and roused J. Arthur, saying as always, "We must do this more often."

But later, as J. Arthur negotiated the maze of streets toward the west side, she set up the familiar bitter litany of complaint about her sister-in-law. She had merely mentioned that Miles was awaiting his medal from the National Music contest when Esther "puffed herself up" and claimed that Kenneth had just won first place in the Ford Motor Company's Good Driving Contest in Iowa. If this was true, why hadn't Esther called her up to brag about it, "as Kenneth can't win a gold star for nose picking without her calling me?"

When J. Arthur said that Kenneth's first place had just been announced, she snapped, "At any rate, it isn't a real *national* award like Miles'!"

"Kenneth still can win the national," J. Arthur observed, "He'll go to Detroit this spring for the final round."

She fell silent. But when they passed the dairy farm of his flute teacher in West Des Moines, she suddenly

187

erupted, "Miles *would* have brought home a First if *you* hadn't kept him awake all night!"

His father said nothing, but for the first time Miles regretted that he had not won a Superior. He saw himself running second to his cousin just like George Kinnick was running to catch up with Jun--only Kenneth Morgan was not the top athlete in the United States or a navy flier. So it still seemed possible that he could catch up. And as he tuned out his parents' favorite quarrel and began to daydream, he resolved to practice hard for the Iowa state championship in the Ford Good Driver Contest next summer when he was old enough to drive.

On January sixth, President Roosevelt gave his annual State of the Union address before Congress. Miles thought that what was later to be called the "Four Freedoms Speech" was the most powerful speech he had ever heard. Once again, as in the fireside chat after Pearl Harbor, the president turned toward a positive vision of America beyond the war. *Our own objectives are clear--the objective of establishing and securing freedom of speech, freedom of religion, freedom from want, and freedom from fear everywhere in the world....*

In a passage that gave Miles a start because it recalled the setting of the first story he had written--which he now intended to call, *"When the Future Was Past"* and send to magazines--Roosevelt said:

If any of our enemies, from Europe or from Asia, attempt long-range raids by "suicide" squadrons of bombing planes, they will do so only in the hope of terrorizing our people and disrupting our morale. Our people are not afraid of that...No matter what our enemies, in their desperation, may attempt to do to us--We will say, as the people of London have said, We can take it. And what's more we can give it back--and we will give it back-- with compound interest.

188

Of course, Miles doubted that the Germans and the Japanese would ever have long range planes able to reach America with suicide bombers. In his view, nothing like the attacks he had sketched in his short futuristic story would ever be possible.

It was early March before a small package addressed to Miles arrived in the mail with the return address of Josten's, a Minnesota manufacturer of graduation rings and high school trophies. His medal was a pretty little silver medallion shaped like a Greek lyre, bearing the words, "National School Music Competition, SECOND RATING," cast in relief. The surfaces of the letters and the lyre stood out and were buffed bright against the dark matte background, and the back of the medal carried the identification, also in relief, "*region two of the national band, orchestra and vocal music association at St Paul, 1941.*" From the medal hung a silk ribbon of red, white and blue stripes.

The next day his name with a list of Adel's several other national contest competitors appeared in the paper again, this time with photos of them holding the medals, the pictures printed almost as large as if they had won a basketball title. That night, second place or not, his parents made a little festivity of it and took him out for a steak at Mack's Cafe.

Miles was proud of the award, but one thing tainted his feeling pride in it with diffidence. The little medal, especially the ribbon, looked from a distance like a real military medal he had seen that was awarded for bravery. And one day as he walked to school with John Hall--who now walked with him every day and pretended great admiration for the medal--he suddenly felt ashamed of that implication and said harshly, "It's not a real medal, you know, and I'm going to put it away. We've got to realize, John, that nothing's ever going to be like it was before."

During Christmas break Jim Winters had come down with pneumonia and died before the beginning of the second semester, and John Hall thought Miles meant their walks to school would never be the same. But Miles never wore the medal on his band uniform the way the oboe player did on hers, and after that, he kept it in a dresser drawer with trinkets and mementos and only looked at it from time to time until he went into the service two years later.

Nor was he able to enter the Ford Good Driving contest, though when school was out, he took the lowest paying boy's job in town, tending Glenn Hucksell's DX station, just so that he could practice driving on the empty truck lot behind it when he could persuade Ferne to leave him the Mercury on her way back from the grocery store. Though he passed his written and driving tests on his birthday and received an official piece of paper saying that he was permitted to drive while his license was being processed, the paper was confiscated by Archie Dillon, and the license was rescinded by the state, due to the trouble he got himself into when Punk, Tiff and Florence Wing decided to visit him at the station one late afternoon in August.

2

His Impediment

So came America's dark spring of the war: It was dark in Europe, and it was dark in Asia. And it would be preferable not to mention that part of it in a story about the midlands of the country, except that what happened on both far away fronts of the Second World War affected what happened here the way shaking the antennae of a mobile shakes its center.

After holding out against the Japanese siege in the Philippines since January, General MacArthur was ordered to Australia, and he and his family left Corregidor in torpedo boats at night. Shortly thereafter, the great island fortress in Manila Bay finally surrendered. On April 9, seventy thousand prisoners began The Death March of fifty-five miles at Marivales, and ten-thousand of them were made to die before they reached the prison camp. The one successful retaliatory strike the American Pacific forces mounted against the Japanese, Major Jimmy Doolittle's bombing raid on Tokyo with 16 B-25 bombers, was merely a heroic gesture that kept Americans' chins up.

Miles went to the Rialto one night because J. Arthur had heard from his brother Chester that the newsreel showed Kenneth Morgan winning the National Ford Good Driving Contest in Detroit. There were a few seconds of Kenneth accepting a set of keys to his first-prize Ford convertible from a Ford executive. The rest of the reel was Franklin Roosevelt holding a press conference on the Tokyo raid in the Oval Office, jauntily smoking a Murad in his cigarette holder, kidding about the advertising slogun (*"be casual, smoke a Murad!"*) and parrying questions from reporters about where Doolittle's attack had originated. Foxy F.D.R. said that it came from "Shangri-La." the never-never land of the movie *Lost Horizon.*

Then on Miles' birthday, in Europe in a bombing raid on Regensburg-Schweinfurt, the Eighth Air Force lost 60 heavy bombers.

Yet the human makeup is such that our individual setbacks, which count for nothing on the world's scale of importance, seem to us to outweigh the wreck of empires. As with Miles in August: since his dream of flying for the Air Force had been foreclosed with his new glasses, which he now wore every waking minute, he had reinvested all his aspirations in following in his cousin's footsteps in the Ford National Good Driving Contest. To this end, he had maneuvered the Mercury around behind the station almost every day to practice backing and parking until he was competent to pass his written and behind-the-wheel test on his sixteenth birthday. The examining officer, Archie Dillon, wrote him a temporary permit to drive while he waited for the official license to be mailed from Des Moines. Then, on the 18th, when he had had the temporary permit only twenty-four hours, Archie Dillon took it away from him and revoked the application. It had been an ecstatic birthday, but it was followed by deepest desolation. After the wild ride he gave the girls, he was forbidden to drive at all; even his practice spins around the truck lot behind the DX were curtailed.

A week later, the fiasco was still the heaviest thing on his mind when Race Berglund arrived home from his summer job in Texas and stopped in at the station after his second day back at work. Miles' buddy was still in a celebratory mood; his bank account now bulged with summer wages and he was sun-tanned and impatient to get started on the fall campaign of double-dating in the Mercury, which they had long planned to pursue as soon as Miles got his driver's license.

At the DX, the heat was stifling. The station was a tiny buff-colored stucco building with a tile roof and a front that was all unshaded floor-to-ceiling glass facing west. The desk against the window was boiling hot in the afternoon. When he had kept the Mercury at the station to practice his driving, Miles had devised a way of staying out of the building and cruising the Mercury around the back lot while still keeping an eye out for a customer on the drive: when a car pulled in, he would stop the Mercury behind the station and hop in through the restroom window, and come out the door into the office throwing a paper towel in the can and excusing the delay as a, "Call of nature."

Now that was all over and the Mercury was inaccessible to him, for all he knew forever, and today, when the sun had passed the zenith, he had taken the office chair back by the restroom window and tipped it back in the shade to finish *The Story of Odysseus and the Tale of Troy for Young Readers.*

Before Race Berglund had gone south, they had had a running argument for a week about which super heroes were the best, Odysseus, Achilles, or someone modern like Superman or Captain Midnight? Both preferred the Greeks to the Biblical heroes like Sampson, or the modern ones, and both agreed that Troy, which they had encountered in Sigurd Fardel's Latin class, was better than Gotham City or Gaza. But Race's favorite super hero had been Achilles, who was the best fighter, while Miles had argued for Odysseus, referring to Achilles dismissively as a bronzed baby shoe ("only Achilles, they bronzed the whole baby except his heel").

At first Miles had begun to identify with Odysseus for the sake of an argument, but he ended by proclaiming the "wily Odysseus" his "patron hero" ("like a patron saint, except he's a pagan"). He especially liked it about Odysseus that while he was a ferocious fighter, he preferred to get his mind around his opponent before he drew his bow: inventing the Trojan Horse, impersonating the old beggar. Miles had told Berglund that if he himself were ever to be a hero--an intention he modestly disavowed--he would fight that way, brains first, then brawn.

Now he had just finished the book and was staring grimly out at the shimmering heat waves in the truck lot, brooding again on the loss of the driver's license he had had for one day, and would get back about the time he went to the service, if ever, when Race, who had worked for the DX himself and knew the drill, came out the restroom window with a Coke and sat down on the ledge beside him and picked up the argument as if they had left off yesterday.

He said that in Texas, Sam Houston was a superhero. And down there they figured everybody at the Alamo was.

Miles picked up *The Story of Odysseus for Young Readers* and thumped it. "The old guys are still the best. *He* is!" he said. In Berglund's absence, his identification with the Greek hero had fed on his discovery that Odysseus was a "wise guy" too. (When Odysseus bested an adversary, he couldn't resist turning back to taunt him, as he had the Cyclops. Miles saw the same trait in himself--like tossing John Hall's shoes on the barn.) "So then," he complained to his friend, why hadn't he inherited Odysseus's golden tongue with women? "Why, Race, man, Odysseus could come out of the sea naked as a jay bird and talk Nausicaa into taking him to the king. And when he got home, Penelope didn't even recognize him, but he talked her right back into bed!"

He had intended to keep quiet about losing his driver's permit, but he suddenly wanted company in his misery, and added with a grimace, "Aw, man, I think I picked up some kind of speech impediment with them. I

194

spend half my nights thinking up what I'm going to say to a girl--I mean: when I'm alone, Race, I'm just like Caesar Romero with his cigarette holder talking girls right out of their drawers, but when I meet them daytimes I'm still as a stone! I go, *'Duh!'*

He thought a minute, and added, "You know Florence Wing...?"

"Fairy? Is she still dating Bruce Cross? Did you take her out?"

"Aw, naw! We walked home from the Rialto together one night--but I couldn't think of a word to say to her all the way to her corner. Which she might not have noticed because it was *Kings Row,* and I could let on I was having deep thoughts about it--but we stood there on the corner forever and I couldn't even say, "See you later." My throat would just go *click--so,* I finally kind of shook her hand?"

"You shook her *hand?*"

"Man, I got a hot flash just doing that!.....*Listen,* Race, she *is something!* you *know?*--but she's a senior next year, going with a graduate."

"Not exclusively."

"Who said?"

"Liz tells me at the store--Liz Sinden sees all *e-vil!*"

"But Bruce has a *car!* Roy gave him full use of the car till he goes to the service, so what's the use? "

"But Bruce'll be gone by Christmas, him *and* his car! And *you,* my man, can be driving her around! And *I'll* be in the back seat with Gail or someone. I'll be helping you talk the way Edgar Bergen talks for Charley McCarthy. I'll put sexy words in your mouth!" He went off into one of his silent laughs.

"No, *you* won't." Miles said glumly, "And neither will I! Liz didn't tell you they lifted my license?"

"Aw, no!"

"I didn't even *get* it. I got a permit that said its coming. But it aint!"

"The *bastards*! You ran over someone?"

"I might as well! What happened, I got the permit from Archy Dillon. no sweat. Then, next day, a Des Moines lawyer left his new Packard for a drain and change while he goes out with Bryce Chapman to look at some land. Hucksell does the work and takes off on his bulk route, and leaves it at the pump for me to fill and move into the shade. It's a grand boat, man,--with an *air conditioner*! White walls! So, okay I fill it up. I've got the key. I start her up, and while I'm still at the pump making sure all the dials are running and stuff, Punk and Tiff and Florence Wing show up and start wishing me happy birthday, and about getting my driver's. *And* they just naturally open the doors and jump in--Punk and Tiff in front, and Florence Wing climbs in the back--and they're going, "*Oh, is this your new car, Miles, your dad's birthday present? Ooooh, take us for a ride, Miles! It's hot. Make the air go through!*"

"So, I rev her up and pull around here, and suddenly I notice that they're all sucking ice cream cones and getting ready to drip on this lawyer's new seats. So I go, 'Whoa, girls, give up the ice cream!' It took every last ounce of my iron will power to say it; I mean, Race, they were wearing *shorts*!

"But I took their ice cream cones! And I canned them in the restroom and brought them some Cokes.

"But when I drop out of that window, Tiff yells, 'Well, if it isn't Batman--Miles had a mask, wouldn't he look just like Batman with his black hair, you know?' So what can you say to *that*? I want to make a wise crack and pass it off, but I'm *speechless*! I hand out the Cokes. And they start yacking--about *toes*! Painting *toe nails*! And Punk and Tiff get their bare feet up on this guy's dash to fiddle with Tiff's toe--which has some kind of bump on it that they invite me to *feel*, man! *So, I'm like putty in their hands, Race!* I should have got their feet off the dash, but I'm just stupidly feeling Tiff's toe-bump, when suddenly I get this weird tingling in the back of my neck, and Florence Wing has got her foot up fiddling in my hair with *her* toes! (making like there's a scar on *her* toe which I'm supposed to pay attention to.) Can you believe this stuff they <u>*do*</u>?"

"Listen, you're going great! You're caressing Fairy's toe!"

"Aw, not quite. When I turn my head, this toe's right in my eye! I can't even focus! But it's at the end of Florence's leg, Race! Have you ever noticed Florence's leg?"

"Betty Grable, on the table!"

"Exactly! So, here they are tipped up and all, and I *look*! And I must just have looked *and* looked, cause Tiff finally says, 'See Miles *blush?* Now he's *Blush*-man!'"

"'Oh, they all go, 'Blush-man Miles!--*titter! titter'*"!

"What did *you* say?"

"Me? I say *nothing*! I turn around; my tongue is stalled. But *the car* said! It starts up, like a mind of its own, and we just: *Zoom!*" He uses his hand to describe a plane peeling off, "And we head into the alley, there! And I suddenly say (you know a stutterer, how they don't stutter when they sing?) Well, I suddenly say like Tyrone Power in *A Yank in the RAF?* (metallic voice). *'Now hear this! Men! We're taking the war to the Krauts tonight! And we're target marker flight and we'll drop our load on Damstel, and the boys'll salvo on our fires! So get it <u>right</u>!'* and such Tyrone Power stuff! *'Here we go, crew, down Bomber Alley!'* And the girls gasping and screaming, and me going,*'Wolf pack country ...(machine guns firing) brrraaaat, brraaat!'* And we tear down the alley behind the taverns to the parking lot behind old Buckmann's hardware, and I crank the spinner and head her right back in! *'Goin' home!'"* And Archie Dillon is out the back door of the East Side and plants his ass in the middle of the alley and holds up his badge...Well, I brake and skid and just clip a stack of beer kegs! He leans in the window and says, 'All right, you're done driving, mister! Get out!'"

I say, "But you gave me a permit! My license is on the way!"

"Well, it ain't never going to get here. For sure!"

Miles fell silent, and Race lit a Chesterfield and expelled smoke with a disconsolate explosion.

"But, the really worst thing, Race, he made the girls get out and walk, 'For safety's sake! Humiliation? And the absolute *worst* thing; with them watching, he sits in the passenger seat and makes me drive it back to the station. No, the worst thing was when I tried to park, I backed one wheel into the *grease pit*!

And, God, then they *all* showed up, Hucksell and the lawyer, and hung around telling me how to get it out. I thought I was going to jail, Race! And that's the story. That's why I wont be driving all this fall!"

The sun behind the courthouse tower was casting a long shadow over the station house when Miles picked up his chair and led his disheartened friend around the station and began to close up.

"When Tiff called me 'blush man,' she ruined my life, *our* lives!" he said ruefully, "You don't know how lucky you are, Race! You can dance with them and talk to them about their cuticles and their box pleats and all they like to talk about. You've got a priceless talent there and you just take it for granted!"

Race Berglund helped bring in the display of tires. Then he headed home across the square. He was not without sympathy for his friend, but his feeling for his own predicament was acute. Double dating in the Mercury with Miles has been a large feature of his plan of personal growth and development for fall. He doesn't know how to drive, and learning would not help, as his mother can not afford a car. But double dating with Miles with some of the girls he has had in mind has practically kept him going through simmering west Texas all summer. He concludes that if he doesn't do something to pull his buddy through his talking block and get his license back, his dreams of long parks by the river and in half a dozen other cloistered venues he has mentally marked for exploration through the fall are dead.

As he scuffs back across the square with his head bowed in striving thought---not unlike the wily Odysseus (peering at Nausicaa through the beach grass), his mind's eye settles on Liz Sinden. She is one of two girls behind the fountain, and the druggist has put her in charge of bossing him around. It was Liz who stuck him with the nick name Race when he went to the basement with her to bring up a gallon of syrup and Bonnie turned out the lights, "*Dick Berglund! What makes you so Racy?*"

Liz's steady boyfriend, to whom she is practically engaged, is still working in Illinois on a blue grass crew. Last night she pulled rank and made Race walk her home when the drug store closed at ten so she could safely take the shortcut along the dark lower end of the park. He knows she will ask him to escort her home again tomorrow night, and he wonders if he can persuade her to let Miles tag along--and maybe show him how to make a move or two on a girl without losing his voice.

The next morning, Race broaches Miles' troubles to Liz. She has heard about the crazy ride he gave the girls, and she doesn't care if he brings Miles along with them when he escorts her home tonight. As to basic courtship 101, maybe she will, and maybe she wont--but in the end, the idea of giving a peach fuzz boy primary instruction in smooth moves seems to appeal to her. Race phones Miles and tells him he has to walk Liz home again and invites him to walk with them. He does not draw a diagram.

There is still some action on the square when Miles closes and locks the station. Liz and Race walk together down 9th St. toward the park with Miles trailing a half step behind. At the gate they follow the gravel past the arch of the Undefeated Team and into the dark part, Berglund chatting up Liz about Texas. Liz is wearing her lime green fountain uniform and her shape stands out in the dark like phosphorescence. Twenty-two years old, an inch more than five feet tall, with a compact little shape and short sandy hair, she has thin lips which she lipsticks fuller, and a smile with a natural ironic downturn at the corners. Her usual laugh is a sardonic snort. Her eyes are gray, her heart-shaped little face is wise. She will not marry Briar, the man she's engaged to, and in fact, will not marry till she's thirty-five. In the meantime she will make a sort of avocation of a series of "tutorial" affairs with several generations of high school athletes. Perhaps, this will be a red-letter evening for her, too, the night she discovers a talent for pedagogical petting.

A block in, Berglund stops directly in the random ray of the street light at the end of Eight Street, and the apprentice is surprised to realize that he has been steering Liz along the road with a protective hand in the small of her back. He now watches bug-eyed as his friend turns and gathers Liz into his arms. He bends over and kisses her with the smoothness of an illusion. They had rehearsed this in the dark basement of the store in the afternoon, but Miles has no idea.

"*Watch* out!" he says, and shys back as if someone had lit a fuse.

Berglund releases her and says, "Okay, now *you*. Miles, pretend to walk along with her a few steps, and then just do like I did. But I'm left-handed, so you would have her on your other side, eh? So stand here! Now you guys walk...Put your hand on her back *here*. Be in charge, Miles! You're her escort. It's your fault if she stumbles! Now,

200

action!" When Miles balks at putting a hand on her back, Liz sighs and turns to Berglund, "Creeps, Race, I'm not going to wipe his chin! Are you sure he...he's not..."

"Not what? Oh! *God*, Liz! If anything, he's too... He gets all steamed up...about *you*!

"Me?"

"Liz, the syrup's there but it just won't pour! I'm trying to help him--but he needs a real woman to...like, advise and consent?..."

"Race, man, forget it! You guys go on. I'll just go home"

"Consent?" Liz snorts, "After the Second Coming I might!"

"That's a very cruel thing to say, Liz! This is, like...first aid to a drowning man, Liz!

"....Oh, Now first aid...Okay, if it's life or death, come here, Miles!" Liz abruptly places herself beside him, "Pretend you're walking me up the steps to my door. Now, Miles, put your hand on my waist." she seizes his hand, "Put it *here*!"

Race applauds ironically, "Now, kind of pivot in front of her so she can't go right in the house...and be talking."

"*Talk*, Miles!"

"Uh, Liz, the P-47 is a long-range fighter plane of low wing construction...."

"For corn's sake, Miles, enough with airplanes, something romantic..." she puts her hand on his shoulder, "Miles, don't you have any sweet nothings you can say, a big talker like you? Say to me, um, like: 'Liz, the moonlight on your face, dah-dah, dah-dah..'"

"And bend down to her."

Here Liz bumps her front against him so firmly that he grabs her to keep from stumbling back, "Oh, Race, he's like a runaway train!"

"Then help him, Liz. What does a girl feel? God, you ought to know by *now!*"

With a sigh of taking on a lost cause, Liz says, "Okay, now; Mr. Miles, when you're with a girl in a dark place talking--and not about airplanes--you are really tuning in to her. You're getting more in touch with her while you're saying something romantic to her. She's no packing crate, Miles, she knows what you're getting ready to do. She's a person just like you are, only different...("A-men to that!") Shut up, Race!...and you've got to find out without outright asking her, if she wants to...I mean...*what* she wants....Sooo, while you're saying sweet nothings, you concentrate on your hands on her back, what they're *telling* you. Feel me, Miles! When I'm not so inclined, I'm like, all back bone. I'm a strange cat. My back is up. I'm ready to claw you.....But when I am so inclined, I'm much more...."

"Slinky."

"Race, I'm *warning* you! What do I feel like now, Miles? Am I going to claw you? Grrrrr! No? Then sneak your other arm around me....For crum's sake, *over* my arm! And careful of the hair! Now, gently tilt my chin up. GENTLY! Yes, *yes*...and all the time sweet nothings, sweet nothings, Miles.......And *NOW* Miles!"

And Miles begins to feel what holding a woman is, and her breath, Sen-Sen! And abruptly, unannounced, out pops Caesar Romero of the night sweats--how did *he* get here? "*Come fill the Cup,*" he croons, " *And in the fire of spring thy winter garment of repentance fling./ The bird of time has but a little way to fly, and Lo, sweet Liz, the bird is on the wing!*" The kiss--a zone of heat that makes him release her like touching fire--Liz holds onto. And Race starts swarming around them like a mad movie director, "Cut. *Cut!* Come on, Enough!"

Miles' arms fly straight out, but for a long moment Liz keeps him locked, her hand behind his head, with

202

surprising strength in her small sinews, holding onto his lips with hers.

"No-no!" puritanical Race, "You don't have to give him the whole course at once, Liz! He's not ready!"

"Oh, he's not, Mr. Freud!" As she steps back, her scathing glance X-rays his crotch and winks up at him with a terrible twinkle that makes him double over as if struck in the gut, "Is this some kind of set up? I'd be safer with a boatload of Marines!..... Aw, you guys, go home!"

But she lingers to pull out a cigarette. Race strikes her light and she blows smoke in his face and turns away, "You *two*!" and starts up the hill, dismissing Race, who follows a little ways waving his hands like a lawyer, and then comes back.

"What are you trying to *do*, get me fired?" he hisses, "You can't do *that*! She's my boss! Gasper gives her the whole front of the store to do as she pleases. I don't know if I'll have a job tomorrow!"

"God, I'm sorry!" Miles says, deeply consternated. They turn back toward the town, and after a minute Caesar Romero speaks "You know, like she said, I could feel her get slinky, Race!"

Saturday is one of those weekends that occasionally come along for Berglund in the summer when Gasper gives him the night off, and his aunt and uncle George, the flourishing attorney, pick him up on their way from Des Moines and take him to one of the dances at the Perry country club.

For Miles the evening at the DX has been busier than usual, three or four fill ups, and once two cars at the pumps at the same time. No time for Odysseus tonight, though he has started to read the end again, where the suitors, unable to bend Odysseus's great bow, have to take their medicine. He puts the book away and glumly takes in the tire display and turns off the sign. He is making one last try at the chin-up bar when he hears his name.

"Oh, Miles, are you going home pretty soon?"

He drops and comes out shaking out his arms.

"Race has gone to Perry." Liz is standing by the pump in her lime-green uniform, "Would you possibly do Liz a big favor?"

"Walk you home?"

"Through the park?"

"I won't have anything to say."

"Oh, you kid me, Miles! All that "fires of spring"? How did you think that up?"

"It was a guy's long poem, Liz."

"You could say it again for me while we walk along? Or, you don't have to. You have an eloquent silence, Miles. You don't always have to be talking to a girl all the time."

He locked the station, and walked beside her with a stark sense of being with a woman on his own. At the South Side Drug, it was Liz's job to rack all the magazines. What did he read when he sat on the floor by the magazine rack reading? Liz said she read magazines that interested her: *Life, The Saturday Evening Post, Colliers.* They found they read the same ones, except *The Police Gazette.* And they got to talking about a piece they had both read about women working in war industries as welders and steam fitters. Liz was very interested that he had heard they were going to hire some women workers at the Des Moines Ordnance Plant. What would the plant do exactly, make guns? He said it was going to make bullets, and they had set the first cartridge machine six months ago and were now open for business making shells. It amazed him that though she wasn't interested in airplanes at all, she exhibited such a lively interest in what he had heard from J. Arthur about the process of making machine gun bullets. They were talking like magpies when they got to her house.

Liz said she was thinking of applying for a job as a machine operator or whatever else they had for women to do out there. She wasn't interested in the WAACs, but working at the plant would be something she could do, "to get out and help the war effort," and it didn't hurt that the wages were much higher than around this town. But, she didn't have a car.

And he told her about the Conards' behind the DX, starting a bus line to the plant that would take workers to Ankeny and back every day. He suspected that she already knew, but she acted so glad to hear about the bus that she made him feel like Mr. I.Q. And naturally, he began to think that she might be inclined to resume his kissing lesson where they had left off Friday. But up on her porch when he opened the screen door, she slid right around and got it between them. Maybe that would have been part of lesson two.

Yet he was so comfortable chatting through the screen with her for half an hour about the new Pocket Book of *Tale of Two Cities*, that when she finally said, "G'-night, Miles," instead of the condescending "Mr. Miles", he had had a very fine time, and walked down the hill taking giant strides and singing under his breath, "*My mama done tol' me, when I was in knee pants, my mama done tol' me, son....*" and was reasonably sure he had overcome his impediment and would never have to mimic an intercom again just to find the words to talk to a girl.

<u>3</u>

Going on War Time

Since America had suffered so many losses in the Pacific during the first nine months (the enormous turning point constituted by the victory at the Battle of Midway in June, was not yet fully understood), autumn might have seen the country sunk in pessimistic desolation, but beneath the few surface changes around Adel, everything began to shift like an awakening sleeper. As the two cement chocks on the west side of the courthouse reminded us where the wheels of our Civil War cannon had stood for seventy years before it went into the first "Turn-in-your-scrap-to-slap-the-Jap" drive, the handful of blue stars on people's front windows made the names of some young men who had not yet had time to establish themselves in the community better known in their absence than they had been when among us. High school juniors who appealed to the school board were allowed to take heavier class schedules so that they could graduate at seventeen and join the navy, though others waited for the draft to take them at the age of twenty-one. Jim Mitchell, a year ahead of Miles, was carrying a heavy schedule to be ready to pass the ASTP test for preflight college training for the Air Corps in the spring. Miles and Race Berglund, swept up in a rush of enthusiasm, returned to school to take extra class work in advanced algebra, which was a prerequisite for Maurice Sinift's trigonometry in the spring and high school graduation half a year early at the end of next fall term. Though they were sixteen-year-old juniors, they expected that the war would still be going on when they reached draft age in 1946 and hoped for something better than infantry duty if they had a year or two of college by then. So they started off to classes that fall in something like a march step, feeling for the first time as though they had a mission, though with their impaired vision, it wasn't clear what it would be.

The slow acceleration of life's cadence was not only in the young. Some thought the lives of grownups would stagnate under the war's deprivations: goods already growing scarce in the stores, food and fuel rationing in the offing, a national speed limit of thirty-five miles an hour already in force, and all the lost naval battles, lost islands, lost battleships on the bottom of the Pacific to weigh morale down--but for the most part, the opposite began to happen. Older people seemed to say to themselves, "Everyone is going to be needed, I'd better get moving!" Miles noticed that J. Arthur, who belonged to the American Radio Relay League, which had merely forwarded emergency messages via a chain of radio amateurs before Pearl Harbor, was suddenly busy relaying vital news from service men to their parents and friends all over the country. J. Arthur had also joined the organization sponsored by the Signal Corps that taught "hams" an extension course in cryptographic analysis, and established a web of amateur radio auditors to listen on all frequencies and intercept the messages of spies and saboteurs trying to betray us. And though J. Arthur now spent more time at his key till late at night, he still taught a class three nights a week in trigonometry for senior boys who meant to get into various special programs of the army, navy and air force.

There were two other radio amateurs in town now who were also working their keys for the Radio Relay League, Maurice Sinift, and a farmer named Bob Freeman on the hill north of the river. The official telegrapher was the agent in charge of the Rock Island station, Ray Wing, who had come to town in 1940 and with his wife Gladys and his daughter Florence had taken the house on the northwest corner of the Morgans' block. Ray Wing was a small, sandy, silent man who wore a white shirt with arm bands and a celluloid visor at work in the summer, and habitually chewed on the stem of a corncob pipe not unlike that affected by General MacArthur. He handled most of the duties of the little railroad station himself, and when the government telegrams began to arrive occasionally, announcing the combat deaths of sons and husbands of county families in the service, he delivered them personally, and would close his ticket window at any time of the day to carry the telegrams out into the county in his aging maroon Chevrolet. Later in the war, when the telegrams became more frequent, people would dread the car's appearance on their street.

Otherwise, Ray Wing seemed happy enough with the duties of the little station, which was on a sleepy trunk line that had carried passengers from Des Moines to the resort town of Milford on Lake Okoboji in northwest Iowa for six decades. It was rumored in town, however, that he used the workshop he had set up in one of the rooms of the old brick station to invent railroad gadgets. Soon after the Wings moved here, though Ray Wing lived modestly-- keeping the decrepit 1932 Chevrolet in the barn behind his house, consuming exactly one glass of beer at the pool hall on his way home from work, going to lodge for his only recreation, content to let his women folk do most of the family spending--people who knew his former neighbors in northern Iowa said he still had a small farm there and owned certain patents on railroad safety signals ("silent sentinels of safety") on which the Milwaukee Railroad paid him a royalty.

In September, Miles heard through the Clarkes that Nile Kinnick was being commissioned in Miami and assigned to advanced carrier training in the Grumman Wildcat. He passed on congratulations through George, but hung up the phone with an empty, hungry feeling that his hero was going where he would never be able to go.

He went to school in the mornings now by way of a detour to Race's apartment, where he waited while his friend had a cup of coffee and a Chesterfield between his paper route and school. Verna Berglund always offered Miles a cigarette, but he declined in order to save his wind and encourage his growth. Though Race still towered over him, he weighed one hundred and seventy pounds and was five feet ten now, and was resolved to get serious about football this year, though he knew he never would convince his old nemesis, Coach Blough, who still called him "Your Royal Slowness," and behind his back, "the flying fuck," for his style of missing tackles with headlong dives.

One day, however, in that standard tackling drill in which running backs were given the ball and allowed to run wild between the sideline and the hash marks as far as they could go through linemen spaced ten yards apart, Miles accidentally discovered a way to catch them, and the next week Head Coach Stollard finally decided that flute playing and football were not mutually exclusive, and made him starting left tackle.

The secret he had learned from biting the dust so many times empty handed was that if you played an approaching runner a little bit lop-sided, no matter how much broken-field dazzle he worked on you first, he would always end up breaking for your weak side. Suddenly Miles even caught Jack Engstrom, a nifty runner he had not been able to lay a hand on before, and he boasted to Race Berglund that he had invented a secret maneuver he called the "Trojan Tackle"--named after Odysseus' wooden horse--"I give 'em the opening and they always take it, and I get there first! I'm in like Flynn!" he boasted to Race, though he hadn't made a "Trojan" tackle in a game.

Then, at the start of the second Friday night home game--full of the steak Ferne had begun to feed him like a burnt offering on game nights--he was the outside defensive end and came loping down under a kickoff, guarding the far sideline as he was supposed to do, and the stocky little receiver suddenly reversed his field and outflanked everyone and met Miles head-to-head at the hash mark on the west side. "Come into my parlor, said the spider to the fly!" Miles said to himself, and the runner obediently broke for his weak side just as scheduled. Miles threw his vaunted Trojan tackle, and the green uniform gave him a stiff-arm and twisted Miles' shoulder between his pumping thighs, and stumbled on for five more yards. But Miles felt the kind of deep hurt in his shoulder that means that member is going to be a long time healing, and he couldn't use his left arm to help himself up off the ground.

It was a shoulder separation, and Dr. Bradley X-rayed it at the office and foreclosed the rest of the season for him with a roll of wide tape and a sling. Abruptly, his season slowed from a sprint to a crawl. He was not only disabled for sports, but just at the time music contests were coming up and everyone expected him to climb right through the eliminations to the National Music Contest again, he could not raise the instrument above his waist. His old prayer to get sick and miss music contest had finally been answered.

There was a new vocal music teacher, however, a serious young woman named Mildred Seevers. She was just out of school, but was an accomplished pianist who could play accompaniments for her groups and conduct like a maestro, and who knew the kind of sound she wanted from a chorus and how to get it. She bought a new music library, arrangements of the Robert Shaw Chorale and a chorus-oratorio of Stephen Vincent Benet's *John Brown's Body*. She selected solo music for individuals, and though she had a drop-dead look that kept the rowdy boys in line, she also had a jolly laugh that endeared her to her students. Miles was soon her willing slave, and she set him to work on a baritone solo of *I Know Why*. At the same time, The

Rotary and the bridge clubs seemed to have noticed the exodus of seventeen-year-olds to the navy and began asking for the boys' glee club and the male soloists to fill their entertainment programs. Soon, following Miss Seevers, Miles was entering at hostesses' back doors again without the flute. He would take his place in a room full of fragrant matrons at the end of the business meeting, stand beside the piano with one hand at his side and his left arm in the sling and sing two songs. Miss Seevers, who was twenty-two that year, had a good ear for songs that reflected the tone of the times, and while General Eisenhower led Americans ashore in North Africa (Torch), she arranged for Miles to stand before the women of the Garden Club and sing, *What Does a Soldier Dream Of?*...

> *..after the long fight's through,*
> *His father and mother, his sister and brother,*
> *His dreams make his wish come true.*

When he sang *Invictus*, everyone thought of the famous flyer, Eddie Rickenbacker and his crewmen, recently discovered alive after three weeks adrift in the Pacific in a small boat, and he sang fervently in a robust untrained baritone:

> *Out of the night that covers me,*
> *Black as a pit from pole to pole,*
> *I thank whatever gods there be,*
> *For my unconquerable soul!*

Though Doc Bradley released him from the sling at the end of November, he would often complain of a twinge in the shoulder and put it on again when he performed. Miss Seevers, who sensed that he did it to add dramatic verasimilitude to the warrior lyrics of the songs, would smile indulgently, "Oh, I'm sure you'll have these little setbacks."

He lobbied for *On the Road to Mandalay*, to acknowledge our English allies embattled in Burma, but because part of the lyric went,

Take me somewhere east of Suez,
Where the best is like the worst,
Where there ain't no ten commandments
And a man can raise a thirst...

the music teacher, now the director of the Methodist choir, set it aside.

Early in his convalescence, one day when he had come out of the gym and pulled off his T-shirt in the hall on the way to the locker room to reset the galling tape, Punk darted up with a pen and scribbled her name on his chest. After that, signing his bandage became something of a fad, and most of the girls in the junior class wrote gushy epigrams on it. He basked in their feigned commiseration, and in the halls between classes would loosen the collar of his shirt and even supply his own pen, always hoping Florence Wing would take the bait, but she passed him by, indifferent to his tinsel celebrity. In assembly, he continued to gawk over the invisible wall that separated the juniors from the seniors at her sleek black head obliviously buried in her book.

Balanced opposing urges seemed to ward him away from her through the fall. He might have caught up with her any day on the way to school, but he had heard that she and Bruce Cross were going to get engaged when Bruce left for service and he obeyed the patriotic taboo against trying to cut in on a girl who had been "spoken for" by a serviceman, though unknown to him, Bruce's sister Charlene had invented the rumor.

212

Though Miles felt that he was standing still, day by day the war was moving him on: November 18th, Congress forwarded to President Roosevelt the bill lowering the draft age from twenty-one to eighteen, and with a stroke of the pen, Miles was less than two years from induction. When Christmas vacation came, he wanted nothing but to stay home and moon after Fairy Wing, but the Morgans took him for Christmas to Ferne's sister's family near Sioux Falls (in 1934, the Haugens had all worked at dipping fruit jars in a tub of swirling yellow, red and blue enamel paint, and later had set the jars out in a stall at the state fair to impersonate multicolored vases in hopes of making a little money to pay their bills). Now Bill Haugen had begun to buy up the other shares of ownership in the small cooperative phone company he had managed--and taken his pay in commodities--through the Depression. Miles' cousin, Bill, 18, who was already an experienced telephone lineman, was going to the Sea-bees in the spring.

On New Year's Eve, Miles went with Bill to the Legion club in the little town of Hartford while the adults went into Sioux Falls to a dance. Big Bill was the commander of the Hartford Legion; young Bill was almost a Seabee and had the full rights of a drinking man in the club, and by nepotism, so did his Iowa cousin. So Miles drank two beers and a "boilermaker" and got tipsy, and they recruited two pasty-faced high school girls and commandeered the telephone company Ford, and Billy drove them all on a wild slalom of figure eights in the snow around the trees of the city park.

Late that winter, Miles was allowed to take the drivers test again. He passed and once more received a permit on probation. The same week, Kenneth Richard Morgan--certified by the Ford Motor Company to be the best young driver in the country--ran his new Ford convertible into a motionless train at a crossing in downtown Ames while chauffeuring a carload of students

213

back to campus. His prize car was totaled, but no one was injured, and Kenneth soon joined the Navy Air Corps cadet program.

It was 1943 already, and though Miles had had his first "toot," and had stolen his first kiss from a strange girl, and his uncle Parker had informed J. Arthur that his son's eyes would definitely pass the test for service now-- whether for full infantry duty or one of the Special Service schools for clerks and bakers, he did not know--Miles still felt like a feckless adolescent.

The Kingdom of Swing

What finally propelled him across some invisible demarcation line was the swing music. J. Arthur had given him a real transcontinental radio for Christmas. The Halicrafters was a state-of-the-art starter set for the ham operator, with a case of crinkled black enameled steel, aluminum dials, meters with jumpy needles for volume and tuning, and enough power to bring in shortwave bands and international broadcasts. When he hooked up the antenna to J. Arthur's, which ran to the chimney of the church without a steeple across the street, he started to hear the bigband broadcasts from Frank Daily's Meadowbrook Ball Room in New Jersey. It was an hour later on the Jersey Turnpike, and he often went to sleep wearing J. Arthur's second best earphones, and was brain-washed till midnight by the hits of the name bands--Harry James, Tommy Dorsey, Artie Shaw(who hired black side men), Benny Goodman, and the black bands: Jimmie Lunceford, Count Basie and Duke Ellington. Glenn Miller's was the quintessential swing band, with its shimmering voicing: "four saxes and a clarinet on top," so distinctive that no one else dared copy it. And he was bowled over by the big band jazz of Woody Herman's *"band that plays the blues,"* which took its jump start from black bands and became Herman's "First Herd," a seventeen-piece power wagon. In its arrangements "hot" swing was embedded with nuggets of multi-chorus jazz rides that passed around the sections like breakneck calls and responses. Hot jump tunes were spaced with romantic ballads for couples doing the fox trot, a lubricious form of moving hug, the tactile illusion of a sweet holding together against the tide of mass separation. The musical icon of that mood was Glenn Miller's *Moonlight Serenade*, which spoke to a million couples who were parting. One night, just as he was nodding off with the music in the earphones, the memory of the Tommy Dorsey dance the eve of Pearl Harbor came back like a revelation. In a flash, he finally understood the gruff deference people had paid to the men-boys in their still-new uniforms--and how the civilians, the waitresses and off-duty cops and deferred farmers had made these boy-men kings of the revel because they saw *It* coming. And he knew in a flash why envy curdled in him when the jitterbugging girls twirled their skirts high to make it a red-letter night for boys they scarcely knew, but hotly clung to, spellbound by the aura of early peril they wore. What stung him was the awakening that he was just over a year away from going in their shoes. And when he fell into deep sleep, cradled in the cadence of the beat, he dreamed he was riding a surf toward the war with all those others in new uniforms. He dreamed the nature of time itself was changing: it was not the demarcation from Eastern Standard to Central Standard Time any more. Decades were over. The transvaluation was pre-war years equal wartime days. And he had joined the universal American present tense of *war time*. What you never would have done before, you did right now, to your own syncopated sound track. When the music woke him, it was the blues, but a new *St. Louis Blues March* now.

In the days that followed, this epiphany, if it was that, merely widened the breach between him and his parents, who still assumed something would come up to keep him home. Still on a short leash with J. Arthur for his joy ride, he could drive the Mercury to away games staying in the little cavalcade of Adel cars that followed the team, while J. Arthur rode the bus with Maurice Sinift talking radio and checking Miles' driving out the back window. If he dated, the car was due back in the driveway before he and his date walked to the dance. To Miles, on his new wavelength, these things were a matter of indifference. He let Race arrange their double dates to serve Race's purpose of providing the best friend of a girl he was pursuing, whose steady, on the team, would only allow her to go with him if a friend went along to "chaperone." So, Miles would deliver Race and the two girls downtown and drive around the block on the way home to see if Bruce Cross's car was in front of Ferry's house, and if the streetlight still fell between their silhouettes. It always did until one night in April they were fused. The next day Bruce Cross left for the service.

When he heard that Fairy had gone to the train with the Crosses to see Bruce off, he went into a decline and stopped going with Race on these set-up dates. In March, he started prowling stag with Jim Mitchell, who had broken up with Molly. They skipped the games and cruised to the Four Corners and back to Woods' Diner till the gas ran out, looking for something, no notion what, until one night in early April:

Something Happened

That night he was riding with Mitchell and Race in one of the garage's Ford convertibles when Jim drew up to three girls walking home from Rainbow and offered them a ride. Miles recognized Tiff and Fairy Wing and Fairy's friend Marylin Gibs, called Gibsy.

The boys got out and they all milled around the car because there wasn't room in a convertible for six. Then

216

Jim put down the top and ordered someone to sit on someone's lap in back now that there was room for their head to stick up. He took Tiff into the front seat beside him and gave Race the outside front where Miles had been because Race's knees were too long for three in the little back seat. He got his sister's head scarf from the glove compartment and tossed it to Gibsy, and Miles sat down in back and beckoned to Gibsy. But Gibsy whispered with Fairy, and suddenly whipped the scarf over Fairy's head, and the "soldier's girl" tied it under her chin and jumped in back and took a precarious seat high on the points of Miles' knees.

They started, and everyone breathed the spring in the wind, and Mitchell forgot about the gas ration and drove them across the old bridge into the country. On the river road he flicked the headlights off. Darkness made the river bottom land slowly emerge till the trees and barns were painted white with moonlight and black in the shadows. Fairy's scarf teased Miles' nose, and her hair flicked his lips, and everybody laughed and sang with the radio, and in the windy back seat, Fairy's body gradually relaxed down his thighs and nestled warm in his lap and her arm stole around his neck to steady her. When Jim turned the headlights on again, Gibsy mock-moaned, "You wanna trade?" and Miles said, "Down, girl! No Gibses need apply!"

They stopped at the deserted farm called Sleepy Hollow and watched the moonlight streaming through the breaks in the collapsing roof, and Miles told the ghost story of the lost Boy Scout, Carl Long, till they all went silent.

Finally someone hooted and began to sing, *"Poor Lil, da-dum dee-yahdah, da-dum dee-yahdah! Poor Lil, da-dum dee-yahdah, da-dum dee-yahdah! One night as she lay in her dishonor..."*

When they were back in town, Jim turned up the radio, which was playing a recorded jazz program of The

217

Hot Club of France from WOI. When they stopped in front of Wings', he kept time to *Sunny Side of the Street* on the steering wheel and Fairy hopped out and tossed Jim the scarf and stood shaking out her hair.

"Sleep tight!" they said, and the front seat sang, *"she felt the hand of the Lord upon her!"* and Fairy retorted, "Hush, we're Methodists!" And Gibsy whispered to Miles, "Be a gentleman!" and he jumped out, too. Fairy said, "He won't be a moment," and waved them all goodbye behind his back while she led him down the side of the house out of sight of the car. Three steps led up to a screened porch in back, and Fairy stepped on the first and turned to face him.

She said she had heard about the ghost Boy Scout at school and was glad to have heard the real story tonight. And wasn't part of it true? He confessed that the Boy Scout wasn't a ghost but his real friend Carl Long, who had actually drowned in Lake Solitude two summers ago. "I'm sorry," she said.

Then his old impediment suddenly caught him by the throat. He stood looking down at her luminous face outlined in her moon-shadow pasted to the house and heard *Sweet Georgia Brown* fading away up Grove Street. He realized that he was holding his breath and exhaled with a sort of gasp, and from some suicidal impulse to be noble, blurted out, "I heard you went to the train with Bruce. You know, Fairy, I wish you two the very best!"

In the silence, she seemed to appraise him and watch him shrink. "I don't *belong* to Bruce," she said at last, "No one but me, myself and I....So, then...goodbye, Mr. Miles Morgan."

After the screen clapped and the back door shut, he stood for a time savoring the bitter aftertaste of his gaffe. Then a light came on upstairs and he moped across the back yard and into the alley. Was he born with his foot in his mouth? He remembered shouting at her here the day he

218

fell off the bike. What had been, just a few minutes ago, the most beautiful hour of his life, had turned into the ugliest, the dumbest--one more self-made social suicide.

But in spite of his blunder, they began to accidentally run into each other often. Without a date, he went to the farewell barbecue for Jim Mitchell and Dan Rainwater, who were leaving after graduation to work on the Alcan highway. She wasn't there, and he sat by the embers of the campfire alone while couples retired to the shadows of the woods to smooch. On the way home, he saw Fairy in the backyard with Sparky on a leash and stopped. She told him about a summer job she had applied for, and said her dog liked him. "Smart pooch!" he said.

Then, on May 10, after her high school graduation, their eyes made a glancing click as her parents and the Crosses stood congratulating her, so he moped around killing time till she was alone. Then he went up to her and put his hand out, but she stood on tip-toe and kissed him on the cheek. He flushed and looked over his shoulder, and there was Charlene Cross glowering at them. It reminded him that Ferry Wing belonged to Bruce, and he stammered out congratulations, and sidled away. A soldier's girl was still a girl in a high tower for him.

But that Saturday night she was with Punk and Tiff and Gibsy and Gloria down-town. They were all in the same booth, and he could dance with her to *Tuxedo Junction,* and walk home with her because Gibsy was along and it was nothing personal.

After that, he deceived himself that their frequent meetings were accidental. He would have Race with him, and Fairy had Gibsy, who lived in the next block, and they would sit down in the booth next to the jukebox and order cherry Cokes dutch. Race and Gibsy knew each other too well from the spin-the-bottle stage for anything to click with them, but in the spirit of matchmaking they would pair up to walk home with the un-couple, and the foursome would sit in the canvas chairs on the Wings' back lawn till ten when the boys would leave together.

Yet Miles was too patriotic--as *he* thought of it--to try to be alone with her again. He knew she and Bruce were still writing, because Fairy would mention what was happening with Bruce in basic training. Did her letters to Bruce talk about *him*? He didn't ask. He felt like a Disney character who could run in thin air until he looks down.

They both wanted to see *For Whom the Bell Tolls,* the film of Ernest Hemingway's novel about the Spanish Civil War. It came to the Rialto, and they went alone, paid their own way, and sat together in an empty balcony. When Gary Cooper made love to Ingrid Bergman in the same sleeping bag, they stopped touching and shifted to opposite sides of their seats. But Fairy cried at Gary Cooper's heroic death (self-sacrificed to give Ingrid Bergman time to get away), and Miles' arm slipped around the seatback to console her shoulder. He felt that she would cry for *him* if he did something like that, and he felt like doing it almost right away.

Bruce Cross's father, as county engineer, had a certain collegial relationship with J. Arthur, and when Miles started lobbying for more allowance so he could pay Fairy's way to the movies, J. Arthur lined up a summer job for him as a rodman on Ralph Cross's county survey crew. There was no way to explain to J. Arthur that he couldn't accept money from Ralph Cross and use it to take his son's girl on movie dates, so Miles called Hucksell and got back his old job at the DX station for the summer--making J. Arthur furious that he would prefer a job with a third the pay. The method in Miles' madness was the prospect of whiling away the long summer evenings sitting with Fairy in the Mercury behind the station. This time he would behave--no joy rides, and no girls but Fairy need come by.

Fire Branded

Then, one night the week before the Fourth of July, when Glenn Hucksell had asked him to keep the station open till ten, and Fairy had promised to stop on her way home from work, he brought the Mercury down for the first time since he lost his license before he got it. Ferne was gratified when he polished his shoes with a dish towel, but put her head in her hands when he left the house in his new slack suit. "What if you have to do a grease job?"

Early on, about dusk, some of his friends dropped by and hung around drinking Cokes spiked with peanuts and talking about the upcoming Fourth of July fireworks show. When Fairy saw the gang and would have passed on by, Miles left John Hall and Race and the others in front and led her around back to sit in the Mercury. She had a new pad of drawing paper and some soft pencils she had bought at the drugstore, and they began taking turns making drawings on alternate pages while Miles sometimes kept an eye on the front through the open restroom window.

He would sketch airplanes, and she would draw head-and-shoulder profiles of brunette girls with full lips and pageboy bobs. He teased her that the faces she drew all looked like her, and when she dared him to draw something besides airplanes, he took the charcoal pencil and told her to hold still while he made his first great sketch "from the life."

As he bent over the page, looking up, then down, the sound of laughter came occasionally from the front of the station, and then he forgot about it. The natural light diminished and the flashing neon sign of the tavern next door gave her mysterious face the tantalizing flicker of a silent movie image and he wadded up sheet after sheet and started over, growing more frustrated the more he hurried

221

against the dark. The way he was holding his tongue finally made her break off the pose to laugh.

He looked up and said in exasperation, "Now you've spoiled it just as I was catching you."

"You've got to catch me on the *Wing*!" she laughed, and tried to snatch the drawing, and they were locked in a mock struggle for the pad when a bottle rocket arched over the Mercury and landed on the truck lot in a shower of sparks.

There was a burst of yelling from the front, and Miles let go of the drawing and opened the car door and listened. Somebody in front said, "It's dying out. Give us a drop, here, John!" Then he heard Race Berglund cry, "*Whoa!* That pump pours!"

All of the four boys on the ramp in front of the station but John Hall had worked at the DX at one time and thought they knew how to manage the two gas pumps. They had been rushing the Fourth by firing bottle rockets from empty Coke bottles at the elderly attendant sitting on the bench in the side yard of the Pure Oil across the corner, lighting the fuses from a small fire one of them had started with a few drops of gas left in the nozzle of the electric pump from the last fill-up. When the tiny fire died down and someone called for more, John Hall had grabbed the hose of the gravity pump and held the nozzle over the guttering fire, and pulled the trigger. This time, a solid stream from the fourteen gallons of red Ethyl gasoline in the glass tower of the pump gushed out of the hose. Bluish fire jumped from the guttering flame on the ramp and ran up the stream of gas and skipped over John Hall's hand and ran on along the hose toward the pump. Miles jumped out of the Mercury and swung through the station window. Coming through the restroom door, he saw a puddle of fire already spreading on the drive and John Hall trying to carry the flaming hose toward the street as though he thought he could throw it away in the gutter. As John ran across the island, the fire jumped from the hose to the steel case of the gravity pump and started to lick around the gallons of red Ethyl behind the glass. When the flaming hose was stretched taut, John Hall dropped it and started dancing, brushing fire from his hands. The others, except Berglund, looked back once and ran across the street toward the courthouse. Race Berglund's eyes popped at the fire licking up around the red gasoline in the glass tower and he ran into the station house door shouting, *"Call the fire department!"*

A vision flashed in Miles' head of the evening phone operator ringing the volunteer firemen from their suppers ten minutes after the DX was a smoldering hole in the ground. He caught a glimpse of the old man on the bench at the Pure Oil rocking with laughter, and suddenly remembered where Hucksell had shown him the fire extinguisher. It was a puny brass job the size of a half-gallon milk bottle, but he snatched it and he ran outside and started squirting a stream of white foam on the burning pump. He had the hopeless feeling that there were ten seconds left to stop the fire licking up the glass tank before the extinguisher was empty. But the foam doused the flames and smothered the flickering hose and part of the puddle on the ramp before it went dry, and he and Race stamped out the rest by dancing like devils on the flickering cement.

When they stood in the blessed twilight with no flames anywhere and his heart still beating like a jack hammer, Miles shook his fist at the old man at the Pure Oil. "You'd go up, too, you old fart!" he shouted, giving the finger to John Hall and the others sidling away across the courthouse lawn. It was still dinner hour, and there was no one else on the square, but he turned to Race with the woeful foreknowledge that there was no way of keeping Hucksell from finding out. Nevertheless, they took windshield rags back to the pump and polished it till there

223

wasn't a trace of soot left, and policed up all the sticks of the bottle rockets in silence before Race left.

"I'll call Glenn in the morning." Miles said fatalistically. He got the tire display inside before he remembered Fairy. He was sure she had fled, but she was still sitting drawing in the semi-dark, and he felt a surge of fondness for her because he felt a little like a Gary Cooper protecting Maria.

"What was all the shouting?"

"They were playing with bottle rockets. It started a little fire."

When he pulled up in front of her house and took his hands off the wheel, they started to shake. He had gone mute again, and she finally opened the door and got out, looking back quizzically under the dim street light. "Well, see you sometime?"

"Tomorrow, sure," he said, feeling belatedly weaker and weaker.

The next day it was Glenn Hucksell who called him first. Hucksell asked him to stop by at his convenience. He didn't say anything about working. Glenn Hucksell was a soft-spoken man, and he seemed calm, but it was obvious he knew, and when Miles started to stammer an explanation he had been rehearsing, he said, "Yes, Miles, Ray Rainwater told me that you put it out, but he also told me you were sitting back there in the Mercury with Fairy. You were in charge." (Yes, sir.) "And if you had been out front it never would have happened in the first place. Would it?" (No, sir,) "I give you the benefit of the doubt, but I thank God a lot more than I do you. You realize what might have happened?" (Yes, sir!) " So, I'm sure you'll understand why I can't have you back. When you stop by and leave the keys, I'll pay what you have coming, which comes to twelve seventy-five. And I wish you luck. But, Miles, just ask yourself, when are you going to grow up and take responsibility?"

From that time Monday morning until Friday evening about nine-thirty when they sat down in the glider on Fairy's back porch and he put his hands to his temples like a man with a migraine and said, "I don't believe it! I refuse to believe it!" and Fairy took him in her arms--it was pretty much the hell week of his life, without one redeeming prospect in it.

At ten he walked to the DX and turned in Hucksell's keys. Glenn Hucksell opened the cash drawer and dug out twelve seventy-five and sent him on his way.

He had rejoined the ranks of the unemployed.

At lunch, J. Arthur must have heard his side of the story from Race because he wasn't as furious as he might have been. But Miles was grounded again; he had no job, and he would now put in his days in the Victory garden until he had some gainful employment. Henceforth, he would find his chores of the day posted on the clipboard on the kitchen door.

Then for two days he sloped about the town with his head down looking for a part-time job at one of the other stations on Highway 6 and the feed store, and the hardware. No one had a part-time job, anyway for *him*, since everyone had heard some version of the fire. It didn't bother him so much when people did not know he and Race had put the fire out, but it did bother him that most people thought it was some kind of a boys-will-be-boys lark. No one seemed to see it as a potential inferno that had threatened lives--the people in the tavern next door--not even Hucksell. When Hucksell found no traces of the fire on the pump, he had decided that the old man had exaggerated, and finally told J. Arthur that Miles could come back to work.

Miles declined, "Well, it was a lot worse than that," he thought with a touch of masochistic pride, and made another axiom of life, "Nobody understands a thing, really, if they just hear about it." But he was through with the DX.

He had missed Fairy at church Sunday and didn't see her the first part of the week as he made his fruitless job rounds. Wednesday was another restless night with indelible visions of the flames, orange-red at the root and tailing upward into little blue vaporous licks around the red gas in the glass tank of the gravity pump. He sat up with the after-image in his head, thinking, "None of you really know! *Death* was right there!"

You Have to Be There

On Thursday, the Germans intercepted the airplane carrying the popular English actor Leslie Howard between Lisbon and London and shot it down. Seventeen persons were lost. The papers mentioned the shock and mourning of the thousands of American moviegoers who had admired Howard for his performance as Ashley Wilkes, the patrician southerner who was Scarlett O'Hara's real love in *Gone With the Wind.* Miles remembered having seen Howard in the film a long time ago, and since then in some movie about the war where he looked very fine in a British officer's uniform. Along with all moviegoers, he felt a pang of sadness at the loss of the handsome actor, as though a friendly acquaintance had died.

The *Tribune* also carried an item from the Polish government in exile in London saying that the Nazi SS tanks and armored cars were still mopping up the last stand of the uprising in the Warsaw ghetto. The Germans were complaining that the uprising had cost hundreds of German lives. The item said that when the rebellion had started in April the ghetto had contained 56,000 Jews. Miles remembered a German-released newsreel of the early days of the uprising showing Germans with submachine guns standing with their boots spread wide apart over pale, frozen-with-fear women and children kneeling with their empty hands raised in supplication for mercy.

That afternoon he finally called Fairy and made a date to come over Friday evening and try to make a really *good* sketch of her. Despite the low week, he was beginning to cheer up. When he had gotten another rejection slip from *Liberty Magazine*, the idea had come to him that his manuscripts might get more favorable attention if he accompanied the stories with his own art work, like the illustrations Jon Whitcomb did for fiction in the *Ladies Home Journal*.

J. Arthur and Ferne had gone out to dinner, and she had left Miles' supper on the stove. He had eaten and was standing at the sink washing dishes, wearing her apron over his slacks and listening to the six o'clock news, when he heard the name, *Nile Kinnick*, and stopped the running water and heard the announcer say, "The former All American and Heisman Award-winning football player of the University of Iowa, now a navy ensign fighter pilot, has disappeared after crash-landing his plane near his carrier in the Gulf of Paria off Venezuela." Engine failure was mentioned. It had happened Wednesday morning.

Miles sat down in the breakfast nook, put his head in his hands and looked at the table top.

When he got up and went out the back door and down the alley to Fairy's it was growing dark. Fairy was sitting in the chaise lounge with the pad of paper and the pencils on the table. She stood up when he came around the garage, and glanced pointedly at the sunset dying behind the Ninth Street hill. "I'm sorry," he said. "I couldn't anyway. Let's walk."

"Where?" she said, watching him with her skeptical eyebrow raised.

"To the park," he said, "You mind?"

"Not if you'll take off your apron." Her eyes prepared to laugh, then stopped.

227

He ripped the apron off and pegged it into the bushes. "Come on!"

She was wearing a knee-length skirt and a yellow blouse and saddle shoes. She walked along beside him in silence, and he said nothing, taking a route through the arch of the Undefeated Team, where he stopped and stood silently looking up at the inscription "1933" before turning west toward the pool. The pool had opened June first, and there were kids splashing under the lights. After a minute at the fence, he turned and started back.

"What is it?" she said when they were almost to her corner.

He stopped and faced her. The light was faint now, but she could see his lips moving wordlessly. Then he took her arm and continued. At Grove Street under the streetlight he stopped again and told her how he had gone around looking for a job, and everyone would bring up the fire. "They don't understand what it *was*, they act like it was a joke! Because they didn't *see* it!"

"I know," she said sympathetically.

"No, you don't," he snapped. "You didn't even know it was burning!"

"Race told me about it."

"The thing I'm saying...nobody really *understands* anything unless they see it with their own eyes! Thousands of Jews are murdered in Warsaw and I didn't feel it as much as I did that Leslie Howard had been shot down! Just because I *knew* him from *Gone With the Wind*! How can we ever get anything right if we only feel what we've seen with our own eyes? There's no...there's no proportion! We're still cave men!" They had turned into her back yard and she took him into the screened porch and they sat down in silence side by side on the glider there.

He kept massaging his hands in an agitated way and finally burst out, "They went out tonight, and Mom left my dinner, and I was doing my dishes and it came on the news that Nile Kinnick's plane crashed off his carrier!"

"I know," she said. "I heard it. I'm sorry."

He gave her a look of outrage, "No, you aren't *really*! You didn't *know* him! They left for Omaha in '33! You hadn't moved here yet. He was our *paper boy*! He was going to be someone special! He was my *friend*!" He stopped, swallowed spastically, and gripped his head as though to lift it off and fix something inside. "But I don't *feel* anything! What's the *matter* with me? I feel *some*thing for Leslie Howard. I want to cry for dumb Leslie Howard. That's silly! But *Nile*; he could have been governor!" He dropped his hands in his lap and sat staring into them. After a moment he said, "He taught me how to kick a *football*!"

"They're still searching for him." she said reasonably.

He turned and looked at her incredulously, "I didn't hear *that*! Then he's *not* dead!" he said. "Then *that's* what will happen! *He'll turn up*!" His face screwed up with the rictus of an arrested sob. His Adam's apple jumped helplessly, and Fairy suddenly turned toward him and took him in her arms. He pushed his face into her hair and his chin into her shoulder and hugged her so hard she gasped. There was so much of sweet reprieve in it that it undid them both. They separated and he stood up. "God...bless you! " he whispered, "He's bound to turn up!"*

Going home down the alley in the dark, his previous black mood magically lifted, and he felt a tingling where his chest retained the soft-urgent impress of her breasts. "What if..." he wondered, since Liz had explained how sensitive girls' backs were, "what if they can make their breasts like bumpers if they don't like you, or soften 'em up if they do? Well, listen, anyway she *does* like me some!" He gave a stiff skip. After that he made himself walk on and think about the Jews. He was sure Nile Kinnick would turn up.

229

Nile Kinnick did not turn up. He was apparently knocked out by his wheels-up landing and went down with his Grumman Wildcat without deploying his life raft. The search found nothing but pieces of the plane. Though his remains were never found, his many friends and fans nationwide continued for a long time to hope. At the time, his death was but one of many, many American losses; but in time, Nile became something of an icon, a symbol of the best of our war-destroyed youth. The University of Iowa football stadium was named for him.

Nor was anything ever found by the search in the Bay of Biscay for Leslie Howard and the seventeen people on his flight. And somewhere in the annals of Enigma, the story of the breaking of the German command code and the code's subsequent use by the allies throughout the rest of the war, the story can be found that Winston Churchill, who had absolute control of the use of deciphered German communications, learned in advance of the German intention to intercept Howard's flight, but reluctantly allowed it to take place for fear of tipping Germans to the fact that the allies were reading their code.

Having pushed the Nazis out of North Africa, the allies invaded Sicily. On the night of July 11 with an amphibious beachhead threatened by Italian forces and a German Panzer division inland, the largest airborne operation of the war so far launched over 2,000 American and British paratroops on Sicily. It was a disaster that nearly caused the Americans to disestablish airborne divisions for the duration. The losses in the air were the result of miscommunication and were all caused by "friendly fire" from ships and allied forces on the ground. An American parachute regiment lost 81 killed and 148 wounded and missing, a troop carrier wing had 7 killed and 83 wounded and missing. Many planes turned back under the withering fire and landed in Africa again with planeloads of dead and wounded paratroopers. A captain who had survived that jump, upon disability retirement from the service in 1944, would post on the bulletin board of the Parachute School at Fort Benning the announcement that he would bequeath to any "Cinderella" paratrooper who could fit them, a pair of shiny, size 12 jump boots he had worn in the jump on Sicily. Miles Morgan would acquire them.

As for the suppression of the Jewish insurrection in the Warsaw ghetto, the Germans finally snuffed out all resistance June 26. In addition to the loss of several hundred German soldiers, some 56,000 Jews who had been imprisoned there also died.

4

Belts and Bandoliers

The Conards, who had long operated a small truck line out of the garage north of the DX station, now had a franchise for a bus line to the new ordnance plant, and had secured some buses the size of large school buses which started their loop at Redfield, west of Adel, and picked up plant workers in Adel and at stops through Des Moines on the way to the plant five miles north at Ankeny. The long ride with its frequent stops made the portal-to-portal time almost eleven hours. But as the fire had made Miles unemployable at home, and Fairy was going to Council Bluffs to the state convention of the Rainbow and then on to Lincoln to spend several weeks with a cousin, the ordnance plant's fabulous seventy cents an hour persuaded him to put on his DX work clothes in the dark Monday, June 7, and board the Conards' bus with Race to apply for a job at the plant.

On the way, people who seemed to him middle-aged, but whose faces had been prematurely ravaged by hard times, nipped coffee from their thermoses and told them horror stories: they wouldn't get a smell of the best jobs, running machines, which required speed but little heft and mostly went to women. Short-term high school kids could expect bottom-level jobs that were dirty, unpleasant and maybe hazardous. *So, enjoy yourselves, boys*!

The Des Moines Ordnance Plant had now been open a year. Sprawled over the farmland on the edge of the village of Ankeny a few miles north of Des Moines, it still had a raw look. The site had been totally cleared by the spring of 1941 when J. Arthur and Miles had toured it with the contractor, and there were still no trees. Now it was asphalt roads, an occasional guard tower and a thicket of rail spurs to the main manufacturing buildings, which were numbered 1 through 4 and 4-A. Set some distance away in still unbroken prairie were a dozen small wooden buildings on a loop of siding. The gun powder was mixed in these buildings and each was surrounded by a high earth berm. At the base of the rough rectangle of main buildings was building #7, a parts warehouse and the location of the time-clock for the floating labor pool. By now, the plant was working full speed, twenty-four hours a day on three shifts producing 30-and 50-caliber machine gun ammunition in belts and bandoliers.

In the hiring offices, the two boys filled out forms and sat through a five-minute interview with a bored personnel man. They had no work experience, were sixteen years old and would be returning to high school in the fall, just kids on summer vacation, probably flibbertigibbets who wouldn't stay a week. Miles said he would like a job that would get him in shape for football. The interviewer raised his head, snorted, marked a notation at the bottom of his form and dismissed him without a handshake. They filled out the form for Social Security cards, were photographed for a badge and told to report for work the next day.

Tuesday when he punched in at building Seven, Miles' wish had been granted; while Race went to the cafeteria, he was sent to be a shell "slinger" in a box car. With a crowd of other laborers, mostly hefty boys too young for the draft, he loaded onto the back of a truck that stopped at every dock to debark the crews to work there for the day. At building Three he was told off with a dozen other young men to a dozen box cars at the dock. The foreman everyone called "Nervous Nelly" hollered, "You, new kid!" and pulled him aside as he jumped off the truck, "You see that there painted on 'em?" he said, pointing to the skull and crossbones stenciled in yellow on an empty wooden shell box by the door of one of the cars. "That means that there box, when loaded with ammo, if you dropped it, could explode and blow this whole place to smithereens! *Handle With Care! boy*! There's some smartasses knocks 'em around. But if a government inspector catches 'em, it's Federal law, you're fired! Maybe do jail time!"

Miles joined a crew waiting for shells in the door of one of the cars. He said, "Ho!" but was ignored. Later, he would understand that they had already seen too many one-day wonders with mom-pressed shirts and no work gloves and "bookworm" glasses. The three slouched in the car door like pauper princes in patched hobo pants and Goodwill shirts with blue tattoos showing through the rips: two stubby fellows with wide shoulders and taut biceps and a third man over six feet, stringy and mal-nourished looking. All cursed and knocked each other about in the easy way of men who have settled into a comfortable crew. When a can of Copenhagen went around, they all dipped, but kept it out of the greenhorn's hands.

Miles decided they were hazing him and made up his mind to show them a thing or two as soon as he got the hang of the job enough to apply Odysseus' mental judo to it. How hard could it be, if these lowballs could do it?

Soon a forklift brought the first load of shells on a pallet and parked it in their door. The shells were in brown wooden boxes with their nomenclature stenciled on them: belts or bandoliers, 30-or 50-caliber, tracer, armor piercing, high explosive, packed in waterproof tin liners in wooden boxes. The weight was stencilled on the side: 76 or 94 pounds. The tall one called Tiny said, "Let's go!", and they seized three boxes and with a running step flung them into the corners of the car with a crash. Miles winced and tried to lift one. He knew he could lift the box if he could get a firm hold. There was a handhold groove at each end, but he had to get his arm under one end and hug the brutal thing to

234

his chest in order to lift it. He staggered to his corner with it, and set it down carefully; then he had to get down on all fours to push it into place.

While he repeated the process with the second box, a furious slamming went on in the other corners of the car, and he was already lagging behind. He simply set down the third box and gave it a parting kick that left it gaping out in front of the dressed rank his mate called Stutt was building from the other side. Stutt called him "*shit-for-brains*" and led him back to tuck his box in flush with the others. "*Get a move on, Delores!*" he shouted.

"But, you're *throwing* them! If you don't handle them carefully they could explode!" All three stopped for a click and stared at him. Then they went back to throwing the boxes. Sweat was already streaming from his head. With despair in his heart, he went back to jerking and wrestling the last box of his first row into place.

When he stood up to get his breath, he saw that they had all built three rows shoulder high and were starting their next one. He had never lifted a ninety-four pound box shoulder high, but he went about heaving the first box onto his shoulder and sliding it into place. But he was now working in his own little cave in the back corner of the car while the other three had filled their quarters almost to the door. And he had expended huge amounts of effort, and was stifling in the airless niche they had buried him in. He would have given anything for a break in the outside world, which was still that mildly sunny spring day he had noticed long ago (in his carefree youth).

He leaned on the pallet and uncramped his back, and suddenly the slam-banging stopped; there was a muffled parley among his betters, and the lanky one said, "Okay, Delores, get out and push the rest of those boxes up front."

So, he got out and stood on the dock and shoved boxes to them from the far side of the pallet, ashamed of the relief he felt to be out of it, while the pigeon-breasted fellow took his spot and quickly brought the load to the front. The other two then filled the gap in front of the door.

It was probably ten in the morning when they finished the car and called the carpenter to block it while they stood on the dock taking a spitting break. They didn't make fun of him. It was much worse than that. They had christened him the tits on a boar. They had nicknamed him Delores. Not that he cared much now; his heartfelt prayer was to get away from the loading dock before they blew it up by bouncing one of these boxes with a skull and crossbones stenciled on it a little too hard! But by handling the boxes carefully, and working like a beast, he had accomplished a fifth of what they had done in the same time. He was soaked with sweat, his hands were raw, he was dead tired, and they were horsing around on the dock like kids at recess.

He had been taken to school by three scarecrows he now looked up to as if they were gods of labor. Oh, to walk away! But there was no bus home till five.

While his erstwhile work mates held a spitting contest with another crew between the cars, Miles moped along the dock brooding on his stalwart father who had ridden the caboose of a stock train from the Nebraska homestead to Chicago with a load of cattle and a gun on his hip at the age of fourteen. He really might have walked back to Building Seven and punched out if the bull-necked one called Stutt had not got nudged off the dock in the horseplay and swallowed a mouthful of Copenhagen with juice when he landed. Before the new load came, Stutt turned green, vomited on the track and staggered off to the infirmary. When Miles, intending to quietly disappear, asked where the rest room was, the atmosphere had suddenly changed, and Tiny said, "I'm goin' that way. Come along, hot shot." and led him down through the building past the assembly lines where the furnaces were

236

annealing and drawing out the brass cups for shell casings. When they went through the packing lines where the finished shells were slotted into belts and bandoliers, Tiny pointed to a couple of boys Miles' age pushing rocker-wheeled buggies the size of shopping carts full of loose cartridges, "Look here, speed ball! Last month one of these guys bumped into something and spilled half a dozen shells on the cement. One hit on the firing pin and went off and shot him--yeah, dead. A high school kid got to be a war casualty without leaving home! That's what scared the shit out of Nervous Nelly. And also the inspectors. But that's not *our* shells. Look there how they pack 'em into the liners? The webbing gives them a cushion, and they go in sideways to how you throw 'em. They wouldn't go off, probably even if you dropped a box off the roof of the car! Don't try it, but *relax*! Ain't nothing going to happen if you sling 'em!"

When they went back to the dock the pallet was in the door. Tiny and Moe now began to show a paternal interest in his work. They still called him "shit-for-brains," but in a friendly way, and Tiny took time to walk him through the process: If you were starting a new car, you had four steps to take, and then, provided you were an experienced loader and hadn't a hangover, and didn't have an inspector looking over your shoulder, you *slung* it two-hand underhand. The box hit the floor and skipped right into its slot. The next row, you slung the box so it snugged up against its outside mate till you left a five-inch space down the center, which the carpenter would block.

At first he still flinched when he did it. But that passed. And Moe showed him how to swing a ninety-four pound box to the top row by using your momentum, like bucking baled hay onto a wagon, and though a box of shells was three times as heavy, if you took that last furious step and swung it up using the swing's momentum to leverage it like a judo throw, you could slip it in up there as gently as a case of wine.

He would soon learn that when the inspectors came to the docks, as they did every ten days, the loaders went back to carrying their boxes and tucking them in like babies. The government men didn't like slinging, but there was a certain collusion. Everyone knew it was safe if you didn't drop one from the top row, and the Pacific was crying for shells, and slinging them loaded the trains five times faster. So word of the inspectors' approach mysteriously preceded them.

Sometime that first afternoon, as he began to produce a little work, and Stutt came back, and his three companions thawed a bit, he learned the reason a newcomer was despised was because a daily quota of four cars a day per crew had been established with the bosses in order to retain experienced crews on the killing job. Any time four cars were finished, the crew had done its day's work. Ace slingers might work right through lunch and finish their quota by four o'clock and take a nap on the stores in the warehouse till the truck came at five. They would go back to Building Seven and punch out and then punch right back in for the swing shift.

Both Tiny and Moe, who were old enough for the service, but had families or deferments for medical problems, counted on the rest they took after their day's quota to replenish their energies to do another shift. They would do this several days a week, boosting their overtime pay to a dollar-five an hour, and to a dollar-forty for a seventh day. Today, by filling Miles' rows when he fell behind, and calling him "shit-for-brains," in a more genial tone, they still managed to finish four cars by a quarter of five.

On the way home while Race described the knockout girls he would be working with in the kitchen of building 1, Miles sat in a coma. At home, he fell asleep over his dinner.

But he scrounged a pair of old garden gloves from the basement, and against all odds made the bus on time the next day. He was stiff and sore, but that day he drew a crew not much more experienced than himself. They struggled and jostled and cursed, but by the end of the day they had stopped running into each other at the pallet and were getting into the synchronized rhythm of that curious dance of the real slingers. They made their quota, and before five had the satisfaction of seeing their car sealed and shunted out for the ammo train to the West Coast.

As summer turned hot and the slingers started to toss their shirts out on the dock and work bare chested, a cluster of women on break from the cafeteria convened at the back doors of the kitchens to watch their half-naked bodies flexing over the shells in the doors of the sweltering cars: Miles and a blond fellow named Louis Freestead of his same height and build, who was from the town of Jewel north of Ames, and a guy from Redfield Miles had played football against, and a burned-out middleweight fighter named Birge, regularly made a crew off that dock. Birge said some of these girls were window shopping and would make a point of sitting down to eat lunch with you if you looked friendly and kept an open place for them at your table and would ride home in your car, if you had one.

So, he learned about the aristocracy of the bottom. Only a couple of dozen stubborn boys and hard-bitten old hoboes out of the ranks of the Depression unemployed worked at the narrow neck of the production flow in the sweltering cars, and kept all the shells made in the five factory buildings moving to the war. That summer, every bullet a Marine fired in New Guinea passed through these few shell slingers' hands, so they were told. He didn't have a car, but when a pretty Drake girl introduced herself in the cafeteria line, saying she had watched him work, he felt like a member of a fist-pumping elite.

But the first two weeks, Miles had nothing left for what J. Arthur called lollygagging. He stumbled off the bus in a daze of exhaustion and went to bed nursing a dozen small injuries and hoarding strength for the next day's job. J. Arthur and Ferne stood back and silently wondered. Of course they had little idea, but knew a transformation of kind, not degree, was taking place in him. They saw little of him; he was late home for dinner, silently ate the meals Ferne kept hot for him and went to bed. But, as the mid-day heat began to run the mercury in the box cars to a hundred-and-five, and the crews worked like devils in the mornings to be almost finished when the heat clamped down, he was able to loaf on the stores till five, and he begin to come out of his funk at home.

Like Rip Van Winkle, he found things changed. Rainwater and Mitchell had gone to the Alcan. Fairy had been elected to a high state office at the convention of the Rainbow, and a picture of her with a little gavel in her hand, wearing a low-cut gown and a string of her grandmother's pearls, her face serious and magisterial, appeared in the *News*. It said she had served in all the lower offices, and now had been voted something like State Grand Love. She came home from country club duty with her cousin by the pool in Lincoln looking like a burnished idol. Had guys there noticed this body in a skimpy swim suit? Guess! Had she flirted? Maybe. Had she dated strange, crude Nebraska boys? You bet! Had she smooched? Sloe-eyed, she smiled her private smile and let his imagination run wild, teasing his anguish till he clammed up. He would not ask about her Rainbow office because thinking of her in a life apart from him intimidated him. In these realms she remained older, more of a person in her own right than he; he felt it and was wary.

240

This was when he forgot about Bruce, and they began to go everywhere as a couple. Deferring to his work, she let him set a lazy pace; they would swim in the evening or go to a show with the summer kids. A boy named Dick Schinn had his parents' Olds at his beck and call, and with his girl, Margaret, took the crowd to the Paramount in Des Moines where Clyde McCoy did a show with a movie trailer. The next week, it was Bob Crosby, "*The Big Noise from Winnetka*," but, as Miles was the only one in the crowd doing hard labor, he made them drop him and Fairy home by ten.

Then they sat down on the grass in her backyard, and he fell asleep with his head in her lap, and she sat very still and leaned on her arms and watched the stars for a long time. He was mortified when he woke. But she assured him he must get his sleep because of his dangerous work. Though his stories about hassles in the cars--how Stutt fell asleep on a load and got sealed in and was being shunted for the West Coast before his frantic hammering tipped off a guard--made her drowsy. She said she could understand his job by the new breadth of his shoulders, and Liz Sinden said Fairy told her he was turning into an Adonis. He would have preferred Odysseus, but he looked up Adonis in the library's encyclopedia and the illustration was okay except for the vines in his hair.

Before Bruce Cross showed up on his delay-en-route to Europe in early August, there began to be erogenous spikes in their moods that were different from the casual romances of the other couples in the crowd. In Dick Schinn's car one night coming from a movie, three couples in a kissing contest while Dick drove solemnly with his arm around Margaret and kept the time on the dashboard clock while the others did movie kisses, Miles and Fairy kissed for ten miles. Soon, at the pool, he taught her under-water kissing, and they dove to the bottom where their bodies could brush and glide against each other. And

241

if you were an older person with sexual experience, watching them for five minutes told you much about their future, but they lacked that experience, and thought it was still play.

When they stayed home and spent the evening together at one house or the other, he got out the portable drawing board and Conte crayon he had bought with his first check and drew her sitting in J. Arthur's chair with her feet on the hassock. He vetted most of the drawings with Fairy and let her take the rejects home to pin up in her room while he backed the best ones with art board and sent them off with short-short stories to *Colliers*, or *Saturday Evening Post*. He always enclosed a stamped, self-addressed envelope in which the rejection slips came back, though some would not come back till after Corregidor.

He had discovered an artist named Petty who did full-page color paintings of luscious, scantily clad girls for *Esquire*, and late one afternoon he brought a new box of colored chalk, pastels, to Fairy's backyard and showed her the full page of the Petty girl sitting languorously on a diving board. They talked about him doing a picture of her like that, and he suggested that she put on her bathing suit and model for him in the same pose on the chaise lounge. "What about the water?"

"I can imagine water," he said.

She had just been shopping for her college wardrobe in Des Moines with Gladys and had bought a new-style bathing suit to replace the old brown one-piece that had two round faded spots on its bottom. The new one was lavender blue with white polka dots and was a two-piece that left a daring patch of midriff bare. A girl named Chili Williams had become the most popular pinup with G.I.'s all over the world in such a suit, and Fairy was eager for him to see her in it, so she went in the house and changed into it and put on makeup and high heels *a' la* Chili Williams, and made a half-facetious grand entrance

242

down the back steps and solemnly pirouetted before him. He put his hand to his eyes and imitated a falling seizure on the grass, and she arranged herself like the Petty girl, leaning back on the chaise lounge with one shoe dangling from her toes over the imaginary water, and he sat cross-legged in the grass below her chair with the drawing board on his knees and worked on the sketch till the sun went down and the shadow spoiled the light. Then he stopped and put the chalk away.

While they examined the drawing, they went on talking in a perfunctory way about things they hadn't ever talked about: Had she ever been in love? She frowned for a long time interrogating a deep imaginary past and finally shook her head.

He grinned, "Present company excepted?"

"You've got a nerve!" she said. "Bruce never talked like that!"

"Then, he never said he loved you?"

"Well?" she said and looked directly in his eyes.

His lips went dry, and his Adam's apple stuck. Mute as of old, he suddenly got to his knees and took her hand, and then seemed to notice that he was in the traditional posture of a man proposing marriage, and froze that way looking truly caught and miserable.

She released him with a chuckle, "Bruce and I never mention love."

"But did you ever feel like that...with *anyone*?" .

She looked at him with a changing expression, "When we moved here, I didn't know anyone, she said slowly, "No boys except my cousins, and no one here at all. And you know what? *You* were the first boy I ever noticed."

"Me?"

The widow Nelda next door, who had been watching them through her kitchen curtains, now appeared with a watering can among the shrubs along the lot line in the twilight.

"Yes, *you*. Do you remember that girl you had a flaming crush on one year, Joann Duncan? Right there across the street. From my window I used to watch you come by and stare at her house.

"For minutes at a time you'd stand, and I would just will you to turn around and notice me. Once you stood such a long time and nothing happened, and you finally threw a snowball at her door."

Her voice suddenly sank to a whisper, and the woman in the bushes stopped watering and stood still.

"Because you seemed so miserable, and of course I was lonely, I'd say, 'Let him notice me!' And one night after my prayers, I said 'Love!' not A-men, just '*Love!*' many times. But don't get any ideas, bud. It didn't mean any one in particular."

Miles bowed his head against her hip, and the widow, who had been silent, suddenly cleared her throat like a ratchet.

"Oh!" Fairy said, and put her bare foot on the ground and tugged his hand to jump to her feet, but he tipped over and pulled her down with him, and they rolled over in the grass laughing like zanies till he let go and she jumped up.

"Evening, Nelda!" Fairy cried, and turned her back on Miles and bent over and switched her hips. "Brush me off!" she commanded, "You've got me all grassy!"

He took out his handkerchief and flirted it over her polka-dot bottom. Nelda's face gaped like an open bin and she made a hissing noise and went in her back door.

"Poor, sex-starved little old thing!" Fairy said, and turned toward the house. Their moment was far away now, and he picked up his drawing and they said goodnight rather distantly. But as he sauntered home with the drawing board under his arm, he kept saying "*Love!*" under his breath.

<u>5</u>

Mania

Miles didn't see Fairy again till Monday night, August 2. Her new office in Rainbow occasionally required her to attend neighboring chapters, and she had been to Ft. Dodge over the weekend. At loose ends Sunday, he had skipped church and put in an overtime shift at the plant to repair the damage his Saturday spending spree in Des Moines had done to his new bank account.

Fairy's admission that she had noticed him before he knew who she was had sent him topsy-turvy into a weekend of bliss. He was still boisterous on Sunday and worked in the box car most of the afternoon bellowing *Praise the Lord and Pass the Ammunition* as he threw the shells, and at the end of the shift, the rest of the crew ganged up on him and tossed him off the dock. It was great fun.

Why ever Fairy had granted him the privileged view of her secret heart he could not imagine. An only child brings to a first love the solitary's closet suspicion of his unworthiness of anyone's affection but his parents', and Fairy's gust of candor had flooded his volatile soul with an aura like a religious vastation. What the widow Nelda described to her friends as their brazen exhibition was to Miles a kind of sacrament of inunction. So, he had still been trailing the shreds of these pink clouds when he and Race hitchhiked to Des Moines on Saturday. They had bought a dozen secondhand records at Gibson's, the storefront record emporium on Grand, and later walked into Gust Manoles' "*Des Moines' Elite Men's Tailor,*" and Miles ordered a custom-made suit (like the suits he saw the stars of the swing world wearing in *Downbeat* magazine), a two-button, single breasted, fingertip length, built-up-shouldered, double-vented suit of fine light weight blue-gray wool worsted with full lapels (while they still had material for them), and two pairs--one matching, one contrasting--of peg-topped, high-rise, full-kneed, fifteen-inch-cuff trousers.

Gust's tailors stood around watching the fitting with Race, and saying, "Yes, reversed pleats, very hep!" in their New Yorky voices. "Like we made for Fiorito when he played the Val Air," they said, egging him on, because they saw he was a boy who didn't even know what "Left dress or right dress?" meant. It would be $59.95 with vest, a week's pay with overtime, just like that, and Gust threw in a tie to make up for not being able to get it right out. He would have to come back for a final fitting in ten days.

Well, they both were flush now. Since he had been at the plant, he had spent little but for bus fare and work gloves and a couple of dates to the movies. So, after the fitting, they went back to Gibson's and bought two sets of tickets to the special appearance of Louis Armstrong and his band at Riverview Park on Friday. It was a one-nighter for the band between dates in Minneapolis and Kansas City. Tickets were almost sold out, and the manager warned them that they would pay double if they waited till the middle of the week. Miles had a master plan already: He would get the Merc and they would make a foursome and go early and have time for the amusement park and then to Satchmo, who everyone said you had to dig this time around because his lip was going and he would be over the hill if you waited till after the war.

And that was the end of the bliss.

On Sunday, a new notice on the bulletin board beside the time clock said he'd been rotated to the swing shift starting Friday night. He got with several others who were being shifted too and they cussed the bosses, but that was all they could do.

Plunged in desolation, he looked up Race Sunday night and gave him his two tickets. Race hadn't asked a date yet, and he took them on speculation. Maybe he could find someone else with a car to double with.

Monday evening, Miles went around to Fairy's and it took him a long time to explain that he had gotten them tickets to Louis Armstrong, but they wouldn't be able to use them because he would go on night shift Friday night. When she took the news with apparent indifference, he began to feel something coming: They were in the yard, and the widow came out again with her watering can, and Fairy picked up the blanket and the radio and led him inside to sit on the glider. The back door was open and Gladys was in the kitchen. Fairy had moved down to sleep on the porch during the hot spell, and her sheets and pillow were on one end of the daybed. He wanted to tease her about inviting him into her bedroom, but it wasn't a jokey moment. Till Gladys turned off the light and left the kitchen, they sat like a couple in an old daguerreotype. Then he tried to kiss her, and she straightened him right up and said, "Don't!" a token slap, but he began to sense that something had made last Friday night a hundred years ago. "You said you used to always...?"

"Well, I don't anything *always!*" *S*he looked away, and took a deep breath, "Speaking of which, Bruce will be home on leave Friday, and we've had a date for his first night home for a long time."

"Aw! *That's* it," he groaned.

She looked at her hands, "It was made a long time before you and I started seeing each other, and I couldn't cancel it now."

He was silent.

"Miles?" she said. "Don't sulk. When I started dating you, Charlene told Bruce about us, and I wrote him back and told him I didn't belong to *anyone*. Which I still

248

don't. And that's all there is to it...my dear," like a woman speaking to a boy.

"Then what did you mean about noticing *me*?"

"Something I wish you'd forget."

"Well, you can't unsay it!".

"After all, he's going overseas," she said at last, "and he's my classmate home on his last leave--and it's just one tiny thing I can do..."

"For the war effort," he said bitterly.

"You shouldn't begrudge," she said. "I'll only see him Friday and Saturday. He's on special orders to leave on Sunday."

"Saturday *too*?"

"Saturday Mom's having the Crosses and a couple of kids from his class over for dinner. You're too young." she said, as if it were facetious.

"All *right* then!" he said, and stood up.

When he ignored the hand she extended, her voice took on a note of sweet reason, "Miles, just try to see it that we're giving up two days of the whole month we'll have together before I leave for school--and Bruce sounds so really lost. Most of his friends are in service, and he doesn't even have any idea what we'll do Friday. He hasn't had a date with a girl since he left."

"When did he say that?"

"On the phone last night."

"So, what *will* you do then--just go somewhere and smooch!"

She gave him a chilling look, and stood gazing out the screen toward the dark street where the headlights of a car were turning toward the river. "Don't you worry about *us*." she said evenly. "Bruce is too much of a gentleman."

He made a strangulated laugh, and an idea seemed to pop right out of his mouth without touching his brain: "Listen!" he said, "What if Race asks Char, and you and Bruce take my tickets and double with them?"

"Oh, *Miles*, would you?" she said, and turned around and hugged him. "You're a really good-hearted person!"

"Oh, yeah!" He opened the screen door.

"We'll pay you for the tickets."

"Forget it But there will be hidden costs, my dear." he lisped like Peter Lorre.

So, he had surprised himself and set Bruce up a swell night. *"Take my girl, please, and I'll throw in the tickets!"* He had done it for the war effort, hadn't he? But when he got home he flung himself on his bed and lay there seeing himself as the guy with the big nose who stands under the window of the woman he loves and woos her for his tongue-tied buddy. "Chump of the week!" he said, and pounded the pillow.

But after a while he got up and phoned Race, who hadn't done anything about the tickets yet, and prompted him to ask Charlene. Miles would take the tickets to Fairy. In a little while Race called back. He had gotten a date with Char, and Bruce would drive.

For Miles, it all worked out as smoothly as shooting yourself in the foot. Friday Bruce drove Fairy to Riverview Park with Race and Charlene in the back seat while Miles went to work in the box cars till midnight, imagining Bruce pawing Fairy in the Tunnel of Love.

At one a.m., when the bus let him off in front of his house, he put his lunch pail on the steps and walked around the block to see if Bruce's car was parked in front of her house. It wasn't. As he moped past, staring hard enough to suck the nails out of the siding, he suddenly knew they weren't in there. And he could see they weren't in Ray Wing's old Chevy sitting in the open garage with one door open. He hung around in the dark by the corner of the garage waiting for them, imagining that Bruce had dropped Race and Char off and taken Fairy to the lovers' lane in the

250

park. (And she would *go*! And God knew how *far*, just because girls suddenly believed they owed something to a guy going overseas!) He smoked his last cigarette at two a.m. and dragged himself home to bed, none the wiser.

The next day was his day off, and he sought out Race and bought his coffee at the Southside Drug, and the method in his madness began to dawn on him: He had really given them the tickets so Race could report on what they did:

"--Yeah, we went to the midway before the dance. No, Fairy didn't hug Bruce in the Tunnel of Love. And no, they didn't dance all that close. Yeah, he put his arm around her on the way home. But we didn't go and park anywhere; She made him drive her straight home, and we sat in front of the house--and talked. Hot time!"

"Talked what?"

"Telling Bruce all the home front news....He hadn't heard the scandal of the year."

"Jimmy Johnson and Lois?"

"Homecoming King and Queen make handsome pregnant pair." Race snorted and butted out his cigarette, "Nine months from queen of the May to a crying shame."

"I thought I saw Lois downtown with the kid in a stroller, " Miles said.

"Fairy kind of doused the fires of love." Race said. "Made Char decide she wanted to go right home."

"Did Bruce kiss Fairy goodnight?" Race shook his head. But, Miles had to persist, like touching his tongue to an aching tooth: "If she took him to the screened porch you probably couldn't see *what* they did."

"Well, they went to the front, but I can't say I was watching." Race butted his Chesterfield in his cup and got up from the booth. "Cool down, man! You're getting into your werewolf phase again. Your canines are growing! Get some sleep."

251

Miles sat in the booth after Race left. So she had been home in bed all the time! But he didn't feel reassured. Maybe tonight Bruce would try to make her quit seeing him.

Gnawing on the thought as he left the store, he almost ran into Bruce Cross coming in with some of the people from the courthouse.

Bruce was a tall young man who looked older than his years in his enlisted man's sun tans with his brown G.I. tie tucked into the front of his shirt and a rifleman's blue badge on his chest. He wore his service school's patch and a corporal's stripes on his sleeves. His cheeks still bore the pock marks of childhood acne, and his complexion had an indoor pallor despite the Texas sunburn on his hands. Miles thought unkindly that his service glasses made him look like an accountant.

But, as their eyes met, Miles had a flashback of Bruce leading an overnight bivouac of young Scouts one cold March day five years ago. They had hiked to a little Scout cabin dug out of a hill in the timber north of town. It had a stove in the center and no electricity and upper and lower bunks around three walls. In the middle of the night John Hall's eggs fell out of his pack in the upper bunk and broke one by one on the head of Jack McCleary in the bunk below. Then chaos in the dark, with someone jumping out of bed and touching the hot stove. But he remembered the ancient authority with which Bruce had quelled the uproar--and himself as a baby-minded tenderfoot wanting to go home to his own bed.

Now, in the doorway, there was that momentary silent click that happens when the image of the woman two men covet stands between them. Then they shook hands and exchanged a couple of strange-dog pleasantries and passed on.

But after nine that night, sitting in the breakfast nook, studiously ignoring Wings' dinner party and working on the sketch of Fairy in the Petty Girl pose reclining on a diving board, he still couldn't stop thinking about Bruce as his mentor. He didn't want to compete with Bruce. When they went on the Scout bivouac that spring he had been a young boy looking up to Bruce as their leader, someone so much bigger and older than he that they weren't even in the same generation. Now, suddenly, was he Bruce's rival? He was sixteen and Bruce what? Bruce would get out of service at, maybe twenty-one? Old enough to earn a living and support a wife and family, get G.I.benefits President Roosevelt had promised service men last month, a G. I. loan or a college education at government expense. And where would Miles be?

Would he be eighteen, nineteen? He tried to take a snap inventory of what was in his head that he could use to make a life for Fairy. He could do one single job of man's work, heft ammo boxes, and that job would be finished at the Duration. Otherwise, he could write the stories and get the rejections, and try to draw pictures: And--he almost forgot--he could play the *flute*! He saw himself trying to support Fairy playing the flute! On a corner in Des Moines? With a tin cup!

Suddenly, he tossed the drawing board in the corner and went out through the back hall where Ferne had finally given up pestering J. Arthur to paper the yellow walls and had started to do it herself. He noticed the new paper had bluebirds on it, and she had set up her table and snapped a plumb line on the wall where she planned to start tomorrow.

He went down the alley, and when he got to Wing's garage he could see the party was winding down; a car had left and another was leaving. He crossed the yard and silently opened the screen door and stole into the dark back porch. In a flicker of heat lightning from the west he could see Fairy's dog, Sparky, lying on Fairy's sheets folded on the end of the daybed. When he silently closed the screen, the dog wagged his tail and dipped his head ingratiatingly, as if apologizing for sleeping on her bedding.

The curtains of the kitchen window were drawn, but they only came halfway up. From eye level he could look right in without being seen if he kept out of the bar of kitchen light that angled across the porch. He saw Gladys Wing was the only one in the kitchen. At the counter across the room with her back to the window, she was scraping plates and stacking them on the drain board. After a moment she went into the dining room and the kitchen was empty.

He stood expectantly watching the empty room like the set of a play after the curtain has opened but before the actors have entered. Several minutes passed. Then Fairy came in carrying some dishes. She was followed by Bruce. They set the dishes on the counter where Gladys had been, and stood talking with their backs to him. He could hear Bruce's voice droning, but could not understand a word because a noisy little breeze had sprung up and bustled through the porch whirring the slats of the half-raised blinds. The kitchen window was the screen of a silent movie: the lighted room, the two actors' averted gestures no doubt expressing what they were saying, but merely inscrutable signs to him. There seemed to be some sort of impasse. Bruce went to the doorway and looked into the dining room and came back and continued, using his hands more urgently in awkward, choppy gestures.

On the porch, the screen door suddenly slapped, and Miles jumped and looked over his shoulder. By the glow of a distant lightning flash he saw the dog hurrying away across the yard toward his house in the garage. The tops of the trees were bending.

In the kitchen, Bruce made a gesture of open-handed appeal while Fairy went on looking down at the dirty plate she had put on the counter. Bruce stood a

254

moment biting his lip, then grasped her shoulders and turned her toward him and crushed her to his chest.

Miles clenched his teeth. Fairy's hands rose and described an uncertain little flutter behind Bruce's back before settling on his shoulders as if embracing a friend of the deceased. As Bruce kissed her throat, Fairy's face, looking blindly straight at Miles, was so mournful that he let out a kind of primal victory whoop, and Bruce, who must have heard it, straightened and started to turn toward the window.

Just then the thunder from the lightning that had driven the dog out of the porch arrived, and a blast of wind and flying drops of rain rammed through the porch, upsetting the candle on the table by the daybed and lifting up a page of newspaper to make a ghostly flight across the porch.

The town's electricity went off, and the kitchen was suddenly dark. Miles heard Fairy yell for Bruce to help her lower the porch blinds, and he lunged out through the screen door just as she opened the door. He missed the step and fell into Gladys's flower bed. He knew he made a racket, but the screen door slammed and he heard Fairy on the porch say, "Sparky runs for the garage when it storms."

Bruce untied the slat blind on the other side of the porch, and it came down with a slap just as the rain came in a solid sheet. Where Miles was, in the flower bed on all fours, rainwater began to run off the porch roof like a waterfall on his head. His hands were soon planted in little pools of mud. His glasses started to slide down his nose, and he smeared his face with mud when he caught them and pushed them up. Above him, the two were lowering the south blind.

Fairy cried, "Let's go!"

Just as a bolt of lightning hit a tree somewhere up the hill, and a great white phosphorus blossom transfixed the courthouse tower like an abstraction, reflex made Miles jump up face to face with Fairy frozen inside the screen with a pile of sheets in her arms. Then the huge crash of it came, and Gladys Wing screeched, "We're all going to the basement!" And Miles took off for the alley. Halfway across the yard, the rain let up and he slowed to a walk, limping along and wiping his glasses on the tail of his shirt. By the time he reached home it had stopped, but his clothes were soaked and his saddle shoes (so long on layaway) were thickly layered with the mud from Gladys's flower bed.

In the back hall he stripped off his clothes and shoes and bundled the stuff up and felt his way through the dark kitchen in his underpants. As he climbed the stairs, the lights came on again and Ferne leaned over the banister above. "A tornado touched down near Waukee! Good gracious! Where have *you* been?" "Nowhere," he said.

Fairy *had* seen him, but when he took his glasses off, the face in the bathroom mirror looked like Al Jolson doing *Mammy,* with white eye sockets and the rest smeared with mud. "Maybe," he thought. He put his clothes over a towel bar and ran a bath.

On the sleeping porch after he turned out the light, he knelt down beside the old bed Uncle Bill style, as he had been doing to try to give his prayers for Nile Kinnick more upward momentum. He now added a codicil asking God not to let Bruce's uniform seduce Fairy. But he couldn't think of a way of putting it that wouldn't sound too selfish to God, and finally left it out, and crawled into the old bed and listened to the storm grumbling away east into Polk County. When the agony of wanting unclenched, he dreamed that Bruce was holding an umbrella over Fairy to protect her from a storm, and the wind picked up the umbrella like a parachute and carried Bruce away.

Painted Stockings

1943 ad in the Dallas County News: ***Genuine rayon stockings, $1.14 while they last!***

Monday morning Adel still looked like an unmade bed. Little had been cleaned up Sunday and there were torn-off branches in all the yards. An old tree was still sprawled across Main Street up the hill, and the street crew was just starting to saw it up. But in the Midwest, after a big summer storm the next few mornings are unusually dewy and brilliant, and everything sparkled and smelled green, though it was going to be hot later.

The moment he opened his eyes, he started worrying again about Fairy recognizing him. Later, when Ferne postponed bossing him around with the wallpaper long enough to answer the phone, he dodged out and headed for Wings'.

Though he didn't know it, what he had been watching from the porch Saturday night was the prelude to an understanding Fairy and Bruce were coming to. Bruce had declared that it was only right, since he was going "in harm's way," that she should be free to date others. It wasn't what he really wanted, but something told him it was what *she* did, and since gallant gestures were in his nature, he said it first. The sudden storm had relieved her of the obligation to make a token protest. And later, when they parted, feeling liberated from the tight little box that everyone had locked her up in just because she had been dating Bruce when he went into the service, she begged off going to the train with his parents and Charlene to see him off.

So, early Sunday, the Crosses stopped at Wings' on their way out of town. The pair had stood beside the car, and Bruce had taken her hand, and she had just begun to feel a stitch of contrition about sending him off to war, as it were, empty-handed when the Mercury crawled by, Miles Morgan rubbernecking at the wheel. He looked, she thought, as though he somehow thought he had the right, and she was furious.

Now, Monday morning she was in no mood to suffer Miles gladly when he barged in just as she was lying on her stomach on the living room floor with the skirt of her old dress hiked up to her bottom while Gibsy finished painting her legs with the patented leg makeup girls were now using when they ran out of stockings. Gibsy had just put aside the *"STOCKINGS IN A BOTTLE,"* and was making a botch of trying to draw a straight seam line with eyebrow pencil down the back of Fairy's leg when Gladys let Miles in the back door and started regaling him about the family adventure during the storm. She hadn't seen the prowler herself, but his darned old body print was still there Sunday morning where he had fallen and flattened her flowers. She thought it was "that Bugger Diamond."

Miles entered the living room and caught Fairy still holding up a hand mirror and critiquing Gibsy's seamline over her shoulder. He burst out laughing, and she snapped, "If you're such an artist, *you* do my seams!"

He appraised her legs from different angles and pulled his lip and went, "Um-*Hmmm!*" But when she said, "Cut that out!" he suddenly snapped his fingers and ordered Gibsy to bring him the colored chalk and the string attached to Fairy's blackboard. Then he took the blue chalk and rubbed down the string and made Gibsy hold it on the top of Fairy's thigh while he pressed the other end against her ankle and plucked it so that it snapped her leg like a rubber band. "Eureka!" he said, and when she held up the mirror, there was a straight blue line down her leg from the hem of her skirt to her heel. He chalked the string again, and they did her other leg, and then he stood up and told Gibsy to follow the lines with the eyebrow pencil. *"You'll*

258

have to do it. It wouldn't be decent for me to draw up there," he grinned, "unless she insists."

"Don't you dare!"

"Say, 'Thank you!' girls."

She could have killed him, lying there like an Exhibit A while he paced around gawking at her legs. Gibsy, too, was fuming. She worked on the seam in silence a minute, and then said, exclusively to Fairy, as though resuming a conversation they had been having earlier about the midway at Riverview Park--"Some guy controls that wind machine behind the scenes and he turns it on when a girl steps over it and blows your skirt up," she said. "Then that bunch of sex fiends hanging around just hoot and whistle! Didn't they ogle *you*?"

"About a dozen," Fairy said, "Service guys. They whistled and went 'Woo-woo!'"

"Weren't you mortified?"

"Yah, and..." Fairy tipped the mirror to look at Miles. "And kind of flattered. Weren't you?"

Gibsy put down the eyebrow pencil and made a face. "Well, *I* will wear slacks the next time!"

Last year in a parlor game Miles had kissed Gibsy ardently, but now that he had fallen for Fairy, Gibsy assumed a disdainful air toward him. "And did Bruce stare at your legs, too?" she asked wickedly, "I'll *bet* he did!"

"Not a blink! He looked me straight in the eye. Bruce is an Eagle Scout, you know," Fairy added seriously.

"Aw nuts!" Miles said and his face turned red, "*I* wouldn't look."

"Nyah-hah!" Gibsy snapped, "You can't take your eyeballs off Fairy's legs now! They're just ready to pop out on the floor an' roll around!"

"They are not!" And suddenly Miles bent over and grasped Fairy's ankles and lifted her up feet first.

"Put me *down*!" Fairy's skirt fell over her head, and when her long hair brushed the floor, she tried to hold up her skirt to hide her panties. "Put me down, *Gorilla*!"

"Look me in the eye, Gibsy!" he commanded, and continued to hold Fairy upside down, gritting his teeth while his face turned purple and Fairy gave up on her skirt and did a hand stand. Then she was face-to-face with his saddle shoes, and they were splotched with mud. A prowler in saddle shoes--she had already guessed. Now she knew. "It was *you*!" she said, as he lowered her to the floor with great care. "*Mother*!" she cried.

"I didn't, did I, Gibsy?" he said. "I looked you in the eye!"

"It *was* you!"

Gladys came in the front door and saw Fairy on her stomach with her skirt hiked up, "What's going on here!"

"Mother, they've done my seams!" Fairy said sweetly, and Gladys, easily put off, bent over and examined them. "Why, I thought you'd never....They're straight as a dye!" she pulled Fairy's skirt down and smiled vaguely at Miles and went into the dining room.

Though Fairy sat up and gave him the look that always made him wither, he had now held her upside down and he felt self-congratulatory and outsized. "Tell her, *Gibsy!*"

"Peripheral vision!" Gibsy said sourly, but the spillover of the private look Fairy gave Miles suddenly made three a crowd, and she soon got up and went home.

They went out on the front porch and sat down together on the swing. She sat and swung her bare feet and they admired her painted legs. She held them out. These matchless legs were now three colors: a reddish rayon-brown that made the band of sun-tanned flesh above seem pale; and above the tan line, the alabaster white of her hips, the vivid impression of which--Gibsy was right--was burned on his retinas.

They sat side by side, and he put his arm over the back of the swing without touching her. It was getting hot, and when she looked out into the sunshine toward the park, the heat made the brick gate of the Undefeated Team shimmer at the end of the street.

She could sense some kind of seismic shift in her feelings. His arm over her shoulder now seemed like a shelter. When she had recognized the shoes, she had thought there was nothing so childish as him spying on her and falling off the porch in the mud. She would have laughed him to scorn, but he had lifted her up like a little rabbit and held her out in the air and put her softly down. So, instead, her heart betrayed her and glowed warm.

And the balance wheel turned to his side, without either of them premeditating it or knowing what had happened. The intuition that had prompted her--the older and more mature--to take the lead in this affair had crumbled because she didn't want to lead any more. He was still like a runaway boy, and a lot the fool, but he was a fool for *her.* And after all, she, too, was an only child. So she gave it up. She closed her eyes and leaned her head against his arm. "Do you still go golfing in the park in the mornings?"

"Not since I've been on the night shift," he said. "I've been getting up late."

"Since detasseling's over, I'm free till school," she said. "If I went to bed early, could I go out with you some morning and you teach me golf? If you wanted to, I mean?" "Well, we could!" he said doubtfully, "I've got all day to sleep. Can you get up?" She nodded. "At five-five thirty, that early?" She nodded,

"Your folks?"

"Be quiet and scratch on my screen, and I'll get dressed and come out. No one will know, if we're back before seven....But stay out of the flower bed." They laughed. Gladys called Fairy to lunch, and they both stood up and agreed he would scratch on the porch screen at dawn.

The noon whistle went off. It wound up and held a high pitch that shrieked over the valley then wound slowly down. Unlike an air raid siren, in Adel it merely meant the noon meal for men who went home for "dinner", or put up the "closed till one" sign and went to Woods' Diner or Mack's Cafe.

Birthday Gifts

Elsewhere--it seemed, everywhere but here--as our deep summer slid imperceptibly through tropic heat toward fall--the War, like a roller coaster slowly topping its climb, gradually began the downhill acceleration toward the end; and since January--marked by the momentous German debacle at Stalingrad and the succession of Red Army tank victories which drove the Wehrmacht back to the Dnieper--started a landslide of worldwide defeats that would cripple the Axis in the next year.

In May the Afrika Corps was destroyed, and the Germans were finally driven from that continent. More submarines were being killed than could be replaced, and Admiral Doenitz terminated the submarine war. The U.S Army entered Palermo. Mussolini was deposed. In the Pacific, General Douglas MacArthur and the navy had started to open the island-hopping campaign at Guadalcanal.

In that South Pacific Theater, on August first, in the Blackett Strait near its Rendova base, an American torpedo boat, PT 109, was rammed and split in two by a Japanese destroyer, dumping the crew into the water. Two men were lost in the collision and never found, but the rest, with several injured, clung to the wreckage and made landfall on tiny desert islands. After four days of perilous swimming between islands in an attempt to avoid the Japanese and make contact with American rescue teams, a future President of the United States--then a PT boat officer clad only in his underwear, and with nothing but his youthful sailing experience on Cape Cod to guide him--led the survivors in saving the wounded and contacting rescuers. On August 8, all were returned safely to the Rendova base.

We had not yet heard of this adventure, but one day at lunch Miles mentioned a story in the *Tribune* about a hospital plane that was crippled by Japanese shell fire as it took off from Henderson Field, Guadalcanal, and later crash-landed on a deserted reef. After ten days clinging to the wreckage of their plane, the twenty-five wounded and the plane's crew were picked up by an American destroyer. All survived.

Miles told J. Arthur and Ferne the story and said that something like this must have happened to Nile Kinnick, only Jun hadn't been found yet.

Ferne shook her head. She had been a close friend of Francis Kinnick when they lived across the street, and she had silently suffered much more anguish over her friend's loss than Miles had. "I don't expect they'll ever find Jun now." She frowned and suddenly lashed out against certain county families who were said to have pulled tricks to get their sons into jobs that deferred them from service.

J. Arthur looked up from his empty plate and said, "Now, Ferne, that's bridge club talk. For one, I know Jack was deferred against his will. He's a tool setter. They are indispensable."

"What about *him*?" she said and looked fiercely at Miles. "He'll be seventeen next week, and he's loading shells. If he goes back to it next summer, and his eyes haven't improved, why shouldn't *he* have a deferment?"

263

Miles started to mention Uncle Parker's judgment that he would pass the eye test now, but she cut him off. They had never really talked about his chances of deferment, but he could tell it had been on her mind, because she knew about the ruling that had just come down from Washington giving certain jobs priority deferments above family deferments because the labor pool was running dry.

Ferne said, "Isn't shell loading a deferment job? Only a *man* can do it--and a pretty able-bodied one to hear this one talk." She turned to Miles, "I think maybe if they offer to defer you next spring when you finish your first term, you should thank your stars and march right back to the ordnance plant." She turned argumentatively to J. Arthur. "I think he *should*! Uncle Bill says loading shells is certainly helping the war effort more than a lot of men that are just pushing paper in Washington. Dollar-a-year men," she said bitterly, "That's what they're worth, while the boys do the fighting and dying!"

"I'm going in when the time comes. That's all there is to it," Miles said stubbornly.

His father tamped his pipe and said to Ferne, "Miles would be about the only one not in it in your family. Jay Gordon and Eugene just joined the Air Corps with Wayne, and Eileen's joined the WAVE's."

Ferne rose and snapped up the empty plates with a clatter. "That's all very well for the West Coast Gordons," she said, "There are five children there." And she looked furiously at Miles as if being an only child was his fault.

J. Arthur said, "Did I tell you Kenneth's volunteered?"

"For what? Tank driving?" she retorted with a stage laugh.

"He's going into the Navy, pre-flight at Iowa State."

Ferne sat down again. "You can count on Esther to always get the best for Kenneth."

"*Ferne*, Esther didn't have a thing to do with it. Give the boys their due. It's their show now. Mothers have to let go sometime." He pushed back his chair.

"I'm going when the time comes," Miles repeated.

"Oh Pfffutt!" As she picked up the dishes again and headed into the kitchen, Ferne threw back over her shoulder, "You men refuse to see! Nile Kinnick is *gone!* Frank Ward's missing, probably dead. And there'll still be many, many more Gold Star Mothers before the dirty Jap gives up!"

Miles sat alone at the table looking down at his calloused hands with one black nail. He could hear her clattering things around in the kitchen. Through the front windows he watched his father swinging along toward town with his disguised polio walk that covered his limp. His straight-barreled pipe smoked ahead of him like the funnel of a complacent steamer.

As long as Miles' weak eyes had assured his rejection or consignment to some Special Service slot, his parents had said nothing against his going, but since the draft age had dropped to eighteen and Uncle Parker had said that service glasses would probably get him classified as A-1 infantry material, he had felt them dragging against it. Particularly Ferne. Though recently J. Arthur had said little, Miles had noticed a perceptible softening of his stonewall discipline and had begun to read it as acceptance if not encouragement. After Miles and Ferry almost ran into J. Arthur on the way home from the early golf lesson one morning, J. Arthur must have known where his Titelists were disappearing to, but instead of a blow-up at the dinner table, he had merely made a clumsy joke about golfing in the dark that Ferne didn't understand. And today he had taken his son's side and trumped her protest about only sons going in by reminding her that Kenneth Morgan

265

had joined up. *Touche'!* So Miles had won his father over. But it gave him the empty sensation of throwing his weight against an unlocked door. Hadn't J. Arthur's been a token resistance all along? All his life his father had felt the shadowy slights of those who knew he was not a veteran without knowing or caring why not. Now, for a vertiginous moment, Miles felt the irresistible tug of that immense maelstrom that was carrying them all into the funnel of the war. Even Fairy assumed he'd be going if it didn't end before his number came up--which she said she prayed for. He had always said that nothing could keep him from going. Now was it the ghost of a second thought that made him sit for a minute looking at his scabby hands and wondering what was so essential about a tool setter?

The first few days of golf lessons, he had taken Fairy's request to learn the game seriously enough, and gravely put his arms around her to correct her stroke. Every other morning at first light they poked the errant balls around the imitation course he had marked out in previous years that started in left field of the ball park and circled toward the river and back around the pool. They would finish as the sun was full up above the river trees and push their bikes up to the pioneer cabin and sit on the broken bench drinking coffee from his thermos and overlooking the unruffled swimming pool and the baseball field and the farthest brownish gridiron of the Undefeated Team with their heads touching like lovers watching a movie. He would tell her that he dreamed of playing fullback his last high school season, but that it wouldn't be any fun without her in the stands. Sometimes, they would talk earnestly about their coming separation ("Will you come home some weekends?"). And sometimes for a minute or two they would share the excruciating empty feeling that it was almost over here for them just as it was getting started.

Probably because he thought she would be unwilling to risk being caught there with a boy, he didn't invite her to go in the pool until the day before his birthday. But Monday morning when he had been bragging about being in the stands two years ago when Babe Ruth had put on a great show standing at the plate hitting ball after ball into the pool, Fairy challenged him to do that with a golf ball. "Name something hard," he said. She wanted him to prove it right then, but it was already too light. "Tomorrow," he agreed, "if you'll promise to dive in and get my ball--ha-*ha!*" But to his surprise she nodded, "A promise is a promise!"

She hadn't yet gotten him a birthday present. When he had taken her to Des Moines with him Saturday to hear the Horace Hite band at the Varsity and pick up his new suit, she had thought of getting him a fine shirt to go with it, but she hadn't brought enough money. And in truth, since what she had earned earlier in the summer had gone into her college wardrobe, she had little to spare.

That night after her promise to dive for the ball, when he showed her the shiny new Argus C-3 camera J. Arthur had already given him, the inspiration struck her that since she was going to wear her new bathing suit under her clothes tomorrow to retrieve the golf ball, she could make him a present of a pose on the diving board for a color snapshot he could use to finish the Petty Girl drawing. She said he could choose. Which did he want, a new shirt? or the pose? No contest, he wanted the pose.

The next morning, he brought the camera, and she wore her Chili Williams bathing suit under a work shirt and shorts. After they knocked the ball around the course, and she tried to take pictures of him addressing the ball ("It won't be fast enough to stop a swing.") he lofted a ball into the pool and helped her over the fence. She found the ball right away in the deep end under the low board and stood for a moment hesitating as the sun topped the trees along the far side of the football field. When he mock-aimed the camera at her, she doffed the work shirt and kicked off her shorts, and straightened up and reached behind her back where she had loose-tied the bra of the suit when she was half awake. "Fix me, " she said.

"Turn around." With a flick of his finger, he untied it completely. It was an innocent jape, but as he tried to retie it, the constable's old patrol car came in the Tenth Street entrance and turned into the pool parking lot. When it passed behind the pool house, Fairy held her nose and stepped off the side and dropped into the pool. Miles dived in over her burble. She went deeper than she intended and fought her way to the surface and grasped the lip of the splash trough and turned to face the pool house as the constable turned off the motor below the berm just under the diving boards. Miles surfaced facing her. His hands bracketed hers, and they looked at each other scarcely breathing as the car door creaked and Archy Dillon got out. They could smell his cigar. Their chests touched and his eyes got round and his face slowly reddened. The constable slammed the car door and started the motor. "Jeezamaria!" Miles whispered, and Fairy saw her top floating on the surface behind him.

As the cruiser wheezed up the hill out of the park, they both stayed catatonically still watching the scare go out of each other's eyes. Then he laughed and ducked under water and scraped his chin against the satiny yield of her naked breast, nuzzling its warmth in the cold water like a puppy.

She seized a handful of his hair and pulled him right up. "No-no! You must treat them both the same or they'll get lopsided!" and she ducked him and fiercely hugged his face against her other breast. When he came up spluttering and coughing, she was climbing out the ladder. She turned her back chastely and stepped into her shorts and buttoned her shirt.

268

"Who told you *that*?"

"Gibsy's sister. Ricky always made love to the same side of her, and now they're seriously unsymmetrical. Get my top?"

She pointed to it, and he brought it up, and they went back over the fence. A while later when he was putting the golf balls back into J.Arthur's golf bag, he suddenly closed his eyes and reeled like a drunk, "Always! I must *always*?" he breathed. "What do you suppose she meant by *that*?"

Later that day Race helped Fairy select a boxed set of Old Spice men's toiletries at the South Side Drug and gift-wrapped it for her. After all, she hadn't posed.

Night Games

Archy Dillon's early morning smoke by the pool made them curtail the dawn swims. But Miles soon sweet-talked Fairy into going out with him after he got home from his night shift. "What's there to do? Everything's closed." But he had the notion of taking some flash pictures of her in different momentous settings of their high school years, "to make drawings of you this winter when you're at school to remember you by."

"A likely story!" But she went along because it appealed to her to run free in the night with him before she settled in for a semester of convent life at the college.

So, when the bus dropped him off in the middle of the night, he started going to Fairy's and scratching on her screen.

Elsewhere, the cities of the Farm Belt had been shaken awake to the night drill of an arsenal of democracy: The trains shunted and whistled and loaded all night in Cedar Rapids (mills and electronics), Davenport (the sleepless river traffic), Ottumwa (artillery shells), Sioux City (the air base). And the Des Moines Ordnance Plant hummed all night and glowed for miles on the horizon north of Des Moines.

Farther away, halfway around the world, the 503rd Parachute Infantry Regiment, 3 battalions, 1700 men, emplaned in 79 C-47s, and covered by a hundred fighter planes, and over-watched on high by three fortresses with General Douglas MacArthur--who jumped up and down in the plane with excitement watching it--flew over the Owen Stanley Mountains and dropped on the Japanese air field at Nazdab, New Guinea. The operation was complete in September. It was the unit's first combat jump, and only twelve were killed.

At one a.m. Miles and Fairy went on their bikes or on foot through a town that still went to bed after the ten o'clock radio news as it had since the Thirties when the radio first began to keep people up after eight. J. Arthur was fond of saying that Adel met his definition of a good town, a place where you could find any reasonable thing you wanted a few blocks from wanting it: somewhere to fix a broken tooth, make a will, buy a dog, forge a harrow.

But after midnight, Adel was one of those villages found in old novels, depopulated by a mysterious force that left the streetlights burning and the distorted reflections in the curved courthouse windows staring at a dead-still square. Or so Miles and Fairy saw it on the quests he laid out like the scavenger hunts of their childhood when they had chalked the walks with arrows and cryptographic rhymes, and chased barefoot in the charmed garden of their childhood games. Now, with those boys gone around the world, and without arrows and no one to run and no one to chase--just these two--they kept to the pretense of gathering valedictory photos of Fairy in the mnemonic places of their high school lives. Though his flash made crude prints that fixed her in a splurge of light and shadow when he processed them in the basement, it made little difference to him, since her shadow form left his imagination room to reinvent her later with his chalk.

In the afternoon before he went to work, he would call and tell her what to wear, and later when he posed her, what to take off. What *she* craved was doing a delicious secret thing. It thrilled something in her to submit this way, because to pose for a man, as any pretty woman understands, is to fix his undivided adulation on her body. (Though she continued to refuse to pose in the nude, "No more of that nonsense. One birthday present a year is all for you!)" Of course he promised, but continued sweet-talking and earnestly schmoozing about the Old Masters whose models had posed in the nude: "Look at Monet! Look at Degas!" And she would smile and promise to celebrate the first day of his Old Masterhood with a pose in the raw. ("But how will I know when you're a Master? Will they give you a gold beret?")

She sometimes seemed to waver, but inwardly had set her will like an alarm clock, to see the summer's end before it came to that. Though she wore only a dressing gown to the school playground one two a.m., and he pushed her in the swing till the skirt flowed back and bared her thighs, and he got one ectoplasmic image of her like a naked angel falling from the black sky. Or another night in the Riverside Cemetery on the steep bluff west of the park where there was a tombstone of polished flat granite the size and shape of a single bed with a black granite cylinder at the head like a pillow: On this sarcophagus he placed her reclining, and spread her hair across the stone bolster for a portrait to be called *The Death of the Maiden*, which failed to turn out.

The night before she left for school J. Arthur let Miles have the Merc and loaned him a gas stamp, and he took her out to dinner at the Moonlight, the disheveled supper club at the west end of University Avenue on the edge of Des Moines which had been Ronald Reagan's favorite spot when he was sports announcer at WHO. The back bar was plastered with blow-ups of the star's favorite roles, *Submarine D-7, Dark Victory, Kings Row*, and Miles ordered whiskey sours before dinner with his heart in his mouth, but the waiter didn't raise an eyebrow.

When their dinners came they ate quietly. Once he raised his glass, "To the last supper!" like a toast, but they didn't laugh at it. After dinner they went to the Passion Pit, a small sunken room with a dance floor, low lights and a juke box. Fairy wore a new heather plaid skirt that was tight over the hips and then accordion pleated to the knee with a sweater set and Spectators--part of her college wardrobe--and they revolved all alone close-hugging in the empty passion pit to *These Are the Things I Love*, *I Surrender Dear*, and *Blueberry Hill,* until another couple came in and punched in Charley Barnett's *Cherokee.* Then they jitterbugged, and he whirled her out till the accordion pleats of her skirt stood horizontal and showed her fine legs.

On the way home, she burrowed under his arm, and he would have taken her to Riverside Park, but Ray and Gladys had gone to bed, and she wanted to stop there and sit in the yard. "Us under the stars here, is how I'll always remember this summer," she said, "You snoring away!"

The widow's kitchen light came on as soon as they closed the car doors, but Fairy tugged him into the garage where the old Chevy squatted with one door open. Since rationing, Ray Wing had only used the car to deliver War Department telegrams, and it smelled of moldy velour and Sparky the dog. When he leaned out to close the door, she held his arm and said, "Hush!" and tapped on the front seat, "Driver, go round the park till we say stop!" she commanded, and sat back and folded her white hands in her lap. He took her in his arms and said, "Oh, God, Christ! It *is* love, Fairy!".

She didn't answer till his hand beneath her sweater had memorized the little buttons on her spine, and he remembered Liz's lesson, to extend his antennae and feel her inclination, and he did and felt that it was all right with her until he leaned back and took her whole body onto his, and their limbs fused like fitted jigsaw pieces for two clicks in the dark old barn, and he breathed, "It *is*! What are we going to do about it, Fairy?"

"Well, not that!" she said, and suddenly turned into an armful of corners and was out of the car tucking in her blouse.

After that, the summer was over, and she went in early by the front door and told him she was leaving too early in the morning for him to come around to see her off, and when they hugged, her face was cool again. He didn't cry, but it was like a funeral.

The next morning the Wings left early and drove to Boone, where they spent the night with Ray's sister's family. These people had a daughter who was a junior at Ames, and she and Fairy would go to the campus together, and she would introduce Fairy to her friends and help her get settled in her dorm. She would spend the winter a two-and-a-half hour drive away from him.

6

Five Minutes of Fame

In the last days before Fairy left for college, they had talked a lot about how they would handle the four months of separation before he joined her at Iowa State at the beginning of the January term. Miles had quibbled about Fairy's continued correspondence with Bruce and been rebuffed, "Stop writing to a *service* man?" Though she would continue to be Bruce's "pen-pal", she had almost sworn that Bruce would never be more to her than a "Platonic" friend, and when he was sure of the inside track, Miles waxed magnanimous and said he didn't expect her to "live like a nun" at Ames--meaning, if she had to have an escort to a prom some time it was okay. But "some (one) time" was writ large in his mind when he said it. After all, their longest separation would be till Thanksgiving. And they assured each other that some Saturday in between she could come down to Des Moines by bus and Miles could pick her up. Then again, another Saturday, he promised to drive to Ames for one of the dances and stay over with the Hill brothers. In that light, the separation seemed bearable.

But as soon as classes started, these pipe dreams collided with the strictures of the war. Fairy had a chemistry lab on Saturday morning, and Miles had one Saturday football game. Ray Wing had designated his sister's house at Boone as Fairy's home away-from-home because the 65-mile drive to Ames at 35 miles an hour to pick Fairy up, and then to take her back to school on Sunday would have used all of his gasoline ration and most of his weekend. In his private estimation anyway, 65 miles wasn't half enough distance between the two "love birds", as he called them now, not fondly.

274

Moreover, though they wrote several times a week, Fairy was soon lonely and found Iowa State impersonal and rigorous. Most of the students were now men in the Advanced Specialized Training Program (A.S.T.P.): V-5s and V-12s in accelerated pre-commission tracks whose rigors fell alike on the civilian students.

At home Miles was soon floundering in his last season of high school football. In the third game of the season, Coach Townsend abruptly shifted Miles from tackle to fullback, a move that caused violent repercussions next door at the Baers, which Miles recounted to Fairy in letters chicken-tracked with exclamation marks:

Lyle Townsend, a civics and American history teacher who had coached all the sports at different times in the last ten years at Adel, had been conscripted to take the helm of the football program again when Coach Stolard decided to resign after the debacle of the Boone game but delayed the announcement till he had a job with a sporting goods company. Jake--Lyle Townsend-- came aboard with the leverage of the Board's desperation, which allowed him to set a new policy he had always wanted to try in coaching football. Since things couldn't get worse, this time around football would be *fun*, win or lose.

In his early forties, the coach was still an extraordinary athlete, and his "football for fun" policy meant that the coach came to practice in spikes and often carried the ball in scrimmages. Having fun also meant using everything he knew about the game in a small school conference where a team customarily ran about ten plays. Fun would be using, in addition to the Y formation he had inherited, the single wing and the double wing, a reverse from the single wing, a double reverse from the double wing, a cross-field lateral with a forward pass, and a new wrinkle on the old Statue of Liberty, among other things. Coach Townsend's lighter touch also meant that at Tuesday practices he would give ten minutes to anyone on the second team who wished to challenge a varsity player for his position. If the challenger won the "head-to-head", he replaced his rival and started the next game. This assured that, fun or not, everyone still ran full speed and energetically bruised themselves and others.

Miles' shift to fullback in the third week was the result of this stricture. Jake had benched Miles the previous game for "loafing". Yet, a raw-boned high school junior, a nephew Lester Baer had brought up from the country to become the next Nile Kinnick and had pressured Jake into trying at fullback to replace a senior leaving for the navy, had never played organized football before, and in Miles' outspoken opinion, couldn't cut the mustard. "*I* slave in the box cars all summer to get ready for football and Rod's out there stumbling over his feet," he wrote to Fairy. "So, Tuesday practice, I challenged Rod Moyers for fullback!

"...Well-well! The halt against the blind," Jake says, and puts the ball on the two-yard line, and tells us to take a turn running it in over Heimberger (240 pounds! probably the strongest human being in this old town!).

"Moyers takes Jake's handoff and runs into Walt, and Heimberger squeezes him like a grape, and the ball flies up and Jack Engstrom takes it in the air and runs 98 yards the other way!

"Ah, so! Jake says. Now you! And I look at big Walt, and go 'Over my dead body!'and I take the handoff and run into Walt's front, and he picks me up by my jersey--(Enclosed, please find the picture from the *News*). That's me *in the end zone bareback*! And that's Heimberger with the disgusted look holding up half a jersey with my number on it! (Fairy, you remember when the Big Ten Photo-of-the-Year was Tom Harmon making a touchdown with his jersey torn off?--well, this is *my* five minutes of fame*!*) So, I'm appointed fullback against Dexter!

"Okay, But *here's* the weirdness!

"J.Arthur comes down Friday morning and says he couldn't sleep because Lester Baer was working on his punching bag in the middle of the night. Ratatattat! Mom thinks he's finally lost it. But, wait, there's a method in Lester's madness...After Moyers sits out Friday night's game, Lester shows up at Jake's front door. Coach is taking a bath, but Lester pushes right past Edith and heads upstairs! (Jake is what--five foot eight? (but did you know he played professional hockey in Canada?) So, *Katy, bar the door*! When Lester Baer bulls into the bathroom and starts ranting at Jake for benching his nephew, Jake gets out of his bath and throws Lester in! Into the bath Lester goes, overcoat and all! Jake had to help him out! Can you see *that*? Nagels across the street saw Lester leaving Jake's house with his coat streaming water and his hat on backward!

"Next day Rod Moyers decides he doesn't want to be an All American and moves back home, and Jean gets her room back. And we beat Dexter, so I'm fullback till further notice!

"More when we're together again-- *soon!* LOVE!"

Miles still couldn't see without his glasses, and in subsequent games often ran up Walter Heimberger's back instead of through the hole the big fellow opened for him. Because he always hit the line at a forty-five degree angle, Miles never lost ground, but he required resistance to keep from falling on his face in the secondary (J.Arthur had a photo of him carrying a bantam linebacker who was keeping him upright by dragging his feet). The Adel team's record ended 5 and 4, proving nothing about the Winning Tradition one way or the other, and Miles admitted to Fairy that his football dreams ended with the last game.

At the end of the season, he went back to music with no regrets. He picked up the flute again and muddled along in the concert band while singing baritone in Mildred Seevers' choir. Soon he was making the rounds of the women's clubs singing baritone solos, his repertoire consisting of wartime hits *What Does a Soldier Dream Of?* and *There'll be Bluebirds Over the White Cliffs of Dover.* In November, Mildred let him try *White Christmas*, a song Bing Crosby had made a hit the previous year.

Then, when Dan Rainwater started his first swing band, predictably, *The Raindrops*, with himself drummer and leader, Jim Mitchell on piano, Herb Robbins and Wayne Fritz on sax, Bud Reams on trumpet and Carl Blanchard on trombone, Dan told Miles he couldn't be in it because flutes didn't play swing. Though Miles was sure he *had* played swing once noodeling around on *Star Dust* in the band room, he swallowed his pride and became the band boy for *The Raindrops.* He would taxi Dan to various dance halls where they tried to sell the manager on booking the band for weeknight fill-in dances. Till the middle of October, most of the pavilions were still open, and there were several country dance halls between Adel and Jefferson, as well as the "White Elephant," in Adel.

Before air conditioning, many of these pavilions in the Midwest were set on small bodies of water bordered by a few cottonwoods in the corn fields where the builders had hoped to harvest some cool breezes on stifling August nights. They uncovered their screen walls June 1st and placed dance ads in the local papers and booked five-piece western combos and polka bands from Minnesota weeknights. On Saturdays they featured territory bands-- bands that had never made a hit record and were well known in only one region, like Laurence Welk before he hit the Big Time.

When Dan finished trying to sell the band for a weeknight gig, the two boys often hung around. They noticed how the leaders watched the musicians get bored playing, *"You do the huckle buck/ / You do the huckle buck!"* and *There'll be Smoke on the Water, on the land and the Sea/ (when our army and navy overtakes the*

278

enemy!) and with the country-western crowd in happy land after eleven, turned the bands loose and let them play hot. Then men stomped and twirled their partners out to arm's length and jerked them back with the force they used during the week to pull the lever on a combine. Small women would leave the floor and momentarily achieve horizontal weightlessness, land with a thud you could feel at the bar and jump right up and go on dancing like sixty.

In the early fall of 1943, through the skittish lighting of the mirror-ball chandeliers that made shimmering sequins on the smoky haze above the dancers, there were fewer men and precious few of them civilians. The men tended to be balding and beer-bellied in short sleeved shirts with colored stitching or white Arrow shirts with sweat spots the size of basketballs between their shoulders. A few 4-Fs limped through the circle-two steps with bad backs or flat feet, and hard-shell 10-beer guzzelers wandered about the parking lots after intermission with impaired balance, peering through the grainy light for their misplaced cars or the cars their misplaced wives had gotten into. Then, the fights would start in the shadows between the cars.

Miles began to notice single women at the dances. Unescorted, they showed up in small groups or pairs at the gate getting their wrists stamped, and though he had often seen little girls dancing together on the edge of the crowd, he now saw grown women dancing as couples.

For all their trying, *The Raindrops* were booked for only one weeknight dance at the White Elephant in town that fall, an audition that didn't make expenses for the house, let alone anything for themselves. Their one paying job was a school dance, the junior prom. Rainwater, who had decided he needed a singer, invited Miles to try out as a "guest" vocalist at intermission. And Since the band had no arrangement for his songs, Mildred Seevers accompanied him on the piano while Dan brushed the

279

drums and Miles stood at the center of the high school stage with a mike and sang *"There'll be Blue Birds over the White Cliffs of Dover."* There was a smattering of applause, and Mildred Seevers opened *"White Christmas"* and he cupped the mike and crooned the Irving Berlin lyrics as he imagined Bing Crosby sang it:

I'm dreaming of a white Christmas/ Just like the ones I used to know...

When everyone stopped dancing and stood around the stage he thought he was dead in the water till he saw they were standing like the crowd around Frank Sinatra at Tommy Dorsey, couples swaying with their heads together in the nostalgia of a spell, while the band stood looking in from the wings as he crooned...*with every Christmas card I write. May your days be merry and Bri-ight/ And may all your Christ-mases be white."*

After that night, he performed the song again by request at an assembly and a Kiwanis meeting, and boasted in his letters to Fairy about the stir he seemed to be making until the music teacher popped his bubble by telling him his instant celebrity was due more to the magic in the song than to his crooning.

He kept telling Fairy he was coming up to Ames to make her a coed (a tradition at the college that a girl was not a genuine coed until she had been kissed under the campanile). But before he worked it out, he fell into a vile mood and began to sting his friends with disdain for the high school and their humdrum company. He went to a dance after a basketball game and stood by the radiators in the dark, bored with the same girls he had played Red Rover with in elementary school and the same air permeated with the stench of cleaning compound and dance wax that he remembered from childhood. And when Fairy's next letter teased him about a name band dance at the Student Union which she seemed to have attended with her roommate, a Pennsylvania girl named Ruth Chen, he was jealous of the roommate. Only to hear from one of the Hill boys, home from Ames the next weekend, that he had seen her at the dance with a handsome V-5.

He felt their "destiny" leaking away without being able to do anything about it, and wrote her a letter naming the dear places on her body he would kiss when they finally got together Thanksgiving night: her sarcastic eyebrow, her down-turned smile--and both her breasts-- equal time, "about a hundred years each, and a thousand for the rest!" In a few days he got a chill reply saying she had left the letter under her pillow and the house mother had read it, and at a house meeting had called her a tramp. "She didn't name me outright, but everyone knew. Now I have to take classes in sex education from the nurse at the infirmary the rest of the semester!" And incidentally, Fairy had accepted her roommate's invitation to go home with her to Pennsylvania over the Thanksgiving holiday.

So, Thanksgiving night Miles went with members of Rainwater's former band to a breaking-up party at a tavern in West Des Moines, and came home and fell over a chair and quarreled with his parents about the beer on his breath. J. Arthur grounded him till Christmas, and he went into a kind of suspended animation and started spending his evenings in the basement at his workbench again. He would turn on the little radio and pin rough paper on the drawing board and try to make sketches based on the flash snaps he had made of Fairy in the summer, marking time till he could win her back at Christmas.

Two days before vacation Race and Mitchell stopped by and they sat around playing *"Chattanooga Choo Choo"* on the little record player till Edward R. Murrow came on. Murrow talked about entering a new stage of the war as impending as a pregnancy, something crucial on the way. (General Patton had overcome the

281

debacle of the jump on Sicily, where American troops had fought against each other for days because their paratroop uniforms looked like the Germans') and the Americans and the British had pushed the Axis off of Sicily and invaded the bottom of the Italian boot, and Italy had secretly surrendered.

The Russians were winning the largest tank battles ever fought, grinding the Germans back to the Polish borders of 1939, and Stalin in the foxy Uncle Joe persona that was popular in the United States, kept calling for an invasion of France. As MacArthur started across the South Pacific in measured steps, the Americans had taken out two hundred Japanese planes and over a hundred ships in a raid on Rabaul.

But it all cost new kinds of bitter losses. The daylight raids of the American Eighth Air Force over the continent lost a hundred and forty-eight bombers in a week, fourteen hundred and eighty trained men. The British, who were bombing the continent at night, warned the Americans to give up the daylight raids.

National news said political pressure to curtail the daylight bombing continued to mount in Washington. "*Time Magazine* reports the life expectancy of a bomber crew is fifteen missions, and a flyer has one chance in three of surviving his tour of duty."

The boys sat by the furnace rolling cigarettes with papers and a bag of Bull Durham. Mitchell had already qualified for Air Force pre-flight training and was expecting his call-up momentarily. He had thought he would go in January, but now said he wouldn't be surprised to be called before the new year. "Sounds like they need me right now." He had a natural ironist's grin and it gave the remark a tinge of gallows humor because they knew it would take him over a year to get through the pipeline. Nile Kinnick had gone in December 1941, and when his Wildcat went down in June 1943 he was still moving toward combat. Nile's next brother, Ben, in flight school now, would not qualify for combat till the middle of 1944. They all knew Mitchell had a long ways to go.

But Miles suddenly saw his friend as another lost flyer. In the corner of his eye, the shelf of model bombers and fighters above the workbench blurred. The prospect of the ruin of *his* Air Force, of the proud invincible Fortresses and Liberators going down by the hundreds made his eyes film, and he looked away from Mitchell. Race made a wisecrack about the Special Services he and Miles were headed for being more dangerous than flying. "Clerks are only lasting three typewriter ribbons now." He said, and threw away his cigarette paper and lit a Rameses. They sat in sober reflection for a minute watching the smoke curl up, and then burst out laughing.

"Christmas assembly tomorrow. I suppose we've got to hear "*White Christmas*" again?" Mitchell said. "Eleanor and Barb got all mushy when you committed it last time; it made them think about their guys in the navy. Fairy ought to hear you sing that tune! She'd cave, man, no more prick teasing." He snorted.

"Hey, Christmas Eve when you take her home," Race said, "Say, 'Fairy, dear, lie down, I want to sing to you.' Four bars should do it."

"Yeah, get it over with," Mitchell growled, "You're virginity's getting to be a drag on everyone. You and Gubser go around looking so ball-busted. Polly won't let him do anything, so he kisses her on the forehead and comes out and lifts his car. I swear! Grabs the front bumper, practically lifts the wheels off the ground!"

Miles thumbed his nose, grinning through his watery eyes. He didn't say he had the Mercury to pick Fairy up from Ames at the bus station in Des Moines Saturday. He said, "If you could sing, you wouldn't have to play that damned piano everywhere."

Leaving the *Home Front*

PART THREE

Leaving the Home Front

Clark Tower — Winterset

SEPTEMBER-OCTOBER, 1971
Volume 21 No. 5

- CLARK TOWER MEMORIAL TO PIONEERS
- SCHOOL'S OPEN – DRIVE CAREFULLY
- NEW IOWA LAWS AFFECT MOTORISTS
- LEGISLATIVE QUESTIONNAIRE FOR MEMBERS

Leaving the *Home Front*

1

A Wartime New Year

To Miles, the Christmas season of 1943 seemed as cold as the Decembers of the Thirties in the Tullis house. His design to spend most of his private time with Fairy was chilled from the beginning because she brought Ruth Chen home for Christmas with her. She didn't tell him in her letter because she knew what he would say. So when he sorted Fairy out of the crowd debarking on the snow-rimmed apron of the Des Moines Greyhound station and kissed her lips--on which a snow drop fell just as she looked up--the fire-and-ice taste of her was a preview of the way the next ten days would alternately kindle and chill his campaign to reclaim her while he danced a hesitation two-step with two pretty girls on his arm and a brace of dates to arrange for Ruth.

That day--was it the 20th? a Saturday anyway-- Ruth gave them their minute alone in the crowd before she stepped forward with her small white bag (she had a monster suitcase in the hold of the bus). A tall oval-faced brunette with sweetly sculptured lips painted vermilion-- wearing a fur trimmed coat with a matching fur hat tilted pertly on her head as Miles had seen Joan Bennett wear one--Ruth had her almond eyes from her father, an American of partly Chinese descent, an optics technician who made something classified in his small plant near Pittsburgh.

Miles' heart sank; bad news in a pretty package.

Not that she was ever really in his way. From the moment Ruth "came out" at a Christmas dance in a green cocktail dress set off by tinkling earrings that winked the color of her eyes beneath her jet pageboy bob, she was the

Christmas star on their hum-drum tree. And Race, who was momentarily between endless loves, caught on with her the first time he dipped her at the end of a set. His six-feet-four made her five-nine feel petite. When they doubled for Les Brown (*and His Band of Renown*), it was Ruth who prolonged the evening with her convert's zest for Race's style of petting (nothing personal) while the Morgans' Mercury idled in Fairy's snowy driveway till the windows fogged.

So Miles was glad to see the last of Ruth when they took her to the Rocket on the thirtieth and sent her home for New Year's. By then, he understood that Ruth was part of the penalty he was still paying for his lusty letter before Thanksgiving. He had already quarreled with Fairy because their intimate moments had been few and often seemed preempted by an aloof dark twin of his complacent summer lover who said things like, "Don't start thinking you own me, Mister. 'Cause you don't!" In fact, she kept him at arm's length till New Year's was almost over and the clock had already struck out the old year.

It marked the third New Year's Eve of the war, which Miles would later refer to as his last New Year's Eve, B. C. "before captivity." It was the New Year's Eve when all able-bodied men still hanging on the home front like the last leaves on the tree, went a little berserk because the legions of their peers were tilting the war toward its climax without their help:

It was the New Year's Eve that British night bombers dropped twenty-four hundred tons of bombs on Berlin. The same New Year's that long range P-51 Mustangs, which would soon escort the Eighth Air Force bombers anywhere in Europe by daylight, started coming off the lines in California.

And it was the New Year's Eve J. Arthur Morgan came home from a midnight party, toasted Ferne as he

288

replaced the dusty-shouldered bottle of Scotch on the shelf of the broom closet, and in silent protest against the reawakened chatter of his neighbor's punching bag (which had hung silent on his basement landing since Lester's immersion in the coach's bath) descended the basement stairs at one a.m. and started laying a brick vault in the fruit cellar under the back porch for a new sound-proof radio room.

And it was the New Year's Eve that an *arriviste* teen-age farmland heiress, whose dipsomaniac parents were on a three-day binge in Des Moines, hosted an open New Year's revel, spread phone invitations as far as Des Moines, opened the big house on the hill above town to all comers, laid the dining table with her father's pre-war liquors and turned out all the lights herself before ten. Shaggy civilians in their forties whom no one had ever seen before arrived from the lower depths of the county, guzzled her parents' booze and settled in.

At eleven, the bemused teens, huddling in the kitchen around the only night-light, heard the thud of someone falling off a sofa in the living room, and someone swear, "What the...!" and someone answer, "This trucker pulled out to avoid a kid!"--and decided they were out of their element. And Miles, Race, Mitchell, Walt Heimberger, Ed Gubser, John Bradley, Gene DeReus and Dick Schinn gathered the girls, Fairy, Punk, Tiff, Polly, Gloria, Lois, Floy, Molly and Margaret, and resacked the home-made wine and the bottle of Iowa State Liquorstore-certified safeforhumanconsumption synthetic Scotch whiskey and the fifth of sloe gin (mother of hangovers) which the girls sipped freely in the benighted belief that sloe gin was nearly non-alcoholic, and picked their way out through the shadows of prone persons entwined on two downstairs beds and a billiard table, sofas and easy chairs and the carpet under the dining room table, and made a convoy to Riverside Park to skate on the Raccoon River ice.

When they aimed the headlights of the cars at the cleared hockey rectangle on the river, Jim Mitchell, who had just received his notice of induction for January fourth, pushed off with giant strokes, performed a graceful pirouette and a great pratfall far out on the ice in the headlights of the three cars and came furiously back to challenge everyone still tying up their skates, "Whoever pushed me, step up and fight! It's a dirty damn way to treat an almost-gol-danged sodjer!"

And it was the New Year's Eve that, on the way back to the square, their caravan joined a midnight traffic jam of half a dozen stopped cars, the police cruiser, the fire engine, the tow truck and a locomotive at the Highway 169 crossing, and everyone got out and stood around Bob Knoll's little roadster, which was lodged like a toothpick in the driving wheels of the locomotive of the midnight train. It was starting to snow again through the headlights, and steam seeped from the locomotive, and clouds of steam rose from the breath of the huddled brain trust trying to free the car. As soon as the train moved, Bob Knoll, who had overlooked the locomotive through a myopia of Iowa State Liquorstore synthetic bourbon because the engine was black and standing still, got into Mitchell's car with his fiancee and joined the festive caravan .

Then all the cars crossed the track and did a circle-the-wagons around the square, honking horns in time for midnight. They made three rounds before the clock struck twelve, and ten circuits altogether before Archie Dillon's old cruiser suddenly appeared beside the Mercury and the constable aimed his spot in the face of Ed Gubser and Polly at the wheel—on whom Miles had conferred the driving in order to sit in back with Fairy on his lap (for old times' sake)--and ordered the Mercury driven home while he considered another cancellation of Miles' license.

It was the New Year's Eve that Fairy took everyone to her house for early coffee while the snow fell straight down till two in the morning, though it was too cold to snow. All had stopped drinking then; Walt Heimberger had left with Lois and the dregs of his father's wine, and the synthetic Scotch had been ditched beside the river.

So, it couldn't have been the alcohol that possessed Miles, who had been too busy chasing Fairy to drink much, to do the parody. When Gladys phoned to say that Ray had slipped the car into a ditch backing out and someone had run into the train downtown so they couldn't get the tow truck till two, it was already after one.

Fairy had just put down the phone in the kitchen, and had started to make more coffee when their turn came to do *A Famous Line from Song or Story.*

So it couldn't have been the alcohol Miles had consumed that made him kneel in front of the little amphitheatre of a dozen couples nodding and waiting sleepily for one last, one last, before letting go of 1943, and he was sober as a church when he grabbed a purple cardigan off the sofa for a cape and a bronze letter opener from the coffee table as a dagger and told Fairy to put her head on his knee. "Play dead; *here!*" And when she laid her head in his lap in a reprise of the *Death of a Maiden* pose he had taken of her on the tombstone last summer and closed her eyes and let her head fall back to show her white throat, and swept the torrent of her jet hair over his thigh, he declaimed, "My mordant beauty!" gravely enough. He had a knack for farce, and when he feigned drawing the bronze knife from her breast, he made his voice quiver *"Ah, Medina! Medina! Awake, fair maiden; know that thou wert the first bosom open--first **blossom** open to my days, and the first star bright of my long night--also other swell things! Awake! Oh, Alas! She shall never more awake to me! O nevermore!"*

Miles held the letter opener under his nose and glared at the point cross-eyed. "*Ah, Medina!...*
The wind in the willow played/
love's sweet melody/
but all of the vows we made/
were never to be!"

Now, it was time for them to all say, *Blueberry Hill.* But the crowd remained silent, and still half-persuaded by the illusion of a bloody blade and Fairy, whose eyes remained closed in a pretty imitation of photogenic death. And suddenly his mouth went dry, and he, too, fell under the spell of his own device: "*This knife that tripped thy dear heart, will I embrace!*" he groaned, "*This blade my last love be, if but one drop of thy chaste blood on its fell tip remain...Now then....Oh thee, cruel priest of pain, perform thy nuptial rite and fuse it with my deepest heart's blood--now! Here! Here!*" and he made as if to stab himself, and fell forward on her breast with a fine expiring gasp, "*And plight our troth in paradise,*" he groaned, *"beyond this scurvy place! Oh, woe!*" he croaked, and succumbed with a final shudder.

A dozen couples were still sitting glossy-eyed with histrionic grief--which is sharper for a moment than real grief--when they heard Ray Wing's old car pull in behind the house.

"Happy New Year!" Gladys and Ray passed through, looking exhausted, waved perfunctorily at the departing couples and climbed the stairs to bed.

*   *   *

The little record player had whispered out the last notes of *Where or When,* and had been clicking like a metronome for a long time when Fairy stirred and looked down as though awakening mildly surprised to find herself unwrapped like a Christmas gift, and her new plaid skirt and navy sweater laid out neatly on the sofa back by other hands. She took her grandmother's pearls between her fingers and looked down through the loop. It seemed the pearls were all she was wearing except her last pair of silk stockings. Miles' face was cradled between her breasts, "*Medina?*" she mused, and ran her fingers through his hair again. Then she arched her back like a cat and pushed him off, "What would my grandma think? Get up! Give me my things. I'm getting cold."

Oh, *don't!*" he groaned. "Oh!" he said and made a grimace as he sat up on the sofa. For a moment a sharp little pang of pity for his pain that she could not share threatened to undermine her will, and they remained in tension, balanced on a sharp divide till the winking lights of the Christmas tree broke time with the mechanical click of the played-out record and she snatched her clothes.

"Nuff !" she said, "Get *up!*"

The streetlights receding toward the square were fading with dawn gray. When he tried half-heartedly to impede her dressing, she said sternly, "Mr. Sweet, are you completely depraved or what? Are you quite sure a hundred years for each would be enough?"

"I know if two people love each other," he said mulishly, "it is not wrong to do loving things."

"There'll be plenty of time for 'loving things' when you come to school." For a moment she watched the lights of the Christmas tree fade with dawn, and frowned. "You don't have a notion what could happen, do you?" she said, suddenly withdrawn and older again. He started to put on his coat, and she hugged him perfunctorily while his arms were tangled in his sleeves. "There's something I want you to see before we leave tomorrow. Now, go lift the car, hon."

His shoes creaked in the snow, and when he saw her peering through the curtain, he gave her a sour imitation of lifting the bumper of the Mercury.

293

She was going back early. His parents were driving him and Race to Ames with their things on Sunday, so he would take her to the Des Moines bus today.

Before three, New Year's day, they were headed out of town, and talking about the room he and Race had got near the campus for the winter quarter. Civilian men had been displaced by V-5s and V-12s in all the dorms at Ames, and he and Race had found a professor's widow who rented rooms to male students just off campus, but it was over a half a mile from her new dorm. The boarding house where he would get lunch and dinner, called Mrs. Tevebaugh's, which fed forty assorted civilian men, under graduates and graduates, was not much closer. In effect, they were on opposite sides of the big campus. Not so hot. And he didn't have a job yet. Fairy offered to ask the new housemother if there were any busing jobs available, but his meal ticket was paid up at Tevebaughs' for the quarter, so he decided not to.

They were approaching a narrow side street at the edge of town, and Fairy said, "Wait. Turn here a minute."

"I think maybe I can get something in campus town," he said. They drove half a block down a gravel dead end street that had turned mostly back to pot holes full of melted snow. There was an old dairy barn with a gaping loft and a leaning shed, a barn lot, and then a small, paint-flaked house before the dead end of the street. He went past the house, then backed and turned around. "What's up?"

"Stop here a minute," she said, before they reached the house again. It was a small one-story house on a rock foundation without a basement. The front had two curtained windows and a door under an open porch that was tilted ten degrees off horizontal across the front of the house. A few things were on the porch: an old swing without chains sitting on the floor, a three-legged kitchen chair, a few brightly colored Christmas blocks, and one of those washtubs on legs with casters and a wringer with a handle. There was a new baby carriage near the door.

"Well?" he said. "This is where old Conner lives. I used to come by with Race delivering papers up here. I heard Conner had the farm once, but he's a famous drunk. What's here?"

"You know about Lois?"

He anticipated her and was evasive, "She was Queen two years ago. With Jimmy."

"You knew they had a baby?"

"Didn't they run off to Missouri to get married?"

Fairy shook her head. "They ran off, but it didn't happen. They went to Washington state. Now *she's* back with the baby. He's still in Pasco working at a secret plant. I guess he sends some money."

He looked hard at the house. There was a privy in back. "Cripes!" he said, "I thought they got married."

"She says they're going to when he gets time off to come back."

"Jimmy probably bought the baby carriage--the old man doesn't work any more."

"That's where they did it," Fairy said. "There on the front steps..."

"What?"

"She lost her virginity to Jimmy the night of their coronation."

"She *did*? How do *you* know?"

"She told us girls. It was romantic I guess. She said there was moonlight...."

He was silent looking at the steps. There was slush on the steps. At one of the windows the curtain pulled back a little.

He put the car in gear and drove toward the highway. He looked at the dilapidated house and remembered the glowing couple in the spotlight of the halftime, and the cheers. "Then it was her I saw with a baby a couple of weeks ago, but I hardly even knew her."

They took the highway toward Des Moines. He looked at Fairy out of the corner of his eye. She sat looking ahead with her hands folded. He thought she was even prettier when she was somber. As they passed through the little town of Waukee, she said, "Miles, I *want* my degree."

He frowned over the wheel. "Is that why you showed me that? That's not us in a million years! We wouldn't ever end up like that! Our folks wouldn't...."

Fairy shook her head. "You don't know what my dad would do! Last night he was laying down the law. He suddenly decided I wasn't going out with you. I was supposed to go along to their old friends' party. They always play cards till twelve. We had a fight in the kitchen and he tried to drag me to the car--by my hair! I was screaming. Mom got him off."

He looked aside. She was biting her lip. He said, "You know, I *thought* he had it in for me. I would try to speak to him every time I met him downtown this fall, politely, like a humble suitor, but I'll be darned if he'd speak to me. Look down and go "Hrumph!" and chew his pipe around. Does he think I'm out to ruin you? What does he have against me?"

"He thinks were doing...." She gave him a down-turned smile of old knowing, "...what we almost did last night. You don't know him, Miles. If something would happen, he wouldn't just hit the roof and get over it like J. Arthur would. Lois-- at least the old man took her back in at home--such as it is. But if you made me pregnant, that would be the end of me for my dad! He'd just wash his hands of us. You know the mad old father blocking the doorway and pointing his daughter with the baby in her arms back into the snowstorm? *Never darken my doorway again!* Well, my dad would *do* that!"

"What does he think--that I'd knock you up and run off...to the *Foreign Legion*? If he didn't take a shotgun to me? Doesn't he think I'd do the right thing?"

"It isn't you so much! He gets that way about anyone I date more than twice. He was like that with Bruce for a while. Any boy could get me in trouble. You're public enemy number one now ....He's not *blind* about us, Miles! But I don't think he's as afraid you'd run away as that we'd be found out. How everyone in church would look at *him*. He's old Pennsylvania Dutch, his folks were. Shunning was a way of life--'*Don't show your face here; we'll leave some scraps outside for you...*'" Her voice broke off while he slowed for a rail crossing. She went on in a wobbly whisper, "When he's like last night, I think he'd rather see me dead!" She ruminated, then added, "But I do honestly think if I went away and came back with a baby and there wasn't any *father*, he'd probably take me in. The *process* would be out of sight; he could imagine it like an immaculate conception. He could live with an immaculate conception."

"Jeez!" he said. "I never dreamed, Fairy!"

"You didn't know I got my hair pulled to be with you?"

Then they were silent the rest of the way to the station. When they embraced at the bus, several uniforms were obviously parting with their girls for a long time. There was a way that everybody looked. He hugged Fairy as though she were the soldier going away. "'to God, I didn't know!" he whispered, "When I'm up there--I didn't know what was *wrong* with you, since Thanksgiving! But I swear you this, Fairy, when I'm up at school you won't have to worry about me...."

She made a wry smile.

"*No*, I swear to God, I *will be good*!" he vowed.

297

2

A Short Course

On January 3, Miles and Race Berglund, bypassing the last semester of high school, settled in at Iowa State College for what was to be--unknown to Miles--his drastically foreshortened college career. J. Arthur Morgan had decreed Miles start in engineering, and Race, already leaning toward law, had taken the path of least resistance and come along. Sunday, they moved into their second-floor room in the home of a professor's widow off the south-west end of the campus--two small study desks, one dresser, a closet and upper and lower bunks. The bath for the three student rooms on the second floor was at the end of the hall.

Impatient to finally be on their own, they had bid Ferne and J. Arthur a hurried farewell--Verna had been unable to come--and with considerable quibbling, arranged their clothes in the closet and put Miles' little Philco and his record player on the shared dresser and flipped for the bunks. In the process, they soon made the acquaintance of their new neighbors, four seventeen-year-old civilians, who, like themselves, were starting college early. Later, after they all trooped to a campustown restaurant for dinner, Miles called Fairy from the pay phone in the hall and confirmed a date with her for Monday night after registration.

In 1944, the State College's core campus was one of the prettiest in the Midwest. The campus of her senior sister in Iowa City stumbled at the foot of the old state capitol and sprawled helter-skelter on both sides of the Iowa River up and down the bluffs between downtown and the university golf course to the west, but Iowa State

College was a discrete land-grant appendage to the town of Ames, connected by a kind of causeway that carried the east-west highway across a half mile of empty meadow from the town to the campus. The center of campus life was the Student Union overlooking the pretty little tree-lined Lake La Verne, and the tall campanile a hundred yards to the north of it. Around the central campus, now drifted with snow, all the old buildings of the original college seemed to have been placed in such a way as to preserve a large irregular green studded with great first-growth trees. Except for the many curving walks leading to the uncleared Pammel Woods to the north, and over the knolls to the veterinary barns and stables that remained out of sight unless you had a class there, the central campus gave a visitor the deceptive impression of a great English estate not unlike Blenheim.

As civilian students were not allowed to have cars on campus, everyone walked miles to and from classes every day; Fairy's dorm was located east of the Union, and Miles' room at the widow's was a mile away beyond the southwest edge of the campus.

At that time, though the architecture of the college paid lip service to a university's traditional foundation in the humanities, the State College's catalog held only sufficient class offerings to meet the requirements of the majors in agriculture, science and technology. The engineering curricula: chemical, civil, electrical and aeronautical, required merely two quarters of English composition, as did agriculture, veterinary medicine, physics, chemistry, zoology and biology. The educational interests of women were thought to be fully accommodated by a home economics major. In 1944, more than half the students were already in the service, enrolled in the ASTP program in which selected naval, army or air force officer candidates did a pre-mobilization college year. Such nonutilitarian studies as music art and drama were deemed

299

superfluous at State because they would have been electives, and the curricula required that a major take only three hours of elective classes in four years. Partly because of the narrowness and rigor of its concentration, the college's engineering and science programs were ranked among the best in the nation.

One singular testimonial to that ranking in the winter of 1945 was that when students entered the vestibule of the chemistry building, they found the east wing of the building blocked off by a temporary wall of rough painted lumber. Above the improvised wooden door was a *No Admittance* sign, and in front of this sign stood one, and sometimes several, uniformed soldiers with M-1 rifles and side arms. Beyond the door, the wing was off limits to everyone except those with security clearance, and these sentries, who were not ROTC students or reserves, but regular army military policemen from parts unknown, examined the clearance of everyone before they were allowed to enter. It was rumored that the east laboratory of the chemistry building was making a secret weapon for the war.

Some of those who did go in and out on security clearance were chemistry graduates whom Miles noticed the first time he ate at Tevebaughs' board table. He was told they were chemistry grad students who worked on a war project being developed beyond the wall, and he noticed that they made up a closed clique of intense, taciturn men, some old enough to be growing bald, who ate together and conversed only with each other in some esoteric patois of physical chemistry. They all wore an air of aggressive assurance that the secret work they were engaged in more than justified their continued civilian status, and Race soon heard in the Union from one of those sage presences who always seem to hover around the periphery of such projects to leak privileged information, that not one person in the whole state, from the governor down to these workers of the inner sanctum, had the remotest idea what they were working on .[*]

The first night: the six new tenants at the widow's convened in a marathon bull session and poker game for cigarettes (which were worth more than money) in the widow's upper hall, missed breakfast at Tevebaughs', and straggled through registration Monday afternoon to finish after dark, harassed, confused and feeling, as civilians, outnumbered, unwanted and distinctly illegitimate. As Miles was not yet familiar with the campus, Fairy had suggested that they meet at the Union after dinner, and he barely had time to return to his room and clean up, skip his first dinner at the boarding house, and hurry back to campus to meet her in the vestibule of the Union.

They sat for a few minutes outside the ballroom with its vast hardwood floor, where Fairy said the big-band all-college dances were held, then went to the cafeteria downstairs and got rubber pie and hard coffee and sat for an hour trading news with the aimless avidity of old friends who have unexpectedly run into each other in a foreign land, though it had been less than a week since he put her on the bus.

Because it was a weeknight, and Fairy had ten o'clock hours, they started for her dorm shortly after nine. On the way, they crossed the snowy field to the campanile, and Miles bestowed on her the long-postponed co-ed initiation kiss. It was to both of them a much over-anticipated anti-climax, and perhaps because Fairy felt the

---

[*] more than six tons of high purity uranium metal in the form of two-and-a-quarter inch cylinders began arriving from Iowa State College at Ames, where one of Met Lab's appointed chemistry leaders, Frank Spedding, had converted a lab to back yard mass production. "Spedding's eggs" increased the value of K.

Richard Rhodes, The Making of the Atomic Bomb

constraint and stilted silence between them as an unlucky omen, as they continued toward her dorm she abruptly nudged them off the walk and led him along a path of footprints in the snow to a rectangular sheet metal structure about four feet high with a large flat metal top and open grillwork sides, that squatted alone in the faint light from a remote lab building. He saw that the snow that covered the campus had been melted around the box by the powerful blast of warm air coming out of the grillwork on the sides. "Leftover from the heating system," she whispered, "It's the only place on campus you can have a smooch."

On the far side of the box a couple were embracing. The girl was seated on the metal top with her legs wrapped around the waist of a boy in uniform. Miles picked Fairy up and carried her across the muddy patch and seated her on the metal top. He pressed between her knees and they kissed again. The warm exhaust heat blew through the grill on their legs, and it was like a cozy roofless room under the winter stars. "Of course, you have to sit up." she said finally.

"Voice of experience?"

She pushed him away, "Ruth came here once. I've never been."

"A likely story."

"Many apply, but few are chosen," she cooed. Her eyes gleamed mischievously into his, "Be nice. Come here."

After a time, he said, "Only a giant could *do* anything this way."

"They say someone did last year--but he was a basketball player." She looked at her watch. "If I'm not in in fifteen minutes I'll have to ring and she'll send me to sex education class again."

He carried her back over the mud and they walked through the bitter cold to the dorm. Other girls were standing around the front door hugging their dates while the house mother peered gravely through the side light. When the porch light came on, he trudged the long walk back up Lincoln Way to his new room. His feet were wet and freezing, and on the way he had a shivering spell.

Thus, his last college date, and the height of his college career.

On Tuesday, he sent Race off, but slept through breakfast again. At lunch time he met up with Race in a strangely silent assemblage of the chem. grad boarders in the dining room at Tevebaughs'. He noticed that no one of the twenty or so grad students at the two tables spoke except the minimum necessary words to move the food around. When he started to speak to Race, the rest of the table suspended their forks in mid-air and silenced him with ferocious stares. Later, as they were putting on their coats in the parlor, a man with a goatee who lived upstairs whispered in Race's ear that there had been an explosion in the secret wing of Chemistry in the morning, and the occupant of the empty chair among the chem. grads, had been killed.

They talked of this accident as they walked to the widow's to get their books for the afternoon. They had heard no sirens. Miles couldn't remember what the victim had looked like.

When he got to his class, he was sweating, though the temperature was in the teens. In the afternoon, as they tramped through the ROTC orientation hike in the woods behind the armory, he began to get goose pimples on his arms For the demonstration problem that was to give the freshmen the feel of things to come, they signed out World War One rifles without ammunition and World War One cartridge belts without cartridges. The ice on Clear Creek had thawed, and Miles was detailed to stand on a fallen log bridge and pass the rifles of the squad across.

He had just passed the first one over and grasped another when a strip of loose bark came off the log under his foot and he fell astraddle the log. Though he kept hold of the rifle on top of the log as he slid underneath with his arms and legs gripping it, the cartridge belt unfastened and fell in the creek. Upside down, he watched it float away with the current and go under the ice. As he had signed for its government value, a substantial fraction of his quarter's tuition, when he had crawled hand over hand to the bank, he waded into the icy water and poked the rifle into the ice and tried to snag the belt with the bayonet, but it was gone. Coming through the woods with his pants soaked up to his knees and pretending to shoot his empty rifle at an enemy bunker, he was the object of general amusement--but owing for the belt, his feet freezing in his only winter shoes, he was too miserable to care.

When the problem was finished and the company was dismissed, he sat on a bench in the locker room of the Armory in his underwear for half an hour after everyone else had left drying his pants and socks on a radiator. They were dry by five, but his shoes, which had never completely dried out after Monday night's immersion at the Heater, squished every step of his mile walk home. In his room, after he took a hot bath, he began to get the shudders again. He skipped supper and went to bed.

Race brought dessert from Tevebaughs', but Miles was sleeping with the covers thrown off and making a peculiar snoring sound. His face was flushed and Race didn't wake him. In the night, Miles' teeth began chattering, and Race got out of his bunk and piled a mackinaw on top of his covers and went back to bed.

In the morning when he woke up feverish and groggy, and his teeth started chattering again, Race used their week's cigarette fund to get a taxi and take him to the infirmary. There he left Miles in the hands of a nurse who took his temperature and started to put him to bed.

By the time Race stopped back after lunch, Miles was gone. J. Arthur, in town for a meeting at Highway

304

Commission, had looked in at the widow's to see how the boys were doing, and had followed their trail to the infirmary. Miles had not seen a doctor yet. J. Arthur took one look at him and bundled him into the state car and drove him to the emergency room of the Methodist hospital in Des Moines.

There they put him on a gurney--burning with fever and sublimely indifferent--and wheeled him to a bed in an unoccupied two-patient room on fourth floor. He had never been really sick before.

When Miles had been in the Methodist Hospital for five days, he came out of his morphine fog already knowing somehow that he wouldn't be going back to school during winter term. Ferne had gone to Ames and withdrawn him from classes just in time to save him from taking failing grades for the term, had gathered his clothes and record player, leaving the radio for Race, paid the professor's widow for his share of the room for the month, and got a small refund for his meal ticket at Tevebaughs'. He could not go back to Ames till fall. Then he would be eighteen and eligible for the draft. All of this--in fact, everything from the first morning when his teeth were chattering and Race had piled the mackinaw on top of his covers--had happened in a fog several degrees removed from reality. But he knew most of it from shreds of the bedside talk of the doctors and his parents that had floated into his head and hung around like smoke in a stale room till he began to come to. Last night the soreness of the pleurisy had subsided enough to let him sleep on his left side. This morning he had felt well enough to sit up on the edge of the bed and bum a cigarette from his roommate. A grizzled elder had filled the empty bed while he was in never-never land, and now sat up and started to talk about surviving the influenza epidemic of "The Great War." His name was Chic Lang, and he reminded Miles he had introduced himself when he moved in. He said the doctors

305

were all windbags, and that Miles had the same thing he had survived in 1918, *influenza*. He described with disdain how they had used their "hearing aids" on Miles' chest and held his x-rays up to the window light and agreed it wasn't pneumonia. Didn't he even remember being wheeled out for x-rays? Chic Lang said they didn't know much, doctors; they had decided to call what Miles had the *grippe*.

Miles sat on the edge of his bed listening to Chic Lang cheerfully telling of people he knew who had died of Miles' disease in 1918. He noticed that Chic avoided talking about what he was in the hospital for now. Miles found his glasses in the bedside drawer and put them on and studied his roommate's ancient chalk-white, unshaven face. The morning light came over his shoulder, and he could see by the crumpled *Des Moines Register* on the foot of Chic's bed that it was deep in January, though he could not make out the date--a double digit in January.

He thought of trying to telephone Ferne to see for sure if he really remembered her telling him she had gotten his registration cancelled and taken his things home. For some reason, he worried about whether she had paid for the cartridge belt he had lost in Clear Creek, because it had been valued at a third of his tuition. Had Paul Hensley actually been sitting in the corner of his hospital room one night telling him the cartridge belt was in the creek under a dead tree? And did Fairy know what had happened to him? Had Ferne said she talked to Fairy?

But sitting up on the edge of the bed smoking a cigarette soon exhausted him and he put his legs under the covers and turned on his good side and went to sleep. When he woke, a nurse was setting up his lunch, and Chic Lang had been moved.

He had the room to himself, and slept most of the time till Ferne came in the Mercury the next morning and took him home. It had been nine days since he came down

306

with the *grippe*. January was almost over, and he was finished with higher education before the service.

3

Square One

His second night home from the hospital, Miles finally got Fairy on the phone. She said she had found out from Race that J. Arthur had taken him to the Methodist hospital in Des Moines. Then Ferne had stopped by when she withdrew him from classes and said he was very sick. Fairy had tried to call, but he had been sleeping. Yesterday she sent a letter (which followed him home a week later).

He told her he had lost weight. "I feel like Samson with a crew cut." Yes, he was home for the rest of the spring term. He had thought of going back to the ordnance plant for the rest of the winter, but when he tried to shovel snow, he realized he wasn't strong enough to do the work. Fairy expressed mock relief that he wouldn't lift her upside down when they got together. He said that they should get married and she should carry him across the threshold.

Self-pity got the better of him, and he said "The first time I go to a pretend war I fall off a pretend bridge. Now I can't go back to Ankeny, but Weir told me I can't come back to high school either. Says 'We've done all the damage we can do.' It's a big har-har to him. But I'm useless here now! I'm back to Square One, Fairy!"

She said in the spring everything would be fine and promised she would be coming home for his commencement in May.

But it proved to be a long winter.

For two weeks he lay about his room while Ferne cooked his favorite meals to put weight back on his gaunt bones. For a while he did little more than file away the rejection slips for stories that had come back from the magazines. The grippe had laid waste to his mental energies, too, and he didn't send the pieces out again, nor did he try to work up any more sketches from the blurry photos of Fairy he had taken in the summer. Some whole days he lived in a lethargic neutral, reading Hemingway's *In Our Time,* and feeling like Harold Krebs, and listening to the soaps on the Halicrafters between the news breaks.

Ferne would make tea in the middle of the afternoon and force-feed him fresh apple pie while he pressed her to retell the family pioneer stories she had told when he was a child, of the first lean-to in Madison County, and the papoose interred in the tree over Clanton Creek, and the panther stalking the children. Out of idleness he looked these forbears up in the yellowed sheaf, *The History of the Clark Family in Madison County, Iowa,* and started to go through the trove of ancestral letters from before the Civil War and list them and put them in chronological order.

Though Miles feigned aloofness to the local news, perhaps in order to sustain the last shred of illusion that he had gone away like everyone else, he listened hungrily when Ferne told him that Ben Kinnick, Nile's second brother, had finished advanced flight training and gone to the Pacific as a bomber pilot. And Bud, the boy whose chest he had sat on the first day of school, had left for pre-flight training in the Air Force. Two of his West Coast Gordon cousins had recently been commissioned: Wayne the athlete was a patrol boat pilot, and Eugene had entered pre-flight training. It made him grumble that everyone he knew was flying, and he silently renewed his vow that he would still find some way to get his wings.

Early in March, J. Arthur came home with an offer for him from Ralph Cross: two months of half-day drafting in the County Engineer's office. Miles went to see Ralph Cross for an interview and decided that the Engineer didn't blame him for cutting Bruce out with Fairy the way

Charlene seemed to. Ralph said Bruce was in England doing fine, though his last letter said he would be quarantined for a few weeks. Miles already had heard this from Fairy, but he said nothing. Where had all the big money gone that he had earned in the summer? He took the job at a fraction of the ordnance plant wages. On the fifth, he would start working three mornings a week at the drafting table by the curved courthouse windows of the Engineer's office. If he didn't rush the project, he figured it would last till May.

Sunday morning, the WHO newscast he listened to before church referred to the Anzio beachhead above Rome that had been taken early in February to outflank the Gustav Line across the waist of Italy, and which had nearly been wiped out by German counterattacks. The latest newsbreaks said that allied airborne regiments fighting as ground troops had filled the gaps and stopped the Germans a mile short of pushing the beachhead into the sea. The Americans had started to retake lost ground. At Monte Cassino the Germans were still holding onto the heights and the Abbey.

The choir was smaller this year, and the only other bass was Cozad, the eighty-year-old druggist who had been in the choir for forty years. He growled the bass parts' pedal tones, and sometimes rumbled the baritone line an octave below the chart. When the anthem was finished he would fold his hands on his ample black vest and go to sleep and snore through the sermon, often breaking out in a series of explosive ratchet snarls and subterranean detonations as if some violent subconscious struggle were going on in him. The congregation seemed to have come to accept the outbreaks as part of the service.

As Miles sat beside the snoozing druggist, his thoughts stitched restlessly from the sermon to Cassino to the life of Christ portrayed in *The Nazarene*, a fictional biography he was reading.

310

He had hoped Ferne's book would reawaken his religious inclination, and had gulped the huge book down as if slaking a thirst. But the Christ which Asch's story described turned out to be little different from the cardboard cutout figure in the pastor's homily about a religious experience of his own: A drunkard the minister had counseled had reformed, and the pastor said that he saw in this not his own work but the hand of Christ. Miles silently questioned: "Where was the hand of Christ when Nile went down in the Gulf of Paria? Where is He, when the thousands of men more worthy of life than your old souse got thrown into that meat grinder at Cassino?"

When the service was over and the druggist awoke with a snort, Miles went home and read the last pages of *The Nazarene* again, and wondered about the author, a Jew now living in New York, perhaps the son of refugees from a Jewish community like the one in Poland the book described--where at this moment all Jews were being extirpated by murder teams of ostensible Christians. "Don't tell me *that's* all God's will, " he grumbled, and felt again on the back of his neck the chill draft of some overwhelming indifference in the world which he had first encountered when his eccentric grandmother, Mary Ellen, had died. "God is so big he might not even notice Cassino, but Christ is our Intercessor? Where is *he* now?" he thought rebelliously. "It's high time He put a word in edgewise here!" But his bleak mood soon gave way to his reawakening sense of personal immunity. Until his illness he had never considered himself even potentially among the millions caught in the abyss of the war. Now, when he took off his tie and sat down in J. Arthur's chair and picked up the latest issue of LIFE MAGAZINE, the pages of visionary pictures depicting the "*post war world*" like a sunny headland of the near future, confirmed his reviving sense of personal immunity.

311

Some time late in March he started to go again with J. Arthur on the long walks over the ditches and through the snow-rimmed mud of the new road that would parallel Highway 6, ten miles to the south between Des Moines and Omaha. Its working designation was Highway 90, and it was already graded from western Iowa to Des Moines. J. Arthur covered some of it every other day and inspected the concrete bridge piers just being poured in deep coffer dams on the Raccoon River bottom at Booneville. Day by day, as the forms were removed and the cranes set huge I-beams on the new piers, the superstructure grew. But the approaches weren't graded, and J. Arthur had to climb a twenty-foot ladder to inspect the construction. At first it had been harder for Miles to climb the tall ladder than it was for J. Arthur, who with his polio-withered leg walked easily on the beams high above the ice-rimmed, flowing channel. Then it had gradually gotten easier. When his strength returned, he grew lazy again, and began to stay on the ground. He would sit in the car with the heater running and read in Huxley's scandalous novel, *Point Counterpoint* while 'Lasses the Super Dog pawed in frustration at the lowest rungs of the ladder and ran around yelping for J. Arthur to carry him up, which he sometimes did.

A character in Huxley's novel of aristocratic ennui in London in the 1920s amused himself by hiring an innocent girl as a maid, seducing her and accustoming her to various forms of sexual depravity, then attempting to degrade and destroy her by showing her a book that defined these acts as abominable sins. Miles mused about what these erotic depravities might be. Wasn't Huxley saying that the real depravity in sex was its impersonal consummation without love?

He and Race had once gone over the pictorial instruction booklet Race had borrowed from the drugstore out of a box containing a diaphragm. It was informative about things they had not known about a woman's

312

anatomy, but had nothing to say about love. Nor could Race, the serious student of techniques of flirtation, shed any light on love. Wordless for once, the usually voluble theorist of the erotic tossed Miles a Trojan condom he had pinched. Though it was a trend for boys to carry a Trojan in their wallets and show it around as a testament of their virility, Miles had noticed the foil wrappings of these condoms were usually shopworn from months of exhibition, and he had unwrapped his and used it as a water balloon in a practical joke.

This particular afternoon, he became aware that the dog's yapping had stopped. The car windows were half open and he could hear voices from above, his father's among them, shouting like a cheering section. When he looked up, he saw that the dog Molasses had finally climbed the 20-foot ladder and was hoisting himself onto the beam of the bridge.

'Lasses' feat marked the beginning of spring. The next time Miles went to the bridge, the dirty lace snow was gone from the river's edge and the river current was swollen and hissing around a big dead cottonwood grounded below the bridge. Now the sun stayed out and made mud everywhere, and 'lasses climbed the ladder and trotted along the beams behind J. Arthur every day. That night, restless with the balmy air, Miles went to the last after-game dance and found Punk alone (he had heard she had broken up with the boy from Redfield Miles had worked with). He danced with her and took her home and stood on her porch talking about getting the grippe and dropping out for the term.

She complained that it had been a boring senior semester. "Why doesn't Weir let you come back and sit in classes? Do you realize, Miles, there are only fourteen guys left in the senior class, all big mechanical-minded farmers! I could crown you and Race for leaving early!"

When he reminded her that he stood before her in the flesh, she said, "Oh, *you* know, Miles! We're practically siblings!"

"Then disown me, sister!" he said like John Garfield. They laughed. Then she said her feet were freezing, and gave him a quick buss on the cheek for seeing her home and said goodnight.

The next week, the week before graduation, Fairy broke up with him, "for good." In their letters they had been planning her weekend home for his graduation and had set a time for him to call about picking her up in Des Moines, but when he called Sunday evening, no one could find her. Monday evening, she came to the phone and immediately started talking over him, heaping a breathless tirade on his head. He said he couldn't understand her, and she repeated herself word for word, as though this speech had been simmering in her mind till she memorized it: Didn't he know what it was called if you made love to one person in your letters and someone else on their front porch?

"I'll tell you what it is, it's called *perfidia!*"

"That's a song," he said with a laugh, which was a mistake.

"Then you probably know what that means from the song *Perfidia!*" she snapped back, It means: 'unfaithful'! It means you're treacherous! I heard you have a new girlfriend."

"From a fortune teller?"

"From a reliable source!"

"No, way!"

"No, *sir*! Adel kids were up here for Science Day, and Charlene told me that you were dating--you know well enough *who*--and Charlene saw you making time with her-- that's what she said, "M*aking time,*"--on Punk's porch after the game. I'm not coming home for your graduation! And I'm sending your letters back! And there'll be a black ribbon around them to stand for something that's dead and over with, Miles!" She began to cry. "So don't call me again! The girls will tell you I'm not in!"

"What about *you* at the dance at the Union with that ugly V-5?" he shouted, but she had hung up the phone.

Of course, he realized what had happened the minute she mentioned Punk. Charlene had been watching him like a hawk, and she must have seen him dancing with Punk that night and followed them home, and--God! *yes!* that little buss on the cheek had done him in!

Now, there was no help for it. In the next two days, when he did call, the girls at the dorm said she was out, and then the housemother, who had formed a low opinion of him after she read his overheated letter, finally took the phone and told him Fairy was going to Boone to her aunt's for the weekend, and his calls were unwelcome. Though he phoned Race and got him to call Ruth to intercede for him, Fairy had already left for Boone.

On the morning of May 10, he talked to Race, who had hitchhiked home for his graduation. Race promised to call Fairy at Boone to plead his case tomorrow. (You *swear* you're clean as the driven snow?) In the meantime, he took a more sanguine view of Miles' plight. There was a party after the ceremony. Race had a date with a girl from Perry who had her own car. "Too bad. You could have doubled with *us* for a change. Why don't you anyway?" he urged. "Pick up someone at the party! Show her that sauce for the goose is sauce for the gander! Fairy'll come back like a yo-yo!" When he saw Miles' woebegone face, he sobered, "Look, Charlene's been conniving to get Fairy back for Bruce. Fairy'll figure that out, sooner or later."

"Later, I'll be drafted!"

But there was something going on around him. In the afternoon, he was robing in the auditorium cloak room when Punk sought his eye across the room, smiled her dimpled smile, and mouthed, *"something to tell you!"* He

315

turned away with a once-burned reflex and slouched into the line as though he carried a banner stenciled "THE WORST DAY OF MY LIFE."

After the prayer, he sat numbly folding and refolding the program while the president of the school board developed a theme about the class's "postwar promise." A retired newspaperman from Des Moines, he had borrowed his title from the current cry of a news butcher on a corner in downtown Des Moines. Since winter, the dwarf who had owned the corner stand near the *Register* for decades had started prefacing his shout of the day's war headline with, "*It Won't be Long Now!*" This week it was Dwight Eisenhower's proclamation about the approaching invasion of Europe, "*It Won't be Long Now!*"

"These young people seated before me," the speaker asserted, "will be the standard bearers of the post war world!" Miles had thought of himself and his peers as *the war generation*; and it seemed that soon now they were supposed to be the "*the post war generation.*" All 25 girls and 14 boys, the editor said, were to lead the way into a new world of peace and prosperity. "*It Won't be Long Now!*" he concluded.

Now the vase with the fan of rosebuds (the class flower) and fern boughs was moved by a custodian in a black suit and a red tie to clear a path for the graduates. The chairs on the stage were rearranged to make room for a table with the pile of diplomas that Coach Townsend would hand to the superintendent while Mr. Sinift called the graduate's name, and the seniors rose. The class edged forward and moved by rows up the steps as their alphabetical predecessors crossed the stage and took their diplomas and shook the superintendent's hand. When Miles' turn came, a gap developed; the girl ahead of him skipped back to her place while he lifted his leaden feet up the steps and shuffled across the other side of the stage with his head between his shoulders. He had been through college. Har-har! Fairy had ditched him--what did he care for this rigmarole? But after he had taken his diploma with his left hand and touched the superintendent's dry claw with his right, something in the spatter of applause like a faint familiar trill stopped him in mid-stride. For an instant he thought he caught a glimpse of Fairy's hair far in back.

She had come after all! But where was she? Not in the crowd of well-wishing parents and friends in the hall after. Ferne and J. Arthur soon carried him away to the Clarkes' (Frances Kinnick's brother), who had invited graduates that had been George's classmates in Adel to a tea to mark his own graduation today in Omaha. The occasion also celebrated Ben's engagement. The middle brother had just received his commission in the Marine Air Corps and Kate Clarke announced that the engaged couple had set their wedding before Ben's imminent deployment as a bomber pilot to the Pacific theater. Neither brother was present, and it was a gathering of mixed emotions over which the pall of Nile's continued absence still presided.

When they got home at six, Miles opened the door and found a note tucked into the door latch.
"Congrats! Where are you? Fairy"

Ferne was surprised by his sudden levitation: Did he have a temperature again? He pretended to be hurrying to the party. He left by the front door and went around to Fairy's house.

The garage doors were open, but the old Chevrolet was gone. He knocked and waited, and knocked once more and went in. At the base of the stairs that climbed to a landing and turned and rose out of sight, he could hear a whispery sound up there. She was in the shower.

The living room looked the same as it had New Year's Eve, except that the drawn shade of the big west window behind the sofa now glowed with the baffled yellow of oblique sunlight, and the Christmas tree was

317

gone from the dining room entrance. He could see part of the dining table, day-lit now by the double windows that looked south down Ninth Street. His antennae told him there was no one in the kitchen. The shower hissed steadily above. He took off his coat and hung it on the hall tree.

What had brought her back?

What he did now, he would not have done in any mood but this giddy sense of resurrection: He removed his loafers, picked up a fat little pillow lying on the purple mohair throw in the corner of the sofa and tiptoed up the steps to the landing where he could look up half a dozen more steps to the second floor hall. He sat down and held the little pillow. She would pass the head of the stairs on her way to her room. Exactly what he intended to do then had not quite come to him--some celebratory, hat-in-the-air sort of thing; perhaps toss the pillow at her feet and yell "All is forgiven!" or something witty, if something turned up.

The shower stopped and he heard the bathroom door open. Fairy stepped briskly from the shadows of the hall wearing only a bath towel. It was wrapped around her head like a turban.

He had already let the pillow fly. When it bounced off her hip, she stopped and looked at him wildly for a moment before she screamed; her bedroom door slammed. The pillow rolled back down the steps.

"Oh, God, Fairy, I didn't mean to...!" he shouted. But what *had* he meant to do? He covered his head with his hands.

From the other side of the door upstairs, she said, "*Now* I know where you are!" with the laughing lilt of exasperation she used when he played the fool. "Go down and Sit! I'll be down in a little."

He slunk down the steps and sat down in the chair by the newel post.

"*Geez! Straighten up and fly right!*" he hissed, and thumped his forehead with the pillow.

"The Hill boys offered me a ride, and I decided to come after all."

"Why?"

Her voice trilled down from upstairs, sublimely goofy, "A little bird told me..."

"*I* told you there wasn't a thing to it," he said. "Charlene..."

"I went to the South Side. Liz says Punk made up with Lock at Christmas. *Ergo*, she wouldn't have been making time with you, hon! Liz says it's Charl trying to get me back with Bruce, 'cause she's told around we're engaged. So you're off the hook--kind of. What were you doing with her anyway, brute?"

"Nothing! Punk and I are practically siblings! Trust me!"

"I trust *Liz!* And she knows *you*, buddy, don't think she doesn't!"

Liz had saved his bacon. "You have much to answer for," he lisped.

For a while only the sound of a hair drier. Then he heard the bedroom door open and she called down. "What's on tonight?"

"Party at Walt's."

"I wouldn't know what to wear. I didn't bring anything." she said.

"You have stuff here!"

Her bare feet pattered on the stairs, and here she was in her old patchwork robe holding two dresses on hangers, "Nothing but this. Aren't you sick of these?" She threw them over the sofa and flung herself down on the other end and kicked off her mules. When she tossed her head dismissively at the dresses, her hair swung around her shoulders and the sunlit shade behind her made a nimbus of a myriad reddish flashes in the whorl of her jet locks.

319

"Dinner at the Moonlight?"

"Or we could just stay home once in a while," she laughed. "We're always eating out."

"What? Where are your folks?" The back light hid her face, and he sprang across the room in two steps and threw himself into the armchair beside her to fathom her expression. She was staring at his stocking feet and suddenly made a cluck of mock pity "Poor things!" and knelt before him and tucked the purple throw around his feet. So he bent over her, and she arched her back to be kissed upside down, and he embraced her and slid out of the chair. When he opened his eyes, the "Medina" of the New Year's *tableau* lay in his lap--one hand over her bare breast and the other forgetting the robe--a Maxfield Parrish maiden in filtered sun motes and shadow.

"They're gone for the weekend." she chuckled from her chest, and her fingers grasped his tie. "Greeks don't wear ties."

"Sheets?"

"Nor shirts." She pulled at his shirttail and got up without closing the robe and pushed him off the mohair throw and spread it on the carpet like a tablecloth for a picnic.

When he had thrown his clothes in a bunch on the chair and lay back and scooped her into his arm, she said, "*Oh, my!*" and covered his erection with the little pillow. She tilted her head back with a critical look at the effect, and took it off again, and tossed it away.

"What does it want for its graduation present?" she asked it in babytalk.

He turned to her, and she to him, and the atmosphere of the room was redolent of her body from its bath: the soap, the Tweed, and the private taste of them imprinted on each other from the New Year's Eve, until their bodies tied the steep close timeless knot in the block of sun-glow on the purple spread. "Go there!" she said,

320

"There *now!*" and then with a helpless flutter, "Don't *stay!* God, *please, Miles!*"

When they put the ruined throw aside, she whispered, "Did you inside?"

"No."

"Swear?"

He crossed his heart. She said that he was dear. Then they lay silent till the chill crept in. When he leaned up to get a cigarette from his shirt, she slipped out of reach and ran up the stairs trailing the robe in one hand with fine indifference.

He dressed slowly, hearing the shower again. In a while she came down wearing the robe and some men's pajamas which she offered him, and "the best side of my bed for all night."

They had a quibble over his leaving. She was still glowing with the energy of the restitution she had made, and the end of all the putting off. But he had come a little down to earth. "If I don't go home tonight, they'll find out from Nelda you were home, and Ferne will tell your mom I didn't come home tonight, and they'll figure it all out. And he'll pull your hair again!"

The serrated shadow of the trees had climbed to the top of the big front window, and the house was in the gloaming when Fairy turned on the kitchen light. But still she must feed him something, not just send him off. As she looked in the refrigerator for the makings of a meal, she was on the verge of tears to let him go.

He wasn't hungry, and there was little in the fridge, but he sensed that it had been waiting under her mind that some day she would make him a nuptial meal. So this was it. He sat at the breakfast table while she made the coffee and toast and scrambled some eggs, and they sat a long time over the last piece of a two-day pie they had found and scraped from the tin, while they talked about Char's scheme to get Fairy back for Bruce. "She thinks she's right.

She's a mess from worrying about him. But what can *we* do? I wrote him again a week ago," Fairy said. "I'll stop if you say."

"You don't belong to anyone," he quoted her.

"*Now* I do, " she said

"Then, you might as well write."

"Anyway, he's still quarantined."

"Till the invasion."

They talked about getting summer jobs together at the plant as soon as her school was out. With his summer's seniority he thought he could get them on the same shift. They could claim the back seat of the bus going home.

The dark came down outside, and from time to time Fairy would get up for more coffee. Each time, her floppy pajama sleeve dragged on his shoulder and the tip of her breast caressed the nape of his neck, and she would renew her offer to set the alarm so he could go at midnight, or sometime.

Finally, he pushed his chair back and said outright that he could not stay and hold off like that again.

"Then, best not..." she finally acceded.

They promised letters right away. And he left by the back door. In the yard, he remembered his coat and went back for it, and almost stayed.

The widow Nelda saw him for the first time as he went back up the porch steps. She thought he was just now coming to see Fairy. While she did up some dishes, she kept time on how long he stayed. He had been with Fairy ten minutes when he left again, and the old woman made a mental note to tell Gladys that Miles had come by, but had left soon enough. She thought Gladys would be pleased.

Fairy cleaned the kitchen and flushed his cigarette butts down the toilet. She put the dresses away and packed the purple throw in her school bag to have cleaned in Ames.

At seven the next morning, the Hill brothers stopped and picked her up, and she returned to Ames having only missed three classes.

Gladys and Ray returned from the night at their home place late the next morning. Fairy had not told her mother she was coming home, and in her phone call Monday from Ames she didn't mention she had been there. Nelda, since she had nothing titillating to report, forgot to mention Fairy's night at home to Gladys, and Gladys thought she had put the purple throw away somewhere for the summer.

Wednesday, Miles received a note from Fairy with the salutation, "Hi, dear trucker! Be patient, hon, soon be summertime! But then we must be good! I've made a New Year's resolution for you about that. Love! Love! *Love*!"

4

It Won't Be Long Now!

When Miles finished the drafting job for Ralph Cross, the tile factory was working one shift again, and he got a job wheel-barrowing the molded clay to the kilns and loading out the fired brick, while he marked time till Fairy finished spring term and they could go together to get summer jobs at the ordnance plant. Working the tile was also a muscle job, but it usually left him with enough juice after dinner for a movie or a game of snooker with some of the crew

But the night of June 5, he had come home early and was at his desk reading with the radio muttering inaudibly on his bedside table when he caught a note in the newsreader's voice that signaled something big coming in on the upcoming invasion. He put the book down and listened. Yesterday, Eisenhower, Supreme Commander, had announced that the Gustav Line was broken and the Allies were threatening the outskirts of Rome. Now, Rome had fallen like a pin dropping in the hush of the world-wide anticipation of D Day, and Roosevelt had just announced, *"One down and two to go!"*

The next day the Invasion began. Edward R. Murrow relayed to the United States Eisenhower's Order of the Day, *"'We will accept nothing less than full victory!' Good night and good luck!"*

Roosevelt returned to the air, *"My fellow Americans: last night when I spoke with you about the fall of Rome, I knew at that moment that troops of the United States and our allies were crossing the Channel in another and greater operation. It has come to pass with success thus far........And so, I ask you to join with me in prayer."*

With J. Arthur and Ferne, he joined the President in the prayer for the success of our arms. Across the table, Ferne's eyes were still closed when he raised his head.

"The largest amphibious invasion in history--tough going on the ground at Normandy!" A CBS reporter in a B-26 Marauder over Utah beach reported the German air force was absent without leave. *"The air is clear!"*

That night the late news announced that some of the Normandy beachhead was a mile inland.

On the ninth, the highway to Cherbourg was cut and the beachhead was forty miles long. On Saturday, it was fifty miles.

By June 12, the invasion of Normandy had succeeded. Eisenhower had proclaimed it: *"Much has happened since the Nazi triumphs of 1940-1941...The tide has turned."*

Everyone in the Midwest suddenly felt as though they had been watching a play from the cheap seats for years and the climax had finally come and the denouement was at hand. The Allies seemed within weeks of winning in Europe. For a moment we went giddy with the illusion that the war was almost over.

At the brick plant, Gene DeReus ran a wheel barrow of wet clay bricks ready for firing up a steel ramp to the kiln and dumped the lot, turning it into a dun-colored mud pile. "Take that, you Kraut!" and walked off to celebrate. "They can call me if they want me back. If not, up theirs!" The rest of the crew worked out the day with more damage done.

Fairy's finals were finished and she had come home that afternoon. That night they made a party and six couples went to dance at Lake Robbins, the pavilion ten miles from town.

While the others danced to the beat of the country band and stamped in happy anticipation, Fairy and Miles stayed in the corner booth, his arm around her and their heads together. Fairy was in a mercurial mood; she reminded him his eighteenth birthday was less than two months away. He said that they never actually inducted you till a month after your birthday. In fact, he was thinking of starting school again at Drake for the fall semester to get in as much of the term as he could before he was called up.

Fairy disliked the home economics major at Iowa State College and wanted a real subject major like history or English, which she could not get at Ames. She said she was going to transfer to Coe or Simpson.

"If I'm at Drake this fall and you're at Simpson, that's close," he said. "Right now, who knows, I might still be here all fall--or maybe not."

She shook her head and frowned. "But what if they call you up right after your birthday? They *could* do that, couldn't they?" A darkness crossed her brow, and she made wet rings with her glass on the table top without looking up. "You know, I haven't heard from Bruce since the middle of May."

"Neither has the family, since before the invasion," he said. "I saw Roy. He's okay, but Char's falling apart."

At eleven, the rest decided to go to Alice's Spaghetti Land. Miles and Fairy got out at her house and went into the screened porch.

"You've never been in my boudoir? Well, Presto!" Fairy pulled on the daybed frame, and the hinged back slid down and made a double bed. Then she put it back. "Don't get any ideas!"

"You've moved down already?"

"It's fresh," she said, "but I've got covers." He looked at the kitchen window. The shutters were closed.

"Oh, they're long gone to the land of Nod."

He got the bed back down.

"Now, is *this* you, *my* you?" he said, "*Come!*"

"Do we need these covers?" She threw the pillows at the head.

"Does anyone need covers on a honeymoon?" When all their clothes tossed on the chairbacks rippled in a draft of night wind coming through the screens like a powder puff, he sighed with a shudder, "This *is* Kismet, *Fairy!* There won't ever be anyone else for us. We *feel* it, Fairy." That was his theory.

"She nodded against his chest, "Please now... Miles, *Please?*"

When they turned toward the night draft, she said, "I don't crush you, this way?"

"Stay till tomorrow."

She kept her head on his chest, "But--did you?"

"No. Scout's honor!"

Then for the better part of June they were often together there. But when Gladys and Ray were around, they took their "honeymoon" to other places. In the Mercury was a place. One night, parked in front of Fairy's house, they saw J. Arthur just in time, swinging by as though taking a constitutional. After that, they went several times to the old garage and the Chevy that Ray Wing drove to deliver War Department telegrams, and which some people had taken to calling the Black Mariah. Or they walked down the tracks to the bridge pier and lay on the concrete abutment one person wide above the whispering current.

They plunged into a maze and lost the thread, and didn't want to find it. One day she blew hot, then cold, and made a spat and sent him home, then phoned and challenged him to prove he loved her for herself without her body. He laughed, "I love your ectoplasm!" She hung up. Gnawed with compunction, he took her to a party, but they ended in a dark room with a chair against the door.

They made movie dates with friends and stood them up because they fell into a dark nest of rugs he threw down beside the workbench in his basement. They went to each other every night like alcoholics to a secret stash of liquor they only thought was hidden because they were already drunk. Their radiant heat set up a supercharged vibration that tripped a primal switch in others and made the girls cluck and the boys fleer and jape and start to follow them.

On his walk, J. Arthur had perceived more than he saw. One night he locked the house when he shut down his rig so that Miles would have to knock when he came home. Then he came down in his slippers, puffed up with sleep and wrath and took his pocket watch from his robe and snapped open the case and stared at the time, and made a fierce inchoate sound. So, Miles left his bedroom screen unhooked and put up to his porch window a painter's ladder that had been left in the tall weeds when the neighbors to the west moved out in May. At two in the morning he climbed into his window and leaned out and dropped the ladder in the grass. At breakfast he yawned and said, "Pass the juice, please." J. Arthur's upper lip turned long and blue as snow, and both their fists were balled. "You *will* be in at my time! You're a seventeen-year-old *boy*! On the verge of the service. If you get her in trouble, what are you prepared to do! You're a damned snot boy! You think because you're big...well, I'll show you big!"

When J. Arthur's voice got soft and reptilian, Miles knew that his father *would* show him, and he almost welcomed the beating he would get, because he knew he and Fairy were over a one-way brink. But Ferne pushed between them from the kitchen, and they turned their backs on each other and sat down.

Miles cursed himself for a monster of lust.(it was more complicated than Huxley thought. Did lust trump love? Did they overlap?) That he kept his vow as best he

328

could, inflamed his desperation, and it became no honeymoon but an ecstatic purgatory, till the night at the end of June when Fairy turned away. They sat in the baseball stands in the pitch dark embracing and quarreling about undressing. As a car came into the park and its headlights raked through the stand, they saw a big man's shadow jump off the far end of their riser. Someone was stalking them. Miles shouted, "Hey!" but it was silent. They quickly left the park, walking down Ninth Street looking back over their shoulders. He had glimpsed the same figure a few nights before, sitting on the railing of the old wagon bridge.

The next day, Fairy went to Des Moines on the bus, and that night she made him stay in and visit with Gladys and listen to "*Mr. First-Nighter*" on the radio while she decided what she would say. Then at the back door she told him she was going to Pennsylvania to visit Ruth over the Fourth. Miles had been pressuring her to go to the plant Friday and get their summer jobs. Now she was breaking the spell. She promised to be back Thursday week.

He was flabbergasted. "God! that's..." he said, figuring, "...the sixth already!" He stormed about the kitchen and harangued, but she had her ticket, which was not refundable, and that settled the argument.

Thursday morning he delivered her to the Chicago Rocket to go to Ruth's. She didn't look like a person going on a holiday. When he kissed her fretful eyebrow to sooth its distracted arch, she shied and looked away blanched and somber.

The honeymoon, such as it was, was over.

On the Fourth of July, when General Omar Bradley ordered every allied artillery piece on the Continent to fire at least one shell into *Festung Europa,* the tile factory crew mounted a progressive celebration, and in De Reus's wood-sided Ford wagon, fueled with hoarded ration tickets and a full supply of mixed synthetic Scotch, sloe gin and fireworks, set off salvos at celebrations in three adjoining counties and ended at a Hugo's Bar and Grill in Des Moines where John Bradley's mother now cooked--since the nurse had reappeared. By this time, a girl named Joyce from one of the county celebrations had stuck to Miles, and the next morning he remembered that he had schmoozed her that he would like to see her again, except that he was going right into the service. At the time, he thought it was a line.

The morning of the fifth, with a hangover, he went to the tile factory and quit. He took the Mercury to the ordnance plant and got back his shell-slinging job starting next week.

Thursday at five o'clock he was at the downtown Rock Island station to pick up Fairy. The Rocket came in and disgorged several hundred people from Chicago and points east, but Fairy wasn't on it. When everyone else had gone, he walked along the platform looking in the windows and then walked back through the cars and looked in the lounge. He had a premonition.

At home there was a letter from Fairy on the dining room table that had come in the morning mail. It had been mailed before the Fourth. The first line told him not to meet the train.

> *I've decided to stay on several days more, then the crowds will be down. I had a terrible ride out. I had to stand for three hours. But after Youngstown a nice soldier gave me his seat. An old friend of Ruth's came to the train with her. His name's Darwin Carling, and he is also going into the service this fall. Except Darwin's been in R.O.T.C and says he will be going direct to O. C. S.*
>
> *I can't think today. I still have to work some things out, then I'll call.*
>
> *What it is, I'm late. From before I left. I'd been waiting for it and hoping I wouldn't need to tell you, but*

330

now I'm pretty late, and I'm usually regular. I know you took care, but in that sex ed. class I had to take the nurse said that IT can happen even when the man does. She said the little devils are very persistent! Don't fret. It's still a false alarm I hope.

Everything in his life came to a standstill. When he had the grippe and they put ice on him to bring down the fever, he was too sick to remember it till Ferne told him afterward. Being less than conscious was merciful; but now whatever he did the rest of the day--like eating dinner--IT was crouched between his eyes and his plate. That night in bed in the dark while a continuous slide show of bits of postwar lives they never would live now played on the ceiling, IT hovered in the foreground like a bat wing.

At around midnight he got up and returned to Uncle Bill's prayer position on his knees and asked God to spare them this once. "God, I'm only *seventeen!*" But he still didn't believe his God attended to such prayers. He got back in bed and seemed to lie awake wide-eyed the rest of the night hearing the tattoo of Lester Baer's punching bag start up at one and go on till nearly dawn, so faint that it made him listen for it when he was trying to think a hundred things at once. He still had the bone-deep superstition that he owed God a penance for what he had done to Fairy.

But what did *she* owe if he had got her into it? If she really *was,* it was she who would suffer--she would never get her degree, and Ray Wing would banish her. (Would the taciturn, mild-mannered little man, smoker of corncob pipes like MacArthur...would he really do that? But he had dragged her by her hair!) It had seemed a million miles away from him then; now here it was! So, if she *was,* what could he do? If they got married, and he was drafted in September, what would marriage help? And

331

where would she go with her baby--*his* baby--while he was in service!

He couldn't bring himself to even consider how his parents would take it--how they would meet their friends-- his parents, who probably still had not totally given up hope that he would become a man.

"Well, here's his manhood for you," the Baers would snicker. "Ha! ha!"

He got up late and moped downtown and was gone all day. He spent the afternoon shooting eight-ball with the certified loafers without knowing whether he won or lost. He was some zombie mechanical man with IT between him and the cue, mumbling prayers under his breath for God to let them off this one time. Though the vision of Fairy in childbirth, perhaps dying, the devil's revenge for his stupid *tableau vivant* of a dead Medina, hung over his head like an epitaph. He stuffed that specter into a black hole with all his might, but it had made a scorched slash through his conscience that would erase the smart-ass swagger out of his life for good.

Saturday, clutching at straws, he looked into the service allotment for a married man. He got a ride to town with Ferne, who was taking two friends to lunch in Des Moines, and got out downtown and went to the recruiting office.

The sergeant looked sharply at his glasses as he sat down and made him take the eye test before he went any further into the process: "If your eyes are weak, we have to get a reading on them before we know where to start." Enlisting was the farthest thing from his mind, but he decided to find out once and for all how his eyes rated with the army, so he took a chit and walked to the Military Recruitment Processing Station around the corner on Walnut. The examination was done the army way, no ducking in for an eye test and getting out. It came at the other end, after you took the whole shebang, naked, in shoes and socks. With his wallet in his hand, Miles stood behind a stubby blond boy and read the chart over his shoulder while the youth had trouble with a line. When it was Miles' turn to take off his glasses and cover one eye and then the other, the letters were the usual blur, but he remembered what they were.

So, he accidentally passed the vision test, and the whole physical examination "one hundred per cent!" The recruiting sergeant, a grizzled, square-faced man with a sandy moustache and a row of serious ribbons, looked up from the results with a quizzical eyebrow, "20-20?" he said, "So, what's the specs for?"

"Prism," Miles said, remembering his uncle's word, "I've got a little prism.

"But I'm not enlisting today, at least not till next week." He told the sergeant he needed to find out the amount of the allowance for a wife.

The sergeant pulled a face, "You know the base pay. And you're married?"

"Not yet."

"My advice: If you're getting married, don't plan to take her with you. She can't live on your allowance unless you've got another source of income. If you try to get an apartment for her near the base, your allowance won't buy a room with a bath down the hall anywhere we'd send you. Can she get a job? Not likely, unless she's a stripper. Heh-heh!

"Confidentially, the way things are breaking now-- I'd wait till you're eighteen. If the Krauts cave before New Year's they may end the draft and re-deploy European armies to the East to finish the little bastards. So, what's your hurry? On the other hand," he grinned, "if her old man comes after you with a shotgun, stop by. I'll keep your papers on file. I can send you to a safe place where no one will shoot you in the pants--not for fornication anyway..." He winked, and looked at his calendar. "But if you sign on, it's a month--maybe three weeks if we expedite it!" He gave a jovial laugh and stood up and extended his hand. "Take care!" he winked.

The next day Miles sat in church and thought about IT as the sermon plodded along and old Cozad snored. He had a stub of a pencil in his pocket and tried to figure on the back of his program how they could scrape up the money to get married.

Then, in the afternoon he went to his room and spent half an hour composing a ten-sentence letter asking Fairy to marry him. Ferne and J. Arthur would let them live in his room and save his ordnance overtime for the baby, and the way they were breaking out of the Normandy beachhead, he might get to work through December before they called him. Then, when he got out in maybe a year, they would have the G. I. Bill to start them out!

Suddenly, it all seemed do-able.

*Listen, hon! The minute you get this, turn it over and write, yes--**YES**!--No, **Phone**! So we can set a date before August! Then get the next train! Get a plane! And I'll take sick time and we can go to Okoboji for a couple of days!*

PS. : Enclose this clip from yesterday's Dallas County News:

Roy Cross informs us that a letter arrived yesterday from son Bruce, who had not been heard from for two weeks. Bruce says he lost his outfit getting off the beach and continued with another company for a time. Bruce says to tell folks he's okay.

Miles mailed the letter before he got on the bus to the plant Monday.

An hour later, sorting mail beside a long-time friend and colleague named Button, Lester Baer turned and asked

334

if he would like to know "how Maxie hits 'em"? August Button knew, as did everyone at the post office, that Lester Baer's cousin Max had once been Heavyweight Champion. He turned grinning and said, "Okay, how does Maxie hit 'em?"

Lester Baer hit him with a right cross that broke his jaw. Then Lester went on a rampage and destroyed everything in back till the post office staff overpowered him. It took four of them to hold him down till Doc Bradley came down from his office and sedated him. He was transported to the veterans' hospital at Clarinda before noon.

The Morgans noticed first that the punching bag had stopped. Then Gladys dropped in and said Lester had gone to the hospital for tests. She didn't say which hospital. The postal staff agreed to keep Lester's breakdown quiet for fear of federal complications. The mail that could be saved was cleaned up and delivered or sent on. The next edition of the *Dallas County News* merely said Lester had been hospitalized for tests. The Morgans got the impression from Jean that it was a kidney stone.

When two days had passed, and his proposal should have reached her, Miles began to wait hour by hour for Fairy's call. Then he decided she would want to answer it by letter. But when it turned the fifth day and there was still no word, he began to think that something had happened to her. She had told him New Year's day that if they got in trouble, Ray Wing would disown her. No have-to wedding would appease him, she had said, only something like immaculate conception. Miles had dismissed it as medieval. Now he took heed and began to fear she might do something desperate to keep it from Ray Wing. He found Ruth's phone number, and Friday night when Ferne had gone to bed and J. Arthur was working his rig in back, he tried to call.

335

It awakened Ruth's mother, who thought the caller was a boy who had been pursuing Ruth. "She's out with Darwin," she snapped and hung up. The next day she told Ruth she thought it was long distance. She thought she'd said, "She's out with Darwin and them." But the two words did not reach Miles. He misconstrued that it was Fairy who had gone out with the boy her letter had mentioned, whom he already resented, the O. C. S. fellow, Darwin, and Miles spent the rest of the night in sleepless consternation, spinning paranoid fantasies on the dark of Fairy with Darwin Carling.

In the morning, his gut tied in a furious knot of self spite, he hitched a ride to Des Moines and completed his enlistment.

Fairy telephoned in the evening and apologized for Ruth's mother hanging up on him. Then she lilted, "Guess what I celebrated last night: We're not in trouble! Hallelujah, hon!" Her low, bubbling chuckle, which he had loved, cut into his heart like a shard of glass.

"What about my letter? What was your answer, if any?"

"What letter? What answer?"

"I've been waiting forever!" he said, his voice rising. "As soon as you said we were in trouble, I wrote. I told you to call. Should I have sent a nickel?".

"I haven't *had* any letter!"

"Well, what *happened* to it! Did it go to Shangri-la!" he cried. "You went out and celebrated with that, that Darwin!"

"Four of us went to a movie...."

"Did you throw away my letter with the other junk mail?"

"*Miles! I never....*"

"Or maybe my proposal slipped your mind!"

"Your *what*? ...."

"In the letter, I asked you to marry me!" He stopped, blackly savoring the abyss of silence. "Wherever it went, it's over the dam now. I joined the army today, babe! I'll go next month!"

"Oh, *God*! Miles! What have you *done*?"

"What have *I* done? Well, someone has done, all right!"

He was silent and the line sizzled. "Are you there?" In the white noise of the line from Pittsburgh, he heard her groan, and his rage collapsed. The letter *had* gone wide somehow. "Oh, my Jesus, Fairy!" Bewildered, he tried to retrieve the pieces of his proposal in his head and blunder it through, "It wasn't a *have-to, Fairy!* It's what I *wanted, what I want!* So, *will* you anyway? We still have time!"

But Fairy sniffled, and drew back. Not that she doubted he had sent the letter. But whatever he had tried to do, nothing had come through to her, and their escape could not close up the abyss of days when his silence had left her to face the prospect of the ruin of her life alone. After the Fourth, she had broken down and spilled her troubles in a sobbing session on Ruth's shoulder. And Ruth had invited her to stay till school began. She would get Fairy a job on the line she worked on in her father's little plant. This, she had done.

In fact, Fairy's intention when she called, underlying her news of their escape, had been to tell him, whatever his silence meant, that she would not be coming back until September. She had started work with Ruth in her father's plant yesterday. His renewed proposal still carried for her the claustrophobic taint of a shotgun wedding. And the prospect of the ordnance job, with long intimate night rides home in the dark of the Conard's bus, no longer appealed.

She hung back and fended off. And it was finally settled by circumlocution. They despaired together over his lost letter, and blamed it for their fearful days. And Fairy

337

promised to think about his proposal and call back tomorrow. And they reconciled of sorts. But when they rang off, the phantom pregnancy still lay heavily between them like a dead child, and neither touched it again.

Then in a few days, due to circumstances at Chen's plant no one had foreseen, Fairy became an inspector for a section of the line with a handsome raise. Her next letter didn't mention it, or that she had taken an unexpected liking to her new responsibility. Of course, they both avowed in letters that IT had brought them closer. But as July turned into August, the idyll of the spring receded in the rear-view mirror of their minds like a half-forgotten sunny childhood lane whose turnoff they had missed, setting them for good or bad on paths more dubious and solitary.

When he received notice of induction for the twenty-fourth of August, they haggled on the phone about her coming home and made various futile plans, including one to meet for a weekend in Chicago, which would require that she take two absentee days, and which both sets of parents forbade, calling it "a one night stand."

Thus, her promise to "come tearing home " when he was called, stumbled on this and that and slipped away, and they had finally resigned themselves to a long-distance goodbye when they talked the last Tuesday. They assured each other that his leaving early was a backhand blessing that would make his furlough come sooner. He promised to call early the twenty-fourth before she left for work, and they said, "Love! Love!" and rang off, both feeling older and somehow punished by the misfortune of the summer for their wicked pleasures of the spring.

5

You'll be Sor-ry!

On June 2, in New Guinea, the 503d Airborne Regimental Combat Team was flown to Cyclops field near Hollandia, and on July 4, two battalions jumped on Noemfoor island, a Japanese-held island 15 miles long by 12 wide, from which the Japanese had been feeding in reinforcements at night for the battle of Biak nearby.

Jumping below minimum altitude on a coral airfield studded with bulldozers and other machinery, the 1,424 men suffered 128 severe injuries. The jump of the 2d Battalion of the regiment was rescheduled, and they made their landing on the beach by LCIs. The 503d drove the Japanese underground and then cleared the island by August 31. This made possible MacArthur's final preliminary island jump to Moratai, just 300 miles from the Philippines.

A source on MacArthur's staff remembered the general, who had been rescued from Corregidor two and a half years before in the dead of night, standing on the beach at Moratai, gazing out to the northwest, "almost as though he could already see through the mist the rugged outlines of Bataan and Corregidor, 'They are waiting for me there,' MacArthur said, 'It's been a long time.'"

General Edward Flanagan later added, "The 503 RCT did not know it yet, but it was to become an integral and active part of MacArthur's dream to return to Bataan and Corregidor."

AIRBORNE, Lt. General E. M. Flannagan, Jr.

The Wednesday before he left for the service, Miles kept his long standing promise to Ferne to visit the relatives in Winterset and be passed in review before them, as they had not seen him since he had yet a foot to grow. A diaspora seemed to have sent many of the Gordons, Clantons and the Clarks to the West Coast, and most of those they did see were the last leaves on the family tree: Hallie, Ferne's mother's sister, who was crippled badly with rheumatoid arthritis; Aunt Lena and Uncle Pres, who had lost their only child to pneumonia her first year of teaching at the small town of Boxholm when Miles was in fourth grade, and had frozen in place huddled over the little shrine of their pretty daughter's last photograph; Al Gordon, eighty-two, Ferne's great uncle, a painter and paper hanger, who had recently fallen off a scaffold and was using a walker. Miles fidgeted with impatience on the hot, leather settees in their flyblown parlors and accepted their vague well-wishing, "Going off to war, is he?"

In the city park at the Clark Tower, which descendents had built of native stone and dedicated to Caleb and Ruth as a tribute to the original seed of the family in the Midwest, Miles and Ferne climbed up the spiral stone stair to the top while J. Arthur stayed in the car. The tower put Ferne in a somber mood, as if it were a memorial to the good times the seven brothers and sisters had seen the last of when their restless father had traded the quarter section of good Iowa farm land for the full section of subsistence land in north-west South Dakota.

Looking over the parapet toward the old stone "home place" beyond the valley, where other people unknown to her now lived, she recited the names of the horses the children had loved, and in her mind's eye saw the landmarks on Clanton Creek where her great aunts were stalked by a panther on the path, and where the Indian child's log sarcophagus had fallen from the tree over the stream near the first lean-to Caleb Clark had made beside Clanton Creek in May of 1846, and where Mary Adeline became the first white child born in Madison County. Miles told her that he had typed these stories out from the scribbled biography of the Clarks that one Judge Lewis had presented before the Madison County Historical Society in 1926 and had left the new typed copy in her folder scrap book.

But as he could remember a time quite recently when he and his friends believed that their own families had been in Iowa forever, and that the real pioneering had all been done by people like Randolph Scott in a "real west" of Hollywood mountains, buttes and treeless plains, it still awed him when Ferne noted that the one hundredth anniversary of Caleb and Ruth Clark's pioneer settlement here was but two years away.

He hazarded that the war would probably be over by then. *Time Magazine* had recently said that Churchill and Roosevelt were soon to meet in Quebec to plan the post war world, and he told Ferne that he and Fairy had talked of moving west when he was discharged, as California seemed a more promising place than Iowa to launch their post war lives. Ferne was silent, looking cheerlessly out over the sear August hillside below, and when she recurred to her old notion that he try divinity school at Drake when he came home, he shied and leaned out over the parapet, and J. Arthur honked the horn, and they went back down.

Thursday, he drove Race to the registrar's office at Drake to complete his transfer from Iowa State. Miles brought along his own transcript with the notion of locking in his Drake enrollment for after his discharge. Could he pre-register now for the semester he got out? The registrar's clerk rolled her eyes, "We don't do that. These veterans we're starting to get now are already marrying and starting families, and we're going to have to clutter up the campus with temporary housing for them next year: And who knows when you'll come back, or for that matter--if.

341

We've still got Japan, don't we? Oh, no, we don't take reservations."

On the way home, Race had him stop at Ma Belle's in the suburb of Windsor Heights to have a beer with some Drake students Race had met. The Windsor Tap was a haunt of Drake's serious teen-age drinkers. Its floor plan still afforded them the anonymity of the speakeasy it had been in the 1920s; behind its everyday restaurant was an "Employees Only" door in the restroom hall that opened on a dark bar with a juke box and a postage-stamp-sized dance floor. There Race introduced him to several girls and four men from the Drake chapter of the same fraternity Race had pledged at Ames. The actives were conducting a pocket rush to get Race to renew his unfinished pledgeship here in the fall and were already on a first name footing. When Race introduced Miles as his friend who was leaving for the service tomorrow, the introductions turned into a series of toasts, and they ordered more glasses and all hefted beers from a half-gallon pitcher, chanting: *Here's to Cardinal Puff for the first time!/So drink chug-a-lug, chug-a-lug, chug-a-lug!*

Some time later, a blonde girl came around the table and sat down beside him to intertwine arms with him and make a toast to their being "shell mates." She had been working at the ordnance plant, and had just quit her job to join her parents at the lake for a break before school started. Her name, he recalled with difficulty in the morning, was Cynthia, or maybe Cindy (she required him to call her Cyn) At the end of their first dance Cyn ordered them Zombies (Belle's own recipe) which they must drink together, again arms entwined, to celebrate their liberation--maybe not so much *his* liberation, she commiserated, massaging his neck as though it would cure him of induction. She toasted him to the bottom of her drink. The Zombie made him cough, so he drank the rest of his at a gulp to preserve his manhood.

They ended in the front of the restaurant dancing where the chairs had already been upended on the tables and they could play the Mills Brothers' *"You Always Hurt the One You Love"* (*the one you shouldn't hurt at all!*). Cyn's ride departed, giving them a dirty look on his way out, and she told Miles how to drive her home--a little ways south of Grand. They were both on the passenger side of the Merc in the shadows of the parking lot when someone pounded a fist on the trunk. Miles caught a flash of Cyn's naked chest in the chrome yellow bar of streetlight when she sat up and hooked her bra. He was going to lock the doors and drive out, but she saw a towering figure coming out of the shadows and panicked, thinking it was her former date stalking her, and jumped out and ran back into the club.

"Sorry about the *coitus interruptus,*" Race said as he got in, "but I'm not walking twenty miles home just because you're having your last fling. What's up? I thought you and Fairy had a pact of purity!"

"...'your own business!" Miles muttered.

"Ol' love 'em an leave 'em!" Race said, "Cyn's slept with half these guys and the rest are waiting. You bucked the line. Listen, man, will you leave her? I need to be well-liked around here!"

"...'m not to be trusted," Miles agreed and started to get out, "You drive."

"Did you forget I don't drive?"

They took the back road home, jerking along guffawing and driving seeing-eye dog style, Race running the accelerator and Miles steering. At the bridges they sped up to put the narrow stuff more quickly behind them. Somewhere the Merc acquired a flat tire on a high curb, and Miles left it in front of Race's apartment and lurched his way home on foot.

Miles and Fairy had planned for a last call early in the morning, but though he dragged himself blindly to the phone, she had left early for work.

J. Arthur and Ferne drove him to the train in the state Ford, and Race, riding along to pick up some of his fall books at the Drake bookstore, went with them to the train. Miles figured Race was making a dry run for his own upcoming induction. Race was now determined to make it over the hurdle of his lazy eye into the service because his rich aunt had two boys coming to college age whose needs would come first and who would go to expensive schools. By Christmas, he would have a semester in on law school. But the Veterans Rehabilitation Act would have to finance the rest when he got out.

On the Rock Island platform in Des Moines, they waited ten minutes for the Rocket for Omaha. Miles picked up his bag and set it down, feeling seedy and blaming Darwin Carling, who shared the car pool with Ruth, for carrying Fairy off early and preventing their last farewell. When he thought of Cyn ("guilty as sin"), he blamed Darwin for that, too, and was grateful for the hangover fog that mercifully obscured his fumbling pass at her in the car.

He was wearing the clothes his mother had laid out, short-sleeved shirt, rayon slacks and his good shoes. In a musette bag he had a shaving kit, clean socks and extra underwear (in case he might have an overnight layover in Kansas City). On top was a purple book, *Judo and Personal Combat,* which he had bought at Hyman's book store to study on the train.

J. Arthur, who had given up cigarettes for a long-stemmed Canadian pipe, dismissed the flat tire and waxed voluble about the utility of beekeeping, his new hobby and the three hives he had bought to beat the sugar rationing.

The Rocket's horn blared, and Miles picked up his bag again. He kissed Ferne. J. Arthur said, "We shall have honey for your pancakes when you come home on leave!"

344

and they embraced and slapped each other stiffly on the shoulders. Miles and Race shook hands, "Tell MacArthur I'm coming!" he called. Standing in the seatless vestibule as the train pulled out, Miles ducked down and waved.

It was night when he changed trains for Leavenworth at Union Station in Kansas City. The new train had several cars of civilian youths going for induction. He found a seat in the middle of a car full of young guys in civilian clothes with little bags like his, all headed for Ft. Leavenworth. The train was still crawling through the outskirts of the city when it ground onto a siding and stopped again. On his side of the aisle, they were beginning to get acquainted and had started joking, awkwardly using the new G.I. jargon, going, "SNAFU! That's, *situation normal, all fucked up!*" when they heard the re-iterant click and ping of another train rolling past. They looked up and stared across into the flashing windows of a Grand Guignol lantern show.

It was a hospital train from the West Coast. Soon the window of a compartment stopped abreast of theirs.

The inductees gawked across into a smoke-filled compartment that reminded Miles of the horrific photos of casualty wards he had stared at in long orgies of morbid fascination with the Adel library's histories of the Great War: By the door to the hall passage there were two duffle bags with the hilts of Samurai swords sticking out. Other Japanese trophies lay about in a disorderly jumble: a rising sun battle flag, a Nambu pistol in a holster, a short sword in a scabbard falling out of a bag that a blond tow-headed boy in shorts and a grubby T-shirt was digging into; he didn't seem to be wounded till he straightened up and tucked a carton of cigarettes under an arm that had a bandaged stump at the end. He caught Miles staring and gave him the finger with his good hand. He tossed the carton of cigarettes to a soldier by the window whose foot was swathed in a bandage that was bigger than his knee and started rewinding the dressing on his stump.

The windows were open between the cars, and the boy with the bandaged leg waved the cigarette carton and shouted, "Where going, girls?"

"Induction Center," the boy beside Miles yelled, "Leavenworth. U.S. Army!" The wounded men all yelled "You'll be sor-ry!"

But they wanted to talk. What was it like in the States any more? Had the slackers punched all the virgins or were there some left? And they wanted to barter. They had more name-brand cigarettes than they knew what to do with, but no cash. The boy on the window side of Miles' seat started to haggle for a souvenir. The one-handed boy offered him a little white silk flag with a rising sun for five dollars. "You got any bloodstained ones?" the recruit shouted. The one-armed boy considered, and said, "ten bucks," and Miles' seatmate handed another bill across. The tow-headed youth swiped the flag on the supperated bandage he had just discarded and handed it back. "Shit!" Miles' seatmate said, and took it with his fingertips.

The tow-head gave them a stare suddenly dead-eyed and old beyond any age they ever wanted to live to. "You get there, you can use your own!"

Their lights dimmed and brightened and Miles' train seemed to move, but it was the hospital train. "You'll be sor-ry!" the combat wounded sang out again as it started to crawl east. As it gained speed, the windows turned into swift flash snaps of mutilated kids, like accelerating tableaus of the carnage of a school bus wreck.

"He said Saipan," Miles' companion said. "Bloody Marines!" He folded his flag and tucked it reverently in his bag.

Their train finally squealed and jerked onto the main line. The inductees were silent till the scattered lights outside spaced out to blackness and they were alone with

346

their own reflections and the black Kansas plains. They started a card game on a suitcase on their knees. The car was quiet the rest of the way.

At Ft. Leavenworth, Miles shot pool most of the day and was sworn in with the rest of his draft about five. The next morning he was issued his uniforms, mess gear and cup, two barracks bags and toilet articles. He packed up his civilian clothes and put in a letter for his parents saying he was leaving in two days, maybe to Texas, and mailed it to Adel.

He took another physical in the afternoon. He was slow reading the chart over the next man's shoulder this time and only caught half of it before he had to take his glasses off. He was written up for a pair of army-issue glasses that only went to men with eyesight 20/60 or worse. He was told the new glasses would follow him to his new billet in ten days. He filled out a personnel form that asked about schooling, bed-wetting and extra-curricular activities. Over *activities* he held the pen a long time before he put down, "music--flute," and listed his second in the National Music Contest. He would have liked to list sports, but he had no distinctions in football. There were two boxes to check if he wished to volunteer for the ski troops or the paratroops. He checked both boxes, but a personnel sergeant who interviewed him at the end of the exam asked him what the names of any Iowa mountains he had skied were, and crossed ski troops out when he couldn't remember any.

That evening he wrote notes to Fairy and Race, and wrote George Kinnick that he had passed by Omaha on his way to Leavenworth. He said he had found out that officers were officers because they had been told where you were going, but enlisted men never knew till "scuttlebutt" tipped them off. He said he heard he was going to Texas.

347

He spent the next day on a coach until a water tower told him he had arrived at Camp Joseph T. Robinson. It was in Arkansas. It turned out to be one of those jerry-built expansion camps slammed together in 1941 with a maze of pitted roads in front of rows of one-story green-lumber barracks set on cement blocks, which had metastasized out of the permanent core of a small pre-war army post. Inside the new barracks were tight rows of double bunks, room only for footlockers to sit on and a stove at either end. They had no running water. There was a latrine with cold showers a half block away.

Here, in a late summer Arkansas heat wave, he began a fifteen-week cycle of infantry basic training that would last exactly twelve weeks.

6

The Bulge

In September, Field Marshal Montgomery made a bold gamble to bring the European war to a quick end. Forces under his command, spearheaded by three divisions of paratroops, would seize the bridges on a road through Belgium and Holland to the Rhine. Then an armored column would dash up this road and secure what the paratroops had taken. The plan, Market Garden, was supposed to open the door for a swift thrust into Germany. Edward R. Murrow, broadcasting for CBS, went along on an unarmed C-47 that released its cargo of paratroops five hundred feet above the German-held terrain and recorded his description of the jump, broadcast to the United States on his return:

[They are] *looking out the windows curiously tension barely suppressed, You occasionally see a man rub the palm of his hand across his trouser leg...In just about thirty seconds now our ship will drop and these nineteen men will walk out onto Dutch soil. You can probably hear the snap as they check the lashing on the static lines. .You hear them shout, "two...three...four...five...six...seven," up to nineteen. Every man out--I can see their chutes going down now, every man clear. They're dropping just beside a little windmill near a church, hanging there. Very gracefully. They seem to be completely relaxed...like nothing so much as khaki dolls hanging beneath a green lampshade.*

Market Garden failed. American paratroopers seized the first two bridges and linked up with the armored column. But by bad luck and command indifference to intelligence from Dutch resistance, the British 1st

Parachute Division (the Red Devils) jumping near the farthest objective, the Rhine bridge at Arnhem, dropped almost on top of two German Panzer units stationed there for rest and refitting. The allied armored column could not reach them, and after a week they were ordered to retire as best they could. Three-quarters of the British were killed or captured:

> However, far from the stumbling advance of the Allies in Europe, General Douglas MacArthur's U.S. Army, with the paratroops of the 11th Airborne Division and the 503rd Parachute Infantry Regiment, was making ready to recapture the Philippines.

WORLD WAR II ON THE AIR, Bernstein & Lubertozzi (narrator: Dan Rather)

It was three weeks before Miles' G.I. glasses came. That Sunday at the Red Cross he put away the horn-rimmed ones Parker had prescribed and put on the service glasses because his right eye had grown weaker, and, ugly as they were with their perfectly round gun-metal-colored frames that gave everyone wearing them a goofy, Harold Lloyd look, the G. I. glasses provided better distance vision, and at that time he was still hoping to qualify as Expert in marksmanship and get into Officer Candidate School. It was a balmy Arkansas late summer afternoon, and he wrote his parents that basic training was shaping up to look like a walk in the park, with everyone on the post out playing baseball or touch football or lying in the sun, and himself expecting to come home on furlough "brown as leather and just as tough!" He had asked Ferne to send his bathing suit.

By the fifth week, that all seemed like a tropic fever dream.

Since then the sky had turned overcast and everything in camp mildewed under a perpetual verge-of-freezing rain. His swimsuit came and was never used. The weather suddenly showed up the expansion barracks as shacks that the wind blew through. On the rifle range the week before bivouac, Miles discovered an Odysseus trick with the sling of a B.A.R. that let its kick walk it across the front rather than up into the air, and scored at the top of the company laying down advancing fire with it, but he could only shoot well enough at 300 and 500 yards to make Sharpshooter, which was not as good as it sounded. The captain had noticed the service glasses and knocked him off the Officer Candidate list. They all suffered the glooms from the endless drizzle more than the piercing chill: A Thursday, when they got back out to the range at seven a.m., the range guard, a married man from Tennessee who had bored everyone with his constant lament about his wandering wife, had shot himself in the head.

The next week, they marched out to bivouac, two weeks in the field while it continued to rain. The guys from the upper Midwest swore that a real freeze would have been better than digging foxholes that filled with ice water faster than you could dig. The second week of it, the whole battalion came down with something. At the beginning there had been 192 men in the company. At the end, 52 men were gone. His platoon of three 12-man squads had shrunk with every sick call till there were only 27 left to straggle back to camp. He told Fairy they looked like they had already been to battle and lost a quarter of their men. He had come to basic training weighing 187 pounds, but when he went to the infirmary the night he got in, he weighed 165. He had a machine-gun cough and thought he was coming down with the grippe again, but at the battalion infirmary a fat doctor with a hangover, furious at being routed out at ten o'clock, read his 103 temperature, chewed him out for malingering and sent him back to the company with some aspirin.

He went to the latrine and spent the rest of the night sitting on a toilet with his overcoat collar buttoned around his chin, writing letters and whooping-coughing. The only good news, he wrote, was that the cycle had been shortened from fifteen weeks to twelve. As to why, you could take your pick of rumors. He didn't think it was because everyone was sick. He thought it had come from high up. The fall of Paris, and Patton driving across France 25 miles a day, had raised the prospect that the Germans might collapse any minute, so the grapevine had it that his cycle would only need to be certified for occupation duty. The bad news: he wrote Fairy that when they took their overseas qualification physical Monday morning, he would probably be bumped from overseas duty to a Stateside supply room clerk, "because of my eyes again. Miles Morgan, only man to ever flunk the infantry!"

He saved Fairy's letters till the last. As he read them in order, he placed the pages face down, then turned them over and read them again. Beside his proposal letter going astray (which had finally followed her home), Fairy had suspected Miles' jealousy over her fictitious date with Darwin Carling had caused him to enlist. Her letters were more circumspect about her Coke date with a red-headed lab partner, and the V-12 Ruth had set her up a double date with, who timidly groped her under the housemother's baleful eye at the front door of West Hall. She complained of boredom with home economics classes after a summer doing "something useful for the first time in my life", and repeated the gossip of the girls about Mrs Berry's mysterious afternoon excursions, from which she returned "happy and fragrant." She said Ruth was probably going to transfer to Penn next year.

He read the letters again and wrote a long portmanteau answer, and toward morning nodded off sitting on the commode.

352

Leaving the *Home Front*

But, Monday morning when they fell out for the overseas physical, the cough had subsided and he had sweated the fever out. Though it was cold enough to snow, the company marched to the infirmary for the physical in combat boots and overcoats. His next letter on Tuesday said:

This is important, are you listening? No <u>underwear!</u> *Nothing else but butt! Ha-ha! We looked like a bunch of dirty old men going to a Rainbow girls' picnic!*

Seriously, the overseas physical is <u>tough</u>*, and I was sure the eyes would get me knocked back to Special Service. But I could see over everybody in front of me again this time, so when I took my glasses off I zipped right through! But where to hide my G.I. glasses so they wouldn't tip them off I was below 20-60? Somewhat of a problem being in the buff and all! But Aha! How bout between my cheeks! Which served very well up to the station where this captain made me bend over and cough and they fell out. So, something fishy here, my man! And back to the chart we go! But before I tucked them in I'd memorized an extra line for safety's sake. So, I'm over the stile! I thought, halleluiah, I'll make dog soldier!*

The first week in November his first letter was postmarked from Ft. Benning:

Hon, you won't believe!--or probably you will from this postmark....The last morning formation at Robinson, Sergeant Herman runs down the list of guys who would go on furlough right away. In alphabetical order, Madden, Moran, Morlock--I wasn't on it! I thought they'd found out what I did and X-ed me off home leave! Then he read off four guys going to the paratroops, who'd ship out for Ft. Benning after the rest had gone home, "Wait a minute," he says. "There's supposed to be five! Oh! Here we are! Miles Morgan!

353

"Whoa," I say, "Not me?!" But I told you I checked the paratroop box at Leavenworth? The captain let it stand! When they dismissed, we five all shouted, "Geronimo!"

So...I've jumped into the paratroops. Pun there! Hey, but we had another physical at Benning to catch you if you had fooled 'em--Oh, Lord, the trouble I've un-seen! More about that crisis later!

Hey, Fairy, no joke! Do you know why the U. S. paratroops are the best outfit in the service? Because they're all volunteers, officers are too, and have to qualify right alongside enlisted men. And no matter what rank an officer comes in at, he goes through the four weeks physical training absolutely under the orders of these muscle guys that torture us with the push-ups--who are all non-coms! They put the officers all in 1st platoon, which is more brutal than the others: If the sergeant catches us goofing off, he says, "Give me twenty-five, sojer!"(meaning twenty-five push ups), but if it's an officer, he says, "Give me thirty, major!"--and if the officer gives him flak for not saying, sir, he'll say, "Sir, give me fifty, sir!" And that major will give him fifty, too, or he'll ship out, major or not. That's why any paratrooper will break a leg for his officers!

But I'm the only one left from our Robinson company now. Two of them got talked into quitting--the first day of A stage before you do anything rough they sit you in the sawdust pits, and the muscle men pace around like tigers and harangue you to quit, and tell you how miserable they're going to make you for four weeks, and tell you to just stand up and you can save yourself all that. But you do, and you've quit, and they ship you before lunch. So two of our guys stood up, and the other two wouldn't go out the thirty-four foot door. I'm the only one left, Mr. Four Eyes--I started wearing my civilian glasses

354

again around here so my G. I. glasses don't give it away that I see worse than 20/30!

But then, if you stay and see it through, it's not <u>that</u> bad, --there's a trick to climbing a 50-ft rope, you know-- and doing a thousand side-straddle hops, stuff. With me, the one hour run almost got me--you know what a flat-foot I am, and we would run the last hour in the morning--on a parade ground about a quarter mile across, divided in half by a dry creek with a little foot bridge. All these companies running w/ noncoms counting cadence, clumps of guys doing the "paratroop shuffle." You run for a half an hour on one side of the creek, then he runs you across the bridge like you're going in, but you just run all over the other side. Double time, never stop. It's not hot but it gets warm! The last twenty minutes you begin to see a body here and there on the ground--guys that collapse. When you head in, the medics sitting on the fenders of the ambulance smoking take their time to get off their butts and cruise around and pick up the bodies. So if you collapse, you just lie there for the rest of the hour--and then you're gone to cooks and bakers school, or where. It's a big incentive to keep grindin'. But we're through with that now. We're running around the airport now, and sometimes back!

And the officers are running with you--Best outfit in the world!

Hey, but next week we make five jumps! What am I going to do with my horn rims?--they'll fly off!.....What would Odysseus do? Something'll come to me! It better!

Why didn't you tell me about Ben Kinnick--or probably you didn't hear about it up at Ames. Last week Mom wrote that Ben's plane was lost on a mission over New Ireland. I looked it up. It's off New Guinea. Remember when Nile went down? Too much of this....

When I opened her letter, I was on night duty in the orderly room. No one was there but me, and I started sniveling. Yah, stuff came out of my eyes. It clotted me all

355

up about that family's luck! Francis Kinnick tutoring me and George after school, and we'd go out to the side yard football game afterward, and Ben would be captain of one side and Nile the other, and Nile would show us little guys how to hold the place kicks. And then Nile won all the football glory in America, all of it!--and it's already over forever! And only George is left. And, I tell you, Fairy, I felt old! So I'm snorting there, and a wise ass in from a pass to Phoenix City says, "What's up, your mother die?"

I said, "Butt off!" and he stuck his nose in and said, "Paratroops don't cry."

I said, "So, sombitch, report me!" (You have to say it just like that in the paratroops or they get really pissed!)

Seriously, though, what'll they do about George Kinnick, Fairy? He's just three months younger than me, and two brothers gone. Would they make him go in when he's lost two brothers? I don't think so. But I know George. He'll go.

Be good, hon. I figure I'll be home in ten days or so! Write quick and tell me what day your Christmas vacation starts. I'll pick you up. Hey, I'm Dreaming of a White Christmas! I figure we'll get ten days.

"Tonight I've been catching up on the news I lost touch with the last two weeks, and since the 82nd and the 101st Airborne were both in the thick in September-Oct., I figure my class will probably go to Europe to one of those divisions. But we won't know till we get back after Christmas.

I already packed my chute today! Next week Geronimo! (though they don't say that any more.) Kisses! Miles

After he sealed the letter, he stayed in the lounge trying to start reading a novel he had picked up at the PX. He hadn't read anything but his judo book for a month and had turned down going to a Danny Kaye movie to finish the letter and start the novel. But he didn't start now. He thought about Ben Kinnick and the war, Ben lost in the Bismarck Sea around the world in the heart of nowhere, mixed with the memory of Saturday basketball in the haymow of Kinnicks' barn. He noticed the war was getting closer The Tennessee married man who had had enough on the rifle range at Robinson was close, and the two troopers making their last qualifying jump last Friday who got tangled up in the air and came down riding a double streamer, were close. And Ferne's letter had said that there were a dozen gold-star names posted in the courthouse now.

He sat over the forgotten book chewing on the pen looking out the window, not following the winking light of a C-47 taking off below the bluff, but remembering George Kinnick swinging like Tarzan on the reinforcing rod across the old bridge the day that looking down gave him such a vertiginous sense of his own fragility that he climbed back down and knew he would never have courage of heights like George.

But when they had hooked his harness to the static line in the door of the tower in B stage--and the guys who wouldn't hook up after they looked down at the troops waiting on the ground thirty-four feet below, had turned back and walked down the steps and off to cooks and bakers school--he had looked down at the ground and jumped out the door and ridden on the risers on the pulley to the sawdust pile. And, guess what? No sweat!

And Monday of C stage with the whole class at attention in formation in front of the 250-foot towers and an I & E officer with a bull horn announcing that he would now have a 180-pound man-shaped dummy wearing a chute released from the east wing of the tower so that the rip cord of the chute strapped onto him would automatically pull and the chute would open and prove to any faint hearts that your chute will fully deploy and let you down softly from just 250 feet. When the chute didn't trip and the dummy, looking just like a man, slammed into the ground in front of them and bounced waist high and showered the front rank with sawdust, then some quit, you bet! Plenty sweat!

But still, somewhere along the way while he had been worrying about courage and how to attain it, his fragility to heights had left him. All this week they'd been telling you that 98% of training jumps were safe--not meaning you couldn't break a leg--just meaning non-fatal. But he knew in his bones that tomorrow the 1,200-foot jump from the real plane would be okay. He said, "I'm 99 and 44 one-hundredths!"

Dear folks, Friday

A lot of things have happened this wk. and I haven't had a bit of time to write.

I have made 5 jumps, and you must admit that is a radical step for a guy who had never been up in an airplane before. It's really the greatest thrill of your life and at the same time it is the biggest scare. (I guess it's always the things that give you a scare that give you a thrill.) I went through the jumps okay without anything but a little riser burn, and will get my wings Sat. We just moved across the Chattahoochee River into the Alabama section of the camp. Not nearly so nice as the old part of the post, sort of like Camp Robinson here.

We are here for training on the order of advanced infantry training (with live ammo). I don't know for sure when I will get home, but most of the troops are only here a week before furlough, so expect to be home in early December. This is not a certainty, though, and might be as much as three wks. I sure would like to come home now, but you know how it is. I got your swell packages and sure appreciated them both. As to the socks, I don't think I'll have much use for them because socks is one think the army gives you plenty of.

I've got a million things to tell you about my adventures as a parachute jumper, but I'm afraid I can't express them in this letter, as I have a hard day ahead and I'm already pooped. I sometimes pal around with Wayne Collins and my old buddy Williamson. We saw Danny Kaye's latest picture, "Wonder Man"; it was really good, the best comedy I've seen in months.

P.S. I hope I'll be sleeping on my porch before long, or have you closed it for the winter?

ALL LOVE Miles.

Dear Folks, Sunday

Well, for furlough I signed up to go to Uncle Maurice's in Puyallup--just pretend to go there-- If all goes well, I'll be on my way to you Saturday or so. If you can spare 10$ please wire it. I am going to have to pay my way home and it will probably cost quite a lot.

I went over to audition for the post band yesterday and I think I may be asked to play in it if we do get hung up here after my leave.

I hope the car will be fixed so that I can go up to Ames and bring Fairy home from school before Christmas. I am going to see if I can't hitch a ride on a plane out of here but that is sort of unlikely.

Gosh, things are sure uncertain...... See you soon.

He would have taken his delay-en-route to Iowa and come back in ten days if a cadre sergeant who was from Iowa himself hadn't taken him aside before he signed for leave and told him that the farther away he was going the more travel time they would give him. Everybody whose home was nearer would come back to the Alabama area and do training till the guys who had signed up for the West Coast came back. He didn't have to actually go there.

359

So, he said he signed up to take his leave at his Uncle Maurice Gordon's in Puyallup, Washington. He got twenty-one days. He could leave after he got his wings Saturday, December 16 and return January 6, and the rest would all be waiting right here doing pushups.

Fairy's last letter said she would have to stay two days after classes let out to finish an Incomplete. He could pick her up the twenty-fourth. She had completed her transfer to Simpson for next term and would be bringing all her things home.

He put notes in the mail telling everyone he would get New Year's at home.

*   *   *

Saturday Miles boarded a little milk train at Columbus that spent three hours getting to Atlanta. He had gambled on the warm weather and wore a new tailored suntan Eisenhower jacket with the red and white patch of the parachute school on the shoulder and the bent wings on the blue infantry lozenge on his chest, but this day was warm even for Georgia and they opened the coach windows and the locomotive belched clouds of soot that billowed in, and the new jacket was hobo-sooty by the time he reached Atlanta and changed to the limited for Chicago.

Genuine jump boots were no longer issued, but the standard G.I. combat boots were universally despised, because the buckles sometimes hooked in the parachute lines and caused a streamer. Real jump boots could still be mail-ordered from the Corcoran Boot Co. in New England, and non-jumping clerks and bakers who had started to wear mail-order jump boots to town to compete with troopers for girls often came back to camp in their stocking feet, having lost them to a safety-minded jumper behind a Phoenix City bar. But Miles had won real jump boots fair and square from a captain getting discharged because of a wound he got from the jump on Sicily. The captain had posted a notice on the bulletin board that he was giving fittings at the orderly room after chow, and any "Cinderella" who could fit his boots could have them and "carry on the tradition." They were size 12-D boots, and Miles had walked away in them.

In the LaSalle Street Station in Chicago, he had the boots waxed and spit-shined again, bloused his pants with two fresh condoms, and bought Fairy a silver ankle I.D. bracelet in a military-jewelry store. He had it inscribed with their first names and a tiny parachute between them before he boarded the Rocket for Des Moines. His new uniform looked like he had ridden under the train instead of in it, but the red boots blazed like a winter dawn.

Ferne and J. Arthur met him at the station in the state Ford. They had driven the Mercury very little since he left because the week before Ferne started work on a machine at the ordnance plant ("to support the troops," meaning him,) she had left it parked on a hill in Des Moines when she stopped for lunch, and it had rolled away, a block downhill, through a crowded intersection and into the window of a pharmacy. J. Arthur had put it in a Des Moines body shop to be fixed in time for Miles' homecoming, but it was still there on blocks waiting for parts. Miles didn't complain, because it was still promised in time for him to drive Fairy home from school the twenty-fourth. Since Ferne had been riding the ordnance bus, she had saved enough gas coupons that he could also count on driving Fairy to Simpson the day before he went back to camp.

The first thing he did when he got home was call her. He said that when he got off the train in Chicago and saw his breath steaming, he knew he was back in God's country.

Fairy said, "Mrs. Berry doesn't like me staying extra days. She's living in the house over Christmas and

361

I'm cramping her style. But she's got to put up with me because my professor's OK'd it." If Miles could come by noon Saturday, they could stop in Des Moines on the way and do some last-minute shopping. West Hall was just off Sheldon, half a block from the little drug store near Tevebaughs', if he remembered. So they agreed that he would get the repaired Mercury from the body shop and pick her up at West Hall about noon and they would come home through Des Moines.

He went to church with Ferne the next day. He would have gone back to the choir but Ferne let him know that she meant to take his arm up the church steps and sit beside him in the pew and introduce him to the new minister after the service. He was for show; he knew it. "Behold, my soldier son!"

So he stood with her for the hymns and kept a grave, attentive mien without a flicker while old Cozad's snores rose to an audible duet with the sermon. The grunts and snorts made him feel at home. Outside afterward, Ferne towed him around, introducing him to people he already knew and informing everyone what he had been doing--unnecessarily, since his starched uniform proclaimed it. She had made him sit around in his pajamas while she washed his uniform and dried it in front of the fireplace. This morning she had ironed it before church. He was the only uniform in church that day.

To Florence Clark, the librarian, and Grace MacLeary, the county auditor, Ferne crowed, "Yes! See, on his cap, and on this shoulder patch--this is not an ice cream cone; it's a *parachute*, which is what he has been doing--jumping--out of *airplanes*!" And while the Quinns and the Royers, who had already lost sons in the war, smiled wanly and passed on, Roy Cross shook hands and plied him with questions about the training at Ft. Benning. Bruce, he said, was in Belgium now, and Charlene, who had started school at Cornell, would be home for Christmas Wednesday.

It was as if he had outgrown the old childish urge to pick his nose every time Ferne boasted about him, and now felt that he was almost what his wings labeled him to be-- almost a soldier. No more. No less. And having kept him in front of the church till she was almost out of audience, and a dust of snow had begun to float in the air, Ferne walked home on his arm talking about J. Arthur's bee hives, which had now displaced the Mercury in the garage for the winter. He was aware, as she was, that the curtains in the front windows of the houses along Ninth St. fluttered as they passed.

He made the courtesy call on the Baers next door after lunch, shook the hand of Lester who had been "cured" and sent home from Clarinda. He accepted the fiction Gladys and the girls effused that they had always known Miles would straighten up and find the manly promise somewhere in himself--buried out of everyone's sight but theirs--till the army finally brought it out.

He heard that Bob Stacy, Nile Kinnick's high school friend, was scheduled to be home from camp on the West Coast over Christmas. Maurice Sinift, the principal, had suddenly thrown it all up and gone off to the navy, though with his wife and child and his flat feet, he didn't have to.

Ferne assured him it wouldn't be long till some of his old crowd would be here; by the time he picked up Fairy on Saturday they should be drifting in. Yes, she'd seen Verna a week ago and thought Dick Berglund was still at Drake, though he had taken his exams early.

After dinner, in the living room he stood on a chair and held the tree upright while J. Arthur fixed the stand. Ferne had not had time after work to get the boxes of lights and ornaments down from the attic, but Miles could try his hand at decorating it after she went to work Monday. They

363

listened to Jack Benny and Edgar Bergen, and when Ferne went to the kitchen to get dessert and J. Arthur nudged the ashtray stand toward him and tapped an extra cigarette out of his pack of *Rameses* in a man-to-man gesture, Miles lit their cigarettes with his Zippo and felt a tug of nostalgia for Sunday evenings at home, though J. Arthur had never permitted him to smoke in the room.

At nine-thirty, his father went to the radio room to keep a date with a ham in New Zealand, and Ferne went upstairs. Miles was standing at the front window watching the snow floating aimlessly up and down through the streetlight in front of the church with no steeple when the martial music of the evening news came on, and a voice that reminded him of Murrow's said, "...*In the Pacific war, American forces combined today in a parachute strike from Leyte to the Island of Mindoro. A Parachute Combat Team attacked the airfield that will complete the last link in MacArthur's island-hopping drive to Manila.*

...The European front, General Alexander Patch's Seventh Army penetrated deeper into the Reich.

"*And Glenn Miller, America's favorite orchestra leader is still missing on a flight from England to Paris where he was scheduled to lead his band, already in France, in a round of Christmas concerts for the troops. Glenn Miller's flight is now long overdue. Miller, 40, is internationally famous.*"

"Oh, shit!" he said, and turned off the radio. Upstairs, Ferne, reading in bed, said she was sorry, "He'll probably turn up."

"That's what they say about everybody." he said and undressed in his room and got into the bed on the cold porch under a mound of quilts and looked bleakly up at the pinprick stars of Midwestern winter. He hoped it would turn out to be a false report. But the losses of the Kinnicks, and Eddie Quirk, J. Arthur's instrument man, who's B-26 had "not turned up," over Italy, had dissipated the

364

optimism that once would have moved him to kneel on the cold floor beside the bed to launch a prayer for Miller from the approved position.

Monday the radio carried so many retrospectives of Miller's career and tributes from so many notables that he only caught one communique on the ten o' clock news about the Seventh Army pressing deeper into the Reich.

On the nineteenth, he hitch-hiked to Des Moines to get a Christmas present for J. Arthur at Iowa Radio. He called the SAE house from Dogtown on the way home. Someone went to call Race and came back to say his room was cleaned out.

He did catch up with Punk playing bridge with two girls and a civilian in the Union, now in the basement of a dorm, and she turned over her hand, and they moved to a corner table to talk.

Yes, she had walked with Race on the way to class the day he went around and got his grades--which were good--but he was feeling very sorry for himself because some veterans were already registering on the G. I. bill, and "poor Richard" was just going in. Speaking of which, one of those vets had refused to buy a Drake beanie from the D-Club boys who always patrolled the Union entrance upstairs with their paddles during registration, and they had tried to whop him. She had heard all hell break loose in the stairwell, and a big fat lineman had come flying out of the stairwell with a broken arm and pieces of his paddle after him. The veteran, she said, was a little bald-headed fellow who had been in some Stalag. She flashed her dimples at Miles, "End of most-hallowed tradition!" She studied him soberly a moment, "What're the German's up to? Will this thing effect you?"

He didn't know what she was talking about. "They've started some kind of a counterattack in Belgium."

He shook his head and waved it off like a fly on his nose. "No way, Jose'! Twenty-one sacred days!" He

365

laughed, and stood up. "Best be...I'm riding my thumb today. Let's hitch together; I'll get a ride quicker."

She laughed and shook her head, "Claudette's coming for me Friday. Will Fairy be home Friday?" He shook his head. "I'll bring her down Saturday."

Miles flagged the Greyhound bus in order not to have to run after cars with J. Arthur's fragile radio tube and didn't think about Punk's word about the Germans till the next day. As no one of his friends was home yet, he had gone to the job with J. Arthur, and was sitting in the Ford twiddling the radio dial for news of Glenn Miller and watching J. Arthur walk onto the bridge with Molasses at his heels when he caught newsbreaks on successive stations about a German counteroffensive in the Ardennes. One said that the Twelfth Army was faced with a large scale attempt to split its front, but that flying fortresses were being called on to blunt the push. The second said that bad weather over Belgium had grounded the Air Force.

On Thursday, he had the house to himself in the morning. He came up from breakfast, and turned on the Halicrafters on his bedside table and instantly heard a fragment of a release: "*...a forty-five mile break in our lines. The Nazi push mounts in power while fog frustrates air blows against the rampant column!*" He snapped it off and started pulling his Glenn Miller records and playing them in a kind of personal requiem for the band leader: *Serenade in Blue* with Ray Eberle and the Modernaires, and *Dear Arabella* with its early-war jokey cynicism about a greenhorn Private Johnny and his fickle girl at home.

At noon, it was as though he were playing a trick behind his own back to turn on Ferne's radio with the WHO noon news, "*...now have penetrated 30 miles from...*" and snap it off before he could start to think about it. He called Sigurd Fardel and asked if he could come up and retrieve *The Anvil Chorus* and some other Miller records he had loaned the band when he went to the service. The director said they would all be gone to an away basketball game in the afternoon; Miles was welcome to pick up his records in the bandroom cabinet. "While you're here, give them a spin on our new console," the director said.

That afternoon, alone in the bandroom, Miles fired up the band's new sound system and put his records on the turntable. The two new speakers in the corners made it sound as if the Miller orchestra was in the room. He sat back and listened to *In the Mood*, and *Song of the Volga Boatmen*, where the whole band audibly pulls the oars, going UGH!, then Miller's *String of Pearls*, and *St. Louis Blues March*, which he had heard at Ft. Benning every day for a month echoing from the speakers on the company street.

Sorting through the library, he found some strange new records of a bass, piano and drum comping on some jazz standards without the solo instrument so that the listener could play the ride on his own horn. Some of the tunes were familiar standards he had heard the combo of the Ft. Benning post band play at the enlisted men's club, and he put Fardel's flute together and tuned it and tried out playing the melody of *At Last* with the combo behind him. The selection of tunes on the album went from sentimental ballads to swing tunes to ease the beginning player into the up-tempo numbers. And when he soon grew impatient with the somnolent *At Last,* and jumped the tone arm to *Blue Skies*, he felt all the intricate, agile lacework of fingering native to the flute, which he had drudged over and over to master *The Whirlwind,* stir to forgotten life in his fingers:

Never saw the sun shining so bright/ When you're in love, everything's right Never saw the days hurrying by/ When you're in love, my how they fly-y!

After the bridge, the flute ran like a deer, and he was double-timing the beat with a break out of nowhere

367

that laid a filigree of waterfall cadenza around the melody. What was *this*? When it ended, he put the flute down and whispered, "Go man!" the way he'd heard the sidemen do in a Phoenix City bar.

Then he ramrodded into *How High the Moon* on the off-beat, and felt the syncopation nudge the ensemble from a freeform cadenza into jazz: He dropped out and tapped the beats, hearing the stiff little combo aching for a riff they didn't have, and he suddenly had the riff, and caught the off-beat again with a four-bar, blues-bent little fugue from *The Red Poppy* that he stitched through *Moon* so fast that he quit thinking and followed the knowing in his fingers, letting his rediscovered technique parse the notes from the *Russian Sailors' Dance* and shake them up and fling them around the chords of *Moon* like dice flung from a cup.

> *Somewhere there's music,/ How faint the tune*
> *Somewhere there's heaven/ How high the moon!*
> *There's no moon above when love is far away, too...*
> *Till it comes true that you love me/ as I love you.*

He put down the flute. The recorded ensemble was rigid and they didn't swing like a live combo, or meld with the flute talking to them, but no mistaking, he had found jazz. On a flute! Allright! He clapped his hands once and sat staring: "Oh, *yeah*, man! " he said.

"What?" said a little girl who had had come down from the third grade room and parked against the band room door listening.

"Sachmo says if you have to ask you'll never know!" he said solemnly. She turned and skipped away down the hall. He polished the mouthpiece and put the flute back on Fardel's desk and closed the band room door behind him.

The playground of the elementary school was empty, but a clump of kids stood in the mud in the middle

368

of the Kinnicks' former football field where Nile had taught him and George to hold the kicks. They were looking at the muddy snow and haggling over whether to try to play with the twilight coming down. Across the corner at the Morgans' old house, someone had torn down the barn where he had thrown John Hall's shoes on roof. He was thinking he would phone Fairy and arrange the time to pick her up Saturday morning.

It was already almost dark when he walked past the lighted courthouse square, the Christmas lights swinging in the wind on the strands strung from the bell tower to the castellated corner towers, and the lighted wreaths over Main Street doing an animated dance over the empty streets gave the square a haunted air. The speakers clanging out *God Rest You Merry Gentlemen*, echoed with an empty hollow fervor.

Going up his front steps, he picked up the *Des Moines Tribune* and looked at the head:

NAZI PUSH CONTINUES
Fog Stops Air Blows at Rampaging Nazi Column/ Americans tighten flanks of 45 mile break/ Situation in Ardennes still serious

He dropped the paper in J. Arthur's lap and his father scanned the headline and said, "I told them at the office that bastard's still got a dirty trick or two up his sleeve."

At the dinner table Ferne asked if there was any possibility he could stay at Ft. Benning in the band. He said he wouldn't, but might try for a band overseas. He had heard that musicians were medics in combat. "Their casualty rates are high; the 101st and the 82nd will probably need some." After he said it, he knew he had made a mistake, and started to kid her about all the socks she had sent him at Camp Robinson.

369

She looked up from her plate. "Every letter from you for three weeks, it was, 'I'm flunking the infantry.' Then, 'I'm going to the paratroops!' We were spinning like tops. Is he in or is he out? We were crossing our fingers, hoping you were out."

"I could have applied for a section 8," he teased. "You can get one of those and get out for acting crazy."

"I know what section 8 is!" she snapped. "If you weren't half crazy now, you wouldn't be in that outfit!"

"That's not the way you sounded Sunday after church," he said. "No, jumping is great! Nothing like it!"

"They don't spend all that money taking you for airplane rides so you can have fun. I worry about the Huns shooting you as you come down, or those wicked Japs."

He looked up at her; she'd never flown, had been born before the Wright brothers had flown, but she had hit unerringly the thought every trooper had had. "Don't worry." he said. "It's all but over--the European side is." He turned to J. Arthur. "Will you call the garage first thing in the morning and make sure the Merc's ready? I don't want to have to wait around the garage half the day before I can head for Ames."

The first sign he took real notice of, though for two days he had been in denial that the Bulge was getting worse by the hour, was at 8:30 Saturday morning. He had been trying to put a call through to a man in West Des Moines, the father of one of his buddies at Camp Robinson. When he reached him and introduced himself, the man said he had just had a call from his son from a port of embarkation in New Jersey and they were flying his whole cycle to Europe. "Ever hear of them flying plain infantry over?" he asked in amazement.

When Miles put down the phone and went into the kitchen, he thought the frown on his father's face meant that the car was going to be late. J. Arthur shook his head,

370

"Still be ready tomorrow a.m. He'll leave it out with the key locked inside. We just take it; I've got the other key." He tapped the front page of the *Register*. "Glad you'll be home with this stuff going on."

NAZI THRUST STILL BUILDING
EISENHOWER URGES GREATEST ALLIED EFFORT

He sat down and read the story. It said the German counterattack in the Ardennes was producing heavy casualties in the worst winter weather of the century, and that fog continued to ground Allied air support.

J. Arthur finished his coffee and went to the office. Miles was sitting in the breakfast nook staring at the newspaper as though waiting for a shoe to drop when the telephone rang and he heard the Steamboat-Annie voice of his Puyallup Aunt Hilda screech, "Oh, it's *you! We had no idea where in the world you were! Did you tell the army you were coming here? You're uncle's been trying to straighten this out with the army! We have a telegram that says your leave is cancelled and you're to report back at Ft. Benning Sunday!*" Her voice was full of zest and recrimination. "*Let me talk to your mother!*"

He passed the phone to Ferne, and abruptly put his head on the table.

He called J. Arthur to try to get the Mercury out today. From his office, J. Arthur called the garage and cajoled and threatened and told them Miles' story, but they still would not have it ready till Saturday morning.

At about 11:15, across from the library on the south side of Adel, Charlene Cross, just home for the holidays, stepped out to get the mail and saw the Black Mariah stopping in front of the house. She began to cry as Ray Wing came up the walk. She took the telegram and carried it in two fingers to her mother in the kitchen. The War Department said that Bruce Cross had lost his life in the line of duty.

Miles called Fairy at 11:30 to tell her that his leave had been cancelled and he would have to take the Rocket to Chicago tomorrow morning to report at Ft. Benning before midnight. "But that's before *Christmas,*" she wailed. "We won't have any Christmas?"

"Yes, we will!" he said, "I'll come up tonight! But I won't have the car." And he began to wonder how he could get there. After a long silence, when Fairy spoke again, she seemed to have come to terms with the ruins of their Christmas plans. "Anyway, Claude Thornhill is playing tonight for the Military Christmas ball."

"Wow!" he said, with hollow enthusiasm, *"Robin's Nest!"*

"Your uniform should get us in."

"Woe to them if it doesn't! But how will you get all your stuff home now?"

"Dad can meet me at the bus in Des Moines. He'll be happy to do it for you."

J. Arthur offered to drive Miles to Ames and stay the night with a Highway Commission radio friend and drive him to the train in the morning, but Miles called the Conard Bus office and got a seat on the afternoon bus to the ordnance plant. From there he knew he could catch a ride to Ames with one of his old workmates.

Ferne fried steak for lunch. Afterward they went to the living room and tried to have an early Christmas. He had brought home a mail order housecoat for Ferne, and gave his father the radio tube the Iowa Radio man without a nose said J. Arthur coveted. His parents gave him a war bond and a hundred dollars cash, and Ferne promised to send him what he needed when he got to where in the world he was going. It was a short and perfunctory festivity, and they were still downcast with the shock from the sudden curtailment of his leave. He had been saving up so many stories, but now that it was over before it started, there was nothing to say. He and Ferne sat waiting for J. Arthur to start a fire in the fireplace, and as the first lick of flame sprang up, the Conard bus honked in the street. Miles picked up his bag and promised to call Christmas Day if he could get through. He kissed Ferne and shook J. Arthur's hand. As he stepped onto the bus he noticed Jean Baer on the front porch waving.

At Building #7, he got off and waited for Richard Speck at the time clock. Speck, who still commuted to Jewell north of Ames in the classy tan four-door rag-top 1937 Ford Torpedo which Miles had nudged him into buying second hand the previous summer, was so surprised and pleased to see him that he volunteered to take him out of his way to Fairy's dorm on the other side of Ames.

On the way, they talked about mutual acquaintances on the crews. Four months had changed the water, and most of the summer slingers were gone. Speck said that Louis Freestead, Miles' steady partner till he went into the navy, had written once from the fleet in the South Pacific. Birge, the old prizefighter who had once knocked Miles wobbly in a friendly sparring match on the dock, had moved on.

It was six o'clock when Speck pulled in to let him leave his bag at the Union, then drove him on to West Hall. They promised to keep in touch.

Fairy's aunt had invited her to lunch at Boone, and her cousin had brought her back to West Hall at three. All of the other girls had left for home, and the house was deserted except for the housemother who poked her head out of her door beneath the stairs when Fairy came in and scowled.

373

Fairy had cleared her room and packed everything except the little lamp and the radio and the dress she planned to wear to the dance, and she was just putting on her coat to walk to the drug store down the block when Char Cross called and informed her of Bruce's death. Char broke down on the phone, and they both cried, and when they hung up, Fairy lay down on her bed. She lay a long time with her hand shielding her unblinking eyes against the dying daylight, and suddenly woke up at the end of dusk from a turbulent dream, and got up and took out of her suitcase the small box gift-wrapped in the paper of a military surplus store that contained Miles' Christmas present, and stuffed it in her evening bag. Then she stood gnawing her thumb nail several minutes and added her nightgown. After her bath, she dressed slowly, frowning in the dark mood of the dream she still could not remember.

She had just come downstairs and turned on the lamp in the parlor when Richard Speck pulled up in front.

When the doorbell rang, Mrs. Berry came to the kitchen doorway with a glass in her hand and watched owlishly as Fairy hurried to the door. "Remember, Missy, just because school's out doesn't mean we don't keep hours." She fixed Fairy with a pointed stare over the rim of her glass. "So...and so on," she finally said, and turned away.

7

Leaving the Home Front

NEWSBREAK:

17 December, American forces have seized the airfield on Mindoro, Philippines, putting them just an island hop from Manila.

22 December, Manteuffel's 26th Volksgrenadier Division and the XLVIII Panzer Corps' artillery close ring around Bastogne, confident of forcing the surrender of the U.S. forces caught there:

To the USA Commander of the encircled town of Bastogne. The fortune of war is changing. This time the USA forces in and near Bastogne have been encircled by strong German armored units. More German armored units have crossed the river Ourthe near Ortheuville, have taken Marche and reached St. Hubert by passing through Hompre-Sibret-Tillet. Libramont is in German hands. There is only one possibility to save the encircled U.S.A. troops from total annihilation: In order to think it over, a term of two hours will be granted beginning with the presentation of this note.

If this proposal should be rejected, one German Artillery Corps and six heavy A.A.Battalions are ready to annihilate the U.S.A. troops in and near Bastogne. The order for firing will be given immediately after this two hours term.

All the serious civilian losses caused by this artillery fire would not correspond with the well-known American humanity.

The German Commander

It had been more than six months since Miles had taken Fairy to the train to spend the summer with Ruth, and they walked apart half-way to the Union, only the crunch of their footsteps in the snow breaking Miles' tongue-tied silence. Half-intimidated by some wild aloofness in her eyes, he drew her under the arch of the campanile to reprise their "coed" kiss of a wartime life ago, and she laughed. And the familiar conflagration started in his chest, and he caught her hand, and they ran the rest of the way with their breath making a single cloud.

The band was playing *Where or When* as they came out of the cloak room and joined the crowd of uniforms and Christmas frocks. Fairy wore a dress he had never seen, of burgundy velvet with a little jacket. On the stand, a girl in a gown of the same color was holding the microphone:

It seems we stood and talked like this before.
We looked at each other in the same way then,

He said, "At first you seemed strange, but you taste like you."

"*But the clothes I am wearing aren't the clothes I wore...*" she responded.

And they finished the verse with the singer, "*But the smile you are smiling you were smiling then...*" and broke up standing in the middle of the floor chortling. When they looked around, was everyone watching because they were playing the fool? Or because of her dark beauty, or because he was the only enlisted man?

They danced close and wordlessly till intermission, and then went downstairs to the cafeteria and sat at a corner table. His coffee went cold and her shopworn piece of yesterday's pie disappeared as they cleared the six months of lines between-the-lines of their letters. She reminded him of their benighted scheme to be close at Drake and Simpson through the fall. Now Ruth had transferred to

Penn and Fairy would start at Simpson after New Year's. "But look where you got yourself..." she said, with a trace of blame in her tone.

"I'd be gone by now even if I'd stayed. So I'll take this..."

The band resumed above. The music drifted down the stairs, and the cafeteria emptied. She looked away. When she avoided his eyes, her face was grave.

"Deep thoughts?" he said, "More than a penny's worth?"

She nodded.

"A dollar then?"

"Oh well, *you're* strange, too. You didn't tell me you were losing so much weight; you're so thin. The paratroops don't feed you."

"I lost it in Basic. The food there was so bad I lived on peanut butter." He told her about the mess sergeant disguising the foul meat under tons of ketchup to get you to take it, then putting a guard on the garbage cans to write you up for K. P. if you threw it away, and how the three nights K. P. after day duty, scrubbing the greasy walls behind the roaring ranges, had taught him to live on peanut butter. "At Benning the chow's fine. I've already gained part of it back. Now, *you* tell me, what's going on at home?"

"It's...." Fairy said. She bit her lip and looked away again and said, "...I'm completely out of touch. I was only home from Ruth's three days before I came back to school. By the way, next summer I'm going back, if the war's still on."

"And live at Ruth's again?"

"Or take an apartment, to be more on our own."

"On our own?" he said skeptically, "I hope Dar's made general by then."

377

She suddenly put down her fork and studied him, "Oh, God, Miles! Tell me you *didn't* volunteer just because I said Darwin was going to O. C. S.!"

"I'm a copycat."

"*Miles*! Darwin's Carling's a complete schmuck! He's got himself a deferment now, has Darwin."

"What made me guess? Now that I'm gone, he can chase you around your new apartment for the duration." He laughed without smiling, and suddenly seized her hand, "Listen: I'm no Eagle Scout like Bruce. *Promise* me you'll wait?"

She shook her head despondently and looked at her watch. "Oh God! How much time do you still have left?"

"To make connections in Chicago? I've got to take the early Rocket. Which will put me in camp late Sunday. The afternoon one, I wouldn't make it."

"So that's what we have?" she said, and spread her hands. "That's *absolutely* all there is?"

"But answer me! *Will* you *wait*? Or will it be like Bruce and me?"

"Oh...*don't*....!" She almost cried out. The same wild look flickered on her face, and her nails bit into his hand. *Snowfall* was echoing down from the great hall--the glittering cascade of Thornhill's piano over the long tolling chords of the brass. They both heard it freeze the moment at some brink--10:30, Dec. 23, 1944--when their time started to run out. She put her finger to his lips, and they got up.

At eleven the band played its theme again, and they danced to it this time hardly moving, rocking each other slowly. Then they sat down on a corner of the bandstand and watched the floor clear and the band pack up. The famous bandleader stood at the keyboard shuffling through the music on the piano rack. The second time he looked their way, he turned and came over. "Merry Christmas! You look like we brought you down."

"*Snowfall's* like a dream of peace," Miles said emptily. Fairy said, "His leave's been cancelled."

Thornhill studied them. "This German uprising?"

Fairy nodded, and Miles saw she was about to cry. He stood up and produced from his wallet a bent envelope in which he had planned to mail the letter he would write to her from the train. The envelope said "U.S. Army Paratroops" in light blue print on the return corner of the white envelope overprinted with a misty blue silhouette of parachutists descending and landing in front of a hedgerow skyline. He handed it to Claude Thornhill, and the bandleader wrote "Best Luck!" and signed the back. They shook hands.

The cloakroom was already empty except for his field jacket and her coat. He took down the musette bag he'd shelved there in the afternoon and gave her the envelope with Thornhill's signature to put in her purse. "The first thing I'll want from you when I get back," he said. "No...the second," and blushed.

They hurried on the walk past Beardshire Hall against the wind and were very cold within a block of West Gate. He steered her into the warm oasis of the Heater and lifted her onto the top. "Better?"

"For the moment," she said. They kissed, and she said suddenly, "Come see my room!" and took his shoulders and slid off into his arms.

"What?"

"I said you never would see it. Now I *want* you to see it. Aren't I fickle?"

"But Mrs. Berry...."

As they climbed the steps, Fairy studied the dark windows, "I think Mrs. Berry went--what do you call it?-- AWOL tonight! She *does* disappear!"

"And if she comes back?"

"If she comes back in the shape she did last night, she'll pay *me* not to tell!"

"You'd blackmail poor Mrs. Berry?" They snickered on the front steps of the big unlighted house, and she left him under the fan light and slipped down the porch to peer in where the kitchen light showed at the back. "No such luck!" she said when she came back, "Berry's sitting there like someone propped her up."

"Will she lock you out?"

"I got a key from a bad girl. And I'm not under Berry's thumb any more. I'm gone!" she said fiercely. "But if she hears us, she'll lock *you* out. I could give you the key to come in later, but her room's under the stairs, and you can't stand around in the cold waiting for her to pass out.

"Let's *go* somewhere!" He tugged her down the steps and they turned south toward Lincoln Way along the black street with their backs to the north wind. He remembered the bus ran on Lincoln till twelve. His watch said 11:40.

The little drugstore in the next block showed a dimmed light. They put their noses to the window and saw someone in the back. Miles rapped on the glass and the elderly druggist came up and opened the door. "Not a fit night." he said. "The register's closed, but there's still a little hot coffee and grounds?" He stood waiting with his head cocked alertly, wondering if they wanted something they couldn't mention.

"I'd like to call a cab?" Miles said. The druggist beckoned him along the aisle to the phone at the pharmacy window. Miles rang the one cab company. "How soon?" he said.

"When we get there."

"I've got ten minutes worth of work here," the druggist said. "That's all I can stay."

Miles thanked him and went and stood by the front window with his arms around Fairy looking over the top of

380

her head at the wind blowing spurts of new snow from the direction of Pammel Woods. In ten minutes the light in back went off and the druggist came up the aisle by the dim glow of the clock over the cash register. He stood with his hand on the door. "Where do you belong, dear?" he said kindly. "School's out, isn't it? West hall? Is Berry still waiting up for you?" He was on the point of offering to drop them somewhere, but the cab pulled up.

They got in. "Downtown," Miles said.

The old Nash cab turned east and wheezed past the Union and along the dry causeway toward town. "Where are you taking me?" He bit his lip, watching the empty soccer field at the edge of the campus pass. "I've never been to *your* room," she said.

"*What?*"

"Since we can't go to mine...?"

He felt like a man who has missed a crucial road sign and finds himself plunging into an abyss. "I don't *have* one! You said Mrs. Berry would be there, so I am sleeping in the bus station." She was silent. He exploded, "I swore not to put you through that again--and go off to God knows where!"

"For once, can't I change my mind?" she said dryly.

It stung him. "Oh, *Fairy!*"

"Did you think I invited you for tea?" she sighed. "God knows you've been gal*ant* long enough now." She leaned her head back against the seat and passed her gloved hand across her eyes in a gesture of impasse. "Did it ever occur to you that I already gave up *my own person* to you last spring? If you had gotten carried away in the heat of your moment some night, what do you think I could have done, dear?" She laughed mirthlessly, "Judo you off the couch?"

"Where now?" They had both forgotten there was someone else in the car.

381

"Sheldon-Munn," he said.

They pulled up outside the hotel and he went in. There were half a dozen uniforms still hanging out in the lobby. He saw no women. "Big night," the clerk said. "No rooms. The sailors are making themselves a Christmas ding." Miles fished in his wallet and put a five on the book, his face burning. "No, *sir*," the young clerk said, looking through the window at the cab, "I *mean*, no room at the inn."

Miles went back to the cab and got in, "No room at the inn," he said. They sat a little apart now. The meter ticked, the motor idling. An ensign went in. Then he came back out and looked at the cab and walked east. "You see?" Miles said, "The clerk's a student type; he wouldn't even take anything."

The driver turned around with his elbow over the seat. "There's a bed and breakfast, huh?" he said. "If you can pass for legit?" They were silent.

Fairy suddenly stirred. "What did he look like? Red headed?" Miles nodded: "Let me *out*," she said, and pushed on his knees. She left her purse on his lap and got out. She reached back and took his musette bag, "I'm not some doxy without any luggage." She went through the door swaying. The meter ticked.

"Just hang on," he said to the driver and went across and looked through the gilt lettering into the lobby. She was standing at the desk making a gesture, her head tilted, the profile of Fairy vivacious. The red-headed clerk was nodding to her cadence and laughing. Then he caught himself, frowned at the register and shook his head. Fairy laid her hand on the page under his eyes. He looked at her hand, and looked up and saw Miles in the window gawking. Suddenly he turned the book around for her.

Two ensigns sprawled in the cigar chairs had been studying her back and talking about her. Fairy smiled at the clerk and left the little bag on the front desk and came back past the navy. "Come," she whispered, "Sign 'Mr. and Mrs. Miles Morgan'...and put '*nee* Wing,' because he knows my 'maiden' name."

Miles paid the cabby and they returned to the desk, she holding his arm so tightly he had to free it while he signed the register. His hand shook all over the page. "I didn't bring our bag because I figured you'd be full," he said.

The red headed-clerk nodded, "When it was just you, I didn't think of the wedding suite. Learn something every day. Lucky you." He slid Miles the room key.

"Leave a call for five o'clock," Miles said.

"Oh. Right!" the clerk said, and snorted.

The room was in a rear corner of the fourth floor. It was not a honeymoon suite. It was obviously a room that had missed the last remodeling of the hotel and had not been rented since. The flowered wall paper was coming off in the high corners, and the oak doors to the "suite" were blocked off. There was an ancient brass bed with a tight chenille cover, a bath with claw-footed tub and a shower on a flexible hose. When he moved the china-painted bowl holding a pitcher to put his bag on the dresser, it left a clean circle in the dust. The smell of the room reminded him of his grandmother's house in winter; it was hot, and the radiator was clanking.

He was thankful for any room. He went to the window and held the curtain back and could see that it had stopped snowing.

"How did you do it?" he said.

"I have a lab with him and he's sweet on me, or was, before he found out I'm married." She embraced him from behind and twinkled her left hand in front of his face. Her little gold ring with the Rainbow emblem had migrated to the third finger with the set turned inside. It made a nice wedding band.

"We're married all right," he said, "and this is our first Christmas." He dug into his musette bag and took out the bottle of French wine he had got by selling the deal in a Black Jack game to a 4th Infantry soldier back from Europe. He had brought it home for their Christmas. He went to the bathroom and looked around and came back with the water glasses. "But no corkscrew," he said. "Corkscrews are banned at the border of Ames. I can knock the top on the radiator."

She took the bottle and placed it on the battered table. "It's more symbolic if you don't drink it."

"If it's symbolic, it can be our Christmas tree, too," he said. Fairy arranged the glasses and the bottle for a good presentation. Then from her evening purse she produced a small wrapped box, which, when he opened it, held a heavy pewter-colored Waltham watch. It was a soldier's watch with a sweep second hand and large luminous numerals. On the bottom of the box was stamped "U.S. Army Signal Corps SURPLUS."

"I was going to have it monogrammed," she said, "but they didn't do monogramming there." "Never mind. It's perfect," he said, putting it on and winding it and setting it. He was glad to have it. His graduation watch had crashed in Basic and now ran an hour or two a day.

The watch might have come from the same military jeweler in the La Salle Street station where he had bought her an ankle bracelet with a tiny nameplate, but they had inscribed the initials on it for him there, and for a little extra had put the tiny parachute between the initials. Fairy poured the links over her fingers, then he cradled her foot in his lap and fastened the chain around her ankle. She held her foot at different angles and admired it. Then she returned it to its box and tucked it in her purse. She said Emily Post frowned on wearing them to bed.

It was after one a.m.--now the twenty-fourth--by the time they finished their Christmas, and Fairy had been in the bathroom and left her velvet dress and turned out the light. He saw that she wore a gossamer nightgown when she came to the opposite side of the bed and pulled back the tight-tucked sheet and the thin chenille coverlet. He finished unlacing his boots and got out of his clothes, and turned off the lamp. He got in on his side, and they lay briefly, high on their opposite slopes with the covers pulled up to their chins, staring at the dark ceiling and feeling the Christmas revels still yammering in the joists of the old hotel. Then he took her into the deep hollow in the center of the mattress where everything that ever happened in that bed, sleeping or loving, had happened. The radiator began pinging and smelled hot again, and he kicked the covers off and she threw the nightgown on the floor.

Later, when he half woke, he found them sleeping close-braided in an arctic chill. He clawed the covers up and scrabbled his T-shirt over her head and fell back into sleep trying to put her arms in.

Then it was hot again, and Fairy slept in the gray dawn light with the T-shirt bunched around her neck like a ruff collar on a naked queen. "Our little Christmas home," she murmured in a dream, and his heart kindled hot in his chest with a wave of such protectiveness that he shuddered as he tucked it down over her breasts. He slept again.

The five o'clock call did not come. He knew somewhere in his head that it hadn't, and knew he was forgetting it. And he forgot it.

It was seven by the time the bath water ran hot. At 8:30 he had called a cab and they stood waiting for it beside the door of the lobby, taking the hard looks of the V-12s who kept straggling downstairs with their smeary eyes that turned covetous at the sight of Fairy's dance dress and her spike-heeled evening pumps.

Then the new plan they had made slipped through on a razor edge: West Hall was deserted--Mrs. Berry had finally taken French leave, and Fairy called home from the front phone and told Ray Wing to meet her at the Greyhound terminal in Des Moines at three. Then, with all her luggage, they were late for the bus and caught it just as it started to pull out. The driver got out muttering and stowed her things underneath, and they stood in the aisle till they could take two seats vacated by a mother and daughter who got off at the Madrid intersection.

They rode mostly silent through the outskirts of Des Moines, thinking what use was talking about the future, which confronted them like a mountain wall, or the present that was finished? So they looked at Claude Thornhill's autograph, and Fairy kept nodding to the tune in her head, bright and pliant with her fingers woven into his.

His train would leave first, so they put her luggage in two big lockers at the bus terminal and took a cab to the Rock Island station. When he smelled the diesel oil and sulfur, the faint impression passed through him that these were the rails below Mary Ellen's house on the Capitol Hill from which the night trains had hooted and fed his dreams of going places in the huge world those sweltering nights when he was little and lay wakeful in the trundle bed on the front porch on East Fourteenth--and now he *was* going out there, and not much wanting to.

When the train lurched, he waved through the grimy window, and other uniforms crowded the other windows waving as he was waving, and other young women besides Fairy blew kisses from the platform.

Then he was gone, and she turned away and walked back to the Greyhound station, where she sat down on a bench near her locker and began to think of Bruce, who had never really been her boyfriend, and began to pray for Miles, who was now her husband.

On the Rocket, all seats were taken again, and he stood in the passage near the door of the women's lounge through Newton, Iowa, till his uniform caught the eye of a pudgy man in an American Legion cap going into the women's lounge with drinks, who gave him the last seat inside among a half dozen couples on their way to a holiday reunion in Davenport. They were all veterans of World War I and their wives, and had staked out the lounge and already started pouring a party into Cokes from paper sacks of Four Roses.

It was just barely disingenuous of him to answer with a nod when they asked if the girl they had seen kissing him goodbye was his bride. It stirred enough empathy that they poured him many drinks to make up for his honeymoon curtailed by the cancellation of his leave. The eyes of the middle-aged women clouded over because he reminded them of the girls they had been when they sent these old men off as young husbands to The Great War in 1917. And by the time the room swam before his eyes, a silver-headed matron had put him down on the lounge sofa with his boots on the arm and his head in her lap, and nursed him beneath the cantilevered shadow of her looming bust, massaging his forehead with ice from her drink till it trickled into his ears.

At Davenport, the Legionnaires debarked and left him rocking comatose on the sofa in the women's lounge across western Illinois till a woman complained about him, and the conductor rousted him out to a seat in the dark coach.

Early Monday morning, once more covered with soot from the little milk train, he got a cab in Columbus and reported to the orderly room in the Alabama area of Ft. Benning half a day late, and they wrote him up and restricted him to base indefinitely. When he threw his bag on his cot in the barracks, his company was as full of holes as if they all had gone to Puyallup, and he flung himself down in his clothes and slept a sleep that draped a scrim of oblivion over Christmas morning.

He woke to the voice from the loud speaker on the pole over the orderly room announcing that paratroop units still besieged at Bastogne had rejected German demands for their surrender. *"Nuts!"* it quoted the paratroop commander's reply. Ferocious cheers came from the adjoining huts. He finally sat up when the P. A. system started braying *Winter Wonderland.*

That afternoon there were plenty of seats on the bus to the main mess for the "Christmas Dinner for Lonely Troopers."

For three more days his comrades straggled in, and went on report and were restricted to base, while in Europe the American relief column continued to hack its way toward Bastogne.

On the twenty-eighth, when his battalion was finally at full strength, the speakers exulted:

American tanks have broken the siege and entered Bastogne! The sky is clear and the air force is again over the German bulge and strafing relentlessly. General Patton has turned his army ninety degrees and is roaring north from Metz to pinch off the German incursion, and the U.S. armies are hacking at the fifty-mile bulge in our lines from both sides.

The speakers played *The Paratroop Hymn* to the tune of *The Battle Hymn of the Republic:*

He jumped into the prop blast with his static line unhooked,
And he ain't gonna jump no more!
Glory, glory, what a hell of a way to die/
Glory, Glory, what a hell of a way to die/

388

It alternated with *God Rest You Merry Gentlemen.* Then, for three days everything stood still in the Alabama area of Ft. Benning.

For the same reason that his Camp Robinson cycle had been flown to Europe, his leave had been cancelled to get troops to Europe fast enough to fill gaps in the front. Though the veterans of the Bulge would not all be relieved till early February, the repulse of the German attack had now ended the crisis. Miles wrote Fairy that he might as well have stayed home over Christmas. No one who had dragged in later had been punished.

After he mailed her letter, their orders came, and he waited in a line of other troopers for a long time to spend his last dollar trying to reach someone at home. He finally left a message at J. Arthur's office that he was on his way somewhere.

His next message came to his parents on a card labeled WAR DEPARTMENT OFFICIAL BUSINESS, with a Fort Ord, California, post mark. It was merely a notice of change of address. Miles had filled in the blanks that said "*Pvt. Miles Morgan, 37758380,* will henceforth receive mail addressed to Casual Co 13, Platoon 2, A.P.O. 21228, San Francisco, Cal."

On the tenth of January J. Arthur received a further note:

Dear Folks,

I am in this new camp, but I can't tell you where I am other than that I am in California, which is still in the U.S., some of the locals assure me. We are under censorship now just as if we were overseas. Mail has been coming through that has been forwarded from Ord, but some went to Benning first. I've been getting 24-hour passes every other day and having some fun, but that was curtailed yesterday, and we are quarantined till shipment.

Now all I'm doing is KP. It isn't bad. Except Bob Hope was up here with his USO show and I had to miss it!

Dad, do you think you'll ever get back on the air? I heard they have lifted the amateur radio restrictions.

PS I'll write more when we're settled somewhere and things are more pacific (to the censor: pacific means peaceful).

Love, Miles

Epilogue

Leaving the *Home Front*

37758380

Corregidor is a tadpole-shaped island of volcanic rock in Manila Bay. It is one of four fortified islands in the bay and lies some twenty-five miles southwest of Manila Harbor. It is only 3.5 miles long and 1.5 miles wide at its broadest point, which lies at Topside (the head of the "tadpole") which is also the highest part of the island, rising sharply to 550 feet. Malinta Hill rises to 390 feet. Years earlier, U.S. Army engineers had dug a tunnel 1,450 feet long, 30 feet wide at the base, and 20 feet high at the arched ceiling, through Malinta Hill...By the time of U.S. involvement in the war in December 1941, the tunnel housed a 300-bed hospital, a storage area, barracks, and eventually MacArthur's headquarters before he left for Australia in 1942.

By February 1945, there was probably no strategic or tactical need to retake Corregidor--it could probably simply "die on the vine". But it was a thorn in the side of U. S. forces because many ships sailing in the narrow straits around the island toward Manila were repeatedly fired upon by Japanese emplacements on the island. Its occupation by the Japanese probably rankled General MacArthur more than anyone else because it was the place from which he had left ignominiously.

The Sixth Army plan called for a combined amphibious-parachute attack on the island. The airborne portion of the assault force, Rock Force, was the 503 Parachute Regimental Combat Team; the amphibious element was the 2nd Battalion, 34th Infantry Regiment, part of the 24th Division.

By the end of January the Sixth Army plan for retaking Corregidor was pretty well set. On 4 February the plan went to Douglas MacArthur's headquarters. The next day, after a careful briefing by the Sixth Army staff, he approved the mission and set 12 February as the target date (With MacArthur's approval, the Sixth Army later changed D day to Friday, 16 February). On 6 February Jack Tolson flew to Mindoro and gave Colonel Jones a "heads up" for an airborne operation that was to seize Corregidor.

AIRBORNE, Lt. Gen. E. M. Flannagan Jr.

After his letter saying he was at a new camp (J.Arthur later learned it was "Camp Anza" at Riverside, California), and leaving immediately for overseas, there was no word from Miles until shortly after 8 a.m. on the last day of February, when the door knocker of the Morgan house clattered as J. Arthur was rising from the breakfast table. Ray Wing was at the front door with a telegram from the War Department.

Telegraphy, the Morse code, was perhaps Ray Wing's only means of fluent communication, and other than the informal engagement of their children--of which his daughter had recently informed him in the heat of a family quarrel--it was the only thing he had in common with J. Arthur Morgan. After handing J. Arthur the telegram, he remained standing on the front steps wordlessly biting his corncob pipe while his eyes grew shiny. J. Arthur read the wire:

The secretary of war desires me to express his deep regret that your son, Pfc. Miles Morgan, has been reported missing in action since sixteen February in the Philippines. If further details or other information are received you will be promptly notified.

When he looked up from the wire, he stared over Ray Wing's head at the top of the church without a steeple for a long time, then heaved a deep sigh and started to return inside without noticing that Ray was still standing there. Then Ray Wing, who had just transcribed the wire from the telegraph, and knew it by heart, as he knew them all now, said only, "Well," and turned away down the steps.

Perhaps, it was as helpful as anything anyone said about Miles' disappearance after the announcement appeared in the Des Moines paper following the list of five killed in action from Polk and Dallas Counties that day:

MISSING IN ACTION:
Morgan, Miles, Pfc.: Mr. and Mrs. J. Arthur Morgan, Adel, Iowa.

Many who called to offer words of sympathy alluded to those cases known to all in which a report of a man missing in action subsequently ended happily with his reappearance after a period of temporary displacement in the gigantic bureaucracy of the eight-million-man army, though no one mentioned the two Kinnick brothers. J. Arthur and Ferne thanked their friends and comported themselves in public, and for that matter, in private, with a level demeanor as though they entirely believed this convenient optimism. And probably for a few days, they did. J. Arthur told Fairy Wing that he considered the lapse in letters from Miles after his last note from Riverside to be due to the kind of Army SNAFU that often lost track of a man and his mail in transit. At first, his theory seemed confirmed when a letter from Miles arrived a few days later:

Dear Folks,
They say censorship has slackened. I'll take a chance and tell you I'm in the Philippines. We moved from one replacement depot to another. Now our guys are with a whole bunch of other paratroopers, most of whom are already on orders to go to the 11th Airborne on Luzon.

395

They are supposed to go by air. I am hoping we will get put on these orders too. On this island there are smashed Jap planes lying around everywhere. There are several airports close. I guess that's why.

I'd like to send you a Philippine souvenir, but it's going into the third month that I haven't been paid, and I don't know when I will be. If I am paid, I will only get around $30. I wonder if my allotments and bonds are coming in. I hope so.

I don't know where you would send anything, so you can just hold off cookies etc. till I get somewhere. Boy, it's still plenty warm here. I would give a lot for some good crisp Midwestern air. How is Adel coming in basketball? I sure wish I could be with you. It probably won't be too long though, I hope. Be sure and take care of yourselves till I get back.

Miles

As the letter was not dated, it momentarily lifted his parents' hopes, till they noticed that the half-obliterated postmark on the envelope dated its mailing in late January. Yet, Ferne passed the letter on to Gladys Wing to relay to Fairy at school--requesting that it be returned--with some hope that it confirmed J. Arthur's theory that the army had temporarily lost Miles.

However, a package soon arrived from a Captain Olson. It was postmarked the first week of March, and contained a few of Miles' personal possessions along with Olson's letter saying that Miles' uniforms and boots were coming separately. Olson said that Miles had been a member of his company and assigned to his plane for the jump on Corregidor until the size of the sticks had been reduced from eight to six men. At this time there had been some reshuffling, and Miles had been bumped to another

396

plane. Olson said Miles had jumped with his squad, but no one had seen him on the ground.

Captain Olson said he had not had time to get to know their son personally because Miles had joined the 503rd as a replacement only a few days before the mission, but he assured them that Miles had already earned a reputation among his buddies as a fine soldier. He added that the Japanese extensions to the cave system under the island had not yet been entirely reconnoitered.

The officer exhibited a natural desire to supply some heartening information to the parents of the missing man, and though he did not possess any, he added that their son had contributed substantially to one of the most successful airborne operations of the Pacific war. Corregidor had been taken, he assured them, with only about half the airborne casualties expected, and only their son and two other troopers were still missing. Olson first crossed out, and then threw away the sheet on which he had written that in all likelihood these troopers had been carried over the cliffs into the ocean by the unexpected wind, and had been substantially higher than the 20 m.p.h. limit prescribed for such jumps.

His missive was cold comfort to Ferne, who pounded her fist once on Olson's letter, making the meager artifacts shudder. These were Miles' bent-winged qualifying pin, a pair of 11th A/B shoulder patches and a spare dog tag containing only his name and serial number, which he had punched out on the machine in the orderly room at Ft. Benning one afternoon when he was doing bored duty there. There was also a small jewelers' box containing the Omega watch his parents had given him for high school graduation, and a receipt for four dollars from a jewelry store in Riverside, California. When she picked up the graduation watch, Ferne howled outright. But it would be the last crack in her composure.

She put these things on the shelf in Miles' closet. She had kept the original box the Omega had come in, and when she learned from Gladys Wing that Fairy had given Miles a watch for Christmas because the Omega was not keeping correct time, she put the Omega in its original box along with the Riverside jeweler's receipt, and sent them to Fairy. The day after they received Captain Olson's letter, Ferne went back to work at the ordnance plant, and she continued working there till the war ended and the plant closed, on Miles' nineteenth birthday August 17, 1946.

J. Arthur, however, went into a decline. Ill health beset him with several ailments in the late winter and spring; first a gall bladder attack that required surgery and several weeks of convalescence. This was followed by attacks of angina pectoris, complicated by a dental condition that required the removal of several infected teeth, one of which was broken off in the socket by J. Arthur's aging dentist, a personal friend from his East High School days, whose faltering efforts caused J. Arthur great pain and unspoken terror of dying from a heart attack in the dental chair. His stress during these sessions caused a relapse in his convalescence from the surgery and forced him to take a leave of absence from his job through the summer.

When he returned to work in the fall, the sideburns of his bald head had grown prematurely white, and Miles' disappearance seemed to have quashed his tireless zest for his hobbies; he sold his bees to a farmer and though he continued to buy parts from Iowa Radio for a new transmitter, he never brought his ham radio station back on the air.

But the mystery of his son's continued absence without a trace did stir in him an insatiable curiosity about the Corregidor assault, and throughout the summer of 1946, as the eight-million-man army was mustered out, took their 24 weeks unemployment allotment and started college under the GI Bill, or bought a home with a GI Loan and settled down, J. Arthur from his improvised convalescent bed on the sofa in the living room initiated a correspondence with veterans of the Corregidor jump, and wrote dozens of letters querying them for any scrap of information of his son's fate:

He learned that in the initial plan 2,000 paratroops were to land on the high point of the island the morning of February 16, 1945, and a thousand more were to jump the next day. He was told that two drop zones on top of The Rock were selected on an old golf course and a parade ground nearby, each barely 300 yards long and several hundred wide, and that both were surrounded by tangled undergrowth and shattered trees that rimmed the 500-foot cliffs above the bay. He learned that casualties of 50% had been expected from the jump.

Veterans wrote him explaining that on the morning of the sixteenth two trains of C-47s flew over these landing zones in single file, each plane having to unload a stick of six paratroopers in six seconds exactly over its zone to prevent the jumpers drifting off the cliffs into the sea. Then the planes returned to Mindoro, reloaded, and repeated the process five hours later.

By September, with the war over, J. Arthur's persistent queries had been bucked up to the executive officer of the 503rd, who sent him a description of the action, drawn from the after-action report. This informed him that the first paratrooper floated down on Topside without arousing any hostile fire at 8:33, and that by 9:45 the first lift, which included the 3rd Infantry Battalion of the 503rd, plus artillery, engineers and the headquarters with the 503's commander, Colonel Jones, was on the ground and assembled on the DZs. An hour later the amphibious assault landed on the beaches, and before the Japanese recovered from their surprise at the airborne assault, the initial objectives of the combined landings were secured.

The officer noted, however, that the casualties of the first jump, Miles' jump, were 25%, probably because the first pass dropped its troops from 600 feet altitude instead of the planned 400 feet, causing some chutes to drift halfway down the cliffs west of the DZs or entirely over them to land on the narrow beaches below. The 503's commander, now on the ground, had immediately ordered the planes down to 400 feet.

He admitted that most of the men of the first drop, Miles' group, did miss their landing zones.

The second lift dropped more accurately at 12:40. In all, 2,050 men of the 503rd RCT parachuted onto Corregidor that day. The officer informed J. Arthur that jump casualties numbered 280: 20 being killed hitting buildings and trees, 210 injured in landing, 50 wounded by Japanese fire, and three unaccounted for. By dusk Colonel Jones had decided that the attack was completely successful and ordered the rest of the 503rd to come from Mindoro by amphibious transport the next day.

Yet, for all the particulars J. Arthur elicited from numerous sources of his correspondence, no one could tell him anything about Miles after he left his airplane.

During his convalescence, J. Arthur read of General MacArthur's return to Corregidor March 2, 1945, in the general's *Reminiscences*:

"I borrowed four PT boats from the Navy and gathered all those who had originally left Corregidor with me. We went back to the Rock the same way we had left it. We had departed in the dark of a somber night. We came back in the sunlight of a new day. In the background, the ragged remnants of our parachutes dangled from the jagged tree stumps, the skeleton remains of the old white

*barracks of "Topside' gleamed down on us, and a smart-
looking honor guard rendered us a salute.*

*"I was greeted by Colonel George Jones, 'I see that
the old flag pole still stands,' I told him. 'Have your troops
hoist the colors to its peak, and let no enemy ever haul
them down.'"*

A Mysterious Sign

Race Berglund, on a troop transport from the States
entering Manila Bay in September of that year--bound for a
clerk's duty in the Judge Advocate General's office at 1st
Cavalry Division Headquarters in Tokyo, though he didn't
know it yet--was playing cards on deck as his transport
slipped by close beneath Corregidor. They all breasted their
cards and gaped up from the deck at the tattered gray
shreds of parachutes still hanging from the splintered trees.
The thought that one of them might be Miles', gave Race a
little electric shock of false clairvoyance. While his buddies
returned to the game, he still stood for a minute locked in
uncharacteristic reflection. The loudspeaker from the
bridge hawked, *"Hear this! Return to quarters and prepare
to land,"* and he glanced at Manila on the skyline. "But he
was probably carried over the cliff," he thought, and
flipped his cigarette back toward the Rock and went below.

The next day in Manila he stopped at a stall because
the Filipino barking his pitch in Pidgin English had a
monkey on his shoulder that was chattering his jaw in a fair
caricature of his master. Of the profusion of curios made
out of jerry cans and shell casings, and the trophy German
Lugers and trench knives transported to the Pacific by the
veterans of the European theater who had been redeployed
for the invasion of Japan before the Bombs curtailed it,
there were pretty Philippine butterfly knives with 5-inch
blades folded into a handle made of a pair of colorful
hinged grips which the Filipinos could flip open in a flash

as they drew them. Race bought his sister's boyfriend one of these knives, and as he had lost his watch in a card game on shipboard, when he spotted a row of secondhand watches, he bought the first one that started to run when the Filipino gave the winder a turn. As the back of the case was badly scratched, he haggled a little, but made a deal quickly because he was shipping the next day and the Philippine pesos he paid for it were no good in Japan.

He wore the watch during his year in Japan, and until a day in the fall of 1946, after he was separated from the service and had reregistered at Drake to finish his law degree. The afternoon his mother took out of her safety deposit box and gave to him the fine Swiss watch she had given his father the year before his death, he removed the secondhand U.S. Signal Crops watch he had bought in the Philippines and put on his father's watch. He was idly turning the old watch in his hand, considering whether to give it to his sister, when he saw something on the back that made him bring it close to his face and examine it with his good eye.

That morning he had gotten together with Fairy Wing for the first time since his homecoming. At the Southside Drugstore, they had had the talk about Miles which they had promised each other in the several letters they had exchanged while Race was in Japan. Over coffee, with a kind of dutiful recitation, Fairy had told him the story of J. Arthur's fruitless quest for some trace of his son. She looked haggard--as who wouldn't, he thought, who had gone through the year she'd had--but she said that things were calmer since she and her father had made peace, and she had temporarily moved back home. She told him that when Miles' status had recently been changed by the War Department from missing to killed in Action, the Morgans had signed his GI insurance over to her.

But what struck Race now from their conversation, was her mention of having given Miles an army surplus

U.S. Signal Corps watch for Christmas when he was home on furlough. Race knew those watches; there were a lot of them around--Walthams with steel cases and green tipped radium dials--and the watch he had bought in Manila was the same kind.

In fact, looking at the back of this watch as he considered giving it to his sister, he had made out for the first time--obscured under the maze of rude excoriations which he assumed a thief had made on the back in an attempt to blot out the original owner's initials--the letter M. connected by a faint scribble to what looked like an almost obliterated ?.W.

The more closely he studied the maze of scratches on the back of the watch, the more clearly he recalled Corregidor and the ragged parachutes on the cliff above his ship, and the more convinced he became that this was the very watch Fairy had given Miles, placed in his possession in Manila by some uncanny Providence. Because, if it was Miles' watch--after all, the inscription on its face bore the words "*water resistant*" not *waterproof*--then surely J. Arthur's conclusion that the wind had carried Miles and his watch into Manila Bay, was highly unlikely.

Race was acutely aware that even now, more than a year after the war, hardly a week passed but that an American or Japanese soldier, or sometimes several, would be rescued from some forsaken island in the Pacific where the war had passed them by. In fact, all the newspapers had recently carried the story of an American sailor, long declared dead, who had escaped Japanese imprisonment months before the war ended, and suddenly turned up walking the wrong way down the runway of Clark Field outside Manila, a skeletal ragamuffin who had escaped from Japanese captivity before the island was retaken, and had been shipped home to Kansas with much jubilation.

Though Race had kept his disclosure to himself when he called Fairy and invited himself over to show her something "uncanny" he had discovered after their talk in the morning, when Fairy opened the door, his heart missed a beat with the excitement of his conviction that Providence *had* guided him to buy the very watch she had given Miles to let them know that Miles had survived the jump and was, very likely, still lost in the Philippines somewhere. It was dinner time, and when Fairy opened the door, he stood holding the watch, explaining that he didn't know what had made him decode the inscription after he had talked to her in the morning, but he had suddenly noticed that the half-obscured letters under the maze of scratches on the back of the watch were part of the initials M.M.+ F.W.

"And this watch has never missed a beat! Do you see what that means? If it's in perfect working condition, it's likely *so is Miles*, somewhere in those mountains on Luzon!" And he put it in her hand with a gesture of momentous bestowal.

Fairy took the watch and examined it, turning it over twice, but without any sign of reciprocal excitement. To his breathless expectation, her face presented a series of involuntary changes as if it were being wrung like a sponge of the life in it. Then with a small down-turned, apologetic smile, she said, "It's the same kind of watch, all right, Race. And the M looks like part of an inscription. But, Race, I didn't put anything on the back of Miles' watch. I got it at that military store across from the Paramount where they don't do that kind of work, and I was going to have DeFord here put something on it before Christmas, but by Saturday his leave was cancelled and he had to hitchhike to Ames to see me at all, and...we made a kind of Christmas...and..." She fell silent and met his eye with some desolate defiance that evoked for Race all her troubles since, "...and I saw him to the morning Rocket...and he was gone."

404

They stood silent a minute over the suddenly devalued watch. "...But what will you do with it," she finally said, "Give it to Ginny's boyfriend?":

"No, I already gave him something." Race felt like a fool now for resurrecting the specter of Miles just when she was probably getting her life back together, but when he shrugged and started to put the watch in his pocket, her hand darted out and repossessed it.

"If *you* don't have any use for it, I ...?" He shook his head, and she took it, "But thanks, Race, for trying."

When she hurried back to the kitchen, the child in his chair attached to the breakfast table where she had been feeding him his supper, was furious. He had thrown his plastic animals on the floor, and Fairy gathered up the toys and took a spoon of the minced ham and dipped it in the plum sauce--the only way he could be tricked into eating the meat--and resumed the precarious business of feeding him through his flailing arms. She had put the watch down on the counter near his tray, and when she turned to get a napkin, he seized it, and his furious little hands covered it with Gerber's plum sauce. She took it from him and wiped the purple sauce off the back to set it aside, but she noticed that her napkin had made the excoriations on the case jump out in a maze of tiny purple cloisonne lines. This purple filigree proved once and for all that what Race had convinced himself were their initials, were merely--in addition to the "M"--some deep random scars.

However, when she held the back of the watch up to the light, she made out, running around the edge of the case, the unmistakable inscription of a series of tiny numbers. For a moment, she tried to remember such a number on the case of the watch she had given Miles. In any event, if there had been one, she had not written it down. And when she wiped the back clean, the tiny digits disappeared.

A complicated story lies behind the number. But as J. Arthur Morgan was the only one who knew Miles' service serial number by heart, for want of that cryptic combination, no one could pose the question that might have started to unlock it.

What became of these people in the years after the war, and whether Miles ever did turn up, and if so, in what condition, would make another story, but this one is over.